KF

Bleak Water

Bleak Water

Danuta Reah

W F HOWES LTD

This large print edition published in 2005 by
W F Howes Ltd
Units 6/7, Victoria Mills, Fowke Street
Rothley, Leicester LE7 7PJ

1   3   5   7   9   10   8   6   4   2

First published in the United Kingdom in 2002
by HarperCollins Publishers

A CIP catalogue record for this book is available
from the British Library

ISBN 1 84505 794 5

Typeset by Palimpsest Book Production Limited,
Polmont, Stirlingshire
Printed and bound in Great Britain
by Antony Rowe Ltd, Chippenham, Wilts.

With many thanks to all the people who gave me help when I was writing this book: Steve Hicks for his advice on police procedure, Ken for all the discussions about the nature of art, Teresa for being a hard taskmaster, Julia for her rigorous editing (bad for the ego but good for the book), Sue and Colin for the use of their flat when I needed seclusion, and Penny and Sue for their valuable feedback on the manuscript.

Special thanks must go to Susan Sanderson Russell and Marjorie Lowe for championing my cause.

People who know Sheffield canal and the towpath will realize that I have taken a few liberties with the geography, and I hope they will forgive me.

For Ken, who taught me everything I needed to know about the madness of artists

And in memory of Susan Sanderson Russell

And this is the occupation known as art, which calls for imagination, and skill, in order to discover things not seen, hiding themselves under the shadow of natural objects, and to fix them with the hand, presenting to plain sight that which does not exist.

Cennino d'Andrea Cennini, *Il Libro dell' Arte*

CHAPTER 1

The grave seemed too narrow for what it was to contain. Eliza shivered in the wind that cut across the high cemetery. She stood with the awkward group that assembled round the burial place, noting with her artist's eye the soil strata where the digger had cut through the frozen ground – the black of the topsoil, the yellow of the clay and down into the darkness of the grave itself.

The mound of soil around the trench was covered with artificial turf, and the grave diggers hung back against the wall, waiting for the interment to finish. The coffin was lowered and the ropes released. The minister stepped forward and said the words that the ritual required. Her voice was low, with none of the forced emotion that Eliza had heard at other funerals. This woman hadn't known Maggie. There was no one here who had been really close to Maggie, not in the last few years. The one person who had been was already here in this burial ground.

Eliza's gaze slid unwillingly to the dark head-stone to the left of the new grave. Polished granite with gold lettering. The inlay of the lettering was fading, but the words were cut deep into the stone and would take centuries of weathering to vanish. They would last for as long as anyone who cared visited this place: *Ellie Chapman, 1989-1998. Love is as strong as death is.*

A man in a dark suit was watching her. He looked oddly formal among the ill-assorted band of strangers who had come to say their last good-byes to Maggie. He'd come into the service late and was now standing to one side of the granite stone. She didn't know him. She didn't know any of the people who were here. Over the years, Maggie's friends had drifted away.

The ceremony was over, and people were moving away from the graveside. Eliza looked at the flowers, all still wrapped in Cellophane that would, once the trench was filled in, be piled on the new burial. They would fade within their wrappings, the messages of sympathy would be obliterated by the weather, and, in a few days, they would be cleared away and destroyed. And then the whole episode would be over.

She found herself walking beside the man in the dark suit. She looked up at him. 'I'm Eliza Eliot,' she said. 'I was at college with Maggie. We haven't met, have we?'

'Roy Farnham. No. I didn't know her well.' He seemed to realize this was a bit brief. 'She consulted me about Fraser's appeal,' he said.

'You were her solicitor?' That would explain the suit.

He shook his head. 'No, I'm a police officer.'

Of course. 'Were you involved in the invest-igation?' The investigation into the murder of Ellie Chapman, four years ago.

'No, but I wrote an article about the appeals system. It ran when the news came out about Fraser. She thought I could get something done about it.' They'd stopped now by the cemetery gate.

'Excuse me?' Eliza turned round. A young man was looking at her, holding a notebook. 'I'm from the *Star*,' he said, referring to the local paper. 'I believe you were a friend of Margaret Chapman?'

'Maggie,' Eliza said. 'Yes, we were at college together.' She looked up at the sky. It was clear and cloudless, the branches of a tree that stood beside the new grave black against the brightness of the sun. A friend of Maggie's . . . How did you answer something like that, Eliza wondered. She was aware of Roy Farnham standing back slightly, watching the exchange. With professional interest?

She had seen very little of Maggie for the last four years of her life. They had been students together at the art school, they'd shared a flat, shared the first excitements and fears of in-dependent living, but by the end of those three, vital years, they had gone their separate ways, Eliza to London to do post-graduate work, then on to work in the galleries in Florence and Rome to study the techniques of the Renaissance masters, and then to Madrid with a coveted grant to study restoration techniques at the Museo del Prado. Maggie somehow remained marooned in Sheffield

3

with a teaching qualification and a baby to care for. They had kept in touch. Eliza had come back to England regularly and had spent time with Maggie and the baby, Ellie, who gradually transformed into a person – a forceful toddler, a lively little girl, an intelligent and thoughtful child. Eliza had liked Ellie. But over the years, other friends, other interests had intervened, and she and Maggie saw less of each other.

Their friendship had dwindled to cards at Christmas and the birthday card and present that Eliza always sent to Ellie. And Ellie always wrote back. Eliza smiled, remembering some of the letters. The last one – *Raed Azile, knaht uoy rof* . . . Eliza had done things like that at Ellie's age. She had once written to her grandmother in hieroglyphics, prompting a rather terse response. And then Ellie had died.

'I don't think that Maggie ever recovered,' Eliza said to the reporter now.

'Did the fact that Mark Fraser is trying to get his conviction overturned contribute to Maggie's death?' He didn't need to ask Eliza to expand on her earlier comment. The murder of Ellie Chapman had become a brief *cause célèbre* four years ago. Eliza could remember Maggie's distraught phone call, could remember going out early in the morning to get the English papers as soon as they arrived, tuning in to the BBC. *No leads in Ellie disappearance.*

'I don't know,' Eliza said. Maggie had campaigned to keep Fraser in jail – not that his early release

4

seemed a likely option. And anyway, nothing would have brought Ellie back.

She exchanged platitudes with the young man though neither of them addressed the question that had hung over the ceremony and hung unspoken in the air between them. Had Maggie's death been an accident? A car crash in which no one else was involved was the kind of polite suicide that Maggie would have committed. On the other hand, she had become erratic, absent-minded and given to drinking too much. She had been drinking when she died.

'Thank you,' the reporter said after a while. 'And you are . . . ?'

'Eliza Eliot.'

'Thank you,' he said.

She looked back along the path to the new grave, the dark headstone beside it. There was a man standing there now looking down at the stone. He looked as if he was reading the inscription. He stood with his hands in his pockets, hunched up against the cold. His cloth jacket looked too thin for the winter day. She couldn't make out his face, but there was something familiar about him. Someone from college? Someone Maggie had worked with?

Roy Farnham came up beside her and they walked together towards the cemetery gates. 'I thought there would be more people here,' he said.

'Maggie lost touch with her friends.' Or her friends lost touch with her in the aftermath of Ellie's death.

'I couldn't help her,' he said. Eliza looked at him. 'She wanted guarantees that Fraser would stay in prison.'

'Do you think he'll get out?'

He stopped and studied the distance while he thought. The cemetery was on one of the highest points of the city, and the hills ran away to the west, a cascade of roofs and winter trees. 'I looked it up after she came to see me. I don't know, to tell you the truth.'

They stood in silence for a moment, then Eliza said, 'It was good of you to do that.'

He shrugged. 'It wasn't much.' He looked down at her again. 'You're local?' He clearly wasn't, but she couldn't place his accent.

'No, but I was at art school here. I came back last summer.'

'What brought you back?'

'I . . .' Suddenly Eliza felt reluctant to go on. He was looking at her, waiting. 'I came to work for the Second Site Gallery.'

He raised his eyebrows. 'Down by the canal? Where . . . ?' Where Ellie's body had been found six months after her disappearance, concealed in deep undergrowth by the towpath, miles away from the place she had last been seen.

'Yes,' Eliza said. He didn't say anything, just kept on looking at her. 'I'd better be going,' she said. 'We're really busy. There's a big exhibition next week and there's a preview on Friday.'

'Oh yes,' he said, with polite interest. Then he

looked at her more closely. 'I read something about that.'

The exhibition had attracted a lot of publicity for a new, provincial art gallery. 'It's Daniel Flynn's latest work,' she said. For a moment, she was back in the streets of Madrid. It was early summer, and the Puerta del Sol was suffused with light. Daniel was laughing at something she had said. Who else had been there? She couldn't remember. There had been a group of them sitting outside the café watching the Madrileños' leisurely drift towards the afternoon. Daniel.

She brought her mind back to the present. 'You must come and see it.'

'I'll look out for it,' he said. A careful non-promise. 'What is it?'

'It's a series of interpretations of one of Brueghel's paintings.' She looked at him. 'It's called *The Triumph of Death*,' she said.

She looked back towards the graves, but the man who had been standing there was gone.

As the day drew on, the sky clouded over and an icy mist began to form, softening the edges of the new grave, black and mounded, a long, narrow rectangle in the grass. The flowers, still in their Cellophane, were piled up on the earth. The chapel of rest was locked up and silent, the business of the day over.

A young girl stood by the grave. Her clothes were summery, unsuitable for the winter weather, light blue jeans, cut off above the ankle, and a sweatshirt with a sequinned pattern across the front, flowers and birds. She was thin, with fragile wrists and ankles, narrow hips and back.

The knees of her jeans were muddy and she had the dirty hands and face of a child who had been playing. The dirt was smeared across her face, and she rubbed tears away with her hands. Then she turned back towards the cemetery gate, her ankles turning as her feet stumbled on the uneven path. She gave an angry shout, and began to run away from the graveside and the burial ground and on to the road where her shoes clattered on the Tarmac.

The chapel of rest was silent in the winter-dead landscape. Most of the graves were old, with mossy stones from which the writing had long ago faded into indecipherability. Next to the newly dug earth, overgrown by the grass and an encroaching laurel, the polished granite of the more recent grave stood out. There were flowers on this grave too, but it was as if the wind had caught them and scattered their petals in a splash of dark red against the black of the earth, a freak wind that had ripped the flowers apart, and strewn their petals across this one grave. *Ellie. Love . . . as strong as death.*

The frozen stillness of the morning thawed to rain, chill, persistent and driving. Eliza turned up the heater in her car as her wipers struggled to keep her view clear. The windscreen fogged, and she had to wind her window down a little to clear it. Her hat was pulled down over her ears, and her scarf muffled round her face, but she still felt cold. It was as if the hour spent in the chapel of rest and standing by the frozen grave had chilled her to the marrow, and it was going to take time for the warmth to creep back in.

The dullness of the afternoon depressed her as she drove back into the centre of the city in a slow-moving line of traffic. The rain splashed up from the road, and she speeded up her windscreen wipers to give herself some chance of seeing ahead. The traffic shuffled forward a couple of yards and stopped again.

The grey of the weather carried echoes of the chill graveyard, and she thought of Maggie alone in the dark, under the ground, dead and gone. And Ellie, with all her bright promise. She wanted to be back in the summer of Spain, or failing that, home in the warmth and colour of her flat, or in the spaciousness of the gallery. The traffic inched past the bus station and then she was on to the confusion of the massive Park Square roundabout. She switched lanes with the expertise of practice, ignoring the impatient horn that sounded behind her, and drove down past the new developments of the canal basin and along the road where the old industrial buildings still stood, unchanged and deserted.

The gallery and Eliza's flat were housed in one

of the old warehouses beyond the expensive and redeveloped canal basin that seemed to be the demarcation line between new Sheffield and the promise of prosperity, and old Sheffield, upon whose flesh the beneficiaries of industrial wealth had fed, and where now there were only the decaying bones. At night, when the gallery was empty, Eliza sometimes felt as isolated as if she were living on a remote island in the Shetlands rather than in the centre of a massive urban sprawl.

She drove past the hotel that seemed to mark the end of the gentrified area and under the bridge to the road that led along the canal side. The change was abrupt. The brickwork on this side of the bridge was crumbling, the surface stained with the water that ran from the broken fall-pipes. Beyond the bridge, there was a narrow alleyway, a cul-de-sac, where old household rubbish was dumped and then left to rot.

She took the turning that led to the canal road and drove past the chained and padlocked gateways of the old loading bays and the canal company offices. She was at the gallery now, the old warehouse looking dark and forbidding in the fading light. It had a mellow brick frontage and arched windows that gave balance and symmetry, and made the building beautiful in the daylight, even before its restoration.

Eliza locked the car and set the alarm. This was an area where you had to be careful. Her mind was already moving away from the events of the

10

morning, and towards the work she still had to do. She noticed that Jonathan Massey's car was parked at the side of the old warehouse.

Jonathan Massey was the gallery director. Eliza had known him for years – he had been her tutor at college, and Maggie's tutor as well. She hadn't been expecting him in today. He'd had some kind of meeting at the education department.

She went into the gallery, nodding a hello to Mel, a young trainee Jonathan had taken on before Eliza's appointment. Mel had dropped out of an art and design course at the local college. They couldn't teach her anything, she'd claimed to Eliza. She was sitting on one of the window sills reading a magazine, *More*, or *Hello!*, Eliza assumed from past experience. She tried to suppress her irritation. Mel was supposed to be working on the opening today, checking the invitations, making sure the replies were in, checking the catering arrangements, while Eliza worked on the exhibition.

'Have you finished checking the invitation list?' she said as she pulled off her hat and unwound the scarf from round her neck.

Mel looked round and shrugged. 'I was waiting for you,' she said. She was affecting boho glamour today, Eliza noticed, a tiered skirt of leather and chiffon, an embroidered jacket, DMs. Mel made most of her own clothes. Her hair, which was currently black, was gelled severely back.

So that's a 'no', then. 'You don't need me to do that,' Eliza said shortly. 'Next time you're waiting,' she began, then decided that she couldn't be bothered. Mel's contract only lasted for another five months, and then she would have to move on.

Jonathan must be in his office. She knocked on his door and went in. He was rummaging through his desk drawer, his back to her. 'Jonathan?' she said.

He looked round quickly. 'Eliza! I didn't . . .' He pushed the drawer shut. 'How did it go?'

Eliza shrugged. A funeral was a funeral. What did you say? 'I thought I'd get on with setting up the exhibition. What have you lost?'

'Oh, just a letter,' he said. 'I'll ask Mel . . . There was a message for you earlier, about Friday.'

'From Daniel?' She'd last seen Daniel six months ago, a brief glimpse in a bar on her last night in Madrid. 'What did he say?'

'No idea.' Jonathan began putting papers back into folders. 'Mel took it.'

'OK.' *The Triumph of Death*. It was Eliza's triumph as well, vindicating her appointment, relatively in-experienced, as curator of the new gallery. But Jonathan had been surprisingly unenthusiastic when she'd suggested that they try for a preview of Daniel Flynn's latest exhibition. 'Flynn?' he'd said. 'He's overrated. And he thinks far too much of himself to come somewhere like this. What's the point? He's only ever been interested in London.' Jonathan and Daniel had trained together at St Martin's. Jonathan's low-key response to the exhibition, the most prestigious the gallery had had since its opening six months ago, had been a constant irritation to Eliza.

The rationale of the Trust that funded the gallery was to bring important and innovative work to the provinces, breaking the stranglehold that London had on the arts scene. 'Daniel Flynn would be perfect,' Eliza said. 'There's a real buzz about his work – a lot of people will come. Look, *The Triumph of Death* is already scheduled for London, but I think he'll agree to a preview. The dates are right and I know this is the kind of setting he's thought about.'

Jonathan's agreement had been grudging. She'd enjoyed showing him the letter agreeing to her suggestion: a one-week preview before the exhibition transferred to London. Even then, he'd had been oddly subdued. 'Must be some kind of gesture towards his roots,' he'd said. Daniel Flynn had grown up in Sheffield.

He was having problems with his own work – a series of photographs around the idea of social exclusion, photographs of children whose lives and origins more or less put them out of the race from the very beginning. The idea was good, but he had been working on it for the past five years, and it still seemed no nearer completion. Which would explain his rather sour response to the success of one of his fellow students.

He'd said, almost as an afterthought, 'That was good work on your part, I suppose.' She hadn't told him about her personal connection with

Daniel Flynn. It *was* good work. She was happy to accept the plaudit, tepid though it was. She looked quickly at the diary to see if anything had changed since yesterday. 'I'll get on with setting up the exhibition,' she said.

Jonathan murmured something. He wasn't really paying attention. Then he looked up. 'Do you need me for anything? Only I want to get off early. I've got tickets for the theatre in Leeds.'

'No, that's fine.' Irritated, Eliza went back to where Mel was looking through a list and ticking names off in a desultory way.

'Daniel Flynn's been in touch,' she said. 'He *said* he's sorry he hasn't been up before but he's been stuck with something in London. Anyway, he's coming in tomorrow.'

'OK,' Eliza said. She hadn't known Daniel was back in England. There was no reason why she should. But she'd thought – somehow – that he was still travelling, that he'd gone to Tanzania where they had planned . . .

Mel was looking at her, and there was a knowing gleam in her eye that Eliza didn't like. She shook herself. 'Right, I'd better get up there. He hasn't sent all the work yet.'

'There's some more coming in tomorrow,' Mel said. 'Didn't you know he was in London?' There was the sound of a door opening and she sat up and became more focused on her work.

Jonathan came out of his office, pulling on his jacket. 'I'll be off then,' he said to Eliza.

'Bye, Jonathan,' Mel said brightly. They watched him go.

Eliza pulled on a smock to protect her clothes. She went quickly up the stairs, trying to put the irritations of Mel out of her mind and concentrate on the exhibition which combined interpretations of detail from Brueghel's *Triumph of Death*, a vision of a medieval apocalypse, with modern imagery and icons that spoke compellingly to a twenty-first century audience.

The windows of the gallery looked out on to the canal: low, arched bridges, the water shadowy in the clouded afternoon. The reflection of the water gave the light a particular quality, pale and clear, and the orientation of the building meant that it was fairly consistent right through the day. As she looked round the long room, she forgot the events of the morning, the sense of oppression and incompleteness that Maggie's funeral had left in her, and felt the work draw her in.

It was almost five when Mel came into the room to tell Eliza she was leaving. 'Jonathan said I could go a bit early today,' she said.

Mel had a habit of doing this – making requests of Jonathan without consulting her. Eliza had had to stamp quite hard on the 'Jonathan said' line that Mel was prone to peddle when she wanted her own way. But this evening, she wanted to be alone with the work, so she nodded. 'That's OK,' she said. 'I won't need you till tomorrow.'

Mel seemed about to say something, then she stopped. 'Shall I lock up?' she said.

'Lock the front entrance,' Eliza told her. 'But leave the galleries. I need to set the alarms.'

'OK.' Eliza heard Mel's feet on the stairs, and a few minutes later, the sound of the outer door closing. Eliza hesitated, then went downstairs. She checked the doors – Mel had locked them. Now she was down here, she might as well set the alarm for the downstairs exhibition space. She punched in the code, hearing the *beep beep beep* and then the continuous tone that gave her about thirty seconds to get out of the room. She pulled the doors closed behind her, and the alarm fell silent. OK, that was dealt with and out of the way. She went back upstairs and lost herself in her notes.

It was dark outside when she surfaced, and the wind was getting up, rattling the windows and making a strange moaning noise as it blew through the derelict building on the other side of the canal. The sound was almost soothing to Eliza in the warmth and shelter. She stretched and stood up. The gallery was silent around her, the work for the exhibition propped around the walls.

She lifted one of the panels and tried it against the wall to get a feel for the height and positioning. It was one of the reproductions from the Brueghel. In the original painting it was background detail, part of the desolate landscape in which the forces of the dead triumphed over the living. Enlarged and brought into prominence, it was a bleak depiction of solitary death.

A bare tree stood against the sky, and a figure hung from it, the head forced back into a fork between two branches so that the empty eye sockets gazed blankly up and the body arched away from the tree. A bolt or nail had been hammered through the two branches, forming a garrotte that held the figure to the tree. The arms were tied and pulled up behind the back so that they bent at an unnatural angle. The legs hung down, the whole figure stretched under its own weight. It was half decayed – almost skeletal, but not quite, not enough. Brueghel had imbued the figure with human suffering and a drear loneliness that had the capacity to haunt the mind of anyone who saw it.

Eliza thought about Ellie, the bright and beautiful child whose life had been cut brutally short. She thought about Maggie whose youth had come to such an abrupt end. She thought about the dark pit and the coffin being lowered into the grave, the earth falling on the lid with heavy thuds that grew fainter and fainter as the darkness closed in.

Madrid

As the darkness closed in on February in England, Eliza flew to Madrid. Spring came early to central

Spain that year. As the plane crossed the Pyrenees the morning sun caught them, the night shadow falling behind as they passed above the browns and oranges of the central plateau, dropping gently down, down to the city that was reaching up to meet her.

Madrid was light and space. The sky was cloudless blue as the bus carried her towards the city, past the lines of trees and the apartment blocks, clean and bright, standing far back from the road.

The *hostal* was in the centre of the city, close to the Paseo del Prado, and even here, at the heart of this European capital, the sense of space stayed with her. The roads were so wide that Eliza, a first-time visitor, hung back at the crossings as the Madrileños surged through the traffic. The exact rules of the driver and pedestrian engagement, which were so clear to her in London, here seemed oddly ambiguous. A light would tell her she could cross the expanse of carriageway, but as she stepped out (her head automatically turning right) a car would bear down and skim past her, seeming to brush her skirt as she leapt for the safety of the kerb, its horn echoing in her ears.

The cafés spilled out on to the pavements, the parks filled the city with air and green spaces. And all around her, the city life, the street life of central Madrid buzzed and swirled. Within a week, it felt as though she had been there for a year. Within a fortnight, she wondered if she ever wanted to leave.

And in her memory, Madrid was always a city of space, even though she soon discovered the narrow streets of Old Madrid, the stifling Catholicism of the churches and the congestion of the relentless traffic. It was months before the city faded into familiarity and then into disillusionment. And even after a long weekend with Daniel in Seville, a trip they made to the coast to Barcelona, Madrid remained her first love in Spain.

'Because of the light,' she told Daniel when he shook his head at her stubborn insistence. 'It's because of the light.'

Eliza put the panel back against the wall. Something had distracted her. She listened. There was nothing but the silence of the gallery and the distant sound of the traffic. It was dark outside. She checked her watch. It was after seven. She needed a break. She turned the lights off and walked the length of the empty gallery. The room was long and high, the floors bare wood, the walls whitewashed, the ceiling supported by pillars that broke up the space. The only light came from the moon, shining through the windows behind her. Her shadow lay across the floor and danced on the wall as she moved. Silence. The double tap of her feet echoed as she walked, heel and toe, tap-tap, tap-tap, as she moved through the long room.

For a moment, she thought there was an echo. The sound of her feet seemed to go on for a second after she had stopped moving. She stood there, listening. She moved again, and her shoes made their light tap-tap on the floor. This time there was silence, then she heard it again, like an echo of her own movement, hush-hush, like soft shoes moving across the floor. *Weird. That's weird.* It seemed to be coming from the downstairs gallery. She ran lightly down the stairs.

'Hello?' she said. The empty space gave her voice an echoing quality. The downstairs gallery was in darkness. She looked round. The main entrance was still locked, but the light for the alarm was out. Someone had switched it off. She felt herself relax. Jonathan. He must have come back for something. She didn't bother turning the lights on, but went through the doors watching the interplay of shade and shadow, the window frame a lattice shape lying across the floor. He must be in his office.

As she moved past the pillars, something caught her attention. A sound? She looked round, but the gallery was empty behind her. Then she saw someone sitting in front of one of the windows, half concealed behind a pillar, hunched forward as though whoever it was, was watching intently something on the canal below. Her heart thumped, then slowed as she realized who it was. It was the young woman who lived in the flat next door to Eliza's. 'Cara?'

The woman jumped, turning quickly, almost overbalancing. 'I didn't . . . I . . .' Her eyes focused on Eliza standing behind her in the dark. 'Eliza.'

She struggled to her feet, hampered by the sling in which she habitually carried her baby, Briony Rose. In the dim light, her eyes looked wide and startled.

She must have used the inside stairs that led to the gallery. There were plans to put in a separate entrance at the bottom of these stairs, but for the moment the occupants of the flats were only supposed to use them in an emergency. In practice, Eliza used them most of the time, and Cara had started following her example.

Eliza looked at Cara. 'Did you turn the alarm off?' she said.

Cara nodded. 'I've seen Jonathan doing it, so I know how it works,' she said. 'I was going to switch it all back on again, honest. I've done it before. I love the gallery. It's a lovely place to sit. I was going to go in a minute.' She was talking rapidly, nervously, her eyes looking beyond Eliza into the gallery behind her. The baby gave a brief cry of complaint.

Eliza bit back the comment she had been about to make. She could deal with this later when the baby was settled. 'I need to lock up,' she said briskly. 'Come on.' She waited as Cara scrabbled round for her bag. 'Here, let me carry that.' She picked up the cloth carry-all that the other woman always toted around with her, and slung it over her shoulder. 'Come on,' she said again.

Cara followed her slowly, looking back over her shoulder at the window. A rendezvous? Was

Cara in the habit of meeting a boyfriend on the canal towpath, or in the gallery? There didn't seem much point when she had a perfectly good flat upstairs.

She headed up the stairs, stopping when she realized Cara wasn't following. 'Cara?' she said.

'I'm coming.' Cara had stopped to look at the poster for Daniel's exhibition, the reproduction Eliza had been looking at earlier, the hanging man. She gathered the baby closer to her. 'It's horrible,' she said.

'I suppose it is,' Eliza said briskly. Cara still seemed reluctant to move. 'Do you want some coffee?' Eliza regretted the impulse almost as soon as she had spoken. She was cautious about socializing with Cara. Eliza felt sorry for her, but she didn't want – she didn't have time for – the demands a lonely teenager might make on her.

'OK.' Cara seemed to make a decision. She looked back at the gallery and then followed Eliza up the stairs. Eliza set the alarm and locked the doors behind her. She thought she heard the echo again as she and Cara walked towards the exit that led to the flats, but when she stopped and listened, everything was quiet. The alarm was sounding its single note, then dropped a tone and stopped. Eliza found herself listening, waiting for the alarm to go off in response to an intruder in the gallery, but nothing happened. She relaxed. 'You really think it's bad, that painting?' Cara said as she followed Eliza up the stairs. She was talking about Daniel's poster.

'Not bad,' Eliza said shortly. 'Disturbing.' Something was nagging at her and she wanted to pin it down, but Cara's chatter was distracting her.

'Why does Jonathan want to exhibit him?' Cara went on. Her eyes were nervous, darting round the walls of the stairway and landings.

'Who? Daniel Flynn? That reproduction is just a part . . . You need to see the exhibition as a whole.' Eliza was trying to fit her key into her lock. She could never get it the right way up. If Cara had been upset by that small detail, then she would find the rest of it devastating.

'I know. I thought . . . It's creepy, that's all.' Cara followed Eliza through the door into the flat.

'Good art is meant to disturb you. But it's only here for a week.' Eliza dumped her work bag and Cara's carry-all, and switched on the lights.

'Hey, nice!' Cara looked round the loft space.

Eliza was pleased. The Trust had run out of money before the loft conversion was complete. Her loft had been renovated to the point of habitability, the roof and the walls repaired, plumbing installed, the floors fixed. She had moved in to bare bricks and raw timbers. She had needed accommodation urgently. There was no time – and no money – for carefully thought out schemes. She had painted everything white and black, had moved in with her bed, her chairs, her lights and her painting equipment. She'd arranged the room carefully to create living and sleeping and working spaces. Now, it looked spacious and inviting, the chairs made splashes of colour close to one of the arched windows overlooking the canal. At the far end of the room, Eliza had set up her easel, and her painting, her Madrid painting, glowed its Mediterranean warmth against the winter night. Behind her, the kitchen welcomed with red tiles and bright pots.

Cara moved over to the window and hovered uncertainly, the baby sling distorting her outline like a misshapen pregnancy. Eliza shifted the papers that were set out on the chairs, photographs, slides, notes, some of her planning for the exhibition. 'Why don't you put it – I mean her, down?' she said.

'She might wake up,' Cara said. 'She cries a lot.' She looked at the child, an expression of bafflement on her face, then went over to the chairs as Eliza went to make coffee, and began to unhook the sling. The baby stirred as Cara put it down, tucking a shawl round it. 'I get so tired,' she said. She slumped into the chair next to the one she had put the baby on. 'It's a lot, when there's only you,' she said.

'It must be hard work,' Eliza said. She wondered what Cara had expected. She poured out the coffee and put it on the table. She looked at the infant's sleeping face. She didn't know much about babies.

'You know,' Cara went on, 'I thought that having a baby would be . . . you know, it would make me special. Now I'm just . . . I dunno.' She shrugged.

Eliza looked at Cara, wondering how to respond to that. Cara was tucking the shawl around the baby as she spoke, and her eyes were shadowed with tiredness. Her face, under the dramatic make-up she favoured, looked thin and pinched.

'Do you need a baby to make you special?' Eliza said.

'I don't know.' Cara frowned. She picked up her cup. 'This is nice.' She leant back in the chair. 'I'd like to have my flat as nice as this. I used to think about it when I was carrying her.' She nodded at the baby. 'I was going to have my own place and make it really nice. I wanted those drape things over the windows, you know, like they have, and I thought all plants and that. And they had such lovely baby stuff, I wanted . . .' Cara's voice faded away as she contemplated the plans she had had. 'I used to think that no one could say you were useless if you had a baby. You've got something to do then. They used to go on at me all the time: "You'll never get anywhere, you've got to work if you're going to pass any exams . . ."'

'Didn't you want to?' Eliza had always been successful at school, had enjoyed shining in a system that had never struck her as too challenging. Her degree had taken her to London, and then to Italy and Spain. Education had opened up the world for her.

Cara shook her head. 'I don't know,' she said. 'I didn't like school. I wasn't clever and they were always on at me, you know . . .'

'So you had a baby?' Eliza said.

The rain drummed against the window. Cara looked out at the canal and sighed. 'It wasn't like that really.' Eliza wondered if Cara had anyone to talk to. She was a solitary figure, drifting through the gallery, cuddling the baby against her in its sling. 'But when I got pregnant I thought, well, it would be nice. To have a baby.' She finished her coffee and smiled at Eliza. She looked round the room again. 'This is nice.' She was curled up in the large chair, and the tense, pinched look was leaving her face. She was as thin as a child.

Eliza finished her coffee. She could see that it was doing Cara good to have some company, but Eliza had things to do. She finished her coffee and stood up. 'Well, I need to get on,' she said. She saw a look of – what? Apprehension? – in Cara's eyes. 'We must do this again,' she said. There was no harm in the odd half-hour spent talking to Cara.

Cara's smile was rather strained as she nodded and gathered up the baby. 'It's been nice,' she said.

Eliza saw her out of the flat, then pulled out the sheaf of notes she had made downstairs. If Daniel was coming tomorrow, she wanted to be ready for him. The rain spattered across the window. It was just the night, just the weather for a couple of hours with Brueghel's macabre vision of the apocalypse.

CHAPTER 2

The road from the cemetery had been dark and wet. Kerry had got lost, taken a wrong turn, and then she had been wandering along dark lanes, like the countryside, where the wet grass slapped at her ankles and green tendrils hung over walls and caught and tugged at her hair. She'd found her way back to the main road eventually, but it was dark now. She looked at her watch.

Lyn would be waiting for her at the café where they always met. She'd be mad if Kerry was late. Lyn was mad at Kerry anyway. They'd had a row about Kerry's dad the last time they met. They always fought about Dad. But maybe Lyn was a bit sorry for what she'd said. Kerry's phone was clutched in her hand and she looked at it again as she pressed the buttons. The saved message ran across the screen: . . . its abut yor dad meet u at the cafy 7 dont b l8 . . . Lyn never said sorry, but Kerry could tell when she was.

There was a bus stop ahead, and she limped up to it, sinking down gratefully on to the wall. She eased her feet out of her shoes – her best ones – and rubbed her toes. Her feet were wet and splashed with mud. She looked up the road, squinting through the rain that distorted the lights and dripped into her eyes. And there was the bus, pulling away from the lights.

She scrambled on board, grateful for the warmth. The driver was friendly and smiled at her. 'You're a bit wet, love,' he said cheerfully. It was almost empty. Kerry pressed her face against the steamed-up window. The bus jolted and rattled, bumping her head against the glass.

She looked at her watch. She should be there by now. She keyed in Lyn's number, but she got the answering service. She keyed in another message: *pls w8.* Please wait. *Please, please wait!*

Lyn never did anything she didn't want to. She used to try and teach Kerry that as well. 'You don't have to do what *he* says,' she'd say, when Dad had told Kerry to go to bed, or tidy her room, or do her homework. But Dad wasn't Lyn's dad. Lyn's dad had left. 'She's jealous, Kizz,' Dad used to say. 'She'll get over it.' And he'd tried to be friends with Lyn, but Lyn didn't want to know. It drove Kerry mad sometimes. Dad would read her a bedtime story, and Lyn would come in and pretend to be looking for something. 'You're too old for stories,' she'd say. Dad would promise to take Kerry swimming. 'I'll take her,' Lyn would say. 'She's *my* sister.' But then she usually forgot so Kerry never got to go swimming.

And then Lyn had gone.

She pressed her face against the window. They were nearly there. She stood at the door fidgeting with impatience. 'Can't let you out here, love,' the driver said. 'Got to wait till we're in the stand.'

And then the doors were open and Kerry was out of the bus and running as the driver's 'Take care, love,' echoed after her. It had stopped raining, but her clothes were wet and her feet were hurting. She ran up the ramp that led to the tram tracks and across the bridge high over the road. That way to the tram and Meadowhall. That way was the old market.

The steps took you to an empty road and a car park, and they smelled of pee. She used to run down those steps with Ellie, both of them holding their noses and laughing, pushing past slower people, excited about the shops and the lights and the people. And Dad used to follow behind laughing at them too, and saying things like, 'Careful, Kizzy, slow down, remember you've got an old man here.' And he'd get them a burger – Ellie's mum didn't like Ellie eating burgers, so it was a secret. Kerry and her dad liked secrets – and . . . Kerry didn't want to think about that.

She tried not to think about the afternoon either, about the way the mist made it hard to see as she walked along the path, about the black rectangle of earth, and all the flowers piled up, dead, like the people in the graves. And the names. They were only names, they didn't mean people, until she saw the stone with the gold letters. *Ellie . . .* Ellie and Kerry.

No Ellie now. She remembered the kids walking past her house that last morning, the day after the police had come and taken Kerry's dad away. They had to walk past that way, there was no other way for them to go, and she waited for them to call out, 'Hey, Kizz, you coming?', waited, didn't run out like she usually did to join the arm-linking huddle on the walk to school, but no one called, and no one looked, not really, just glances that Kerry could see from behind the nets where she was watching, and their faces were tight and frightened, and they said things to each other as they passed and they cast their eyes over the house again, and then they ran off up the road.

And she'd gone to see Maggie. Maggie used to talk to Kerry when Mum was ill. 'You're fine, Kerry,' she'd say. 'You're a great kid.' And she meant it. Or Kerry had thought that she meant it. But Kerry had gone to Maggie and Maggie's face had been all twisted and blotchy, like Mum's was, and she'd looked at Kerry as though she hated her. 'Get away from me,' she'd said, and she hadn't shouted it, she'd said it in a cold, dead sort of way. 'Get away from me, you . . .' And someone had come to the door and pulled Maggie inside, and had looked at Kerry in the same way as she pushed the door shut. And all Kerry could hear was the crying.

And Dad had gone to prison. He wrote to Kerry.

Once a week, the letters came, and Kerry wrote back. But they couldn't say anything real to each other. Kerry couldn't write about what it was like at home with Mum, or what had happened at her last school and the place they'd last lived. She could still remember the voices in the night, *Paedo! Paedo!* And the sound of breaking glass as a brick shattered the front window. She couldn't tell Dad about that. And he wasn't telling Kerry anything. He said things like *It's not so bad once you get used to it* and *Don't worry, I'll be home soon.* Only he didn't say that so much now. In his last letter, he'd said, *Prison changes people, Kizz . . .*

She didn't watch the TV news, she didn't read the papers. The teachers said they all should. But Kerry didn't want to read what they said about her dad: *Pervert. Monster. Evil.*

She was there – Victoria Quays, the entrance to the canal basin. The water was black, reflecting the white of the moon. She hurried across the cobbles, her feet turning on the uneven footing, towards the café.

She pressed her nose against the window. Lyn? The café door opened, and some people came out. Kerry bit her fingernail. She could see through the steamed-up windows. There were only a few people, and she was sure . . . She kept looking. Lyn wasn't there.

She tried Lyn's number but got the answering service again. 'I'm here,' she said. 'I got it.' I got the message. That was a daft thing to say. Of course she'd got the message. Lyn knew that. It was so late, she'd got fed up and gone.

She didn't want to give up yet. She could walk along the towpath, walk to the gallery. Maybe Lyn was there. She could see the faint gleam of the water ahead of her. The city lights made an orange glow against the sky but the path itself was in darkness. She hesitated a moment, then stepped out of the light into the shadow of the first bridge. The air was cold and damp and the ground felt soft and slippery under her feet.

She could see a faint gleam beyond the tunnel mouth and the dank smell of the water closed round her. Now she was feeling her way, her hands pressed against the curving stone wall that came down low, almost to her head. The water lapped against the brick in a sudden flurry of ripples as though something had disturbed it.

As she came out of the tunnel, a shape formed itself in the water, a moored boat, dark and featureless, half concealed in the shadow of the bridge. The boards of the deck were grey and uneven. The path seemed to be petering out now, the buildings coming right to the water's edge. She was faced with a blank brick wall. She was on the wrong side of the canal. She needed to go back to the canal basin.

The moon came out and the reflection of the canal side appeared in the water. The water was still now, and she could see the walls that lined the path, the bushes and the path framed in the mirror of the canal. She turned back, and the darkness faced her, the black mouth of the tunnel, the smell of the canal that had rippled as though something was moving through the dark water. She didn't want to go back that way.

Her throat felt tight. She turned round again, and the boat was low in the water beside her, and a brick wall in front of her. She looked back, but the tunnel waited, trapping Kerry between the canal and the wall.

Eliza couldn't sleep. The sheet kept twisting up as she tried to find a comfortable place to lie, and she felt too hot, then she felt too cold. It was raining again, and the steady beat on the window became an irregular rattle as the wind blew the rain across in a flurry. The roof creaked. She turned over and punched the pillow into shape again. She settled down and curled her arm round her head. Deep, slow breathing, relax into the bed, just let go and melt away . . . There was a clatter from the other side of the wall, like the sound of something dropped on to a bare floor, rolling to stillness. She was awake again.

She was thinking about Maggie, and about Ellie. Seeing Cara's baby tonight had reminded her of the first time she'd seen Ellie, a tiny bundle in Maggie's arm. Eliza had been more engaged by the older Ellie, the bright girl with her mother's talent for art and a delight in words that seemed to be her own. *Raed Azile* . . .

Images from the exhibition began to form in her

mind. She didn't want them there, not now. Suddenly, she wanted no part of that medieval dance of death. She turned over again, disturbing the quilt. A cold draught blew round her. She looked at the clock. One a.m. Tomorrow was going to be difficult. She needed to get some sleep. She could feel the draught again. She knew what it was – it had happened before. Cara must have come in up the outside staircase earlier and not shut the door properly, so it had blown open.

She braced herself and got out of bed. It was freezing. She pulled her dressing gown round her, shivering with cold, and looked out of her door. The passage was in darkness, but the door was open and banging in the wind. There was water on the floor where the rain had blown in. She pulled it shut, banging it hard to make sure it locked, half hoping that Cara would hear it and realize what had happened.

She huddled back into bed, her hard-won warmth gone. Someone was moving around on the other side of the wall. She could hear soft footsteps moving backwards and forwards, backwards and forwards. The baby had cried almost every night since Cara had moved in.

The rain was heavier now, and she could hear the drips from the gutter hitting the fire escape. She drifted into the suspension of time that was neither sleep nor wakefulness. Her thoughts were starting to fragment into dreams. Then she was awake again. She had a residual awareness of a sudden noise.

She listened. Only the rain and the blowing wind. Sometimes it blew through the broken roofs and windows of the canal-side buildings, making a shrill, wailing cry. She could hear the sound of the baby on the other side of the wall. She glanced at the clock again. Two. She was wide awake now. Maybe she should get some cocoa or something.

She needed to sleep. She'd try the hot-milk treatment. She got up and went over to the fridge. There wasn't much milk left, but there was enough. Just. She tipped the milk into a pan and lit the gas, yawning and shivering slightly with the cold. Maybe she should curl up in a chair in front of the fire, drink her milk and try and drift off to sleep there.

The milk was starting to froth. She poured it into a glass, and sprinkled some chocolate on the top. She wrapped a blanket round her shoulders and curled up in the chair. The rain drummed on the skylight above her head. The wind was rising and the window rattled. She heard the staircase creak, and for a moment she thought there was someone out there, but it was only the wind making the building groan and rattle.

The crying had changed to hiccuping sobs. Eliza shifted restlessly. There was nothing she could do. She sipped the milk and tried to shut the sound out. The milk was warm and soothing, and the chair felt soft and comfortable as she sank back into its cushions. Her eyes were heavy now and she let the empty glass drop to the floor. Soft and warm.

A sob, and silence. A sob and silence. She was looking for the baby. The corridor was long and there were doors and the baby was behind one of them, then she was in the gallery and the painting on the wall was the graveyard, and she protested because she didn't want that painting. 'You must.' It was Maggie's voice, and she laughed. She reached out to the painting but as she touched it, it fell apart under her fingers, the paint flaking away, falling off the canvas and vanishing as her hands dug deeper and deeper into the darkness, through the black of the topsoil and the yellow of the clay and then it was the canal and she could see the figure reaching up and up from the depths of the water, from the painted grave.

And then it was morning, bleak and dreary. She woke in the chair feeling stiff and cold. The rain had stopped, and on the other side of the wall there was silence.

The empty buildings were a faint presence in the dawn now, their dilapidation becoming apparent as the sun rose higher. The converted warehouse looked incongruous, new. The water lay still, gleaming in the faint morning light. The canal was little used here.

A bridge crossed the canal further down the towpath. The canal ran under the road through a short arched tunnel. The bridge was a silhouette as the sky lightened, the water in the tunnel opaque and black. The sky was heavy with clouds, promising more rain. The sound of the early traffic disturbed the silence, and the smell of car fumes drifted through the air. The light crept across the water, across the mouth of the tunnel, reflecting up on to the brickwork. The colours began to appear, the dull green of the undergrowth on the towpath, the black of the sodden ground, the reds and yellows and blues of discarded crisp bags, soft-drink cans, cigarette cartons. It illuminated the crumbling brickwork, the weeds growing in the pointing. The shadow of the tunnel lay sharp across the water which moved slightly as the wind disturbed it, slapping against the side of the canal.

The rain was starting again, making the light dull, making the surface of the water dance. And there was something in the water under the bridge. It was like a tangle of weed and cloth, half in and half out of the shadow, sinking into the oily water. As the water rippled, the bundle moved slightly, rocking gently in the eddies. Rise and fall back. Rise and fall back. And sometimes as it moved, a faint gleam of something almost blue white gleamed through the water in the thin morning light.

CHAPTER 3

Roy Farnham was tired. His head was aching and his mouth felt dry. The call had come through shortly after six, jerking him out of a deep sleep. He'd sat up late the night before. It had been after one by the time he'd got to bed, and then the burial he'd been to had lodged in his mind, the dark cemetery and the funereal shrubs, the sparsely attended service. What a waste of a life.

His mind had drifted to the woman he'd talked to, Maggie Chapman's friend – what was her name? Eliza. She'd been striking in a long black coat, her fair hair escaping from under her hat. Maybe he should drop in at the gallery, see this exhibition . . .

He'd slept, woken, slept again. And now, as the heaviness of true sleep was carrying him away, the phone, the fucking phone was ringing and he was back on duty and he was going to have to answer it.

He rolled over in bed and picked up the handset. 'Farnham.' As he was speaking, his hand was groping around on the bedside table where he'd dumped a packet of aspirin the night before. He popped a couple out of the foil and sat up as the bitter taste of salicylate filled his mouth. He looked at the clock display on the stereo: 6.15. 'OK,' he said. 'OK, I'll be there.' He gave the instructions more or less on automatic pilot, then lay back for a minute as he got his thoughts in order. A body in the canal – suspicious death. *Shit*. Not a murder, not on his first day back. A young girl, they'd said. With a bit of luck, it'd be an accident. Or suicide.

The room felt cold as he pushed back the quilt. The heating wasn't set to come on until seven. He pressed the advance switch, but the warmth hadn't really begun to permeate the flat until after he'd showered and dressed. A fine rain was falling as he left the house, and the steering wheel was cold under his hands.

It was colder by the canal side. A body in the water always has the potential to be a suspicious death and the early summons had put the responsibility for the decisions squarely on Farnham's shoulders. His hopes for a simple accident or suicide faded as he stood on the canal bank, listening to the pathologist with deepening resignation. He didn't want another murder inquiry. But the body that was pulled from the water allowed for little doubt. 'Whoever put her in there made sure she wouldn't come up again,' the pathologist said. She pulled the matted hair away from around the neck, and showed Farnham the cord that was twisted round the woman's throat. It was attached to a bag. 'There's a brick or something in there. Pulled her right under. Poor girl.'

Farnham, crouched on the canal side, felt the wind cut through his jacket as it funnelled through the archway of the bridge. 'Suicide?' he said.

'Mm.' The pathologist looked at the cord assessingly. She didn't sound convinced. 'It's possible. But look at her hands.' She showed Farnham the damage to the fingers. They were bruised and misshapen, and there were faint marks on the wrists. 'That's pre-mortem damage,' she said.

Farnham stood up, feeling his knees protest. He wasn't forty yet, for Christ's sake. He needed to get to the gym, cut down on the beer, start . . . After this case. He'd think about it then. He looked at the dark water of the canal. The wind ruffled the surface, sending ripples lapping against the stonework. 'I'll get a team down there,' he said. They'd need to search the water under the bridge where the body had been found. They'd need a search team along the canal bank, along the canal itself – house to house – or boat to boat. God help his budget.

He looked down at the dead woman again. She seemed young, very young. The pathologist stood up beside him. 'I'll tell you something else,' she said. 'There's a baby somewhere. This girl had a baby not so long ago.'

Farnham closed his eyes. This was all he needed. 'OK,' he said. 'We'll get on to it.' The rippling water reminded him of the sea. A dead woman in the water. A baby. What were they going to find when they searched the towpath and the canal? He pinched the bridge of his nose, and rubbed his eyes with his fingers. 'OK,' he said again. 'Let's get started.'

Eliza put down the phone. She'd been talking to Maggie's landlord. Maggie had named Eliza as her executor, and suddenly, all of this was her responsibility. She'd contacted him shortly after Maggie's death to let him know what she was going to do about the flat. 'The rent's paid to the end of the month,' Eliza had said, the first time she had talked to him, when Maggie was just two days dead. 'The flat will be cleared by then.' After Flynn's exhibition, when she could give it her full attention.

But he'd phoned this morning with worries about security. The upstairs flat was unoccupied and the house was standing empty. 'Word gets around,' he said. Someone had been seen hanging round. Eliza doodled flowers on the pad by the phone as she listened.

'I'll get to it as soon as I can,' she said. The flat was a nagging irritation, but he had a point. An empty flat was vulnerable. There was little, if anything, of value there, but she didn't want Maggie's place vandalized, her books, her diaries, her photographs – all the memorabilia of Ellie – damaged or destroyed.

After she hung up, Eliza contemplated the task she'd set herself. It probably wouldn't take long. She found the prospect of sorting through the remains of Maggie's life depressing. She'd get started on it as soon as she had a couple of hours. She tried to put it out of her mind. She made breakfast and stood at the window watching the canal as she ate toast and drank coffee. Daniel was arriving today. She felt a twist of emotion in her stomach which she found hard to analyse. Excitement? Fear? Anger? It was the way she always felt when she was about to do something new, something that presented her with a challenge, that was all. But she dressed carefully, twisted her hair on top of her head the way he used to like it.

The gallery was busy when she came downstairs from her flat. Mel was unpacking boxes on the floor, surrounded by polystyrene and bubble wrap.

'Hi, Eliza,' Mel greeted her. Her hair, which had been black the day before, was pale blonde, carefully tousled. 'This is that stuff from Daniel Flynn.' She ran her eyes assessingly up and down Eliza. 'You look nice. Jonathan, Eliza's got dressed up for Daniel Flynn. Doesn't she look nice?'

Eliza felt her face flush. Jonathan looked up. 'Mm,' he said vaguely. Mel smiled.

'What time did Flynn say to expect him?' Eliza started checking through the post.

'Sometime this morning.' Mel shrugged. 'He didn't say.'

Jonathan looked up from whatever was absorbing

him at the desk. 'Have you had a chance to talk to him properly, Eliza?'

'Not really. I sent him a couple of e-mails, told him what I was planning. He didn't reply, so I'm assuming it's OK. I haven't managed to get him on the phone. Everything's in hand for Friday.' Eliza kept her voice casual.

Jonathan was checking the diary and opening his post. 'Oh, not again. Get a letter off to this guy, Mel. It's the third time he's sent me some photos of his stuff. If I was looking for wannabe pre-Raphaelites I'd go to the greetings-cards section in Smith's. At least I'd get someone who could handle paint.'

'I'll do that now,' Mel said. 'While I'm waiting for Eliza.'

'Thanks.' He flicked through the diary. 'We've got more school kids in tomorrow. I'd better deal with that. You know, I thought I was an artist, not a child minder.'

Eliza ignored this as she checked through her own post. It was just Jonathan's usual complaint. He always moaned about the school visits – and almost always dealt with them himself. Jonathan liked children. He was a good teacher – she knew that from her own student days. But he was surprisingly good with kids; serious and sober, but able to hold their interest and arouse their enthusiasm. It was a side to Jonathan she never would have suspected.

The post was dull – some advertising and some

44

charity leaflets that went in the bin, an invitation to a private view that might be worth going to, and some art catalogues she put on one side for later browsing.

'. . . like some kind of charity for homeless kids.'

'What?' Eliza hadn't been paying attention.

'I said, this gallery is like some kind of charity for homeless kids.'

He was bitching about Cara again. He'd taken against her, almost from the time she'd first moved in. Jonathan would have preferred the flats to be let at full market rents, rather than the 'affordable rents' – high enough in Eliza's opinion – that the Trust required. He thought that the flats should be taken by 'young professionals', not the socially needy. 'That's what you get for using taxpayer's money,' Eliza said. She remembered the night before, the shut-down alarm. 'By the way, Cara . . .' She stopped. 'It doesn't matter. Come on,' she added to Mel, 'let's get this lot upstairs before Daniel Flynn gets here.'

Mel pulled a letter off the printer and put it in Jonathan's in-tray. 'OK.' She sighed but stood up and she and Eliza began moving the boxes that contained Flynn's drawings and sketches towards the lift.

Once they had moved the boxes into the upper gallery, they began to sort the remaining pictures, matching the numbers with the plan that Eliza had set out the night before. So far it was all going smoothly, and they should have everything set up in plenty of time for the opening. She made a mental note to go over the invitation list for the private view and make sure that no one had been left off.

Mel's voice interrupted her thoughts. 'Oh God, look at this!' She was holding up a photo-assemblage, in which, against the barren incandescence of the Brueghel landscape, a man in the unmistakable uniform of an officer of the Third Reich was placing a noose round the neck of a young woman. The woman's hands were bound. Eliza could see the fastidious care with which the man was positioning the rope, the concentration on his face, the woman's white-faced fear. 'Is it real?' Her eyes were bright.

Eliza nodded. She had seen the photograph before – in fact, she had drawn Daniel's attention to it. It was one of a series taken towards the end of the war when Hitler's army was in retreat. 'The triumph of death,' she said. 'Flynn's right. Brueghel's images don't do it for us any more.'

'It's gross,' Mel said.

Eliza wasn't going to argue with that so she didn't reply. She stood for a minute, looking down at the canal. There was some sort of activity further up on the towpath. She'd been aware of people hurrying past and now, as she looked, she saw a couple of police officers. There must have been some kind of trouble down there in the night. She shrugged, dismissing it.

She closed doors, shutting off the hum of activity

from the floor below, and let the silence of the gallery close around her. She had work to do.

Madrid

The silence of the museum closed around Eliza as she walked through the high, light corridors. These were the times she treasured at the Prado, the early mornings before the gallery got too busy when she could have the spaces and the paintings to herself.

Her interest in the early painters had brought her to the rooms where the sixteenth-century Flemish paintings hung. They had developed techniques that produced paintings with a clarity and depth, and a saturation of colour that has never been surpassed. The big attraction for visitors was *The Garden of Earthly Delights*, Hieronymus Bosch's enigmatic depiction of heaven and hell. The colours, after all the centuries, were still vivid and clear. Eliza had spent a long time studying it.

But gradually she was drawn to a smaller panel that hung on the far wall. From a distance, it looked dark, but closer, the detail began to appear, a bleak coastline, a sluggish river, fires that cast a sombre glow across a landscape where death marched as an army. Brueghel's masterpiece: *The Triumph of Death*.

The painting exercised a fascination over her. She was intrigued by the meticulous techniques that had kept the paint so fresh, the luminescence of the water and the incandescent glow that suffused the landscape. Brueghel had probably worked with tempera white heightening into the wet or on the dry imprimatura, beginning with the highlights of the flesh . . . It was a painting that drew the eye, as the army of death advanced across a desolate landscape, hunting down and slaughtering the living, men, women and children, with a pitiless dedication and terrifying cruelty.

'*Un cuadro interesante*, no?'

She looked round. Two men were standing behind her, studying the Brueghel. They were both tall, casually dressed, one with Mediterranean-dark hair, the other with the fairer colouring of the north. Something about them said 'artists'. The dark-haired one seemed familiar. He was the one who had spoken, and she realized he had been talking to her. She tried to frame a reply in her still rudimentary Spanish, when she recognized his accent as English. 'Yes,' she said. 'But I always think that this is the wrong place for it.' Where had she seen him? Had he been in the café the night before?

'Where else would it belong but among the Boschs?' the other man said. Her artist's eye analysed his face – tanned as though he spent most of his time outdoors, Slavic bones. His dark glasses reflected her gaze.

'I mean the place,' she said. She gestured at the high, clearly lit gallery. 'It ought to be in the shadows, I don't know, in a dark corner of an old church,

and you'd come across it out of the blue. Or . . .'
She'd been thinking about this painting for weeks.
'I know it's medieval, its ideas, but there's something . . . I'd put it in a current setting. A cityscape,
industrial ruins, show people a modern triumph of
death.'

The dark-haired man looked round the room.
'That's the problem with a place like this,' he said.
'It's decontextualized. Stuck here, it's history,
superstition.' He moved closer to the panel. 'It's
a fifteenth-century video nasty,' he said after a
moment. 'Someone's cut that bloke's eyes out. If
it is a bloke.'

There was an element of the video nasty in the
relish with which Brueghel had depicted torture
and death. 'They were into death, the apocalypse,'
she said. 'Like we are now, I suppose. The end
of days, all that stuff.' In the foreground, a
body lay in a coffin, its head resting on a bundle
of straw. It reminded her of something she'd
read recently. ' "Do not apply any pink at all,
because a dead person has no colour; . . . and
mark out the outlines with dark sinoper and a
little black . . . and manage the hair in the same
way, but not so that it looks alive but dead . . .
and so do every bone of a Christian, or of rational
creatures . . ." '

'Cennino Cennini,' the other man said. The
fifteenth-century artist whose manual of painting
techniques illuminated the world of Renaissance
art for later centuries. 'How to paint dead flesh.'

Eliza was surprised he'd recognized it. He had taken off his sunglasses to look more closely at the picture and at her. He narrowed his eyes as though the light in the gallery was too bright. 'Cennini. "A dead person has no colour . . ." He's wrong, you know. The dead decay. We don't see it in modern times, not in the so-called civilized places. They have colour. We never see that, it's all hidden away, burned, buried . . .'

Eliza thought of Ellie in her bleak grave.

He slipped his glasses back on. 'Someone should do an exhibition, isn't that right, Daniel?' He seemed amused.

Of course! She knew why the dark-haired man seemed familiar. 'You're Daniel Flynn, aren't you?' she said. He had had a show in London two years ago that had caused a sensation among the critics and an interesting scandal when a fellow artist accused him of plagiarism. He was attractive, bohemian and controversial. Since then, his name was everywhere, his photograph in the magazines and Sunday papers. She should have recognized him at once. 'I didn't know you were in Madrid.'

'I got here a few days ago. I'm travelling, looking for what to do next. This is Ivan. Ivan Bakst.' The name wasn't familiar to Eliza. They shook hands.

'Eliza,' she said. 'Eliza Eliot. I'm here on a temporary contract.'

The two men had met up in France, Flynn told

her. 'We knew each other in London,' he said. 'Years ago, when I was at art school.' Bakst had been travelling the European waterways. He'd left his boat near Lyons, and the two of them had come down to Spain together.

'Are you staying?' Eliza said. They looked as though they would be interesting additions to the small expatriate community of artists that had assembled in Madrid that summer.

'We're going across to Morocco,' Flynn said. 'Tangier. And then further south, Tanzania, maybe, Ivory Coast.'

'I've never been to Africa.' Eliza and Flynn were drifting away from the painting now. Bakst remained studying it.

'Spain's almost there,' Flynn said. 'It's easy to forget. The Moors occupied most of it. I don't know, I might stay for a while.'

'You could spend a year going round the galleries here,' Eliza said. Not that she'd done as much gallery visiting as she'd planned. The social life in Madrid was too enticing.

'Why bother? You might as well visit Lenin's corpse,' he said.

'What?'

'It's what these galleries do to art. It isn't allowed to die. It doesn't go through the natural processes. A place like this is a mausoleum. Or a trophy hall. Dead art.'

Ivan Bakst had come up behind him as he was speaking. He gave Eliza a cool smile as though the two of them were sharing a joke. 'You do well enough out of galleries, Daniel,' he said.

Flynn laughed. 'So I should turn them down? Look, the money lets me keep working.' He looked at Eliza again. 'We've just got here. Show us around. Have a drink with me. Tonight.'

She looked at him. His face was thin, long-jawed. Against his dark hair, his skin had the almost translucent fairness she associated with the west-coast Irish, the Spanish. His eyes were blue.

'OK,' she said.

The flats were a concrete cliff towering up into the sky above her. It was dark, but her eyes were straining upwards because she knew it was coming, soon, and she wasn't going to be able to stop it. She tried to duck away from it, get out of sight, but it was coming now, hurtling down towards her and . . . The sudden ringing alarm jerked her out of the dream and she threw her arm up instinctively to protect herself and then she was awake, breathing fast, her heart hammering. She lay there staring at the ceiling. That dream again. Shit! Detective Constable Tina Barraclough rolled over and picked up the phone. 'Yeah?' Her voice sounded hoarse.

'Tina? Where the fuck are you? You're supposed to be here. Now.'

Dave West, her partner. She looked at the radio, and groaned. It was after seven. She'd forgotten to set the alarm – no, she could remember now, she'd come in after three and switched the alarm off. She didn't want to be jolted out of sleep. And she was going to be late again. 'Shit. Where . . . ?'

'Look, there's been an incident down by the canal. We're supposed to be there sorting out the house to house. I've covered for you – I said you were heading straight down – so you'd better be there.'

'OK, OK. I'll . . .' As she was speaking she rolled out of bed on to the floor, where she lay for a minute, holding her head and trying to gather the pieces of the day around her. The remains of her dream fell apart inside her head. Something about falling . . . The phone was still talking at her. Dave, trying to tell her the details of the incident. 'Yeah, yeah.' She couldn't get her head round it. She'd gone clubbing the night before.

She unravelled herself from the sheets and stood up, promising Dave she'd meet him at the canal basin in half an hour. She felt strung out and sick. It had seemed like a good idea at midnight, a bit of speed to get the party mood going. Now she wasn't so sure. Ten minutes on the exercise bike might bring her round, but she couldn't face that. She went through to the bathroom and turned on the shower, then she sat on the edge of the bath, holding her head. She was horribly aware of her stomach, her throat. A cold sweat was breaking out over her body, and she felt light-headed and dizzy. She didn't know how she was going to get through the day.

She toyed with the idea of calling in sick. But that wouldn't be fair to Dave. He was covering her back, and she'd let him do that a bit too much lately. They'd both been involved in a not very successful investigation into some recent drug deaths. A batch of pure heroin had turned up on the streets and effectively culled three unwary users. The outcome had been the arrest of a few minor players, a slight shift in the hierarchy on the streets and a return to business as usual. The source of the heroin had not been established. It had been an uncomplicated case, but she hadn't managed to get on top of it. Tina should have had her promotion by now, but her reputation as a good and reliable officer had taken a bit of a hammering recently. She had to get her act together, for what it was worth.

She struggled to recapture the details of this new case that Dave had tried to tell her. A body in the canal. A murder. He'd said who was in charge, and she couldn't remember. Shit, she needed to know that. She could phone . . . no, she'd remembered. DCI Farnham. Roy Farnham. That was the name Dave had said. Farnham had come across to Sheffield from Humberside, and he had a reputation as a high flier who didn't suffer fools gladly.

A murder was a good, high-profile case to be involved in. So why did she feel the drag of depression as she thought about the things that the investigation might uncover. And the feeling, at the end, that you had done little, if any good. She thought about a tower block on a summer night, the cars, the lights, the voices shouting, and the flicker above her that became the figure plummeting down from that dizzy height . . . She shook her head. That had been three years ago. There was a murder case, she was on the team, and she needed to do a good job to try and get her stalled career moving again.

A few minutes under the shower revived her a bit, but when she looked in the mirror, she still resembled Dracula's daughter. *Fuck it!* Why had she let herself get talked into the speed? It would have been OK, otherwise. Today, she needed some artificial aids. She took a small twist of paper out of her bag and opened it carefully. Better than she'd thought. There were still a good couple of lines there. She tipped a tiny bit out, cut it and breathed it in, her eyes watering as the numbness hit then a sharp pain deep inside her nose. Then she felt the magic start to work. Her head cleared and the cold, sick feeling retreated. Her energy was returning – she'd have to be careful not to go hyper when she got to the canal. They'd spot it.

She crammed her stuff into her bag and went down to the kitchen. Pauline, one of the women she shared the house with, was there, eating cereal and reading the paper. 'There's coffee,' she said, without looking up.

Tina poured herself a cup. 'Oh God, last night, I don't know what I thought I was doing it was stupid crazy but hey there's something going on down by the canal could be a good case for me so I really, really need to get . . .'

55

Pauline looked at her. 'I'd come down a bit before you get there,' she said.

'Yeah, yeah, OK.' Pauline was right. She'd need to watch herself. She gave the coffee a miss, forced down a slice of bread and marmalade and headed for her car, the energy suddenly singing in her veins. The rain stung her cheeks and she felt a great surge of optimism as though, after all this time, she'd found her real self, that relaxed, confident self that lived inside her and was so often – these days – inaccessible.

It was half an hour before she'd managed to force her way through the city traffic to get to the place where Cadman Street Bridge crossed the canal. She was aware of Dave's reproachful glance as she arrived to be given her instructions for the day.

Eliza and Mel spent the first part of the morning moving the display boards around to get the angles right. 'I want to make a link with the canal,' Eliza explained to Mel. 'Look at the water on the Brueghel. And the bridge. It's just . . . I don't want people to look at it and think, "Oh, old master," I want them to look at it and look out of the window and think, "This is here. This is now."' She straightened the enlargement of the hanging man on the display board in front of her and stood back.

'Is that what Daniel Flynn says?' Mel asked. She brushed dust off her trousers.

'No, those are my ideas,' Eliza said.

Mel pulled a face and sat back on her heels. 'Can we have a break? I'm tired. Shall I go and make some coffee?'

Eliza translated this as Mel wanting a chance to get away from the drudgery of setting up the exhibition space. Whatever Mel's motives were, coffee was a good idea. 'You'll have to go to the café,' she said. 'We're out of coffee here.' She reached for her purse. 'I'll have a cappuccino.' Mel was looking out of the window with interest, and Eliza remembered the activity she'd noticed earlier. 'Maybe you can find out what's happening,' she added.

Mel gave her a bright smile. 'Yes,' she said. She went to get her coat.

While Eliza was waiting for Mel, she went downstairs to see if there were any messages for her and to see if Jonathan wanted her for anything. His door was ajar, and she could see him in front of his computer. She knocked, and pushed the door open. 'Hi.'

He jumped and twisted round in his chair. 'Don't *do* that, Eliza. Get some shoes that make a noise.'

'Sorry,' she said.

'I didn't train to spend all my days writing reports,' he said. 'Eliza, *what* was that about Cara?'

So he hadn't missed her evasion. 'It'll keep. Anything new?'

He shook his shoulders irritably. 'No. You could write this report for me . . . No. Let me know when Flynn gets here.'

There wasn't too much of the morning left. She was beginning to think that Mel had got the message wrong. She checked her watch. It was almost half past.

Jonathan's window caught the sun. The room was light and airy. Eliza thought it would make a good seminar room when they managed to expand the educational side of the gallery. There were posters on the walls from exhibitions Jonathan had particularly admired, including his own big success from over ten years ago now, a photographic exploration of England's industrial landscapes, abstract shapes against the wildernesses that were encroaching on the urban decay. Jonathan's skill as a photographer, and the depth of ideas behind it, had attracted a lot of critical acclaim. But he'd never produced anything of a comparable quality.

'About Cara . . .' she said. Jonathan needed to know that Cara had got through the gallery alarm system.

He looked up from his work, his face expressing irritation. '*What* about Cara?' he said.

'She'd let herself into the gallery last night.'

He looked at her in silence. He didn't seem surprised, more irritated and a bit anxious.

Eliza went through what had happened, her encounter with Cara, and Cara's claim that she'd learnt how to work the alarm system by watching Jonathan. His face grew tense as he listened to her.

'Rubbish,' he exploded. 'Bullshit.'

Eliza shrugged. 'That's what she said.' He seemed more upset by that than anything else. Jonathan didn't like to be seen as fallible. But now she thought about it, it did seem odd. When would Cara have watched Jonathan setting the alarms? 'Anyway, I thought you needed to know,' she said.

'You should have told me sooner.' His face was angry. It didn't bode well for Cara. 'I'm getting on to the Trust. We never agreed to this sort of thing.'

'Do you want me to do it?' Eliza thought she could soften the message a bit, get the Trust to impress on Cara the importance of the security systems without getting her into major bother.

'No.' Jonathan was adamant.

Oh well. He had a point. Eliza looked at her watch again. Mel was taking her time with the coffee. She ran back up the stairs and went in to the upper gallery, pleased that the placing of the display boards hadn't diminished the sense of space and light. She crossed to the other side of the room, to look at it from a different angle. Good. And from here, she just had to turn her head and she was looking down into the dark waters of the canal.

Then she was aware that someone was standing behind her, and hands lightly touched her shoulders. '*Un cuadro interesante*, no?'

She spun round, her heart hammering, and Daniel was there, smiling at her a bit warily, a bit cautiously, as though he wasn't sure of his reception. 'Daniel!' she said. Then, 'You frightened me out of my wits!'

'Sorry,' he said. 'There was no one downstairs.'

It was so long since she had seen him that she had been imagining him more and more like his publicity photograph, which portrayed him in chiaroscuro, brooding and shadowed. But without the photographer's art, he was ordinary, the Daniel she had known in Madrid, with dark hair, blue eyes and a friendly smile which became less guarded as she smiled back at him.

'It's been a long time,' she said. 'How are you? What have you been doing?'

'I'm OK,' he said, still slightly careful. 'I've been working. I left Madrid a few weeks after you – kind of lost its charm then.'

'Where did you go?' she said. She thought she knew the answer. *Africa. Tanzania.*

'Whitby,' he said. 'I've got a flat on the coast there.'

Whitby. She wanted to laugh. 'You should have come across,' she said. 'We could have – I don't know, something.' He'd been so close, and he hadn't bothered to get in touch.

'I was working,' he said. He moved across to look out of the windows. 'This canal,' he said. 'It's like the Brueghel landscape – you've even got the arched bridges and the dead trees.'

'They're alive in summer,' Eliza said.

'Artistic licence.' He looked at her. 'I've never

forgotten what you said that time we were looking at the Brueghel together.' His gaze moved to the canal, and he was quiet for a moment as he looked out of the window, frowning slightly. 'I like what you've done. I knew you'd understand this exhibition.'

The slight tension that had been inside her all morning relaxed. That was the one factor she had been unable to control. Daniel might have hated her ideas. 'Good. I'd better tell Jonathan you're here.'

He shook his head. 'It'll keep.' He was leaning against the window frame, looking out at the canal side. 'So how do you enjoy being a curator?'

'I love it.' That was true. Eliza enjoyed interpreting other people's work, presenting it in ways that would make people look carefully, think about what they were seeing, think about art in its context, not as a series of isolated pieces stuck like relics in an exhibition.

'What about the painting?' he said. 'Your own stuff?'

The Madrid painting that was on her easel upstairs. She had discussed it with Daniel months ago when it first began to form in her mind. She had wanted to do – a modern triumph, not of death but of life, something that would encapsulate what Madrid had come to mean to her. She had been brought up in the far north of England where shadows and light merged, where night and day segued one to the other in an indeterminate creep of time. Madrid was of the south – a place of hard shadow and saturated colour. That was what the painting would celebrate.

But as Sheffield had closed around her, the dark winter, the solitary life she seemed to have chosen here, as though she didn't want to commit herself to this place for longer than was necessary, didn't want to make the ties that might hold her here, the painting had changed. The shadows of the north began to creep around the edges, the colours began to fade, and she realized that the painting was growing under her hands, turning into something different from what she had originally planned.

But she didn't want to talk to Daniel about it, she realized. They had discussed everything in Madrid. But this wasn't Madrid, and Daniel was different now.

She shrugged. 'It's easy to get distracted,' she said ambiguously.

He pushed himself upright. 'But you are still painting?'

'Oh yes.'

'Show me what you've done,' he said. 'Show me what you're working on at the moment.'

For a second, she thought he meant now, but he was looking round the gallery again. 'I need to spend some time with this,' he said.

'I'll leave you to it for a while, shall I?' she said.

'No. Walk me round it. Tell me your ideas for the rest. Then we'll do the official welcome bit, OK?'

Eliza felt her slight depression lift. She got out her notes, and they went through the exhibition together, talking through problems, sharing ideas, disagreeing once or twice. Eliza saw Mel in the doorway at one point, looking a query. Eliza shook her head, wondering what had taken Mel so long, and she disappeared.

It was getting on for midday before they had covered everything. They had spent the time walking round the gallery, sorting through the pictures, experimenting with different arrangements on the walls and display boards. They had fallen back into the swift exchange of ideas that had marked their relationship. They talked about the things they missed, the people they'd been friendly with. 'Do you remember . . . ?' they each kept saying, and then laughed as they thought about the places they'd gone to, the things they'd seen, the things they'd done. 'It's Madrid comes to Sheffield time,' he said. She looked at him. 'Ivan,' he said. 'He's been in touch. He's coming through South Yorkshire in a couple of days. He'll be here for the show.' He smiled at her.

Ivan Bakst. She couldn't share Daniel's enthusiasm.

Then he stopped abruptly and looked away from her, out of the window towards the canal. The sun had gone in and the light had faded. 'I think that's it,' he said. She had the feeling that his attention was elsewhere. The words seemed to die in the air between them.

The upstairs gallery was very quiet. She had expected Jonathan to come up to see Daniel – Mel would have told him that Flynn was here – and she had half expected Cara to appear, drifting into the gallery from her flat, eager for company and conversation, but there was no sign of her. Eliza remembered the crying in the night. Suddenly, she felt tired and had to suppress a yawn. He noticed and said, 'You've been working all morning without a break. You should have said something.'

Eliza shook her head. 'Bad night,' she said.

They were at the entrance to the gallery now, at the reception desk. Jonathan's office was to their right. 'Look.' He checked the time. 'I'm running late. I'll get off now – I'll give Massey a ring later. Tell him everything's fine, just go ahead as we agreed, right?'

Eliza was surprised. She didn't know what to say. 'Oh. Yes, all right.' She'd expected him to suggest some kind of further meeting, a drink, *something*. She wanted to talk about Madrid, put some kind of closure on their relationship, the closure it had never properly had. 'When . . . ?'

'I'm going back to the east coast today,' he said. 'I'll be back for the do, don't worry.'

Today. 'OK, fine.' She watched him as he left the gallery. He stopped once he was outside, as though he was getting his bearings, then he turned away from town, towards the road that crossed the canal over Bacon Lane Bridge. There was a route on to the towpath there, she remembered. She shook her head, confused. She'd better go and see Jonathan.

He wasn't in his own room, he was in the general office talking to Mel, who looked up with alacrity as Eliza came in. 'Where is he?'

'He's gone. He was in a hurry. Jonathan . . .' She could hear her voice sounding flat.

Jonathan shrugged. 'He's known for it,' he said. 'Lots of enthusiasm, lots of *How wonderful you all are*, then he loses interest and fucks off.' She was surprised at the hostility in his voice. 'He's OK with what you're doing?'

'Yeah.' Eliza sagged. 'He thinks it's wonderful.' She looked at both of them. 'Well, haven't I earned a coffee?'

Mel looked back at the gallery entrance, where Daniel had disappeared. Jonathan shrugged. 'Don't worry about it,' he said again. 'Look, I've got a meeting in town. Tell me about it later.' He looked tired and edgy, Eliza noticed, as he left. He seemed more and more weighted down with admin – meetings, reports, more meetings.

'What happened to you?' she said to Mel after Jonathan had gone. The canal basin was only ten minutes from the gallery, but it had been almost an hour before Mel had come back with the coffee.

'I had to go round by the road,' Mel said. 'The towpath's closed off.'

'Closed off?' Eliza switched the kettle on. 'Do you want some?' She'd have to make do with instant.

'Yeah. It's all police and things.' Mel started digging in her bag and pulled out her magazine. For her, coffee meant a cessation of work. 'I started walking and before I got to Cadman Street Bridge, there was tape across the path and a couple of policemen.'

'What's happened?' Eliza had forgotten the activity she'd noticed from the window earlier that morning.

'Well, I stopped and talked to them,' Mel said. She was an incorrigible talker, an incorrigible flirt, and the men watching the path would have been more than happy to oblige her, Eliza was sure.

'So what did you get them to tell you?' she said.

Mel smiled, pleased. 'Well, not much,' she admitted. 'One of them said he might drop in later. But they said' – her voice dropped and her eyes gleamed – 'that they'd found a body in the canal.' She shivered with manufactured excitement.

'Drowned?' Eliza said. She thought about the still, dark waters. They might be still, but they were cold and dangerous. People had drowned there before, and would again, but she, like Mel, was more intrigued than horrified by the idea of disaster and death on the towpath, close to where they lived and worked.

'He didn't know,' Mel said. She dismissed the subject. 'Can we have lunch now? I got a sandwich.'

Eliza looked at her watch. It was after one. 'OK,' she said. She had a Marks and Spencer salad in the fridge from yesterday. They could take half an hour.

Mel settled down with her magazine as Eliza made coffee. 'Where's he staying?' she asked.

'Who?' Eliza poured water into the cups. The sour smell of the coffee made her slightly queasy.

'Daniel Flynn,' Mel said impatiently. 'He looks really sexy in the photograph.' She gave Eliza a speculative look.

Eliza concentrated on her coffee. 'He's OK,' she said, keeping her voice neutral. She listened to Mel as she talked about Daniel, the things she'd read about him, the things she'd heard, his involvement with this famous beauty or that famous beauty, things that Eliza would really have preferred not to hear about, but of course Mel didn't know, and Eliza had no intention of letting her find out. She tuned out the sound of Mel's voice, responding with an occasional 'Mm', and let her mind drift.

And she kept coming back to Daniel. She'd managed to push him out of her thoughts for a while, but during the next few days, that was going to be hard. She'd need to keep herself focused on the work. She thought about the pictures and photo-montages that had surrounded her all morning. Daniel had liked her idea of using the Brueghel as a focus, drawing the viewer in through the greys and blacks and blues of some of the images to the centre of incandescence where strange winged creatures flew above a river of fire and screaming children fled a napalm hell. Suddenly, she was impatient to get back to work.

'OK,' she said, finishing her salad. 'Let's get on with it.'

Mel, silenced in mid sentence, looked put out. 'Jonathan wanted me to . . .' she began.

'And I want you to help me get the room set up,' Eliza said. She had just about had enough of Mel, and for once, Mel shut up.

They worked until late in the afternoon, then Mel said, 'Eliza . . . ?'

Eliza was angling a display board. 'Yes?'

'Jonathan said I could finish early today. I'm going to the concert. He said it was OK with him if it's OK with you.' Her voice was unaccustomedly diffident.

Eliza nodded. She'd worked her bad temper off, and she had no reason to keep Mel. They'd made good progress. 'Fine. I think we've done as much as we can. I'll go on for a bit. See you tomorrow. Make sure the door's locked.'

She listened as Mel's footsteps faded down the stairs. She was glad to be by herself now. She could walk round, absorb the design that they'd carefully set up, note places where it needed refinement or alteration, begin to get the feel of the exhibition as a whole. Flynn would be back on Friday for the private view, and Saturday, they were opening. She needed to check the arrangements for the private view again, check with the caterers, see if there were any last-minute invitations to be sent out.

She was holding up another of the enlargements from Brueghel's original painting, the depiction of death on a red horse, this one taken from the centre of the painting where all the re-enactments of death took place in the orange glow from the fires that suffused the dead landscape, when something made her jump – *Too much time with the old masters* – and she realized that there were two people, a man and a woman, standing in the doorway watching her. Mel must have left the door unlocked. She sighed. 'The gallery's closed now,' she said. 'We open at ten.'

The woman looked at the painting Eliza was holding. 'Death on a red horse,' she said. 'I thought it was a pale horse.' She moved round until she could see the picture more clearly. '"And behold a pale horse; and his name that sat on him was Death,"' she said.

Eliza recognized the words. 'Revelation,' she said. The fading light fell on the woman. She was a Goya portrait, with full lips and dark eyes, her oval face framed by black hair. She looked pale and tired – a Goya with a hangover, Eliza diagnosed with the expertise of experience. 'I don't think Brueghel was painting Death specifically. I think they're all deaths, if you see what I mean.'

The woman nodded, still eyeing the painting. 'It's . . . striking,' she said. Her tone changed. 'You're Ms Eliot, Eliza Eliot?' Eliza nodded. The woman took something out of her pocket and held it up for Eliza to see. 'Detective Constable Barraclough,

South Yorkshire Police,' she said. She looked too exotic to be a policewoman. 'And this is DC West.' The second officer nodded at Eliza.

'We're investigating an incident on the canal bank last night,' DC Barraclough said. 'You live in the flat upstairs, don't you?' Eliza remembered Mel's story of the closed-off towpath, the body in the water. 'We're trying to put together a picture of what happened. Did you notice anything unusual last night?'

'Unusual?' Eliza shook her head. 'How do you mean, "unusual"?' An incident. A feeling of unease was beginning to stir inside her. What, exactly, had happened on the towpath last night?

'Anything that sounded like trouble, a fight? Even kids messing around?'

Eliza shook her head again. She couldn't remember anything like that. She remembered the noise of the storm.

'Do you get a lot of people along the towpath at night?' DC Barraclough said.

'Boats go by sometimes. Kids occasionally. It's usually pretty quiet.'

'But you didn't hear anything like that last night?'

'It was very stormy, so that kept me awake. But . . .' Eliza shrugged. The sound of bad weather wasn't what this woman was looking for. 'Have you asked at the other flat?' she said.

DC Barraclough looked surprised and checked her notebook. 'The other flat?' she said.

'There are two flats,' Eliza said. So much for efficiency.

'Who lives there?' It was the man this time. DC Barraclough was flicking through her notebook, frowning.

'Cara . . .' Eliza realized she didn't know Cara's second name. 'A young woman and her baby,' she amended. 'She's called Cara. I don't know her . . .'

She was aware of a beat of silence, then DC Barraclough said, 'There's a baby?'

'Yes.' Eliza saw the two police officers look at each other. 'Is something wrong?'

'Have you seen her today?' the other woman said. 'This Cara?'

Eliza shook her head, suddenly feeling uneasy. She remembered wondering why Cara hadn't come wandering into the gallery the way she normally did. She remembered Mel sitting back on her heels, her eyes bright with excitement as she talked about the police on the towpath and the body in the canal.

DC Barraclough didn't answer her. She was talking on her radio.

The Second Site Gallery wasn't far from police HQ. Roy Farnham was there within fifteen minutes of getting the call. He pulled into the car park in front of the old warehouse, aware, with part of his mind, of the beauty of the old brickwork, the elegant arch on the windows and doors.

71

One of the officers was waiting for him. He'd noticed her before, the DC who always looked as if she had just got out of someone else's bed. Tina Barraclough. What was it he had heard about Barraclough? Some kind of crack-up after a case that went bad a couple of years ago? There had been something about a suicide, a young man had jumped from a tower block . . . He couldn't quite remember. He noticed that she looked rather ill and ragged as she came over and told him quickly about the young woman, known only as 'Cara', who lived in a flat above the gallery with a baby, and who hadn't been seen that day.

'Can we get access?' he said.

Barraclough shook her head. 'Dave West's been up.' She indicated the blocked-in stairway running up the outside of the building. 'The bottom door was open, but the one into the building is locked.'

Farnham could hear the pathologist's voice from early that morning. *There's a baby somewhere. This girl had a baby not so long ago.* 'We need to get in.' As he spoke he was aware of someone coming from the gallery, a woman. He recognized her as she looked up. It was Eliza Eliot, the woman he'd met at the Chapman funeral – he'd forgotten for the moment that she worked at the gallery. He'd hoped if he saw her again it might be in a less formal setting. A funeral and a murder inquiry. *Christ, Farnham, you know how to show a girl a good time.* 'Miss Eliot,' he said. He saw recognition in her eyes. 'You told my officers you haven't seen the woman who lives upstairs all day. Is that unusual?'

'Yes.' She rubbed her arms against the cold. 'Yes, it is. She usually drops into the gallery at some time. She's a bit lonely, I think . . .'

'Is there another way into the flats?'

'I'll get my key . . .' she began, then said, 'There are stairs in the gallery. It's quicker that way.' He followed her into the gallery, past an empty reception desk and through a turnstile. The gallery was empty, the long downstairs room in darkness. He could see the shapes of pictures on the wall, objects standing on the floor space, making odd, shadowy shapes in the fading light. Eliza Eliot led them to the back of the gallery and through a door that opened on to a staircase. She ran ahead and opened a heavy door at the top of the stairs.

Farnham found himself in a long, straight corridor. There were two entrances on the corridor, open lobbies that led into the individual flats. The door that led to the external staircase was at the far end.

'That's Cara's,' Eliza Eliot said, pointing to the first door.

Barraclough looked at Farnham, then knocked on the door. There was silence. She knocked again. 'You heard her in the night?' Farnham said to Eliza.

Eliza nodded. 'She was seeing to the baby. It was crying.'

Barraclough's face was tense as she listened. 'There's no one there,' she said, addressing herself to the other officer.

Farnham nodded to West, who stepped back and kicked the door over the lock. It gave a bit. He kicked it again and it flew open. The small entrance lobby was dark. Farnham heard the click of a light switch, but nothing happened, then Barraclough's voice said, 'The light isn't working,' then, louder, 'Cara? Police. Are you all right?' He shone a torch at the ceiling. There was a bare bulb hanging from the light fitting. He went ahead and pushed open the door into the flat. The room was dark apart from the flicker of a candle. Heavy curtains were pulled across the window. It was icy cold. He pressed the light switch, but again, nothing happened.

West was over by the window, tugging at the curtains. They fell away, landing on the floor with a thump, releasing the smell of dust. They were just old blankets hooked over the curtain rail. In the dim light, it was like being in a child's room, the nursery print on the bedspread, the teddy bear and the doll propped on the floor by the bed, the sheets and pillows disarranged, a rocking horse pushed against the wall at one side. There were the remains of a sliced loaf on the worktop, a mug, an open milk carton, a baby's bottle, unwashed. There was a cupboard on one side of the room, the doors hanging open, and beside it a chest of drawers, the drawers pulled out, stuff scattered over the floor.

He heard Barraclough's exclamation. She was leaning over a cot that was pushed close to the window. Farnham felt his heart sink as he saw the motionless shawl-wrapped bundle. He was already speaking into the radio as Barraclough began to run her hands over the infant. He saw Eliza Eliot standing by the door, her hands pressed over her mouth, her eyes shocked. He nodded sharply at West, who began to usher her back, back towards the door of the flat, the landing.

Then Eliza was outside the flat, and the young man was looking down at her. He was holding a photograph. Eliza noticed that he held it carefully, protecting it from his fingers with a tissue. 'Is this her? The woman who lives here? Cara?'

Eliza looked at the photo. Cara smiled be-wilderedly back, a very new baby held awkwardly in her arms. 'Yes,' she said. 'Look, what's . . . ?'

Roy Farnham came out, still talking on the radio. His voice sounded brisk and efficient, and somehow this was more reassuring than shouting and urgency and exclamations. He looked at her. 'We'll need to talk to you,' he said. 'Would you wait downstairs?'

She shook her head. She found herself persuaded, firmly and inexorably back down the stairs to the gallery, back into the office where she sat down heavily. The sound of a siren was already audible in the distance, coming nearer and nearer. She was shaking. She looked wordlessly at the young officer. She couldn't understand what he was saying. 'I don't know,' she kept saying. 'I don't know . . .' She tried to listen to what was happening two storeys above her, heard the sound of feet running on the outside staircase and silence again.

Cara. Cara's baby. She had a sudden vision of Ellie as a tiny bundle in Maggie's arms, of Cara putting the baby down on the chair in her flat in response to Eliza's clumsy invitation. 'I've got to . . .' she said, and stood up. She went to the gallery entrance, ignoring the efforts of the young man to keep her back.

Two paramedics came down the stairs at speed, one of them carrying the tiny bundle that must be Briony Rose. The siren was still sounding as the ambulance drove away. Like a sleepwalker, Eliza went up the stairs to the exhibition space, and stood in front of the reproduction of the Brueghel that formed a centrepiece to the exhibition. 'Miss Eliot?' She heard the officer's voice behind her.

A river flowed across the scene, a bloated corpse drifting on the oily surface, another sinking beneath the water under an arched bridge. A burning tower dominated the landscape and the armies of the dead pressed forward.

CHAPTER 4

Kerry's diary

Ellie's mum died. I went to the funeral but I went late because I didn't want anyone to see me. It was creepy because there was all earth in a pile where she was buried, not like the other graves, and the flowers were all piled up. I don't want to be buried when I die. There was a grave with Ellie's name on it and someone had put red flowers on it. I felt sad when I saw them . . .

I got lost and I was late. Lyn wasn't there. She'll be mad with me. She said that it was about dad. I don't understand what she means. She told them things about dad. It wasn't her fault. Dad says. Only now she says something else only I've got to see her. And now she'll be mad at me.

Kerry heard Mum's footsteps on the stairs and she pushed her diary under the mattress. The footsteps came to her door and stopped, then they shuffled past and she heard the sound of

Mum's door shutting. That would be it for the night. She'd left Mum downstairs in the kitchen. Mum had been nice at tea, she'd asked Kerry about school and about her friends and all the things they used to talk about. Kerry had pushed her oven chips round the plate and tried to say the right things, but Mum had her big green mug at the table, the one she pretended had tea in it. 'Tea without milk,' she'd say with that laugh that wasn't really a laugh, as if Kerry was a kid, as if Kerry didn't know. And after a while, she began.

'Where were you on Monday night?' she said.

Kerry thought that Mum hadn't noticed how late she'd been. It must have been ten-thirty when she slipped her key in the lock and crept in, shivering with something that was more than cold. 'Stacy's,' she said. She dipped her chip in the bean juice. The thin pink liquid dropped on to the cloth.

'Kerry!' Mum jumped up and came round the table to where Kerry was sitting. 'That mess. On the clean cloth!' She seemed about to cry. She grabbed Kerry's arm. 'Clear it up!' she said, trying to rub the stain out with the sleeve of Kerry's top, her best top that she'd sewed the sequins on to herself to make it look right. Kerry jerked away and she felt the sting across her face as Mum's hand slapped out. There was silence.

Kerry looked down at her plate. She knew what was coming next.

'I'm sorry, sweetheart, I'm sorry, Kerry, I didn't . . .' And she hugged Kerry against her, against the chemically smell and the smell of cigarettes and sweat.

The tablecloth was mucky anyway. There were stains all over and some of them were from where Mum had splashed her drink over the table when she talked and laughed and waved her hands around. 'Why don't you bring Stacy back here?' Mum said after a while. 'You could have a sleepover, I know that's what you all like, having sleepovers. Do you remember when you and Ellie used to have . . .' Her voice trailed off and she picked up her mug and drained it. 'I need some more tea,' she said.

'I'll get it,' Kerry said quickly. If Mum didn't have any more now, she might go to sleep and then maybe she wouldn't be so bad in the morning.

'No, you stay where you are, sweetheart,' Mum said. 'You've been busy at school all day. I'll get it.'

Kerry slid off her chair. 'You've been at work . . .' she began, and saw Mum's eyes slide away and knew that Mum hadn't been to work, again. 'I'll get it,' she said.

'I said, I'll get it!' The shout was sudden and sharp, and Mum went into the kitchen and slammed the door behind her. Kerry sat at the table and squeezed her eyes shut tight. Her arms felt tingly and itchy, and she rubbed them. Then she pushed up her sleeve and dragged her nails across the skin, but the jumpy feeling stayed so she did it again and again until the skin was all sore, and the pattern of fine red lines that criss-crossed her arms stood out, red and angry. She could hear Mum moving around in the kitchen. She called out, 'I'm going to do my homework.'

Mum's voice sounded muffled. 'You . . . do that.'

Now Kerry was sitting on her bed. It was dark outside. The streetlamp wasn't working, but she knew it must be late because the kids who played out on the estate had gone in. She yawned. Mum ought to know why she didn't bring Stacy home, or anyone. She had brought Stacy home once, and Mum had been OK at first. Kerry had seen Stacy's eyes going round the room which was so different from Stacy's house. Stacy's house had all cushions and dried flowers and little ornaments, and three different curtains on the windows.

Only then Mum had started talking about where they used to live, and how it had all been different. Kerry had said, *'Mum!'* in anguish, and Mum had started shouting and then she'd gone to sleep in the chair. The next day at school, Kerry had seen Stacy whispering with some of the other girls, but no one much liked Stacy anyway, so no one said anything.

Kerry turned the light out and curled up under the covers. She'd bunked off school and now she'd be in trouble, but she'd dreamed, that night. She had dreamed about Lyn, about the canal and the towpath, that she was on the towpath in the dark and something was chasing her, and her legs wouldn't move as though the air had got thick, like treacle. She remembered looking back through the arched tunnel, and the sound of something in the water. And then it had been a bright, hot day, and the river was glittering in the sun, and there was Ellie, only she was walking away from Kerry, faster and faster, and no matter how Kerry called, she didn't turn round.

She woke up in the darkness. Her face felt wet. It wouldn't go away – the grave with Ellie's name on, and the flowers all red like the jumper Kerry had been wearing that day. She wanted to see Lyn. She couldn't talk to Mum, and she couldn't talk to Dad. She used to talk to Maggie, but Maggie sent her away. And now Maggie was dead too.

Maybe Lyn had been waiting somewhere else. Maybe Lyn had tried to get in touch. Kerry hadn't looked at the phone, left it buried at the bottom of her bag, trying not to think about the way the water in the canal had swirled and rippled as though something was moving through the water, stealthy, silent, intent.

Tomorrow was the day for a letter from Dad. He used to write every week, but lately . . . Maybe she could tell him what Lyn said, maybe Dad would know what she meant, and he could tell Kerry what to do. As she drifted back to sleep, things began to look a bit better. *Its abut yor dad meet u at the cafy 7 dont b l8 . . .*

It was shortly after eight the following morning when DCI Farnham called his full team together. The canal death was now officially a murder. Tina

Barraclough shook her head to clear away the fuzziness left from the sleeping pills she'd taken the night before. At least the pills meant she didn't dream. Dave West had saved her a place, and she picked her way through the group to sit next to him. 'Who were you up to last night?' he said.

So she still looked like shit. Oh well. 'No one you know,' she said.

Farnham's manner was quick, efficient, dispassionate as he gave an account of the post-mortem report which confirmed what they had already worked out – the woman they had fished out of the canal had been murdered.

'We've got an initial identification,' Farnham said. 'She lived in one of the flats above the gallery – called herself Cara Hobson. We need to confirm that, find the next of kin, OK? She was murdered. There may have been an attempt to make it look like suicide, but it was pretty half-hearted.'

'Maybe whoever it was didn't mean to kill her,' one of the officers suggested. 'Panicked and dumped her in the canal afterwards.'

'She drowned in the canal,' Farnham said. 'That's the cause of death. But the initial post-mortem findings suggest we're looking at something that was planned.'

Though Cara's arms and legs had been free when her body was pulled out of the water, there were marks around her wrists and ankles that suggested she must have been tied at some time before her death. A cut cord that matched the marking on the wrists had been found in the water. 'There's no flow in the canal,' Farnham said, 'so anything that fell off her would still be close by. We haven't found her bag, or a purse. Her money, her cards, her keys – they're all missing.'

The damage to Cara's hands had been noted when the body had been lifted out of the water. 'They aren't defence wounds,' Farnham said. 'And she didn't break her fingers trying to pull the cord off her neck. They were broken before she died – someone twisted them until they snapped.'

There was a murmur around the room. Farnham held up a cloth sack with a drawstring. 'This was round her neck, weighted with a stone. It's the way you drown a dog, throw it in the canal with a brick round its neck. But the post-mortem suggests – this isn't definite, but it's probable – that she had already drowned before the weighted sack was put round her neck.' He explained about the marks from the drawstring that had been twisted round Cara's neck. 'There's very little bleeding into the soft tissue – it might have been an after-thought, make sure that her head stayed under the water just in case. There was no attempt to hide the body – she was caught in the mud. If she'd been pushed away from that, she'd have sunk and we probably wouldn't have found her for a while.'

And the immersion had destroyed any physical evidence of Cara's killer that might have been on her body. 'What it does mean,' Farnham had said, 'is that whatever happened took time, and it wasn't quiet. It's unlikely she was attacked in the flat. The woman next door didn't hear anything. No one heard anything on the canal bank. There's somewhere else. He spent some time with her.'

The pathologist had not been able to come up with a close time of death. The cold of the water had made this even less certain than it usually was. Cara could have died any time between mid-evening and shortly after midnight the night before. She'd been dead for at least six hours when she was lifted from the canal at six-thirty that morning.

Tina's mind went back to the flat, the dim room, the light switches that hadn't worked, the heavy blankets over the windows, the flickering light of the candle. She missed the next bit. West nudged her and she hastily reconstructed what Farnham had asked – what time had Eliza Eliot heard Cara in the flat. 'Around midnight,' she said. 'She's coming in today to go through her statement.'

Farnham considered her for a moment then moved on. Tina breathed again. She could remember talking to the Eliot woman the evening before, struggling against a headache and a fatigue that threatened to overwhelm her. Eliot had been emphatic about hearing Cara, but had been uncertain about the time. 'It was – I think I woke up,' she'd said. 'I think I'd been to sleep. So it must have been – I'm trying to think of something to give me a fix.'

84

'Well, was it before midnight or after midnight?' Tina had been desperate to get home, lie down, get over the speed hangover that was getting worse and worse.

Eliot had looked at her. 'I'm not . . .'

'We just need to get a general idea.' If she didn't get out of here soon, she was going to be sick.

'. . . before. I think.'

'If I say midnight?' Tina said.

Remembering this, she felt her face flush and she concentrated on her notes to hide it. But it sounded like midnight was about right.

Farnham was winding up. 'There was some disarrangement in the flat,' he said. 'Pillows displaced, stuff hanging out of drawers and cupboards. It doesn't look like a struggle – but we can't rule it out, not until we've got the forensics anyway.' The candle had been burning for about eighteen hours – but that gave no indication of the time she had left the flat.

There was one more thing. Cara Hobson had been picked up on Broad Street and charged with soliciting three weeks earlier. Tina had been aware of a change of atmosphere in the room, a murmur that ran round the team. She thought she detected a certain relaxation in some of the men. A puzzling case had suddenly become a simple one. A prostitute. It was unfortunate, but these things happened. Occupational hazard.

★ ★ ★

Tina was assigned the job of going through the stuff that had been taken from Cara Hobson's flat. It was something one of the uniformed officers could have done, and Tina wondered if Farnham had noticed her late arrivals, the signs of hangovers, the lapses in concentration. She *had* to get her act together. She sorted listlessly through the pile of papers, and tried to stop herself from looking at the clock. Eliza Eliot was coming in later that morning to go over her statement. That would give her a break.

If only her head didn't feel so woolly from the sleeping pills. She could try and wake herself up with some . . . She dismissed the thought. Using the last of her coke might liven her up for the moment, but she'd come crashing down later. She started on the task of going through the stuff the search team had brought from the flat.

She remembered her first impressions of the flat – a strange, dim nursery lit by the flickering light of the candle. The nursery effect – more of a child's bedroom effect, Tina thought, came from the toys scattered round the room – toys that were far too old for an infant: a rocking horse, a doll, a teddy bear, all larger than the baby herself; a counterpane printed with nursery-rhyme motifs. Presumably Cara was trying to create some kind of idealized child world for Briony Rose. One that she hadn't had herself? *Hold that thought.*

She sorted through the clothes. Cara had favoured shapeless, baggy clothes, jeans with floppy, flared

86

legs, loose-fitting sweatshirts, but there were one or two unexpected things – a basque, lacy stockings, what looked like an old-fashioned school tunic – odd things for a woman of Cara's age and tastes to be wearing.

'There's not much here,' Dave West observed. He had been taking witness statements, and had come along to offer a hand to Tina more as a gesture of support than because she really needed it. He started sorting through a box of papers.

According to Eliza Eliot and Jonathan Massey, Cara had lived in the flat for about three months. There should have been bills: utilities, council tax. There should have been some kind of evidence of Cara's income: bank statements, Building Society books, benefit books. But there was nothing. There should have been personal stuff: addresses, phone numbers, some kind of reference to friends, to appointments. But again there was nothing. No one at the gallery reported seeing anyone visiting her – in fact, Eliza Eliot had specifically mentioned the solitary life that Cara Hobson had lived.

There was no phone installed. 'Is there a mobile?' West said.

Tina checked. It seemed logical, but there was no sign of one, and no record of any account. 'That'll need looking into.' Tina made a note. A mobile could contain a lot of useful information. Cara's killer could well have taken it, thrown it away. 'Do you think someone cleared the flat out before we got there?'

West shrugged. It was possible. 'Anything from forensics?' he said.

'The identifiable prints in the flat were Cara's. There's a thumb print that can't be matched to anyone yet. They're still looking at that one. Apart from that, there's no evidence of a break-in.' But stuff had been pulled out of the drawers, scattered around. A search, or the general mess that nineteen-year-olds tended to live in? The flat itself was bleak and comfortless – the walls new plaster, the bathroom untiled, no cooker, bare boards on the floors.

Having finished with the clothes, Tina began to go through the piles of papers that Dave had been sorting out. It was like he had said. There wasn't much. 'I'm going to talk to the people who rent the flats,' Tina said. 'This Trust or whatever it is.' She began going through her notes, looking for the number.

'Here,' Dave had found it.

She negotiated her way through the electronic answering system, pressing buttons as an automated voice issued instructions, until she made contact with a human being. The woman at the other end of the phone admitted that she did know something about the Second Site flat, took Tina's number and said she would phone her back.

'She said "flat".' Tina remembered that they'd gone to the gallery expecting to find just one residence.

'Doesn't give you a lot of confidence.' West was

packing stuff back into the boxes. 'If the boss can get anything out of this lot, he's a better . . .'

The phone rang. 'We have one tenant,' the woman from the Trust informed Tina. 'Ms Eliza Eliot. She took the tenancy of the flat in August last year, as soon as it became available.'

'And the other tenant – the other flat, I mean,' Tina said. 'Cara Hobson and her daughter.'

'There is no other flat,' the woman said.

Surprise silenced Tina for a moment. 'Of course there is,' she said. 'That was where Cara Hobson was living.'

'Well, I'm sorry . . .' There was the sound of papers being moved around. 'Let me go and check.' Tina put her hand over the phone, and looked at Dave. She raised her eyes and pointed to her head. *Brainless.* Then the woman was back. 'There are plans for a second flat,' she said. 'But the conversion isn't complete. There are no plans to finish it before next summer. There's only the one flat at present.'

Tina thanked the woman and hung up. 'Hobson must have been squatting,' Dave said, when she told him.

Tina thought about it. It explained the comfortless, unfinished appearance of the flat. But it seemed like an odd place for a squat. It would have been the simplest thing in the world to exclude her from the building – secure either of the access doors, and Cara would have been unable to get back in. On the other hand, if this was purely a temporary residence, it would explain why Cara had so few possessions and the lack of any paper evidence of her existence.

She expressed these doubts to Dave, who shrugged. 'Who knows why they do anything?'

Who can understand the mind of a prostitute? Tina translated. *Who cares?*

'What about this?' Dave had a couple of sheets of paper in his hand and was unfolding them. She looked over his shoulder. They appeared to be press cuttings, photocopies of newspaper reviews. 'Arty stuff,' Dave said, dismissively.

Tina read through the first one, aware of a flicker of interest outside the routine of basic detective work that was – OK – important, but dull, dull, dull.

Gonna roll the bones!

Arnolfini Gallery, Bristol, until 9 September

'Entropy' is an intriguing exhibition of film and computer images that is worth a visit. Ivan Bakst's time-lapse animation, and the reworkings of stills into abstract designs turns the process of death and decay into something that has a strange if macabre beauty . . .

There was a photograph – a dead fox with its teeth pulled into a rictus snarl, the eyes fallen in. She checked the date: 1999. The second cutting was another review of the same exhibition. Tina read it. This review was dismissive. *An obsession with death . . . cliché . . . gratuitous detail . . .*

She looked at West, who shook his head. They didn't mean anything to him. She turned them over. On the back, someone had scribbled: *J – thought you might be interested.* J? Jonathan Massey? She made a note to follow it up, and another to chase up the details of Cara's arrival in the flat, then went back to her search through the paperwork. There was nothing else.

CHAPTER 5

When Kerry woke up, she felt better. She got up early and ironed the grey skirt and maroon jumper that was what they made you wear for school. She'd taken the skirt in, and turned up the hem. She'd asked Mum for some money to buy a top, one of those with eagles and flowers like she'd seen Samantha Mumba wearing, but Mum had said, 'I haven't got money for T-shirts, Kerry. Don't go on.' So Kerry had got out her tiger one that came from the World Wildlife Fund, and she'd jazzed it up with sequins and things, but she couldn't do much with the jumper.

She put on the top, pulling the sleeves down to cover the fine tracery of cuts that ran up the inside of her arm. It was chilly, but she draped the jumper carefully round her shoulders, tying the sleeves loosely at the front. That looked better. The skirt felt loose. She was going to have to take it in again. She brushed her hair and looked in the mirror. If she'd washed it yesterday, she could have worn it loose like Buffy. She tied it up with a band. She looked in the mirror and smiled at her reflection. Buffy smiled back. That was all right.

She went downstairs. There was post on the mat. She picked it up. A letter in a brown window envelope. A bill. It was in red with *Final Demand* written above the address. A letter addressed to Mum – it was from the school, Kerry recognized the postmark. She slipped it into her pocket. No letter from Dad.

Mum was in the kitchen, and she looked up as Kerry came through the door, picking up the green mug that was beside her. She was still in her dressing gown. 'Are you off now?' she said. She smiled, but she sounded anxious and there was a flat, strained look to her smile. She wanted Kerry to go. That smell, sweet and penetrating like nail polish, hung round her. Kerry knew what that meant.

She got down the cornflakes. 'You want some, Mum?' she said.

'I'll get something later.' Mum lit a cigarette and watched Kerry pour milk on to her cereal.

'Aren't you going to work?' Kerry could hear her voice sounding small and angry. She put the brown envelope on the kitchen table. 'You'd better go, because there's another bill you haven't paid.'

Mum stared at the window. 'Oh, Kerry, don't nag,' she said. 'Hurry up. You'll be late.' She shifted restlessly from foot to foot. Kerry wanted to say something, but Mum looked at her so blankly that she couldn't think of anything. She picked up her bag and looked in the mirror again. This time it was just Kerry who looked back, but somehow she couldn't care about it any more.

She left the house, heading towards the bus stop, her feet moving slower and slower. She opened the letter from school as she walked. It was the usual stuff. *Dear Mrs Fraser* . . . Mum didn't call herself Mrs Fraser any more, but the school kept making that mistake, because Kerry went on being Kerry Fraser. *Dear Mrs Fraser* . . . Kerry pulled a face. *Blah, blah, blah . . . unexcused absences . . . blah, blah* . . . She was about to screw it up and throw it away, when a phrase caught her eye: . . . excluded for a period . . . She read the letter closely, but it was all right. She wasn't excluded, but she had to stay after school on Friday. She would be excluded if she missed that . . . without good reason . . . At least they couldn't phone Mum now. She remembered the last time the school had phoned. Mum's eyes had looked tired. 'I can't cope with this,' she'd said. And Kerry had felt cold inside. What if Mum sent her away? What if she put Kerry in care? That's what she'd done to Lyn. Then what could she do to help Dad?

But the phone had been cut off. That was another bill Mum hadn't paid. Kerry had told Lyn, and Lyn had pulled one of those faces, but she'd given Kerry the phone. 'Don't let *her* get it,' Lyn said. 'I worked hard to buy that.'

She kept it deep down in her bag, where Mum wouldn't see it, and she kept it switched off so it wouldn't beep and give her away. She switched it on now. She wanted to call Lyn, but if Lyn was mad at her she might not talk. She thought for a moment, then keyed in *sori I woz l8*. She pressed 'send', holding her breath. Was Lyn so mad she wouldn't get in touch? She sat on the low wall by the bus stop, the phone in her hand, watching up the road for the bus. It didn't mean anything if there wasn't a reply. Lyn's phone might be switched off, she might be busy, *anything*.

She could see the bus in the distance now, pulling in to the stop further along the road. She was about to stow the phone safely in her bag when it beeped. She nearly dropped it. The message signal was flashing. She felt breathless as she pressed the *read* button. It was all right. Lyn wasn't mad at her – Lyn was worried. The letters ran across the screen.

RUOK?

Eliza got up early and watched the sun rise over the canal. She hadn't slept much the night before. Every time she began to drop into sleep, she thought she heard those soft footsteps again on the other side of the wall.

By eight, she was dressed and breakfasted, and glad to go downstairs and start work, to get back to the world of the normal, the commonplace, the everyday.

Jonathan arrived late. He'd had a bad night, he explained irritably, and he didn't want to spend all day shut in his office in the gallery. That reminded Eliza she was supposed to check and sign the statement she'd given to DC Barraclough the day before. She was probably the last-known person to have seen – or at least to have heard – Cara alive. Jonathan sighed when she told him.

'I've got to go out,' he said. 'I've got a meeting and I don't want to leave Mel on her own.'

This was the first Eliza had heard of any meeting. 'Can't it wait? Mel needs supervising.' *Or she'll spend all morning with her feet up and her magazines.*

'Mel's fine,' he said.

She looked at him. He seemed tense and anxious. 'What's wrong?'

'Oh . . .' His sigh was audible. 'The police have been in touch. They've searched her flat, and the stairs, and now they want to look over the gallery.' So that was the reason for the sudden appointment. He didn't want the hassle of dealing with them. There was nothing she could do about that. 'When will you be back?' he said.

'I've no idea,' she said, more sharply than she'd intended. 'I've never been involved in a murder inquiry before.'

He looked a bit shamefaced at that. 'I know,' he said. 'Oh, well, you'll have to go. Oh, I suppose I can rearrange things.'

Eliza left early for her appointment. She wanted ten minutes to herself with some decent coffee before she had to think about Cara again, about Cara's death, about the shabby flat and the still bundle in the cot. She walked along to the canal basin, to the café, and sat in the window in a soft chair, watching the boats, people coming and going along the towpath. Something caught her eye. A picture in a newspaper being read by a young man, glimpsed as he ambled by.

There were newspapers in the racks and on the tables. She went to look, flicking through the nationals, not seeing what she was looking for. Then she saw that the early edition of the local paper was out. She opened it, and the photograph looked back at her. Cara and Briony Rose. She put the paper down on the table in front of her. What had she expected? Of course it would be in the local paper. It was probably in the nationals somewhere. She looked at the headline. She read it once without taking it in, then she read it again. CONCERN FOR CHILD IN PROSTITUTE KILLING. It must be the wrong story. The story didn't go with the picture. It . . .

She read the article slowly, her heart sinking. The police were treating Cara's death as suspicious; and they believed that Cara had been a prostitute. She had been out on the streets the night she was killed, the article said. That was ridiculous. Cara hadn't been a prostitute. She . . . But Eliza's rejection of the idea was starting to lose its force. The gallery was very near to the red-light areas of West Bar Green and Corporation Street. Eliza had seen the prostitutes waiting at the kerb side often enough. And Cara had been young, lonely and poor.

But the main focus of the article was the baby. Eliza had a feeling that, if it hadn't been for the involvement of the child, Cara's death – Cara's murder? The police hadn't said anything about murder – would have merited only a brief paragraph on an inside page. She read on. Briony Rose had been hypothermic and dehydrated when she was found, having been shut in the flat for over twelve hours. She was still being treated, but was 'expected to make a full recovery'. Cara must have left the baby while she went out to work. And then the editorial rehashed Ellie's murder in a dramatic 'canal of death' paragraph.

She read through the article twice, trying to make sense of it, then she looked at her watch. *Shit!* She was late. She grabbed her things and ran along the road and up the hill towards the brick block that housed the police headquarters.

'Ms Eliot, thank you for coming in.' It was DC Barraclough, the young woman Eliza had talked to the day before. She was still tired and heavy-eyed. It looked as though she had a social life to match her appearance. 'I know you're busy at the gallery.'

'It's the private view on Friday,' Eliza said, moving automatically into PR mode. 'Why don't you come?' she added, remembering the woman's interest – *I thought it was a red horse . . .*

DC Barraclough looked surprised. 'Maybe I will,' she said.

'I'll send you an invitation,' Eliza said.

The other woman focused on the papers in front of her. 'There's one or two things in your statement I wanted to check . . .' she said now. She frowned as she looked round the room. 'Thank you for coming in,' she said again. She shook her head, trying to organize her thoughts.

'Before we start . . .' Eliza said.

DC Barraclough shot her a quick look and waited.

'The baby,' Eliza said. 'Briony Rose. How is she?' She couldn't get the image of that still bundle out of her mind.

'She's doing well, she'll be out of hospital soon.'

'What's going to happen to her?'

DC Barraclough shook her head again. 'I don't know,' she said, taking out a sheaf of notes. 'That's in the hands of social services. Now,' she changed the subject briskly, 'let me run through those timings with you again,' she said. 'We'd like to get them a bit more specific.'

'You said it was a general idea you wanted,' Eliza said. She felt a mixture of relief and anxiety about the baby.

'Just a bit more specific. You closed the fire door a bit before midnight –'

Eliza nodded. 'It must have been, because I heard her walking around in the flat later.'

'– and then you say you heard the baby crying, and that was when you heard Cara? Can you remember the time?'

'I remember I looked at the clock,' Eliza said. 'I

was so fed up about being woken up again. But I can't remember what time it was. You said it must have been around midnight.' She frowned, thinking back. That was the way it had happened, wasn't it?

She saw DC Barraclough look past her, and turned round. A tall, fair-haired man had come into the room. It was a moment before she recognized him as Roy Farnham, the man from the funeral, the man who had been at the gallery yesterday, taking charge when they found the baby.

'Thank you for coming in, Miss Eliot,' he said.

'Eliza,' she said. He nodded and looked thoughtfully at DC Barraclough, whose face was a bit pink.

'Is everything all right, Barraclough?' he said. His voice was polite, but DC Barraclough looked more flushed. He turned to Eliza. 'I'd like a clearer idea of the evening. Can we go over it again?'

She nodded. 'I was explaining to DC Barraclough,' she said. 'It's really hard to remember.'

He dismissed that. 'Don't worry. Let's see what we've got here.' He took her through the evening with Cara, the time Cara left her flat, what Eliza had done next. 'You don't give yourself much time off,' he said with a quick smile. She smiled back. 'Right, so you worked for – what – all of the evening? Did you do anything else?'

'No, I worked, then I felt tired, so I got ready for bed.'

'And then . . .'

'I went to bed. I read for a while . . .'

'Let's go through that again,' he said. 'It was about half past seven when you went upstairs with Cara Hobson. You had coffee and then she went – how long did she stay?'

'Oh, only as long as it took to drink the coffee. Twenty minutes or so.'

'OK. So about half past eight, you started working. How much work did you get through?'

'There was a folder of stuff – I got that finished. It must have taken me more than a couple of hours . . . Yes. The news was finishing – I meant to watch it and I missed it.' He didn't say anything, just waited. 'I had a shower,' she said. It was coming clearer.

'So it would have been about eleven by the time you got to bed.'

She nodded again. 'And then I read until I began to fall asleep, you know.'

'And something woke you up?' he prompted.

'It was the draught from the door,' she said. 'There's a fire door leading on to the steps, and sometimes Cara didn't shut it properly when she came in. I had to get up and shut it.'

'So you were wide awake,' he said. His smile was sympathetic. 'And an early start the next day?'

She looked at him. 'I remember now, I looked at the clock. It was after one. I was really pissed off. And that was when I heard the footsteps. I was trying to get to sleep, but I could hear Cara walking around with the baby.'

'And then . . .'

She frowned. 'Something else woke me up later, I remember that. I spent the rest of the night in the chair. The baby was crying. But it was something else woke me up.' She shook her head. She didn't know what it was.

'Someone going out? Opening the fire door?'

Eliza shook her head. 'I wouldn't hear that. I don't know what it was.' In her mind, she could hear the wailing cry of the wind as it blew through the empty windows of the derelict buildings. She shook her head. She'd be guessing now. 'I made myself a drink. It was about two, I think. I'd forgotten.' She felt pleased with herself for remembering.

Farnham nodded. 'Did you hear anything else from Cara's flat? Apart from the baby.'

Eliza thought. 'No, it was only the baby. I don't remember hearing anything else.'

'OK,' he said again. 'And you didn't see Cara at all after she left your flat?'

'No.' Eliza remembered Cara as she walked towards the door. Hindsight – was it hindsight? – made her a sad and lonely figure. 'No, I didn't see her again.'

He stood up. 'Thank you, Miss Eliot, you've been very helpful. DC Barraclough will sort out your statement with you.' Eliza was aware suddenly of the other woman as a silent presence in the room, aware of a tension in the air.

'Listen,' she said. 'There was something I wanted to know . . . I don't know if you can tell me . . .'

Farnham waited, his hand on the door.

She knew he must be busy, but she had to ask. 'The paper,' she said. She could see his expression changing, becoming cautious. 'They said something about the canal, they called it "the canal of death" and they mentioned Ellie Chapman. Why are they making a connection? Is it just the canal?'

He looked at her. 'You knew Ellie,' he said. He seemed to hesitate, then he said, 'We found Cara Hobson's body near Cadman Street Bridge.'

Of course. The place where Ellie's body had been found dumped in the undergrowth by the towpath, an accidental find. The police were searching the towpath after a junkie had OD'd in a boat moored by the canal side.

'It's a deserted place,' he went on, 'but it's bang in the centre of the city – and there's a lot of dodgy places close by, you must be aware of that – a good place to shoot up, a good place to take a punter. A good place to dump a body.' He looked at her to make sure she understood. 'There's no other link,' he said.

It was gone twelve by the time Eliza left the police station. Somehow, she had expected the news of Cara's death to have more impact, for the people going about their business in the city to be concerned, aware, talking about the death that had occurred in their midst. Eliza only felt that sense of involvement, that sense of something cataclysmic having happened, because she had known Cara. Otherwise, would the death of a prostitute have weighed heavily on her mind?

The thought depressed her and she returned to the gallery in a bad mood. The police had been and gone. The search of the gallery had revealed nothing, and Jonathan was preparing to leave for the meeting he'd been agitating about earlier. She showed him the paper and he scanned it in trepidation. 'They mention the gallery,' he said.

'Well, they would.' Eliza hung up her coat and pulled on the smock she used to protect her clothes when she was moving stuff around. 'Cara lived here.'

'She lived in the *flats*, Eliza. They're nothing to do with the gallery.' He rattled the paper irritably.

'Yes, well . . .' Eliza's mind was moving between the events of yesterday and the work she still needed to do.

'I knew it was a bad idea letting the flat to that child,' he said. 'And now we're going to have all the pimps and kerb crawlers knocking on our door. It was bad enough when it was a kindergarten, but now we're a fucking brothel.'

'What other kind of brothel would there be?' Eliza said wearily. 'Shut up, Jonathan.'

He looked a bit abashed. Eliza wasn't really angry with him. He'd had a stressful day, the preparation for the opening disrupted by the visit from the police team. She supposed he was just dealing with it in his own way. He pulled his coat on. 'I won't be back today,' he said. 'Phone if anything urgent comes up.'

'It won't,' Eliza reassured him. She made herself

some coffee – *instant, yuk* – and took it upstairs so that she could get on with her work for Flynn's exhibition. She was behind now. But the words 'suspicious death' kept resonating in her mind, and she kept thinking of feet moving silently through the gallery in the dark, in the night, a couple of floors below where she slept, coming to the stairs, beginning their stealthy climb . . . *Stop it!* 'Drama queen!' she said out loud. No one had come into the gallery. The police had checked. The paper said that Cara had gone out, gone working, leaving the baby alone in the flat.

Cara had been in the flat during the night – Eliza had heard her. She must have gone out after that. She could remember the sound of crying. The crying had sounded almost hysterical, and then it had gradually faded into hiccuping sobs, and then into silence. Eliza stood still in the empty gallery, the light from the low winter sun casting long shadows across the floor. What had been going on, on the other side of the wall, in the dark, in the night, when she, Eliza, had been curled up in her chair, drinking cocoa, slipping away into dreams?

Madrid

Eliza's eighteen months in Madrid slipped past her like a dream. Once Daniel Flynn had arrived, time seemed to kick into overdrive in a whirl of excitement, of art and books and travel and sex and wine.

It was a month since they'd first met. Their relationship had taken off with a giddy speed that still made her uncertain about its status and durability. In her experience, a swift tumble into intimacy was usually followed by an equally – but less pleasant – tumble into indifference or enmity. His arrival in Madrid originally had been a random zag in an unplanned drift around Europe. But he'd prolonged his stay in Madrid, taking a summer rental. Ivan Bakst, the man he'd been travelling with had moved on, but Daniel had stayed. He'd started spending a lot of time at the Prado, his status as a rising young artist making him a welcome visitor, gaining him entry when the museum was closed, and giving him access to off-limits areas, such as the workshops where Eliza was now.

She picked up her magnifying glass. The portrait on the easel in front of her was illuminated by a raking light, showing the brush strokes that a living artist had placed on the canvas almost five hundred years before. *Portrait of Sophia*. She moved the glass across the surface, studying the paint. The picture had been damaged at the bottom left. She could see the multi-layered structure of the red paint of the woman's cuff. She made a note.

Daniel would be upstairs in the Flemish rooms, studying the Brueghel. He was beginning to share her obsession. He was searching, he'd told her. He knew what he wanted his next work to be about, but he couldn't decide on its form. He was an eclectic artist, prepared to use any materials that came to hand and seemingly competent in most traditional and non-traditional media. He found Eliza's interest in Renaissance art hard to understand. 'It's gone, it's past,' he'd said once when they'd discussed it. But he was spending more and more time in front of *The Triumph of Death*, more and more time listening to her ideas about it.

Later that morning, they met for coffee in one of the pavement cafés that abounded in the city. They sat in the sun as the waiter came over to fill their cups and take an order for *churros*, the sweet batter sticks that Eliza had developed an addiction for.

His exhibition was starting to come together in his head, he told her. He wanted to focus on *The Triumph of Death*. 'I want to put it in a current setting,' he said. 'A cityscape, industrial ruins. I want to show people a modern triumph of death.' He had a small reproduction of the Brueghel, and he wanted to pick her brains about its background, the nature of its composition. The waiter put a plate down in front of her and he helped himself.

'It's heavily symbolic,' Eliza said. She dipped her churros into her coffee, and let the crisp sweetness melt on her tongue as she thought about it. 'It's a series of tableaux that people would have recognized. You'd need some modern equivalents. Look here, for example –' She pointed out the fallen woman about to be crushed under the wheels of the death cart. 'She's holding a spindle, and the scissors in her other hand are about to cut the thread. That's Fate. When the thread of your life is cut, you die. I don't know what that image would mean to a modern audience. Or here, the lovers.' They were singing to each other, absorbed, close, doomed, as Death added his counterpoint to their duet.

CHAPTER 6

Farnham's summons came sooner than Tina expected. She'd gone back to the incident room and was sitting at her desk making a pretence of going over her notes. She just needed a few minutes. Her eyes were starting to close, and she jolted awake as Dave nudged her. 'Get a grip,' he muttered. Farnham was coming into the room.

He looked at Dave. 'There's someone waiting for you in interview 2, West,' he said. Dave vanished with alacrity.

Farnham stayed where he was, looking at Tina. She felt a twist of nerves in her stomach, and swallowed. She could remember the way he'd looked at her as Eliza Eliot was leaving, a long, assessing look.

He said. 'My office. Five minutes.' He went out through the double doors, towards his room.

Tina took a deep breath. OK, better to have it out in the open. She went along the corridor and knocked on his door. He was sitting at his desk, a sheet of paper in his hands, a witness statement. He looked tired. 'So, Tina,' he said, his tone conversational. 'You're planning a move to Traffic?'

'Sir?'

He leant back in his chair. She shifted her feet nervously. The bastard was going to keep her standing. 'You don't know what I'm talking about,' he said. 'OK, I'll tell you.' He looked at her. 'First briefing, late. Second briefing, late. A less charitable man might say hungover, as well. First interview – you not only don't get the crucial detail, you suggest a time to the witness. The wrong time, as well. Second interview, I come in and find you halfway through doing the same thing. We've got the correct times now, but Eliot changed her story – any defence lawyer could make hay with her in court.'

'I'm sorry, sir,' she said.

'You could have chosen a worse way to muddy the waters,' he said, 'but I can't offhand think of one. Cara Hobson – remember Cara Hobson, Tina? – Cara Hobson had been dead for at least six hours when she was found. Now, if the Eliot woman is right, and she heard someone in the flat at one – rather than midnight – then it wasn't Cara Hobson.'

Tina felt her face flush. She hadn't thought of that – it was so blindingly obvious, and she hadn't even thought about it. She saw Farnham register her response. He knew.

'If you screw up again, you're off the case, right? You're still on it now because I'm short-staffed. Understood?'

She nodded.

He kept his eyes on her, tapping his pen on the desk. Then he relaxed slightly. 'Anything in the stuff from Hobson's flat?'

The sudden switch of direction confused her for a moment, and she stammered as she tried to reorganize her thoughts. 'There's this,' she said, holding out her notebook.

He looked at her. 'Yes?'

She flushed. *Get a grip, woman!* 'The flat,' she said. 'Cara's flat.' She told him what the woman from the Trust had said.

He frowned. 'So she was living there unofficially?' he said.

Tina nodded. 'Like a squat,' she said.

He thought about it and shook his head slowly. 'Doesn't make sense. She'd need keys to the outer doors. Someone must have given her those.' He balanced his pen between his hands. 'I wonder why no one spotted it . . . OK,' he said after a minute, 'find out who had keys, who had access to them. She must have got them from somewhere. Anything else?'

She showed him the reviews that West had found, with the scribbled note to 'J'. Farnham read through them quickly and raised his eyebrows. 'You know about this stuff, Barraclough,' he said. 'What's all this death stuff got to do with anything?' He looked irritated.

Tina hadn't thought of herself as an art expert. 'It's . . . they've always done work about death,' she

111

said. 'This kind of thing is fashionable, I suppose. You know, Damien Hirst and dead cows and things like that.' *Full marks for erudition, Tina.*

'OK.' Farnham rubbed his eyes with his thumb and forefinger. He looked like a man with a bad headache. 'If these are Massey's, we need to know what they were doing in her flat.'

Tina felt herself slump as she went back to the incident room. Her eyes felt heavy and her head felt full of cotton wool. She checked her watch. If she tried an artificial boost now, she probably wouldn't be hit by the come-down too badly until she came off shift – only a couple of hours to go. She picked up her bag and headed for the ladies.

The classroom was noisy and it smelled of chalk. Kerry laid her arm across the desk and rested her head on it. She was bored. She yawned and sucked her pen.

'Are we keeping you awake, Kerry?' Mr Nixon. There was a flurry of giggles around her.

'Sorry, sir,' Kerry said, sitting up again. He was looking at someone else now, so she slumped forward over her book. The electronic beep of a mobile phone penetrated the voices and the scraping chairs. Kerry jumped, and felt her face going red. She'd forgotten to turn her phone off. Mr Nixon looked round. 'Whose was that?' he said. 'Come on, you know the rules. Switch it off.' He looked round the room. If he saw whose it was, he might confiscate it. Kerry had kept her head down, praying that another message wouldn't come through. Then some of the lads started up, and Mr Nixon went across to deal with them. Kerry breathed again, and slipped her hand into her bag to switch off the phone. She saw Stacy looking at her accusingly, and glared at her to keep her quiet. The maths lesson dragged on.

At break, she went straight to the toilets. Stacy trailed after her. 'That was your phone, Kerry, I heard it.' Kerry looked in the mirror, pretending to be fiddling with her hair. 'I saw Martin Smith at the bus stop this morning,' Stacy said, and giggled. She wasn't really interested in the phone. She wanted to talk about Martin Smith. She had been going on about the Year 12 boy for weeks. Year 12s didn't look at the girls from Stacy and Kerry's year, Kerry could have told her that. She stood in the queue in a jitter of impatience as Stacy checked her make-up in the little mirror she carried round with her, fiddled with her hair, talking on all the time. Kerry wanted to scream.

When a cubicle finally came free, she locked herself in and checked the phone. The message icon was flashing. She pressed 'read', her fingers clumsy with impatience. The words ran across the screen before she could take them in properly. She pressed 'read' again. *ITS ABOUT YOUR DAD FDAY SAME PLACE 5.00.* About Dad. *Friday, same place.* Friday. That gave her time to plan. Five o'clock was after school, it would be all right . . . Then she remembered the letter. *Will be required to stay*

113

in school on Friday . . . to complete the work missed during her unauthorized absence . . . without good reason . . . excluded . . . Her mind flew into overdrive. She had to be there on Friday. What if Lyn changed her mind? *A good reason . . .* Maybe she could get one, maybe . . . An idea was beginning to form in her head.

Stacy was in front of the mirror as she came out, tugging impatiently at her hair with a comb. 'I'll do your hair,' Kerry said. Kerry was good with hair. Stacy stood still while Kerry wound it round the brush and pulled it back. 'Just pin it for now,' she said. 'If you wash it, I can do it properly. I can do it so it flicks up, you know?'

Stacy looked pleased. 'Let's go to my house after school.'

Kerry pretended to think about it. She didn't want to go home anyway. 'OK,' she said.

Jonathan Massey projected 'media' and 'arts'. The dark jacket and shirt, the studied carelessness of the open collar proclaimed his status. Farnham wasn't sure about the brutally short hair, the small beard and the dark frames of his glasses. He had a feeling that these were no longer the mark of someone at the cutting edge – they were the mark of someone who was letting fashion get ahead, who was losing the battle with staying young.

Farnham had done his research into Jonathan Massey. A provincial gallery, an administrative job, was a come-down for someone who had,

114

briefly, shown potential for renown. His career as an artist seemed stalled, his personal life seemed oddly bleak – no partner, no marriage, no children. Jonathan Massey was a disappointed man and disappointed men sometimes vented their frustrations in less than social ways.

But he seemed co-operative enough. Farnham took him through the evening of Cara's disappearance again. Now he had something closer to the correct timing – he tried to push the distracting anger away – he had a clearer idea of the times he needed to cover with Massey.

And Massey seemed to be in the clear. He'd been in Leeds. He'd gone to the theatre. 'The Leeds theatre is still better than Sheffield,' he said, irrelevantly. He'd gone with a friend, and they'd had something to eat afterwards. They'd gone back to her house, and he'd stayed the night, driving back early the following morning. He gave them the name of the friend with a slightly impatient twist of the mouth. 'Patricia,' he said. 'Patricia Carr. I don't want her embarrassed,' he'd said. Farnham wondered what the nature of such embarrassment might be, whether it might prove potentially useful.

He took Massey through the workings of the gallery. He was curious about who might have had contact with Cara in the course of the working day. 'We don't get many casual visitors,' Massey said. 'We're mostly for schools and colleges at the moment. The upper gallery is the one that will bring the public in, and that isn't open right now. We're hanging an exhibition. Private view this Friday.' He looked worried, as well he might, Farnham thought. This must be his big night coming up, and there was murder on the doorstep and a police investigation getting entangled with the last-minute preparations.

'But who comes to the gallery apart from you and . . .' Farnham checked his notes.

'Eliza Eliot and Mel Young,' Massey finished his sentence off for him. Farnham ran the names through his mental inventory. Young? The trainee. He waited for Massey to go on. 'Oh, I see what you mean. Well, we've had deliveries, of course. I can give you a list. We had people from the Trust round a couple of times.' He thought. 'There were the decorators finishing off. But that was about a month ago.'

The usual traffic in a small operation. But all these people needed interviewing. 'What about upstairs?' he said. 'The flats?'

Massey shook his head. 'I wouldn't know about that.'

'Who would?' Post, deliveries, repairs – there could be a long list there. 'Would the Trust keep records of any repairs, anything like that?'

Massey shook his head. 'I don't know. You'd have to ask Eliza. Sometimes the post came to the gallery,' he added. 'I know that. It was one of the reasons Cara was always down here. It gave her an excuse, coming to check her post.'

'She was a problem?'

Massey looked weary. 'I had nothing against her,' he said, 'but she was always there. When you're setting something up, you don't want people under foot.' He was indignant at the suggestion that Cara had learned the alarm codes from him. 'Certainly not,' he said emphatically. 'I never set the alarm when she was around.'

He was less clear about why he hadn't simply solved the problem by banning her from the gallery. 'It's the flats,' he said. 'The linking door – it helped Eliza to have access, and we'd just got used to using it.'

'And you never contacted the Trust about her?' No one, apparently, had ever alerted them to the fact that they had a squatter on their property. 'What would they have done?' Massey said. 'The gallery is nothing to do with them. It was our problem.'

Farnham showed him the reviews that had been found in Cara's flat. He glanced at them irritably, then looked more closely. 'Where did you get those?' he said after a moment.

'They were found in Cara Hobson's flat,' Farnham said, watching him carefully.

Massey went red. 'Well, I didn't put them there,' he said, returning to his original defensiveness.

'No one is saying you did,' Farnham said. 'But they were found in her flat. Perhaps you'd like to tell me about them.'

'They're cuttings.' Massey looked at him. 'I sent

for them. Someone suggested he might be good for us at the Second Site. So . . .' He shrugged. 'Last time I saw them, they were on my desk,' he said. He couldn't account for their presence in Cara's flat.

'Where is he now?' Farnham said. 'This Bakst?'

'I don't know.'

An inconsistency. 'So how were you going to contact him, if you wanted him to do an exhibition?'

'I hadn't got that far,' Massey said. 'It was only a suggestion.'

'And you're not aware of any contact between him and Cara Hobson?'

'I have no idea,' he said firmly. He didn't know anything about Cara. Men had not come to the gallery looking for her. He began to look uneasy at the direction Farnham's questioning was taking. 'I don't know anything about her social life,' he said. 'I don't think anyone did.' He refused to speculate any further.

Triumph at Canal of Death

The 'Triumph' of Sheffield's latest entrant to the arts scene, the Second Site Gallery in premiering Daniel Flynn's new exhibition, The Triumph of Death, *became grimly ironic with the discovery of the body of a young woman in the canal . . .*

Sheffield canal is no stranger to mysterious and violent death . . .

. . . and in 1998, the body of nine-year-old Ellie Chapman was found by the towpath near Cadman Street Bridge, and close by, on a boat moored on the canal side . . .

Now, days before the exhibition is due to open, this latest tragedy has local people asking . . .

The phone rang as Eliza read the article, a feature in the arts pages of the local paper. She ran her fingers through her hair. She should have expected it after what had happened. She picked up the phone. It was Laura, a friend from college days who had, like Eliza, gone into arts administration. Eliza, Laura and Maggie had shared a flat in their second year, and all of them had had their dreams. And they'd all done well enough, Eliza had supposed in the years that followed. Maggie's ambitions had been curtailed a bit by Ellie, but she'd gone into teaching and had been doing well at a local primary school. The school where Mark Fraser taught. Eliza could remember the letters when Maggie had talked about Fraser – his kindness, his problems with his alcoholic wife and dysfunctional stepdaughter, his lovely, lively child who was Ellie's best friend . . . She didn't want to think about that.

They'd all done well, that was the thing. Laura had worked her way up arts administration in local councils, and had come back to Sheffield a couple of years before. But now, to Eliza, it didn't look like success at all. Maggie had stayed put and substituted teaching and Ellie for her dreams of creativity. And Laura and Eliza had ended up back where they had started, but servicing the art of others, not producing their own.

'Eliza?' Laura's voice was puzzled.

'Sorry. I was miles away.'

'We haven't met for ages,' Laura said. 'You're working too hard. Let's have a drink. I've been reading about lurid events at your gallery.'

'Yes.' Eliza could hear her voice sounding flat.

'Sorry,' Laura said. 'It's a bit close to home really, isn't it?'

'I knew her – the girl who was killed,' Eliza said. 'Oh, not well,' she added quickly as she heard Laura's shocked drawing-in of breath. 'She lived next door to me.'

'That's close to home,' Laura said. Her voice became brisk. 'Well, you're definitely going to need a drink, then.' They arranged to meet later, at the pub on the hill near the Wicker Arches. Eliza put the phone down and looked at her watch. It was after six. She needed something to eat, but first she needed to do a final check on the gallery, make sure everything was secure.

The story in the paper about the events that had taken place a few hundred yards from her window, albeit four years ago, was weighing on her mind. Jonathan had left the gallery shortly after lunch and she had been on her own for most of the afternoon, apart from Mel, who had been uncharacteristically subdued.

She looked out of the window. The sky was clear, and the chill in the gallery, which she hadn't noticed engrossed in her reading, told her that the night would be cold. She cleared her desk, and locked the door of her office. The upper gallery was dark and silent now. She needed to check the downstairs and set the alarms before she left.

The gallery was in darkness as she went down the stairs, but there was a splash of yellow light from the open office door, making an odd, abstract shape. 'Jonathan?' Eliza said. She went to the door and tapped.

He was sitting at his desk, engrossed in something on his computer. He jumped and looked up. 'Eliza. I thought you'd gone.' He looked back at the screen. 'I'm shutting down,' he said. He looked tired, as well he might, Eliza thought. The tinted glasses he habitually wore concealed his eyes, but there were sharp lines beside his mouth, and his beard, normally meticulously groomed, looked a bit shaggy, as though he hadn't taken the trouble to trim it recently.

'I'm just finishing,' she said. 'Listen, I'm meeting Laura for a drink at the East House later. Do you want to join us?'

He shook his head. 'No. I'll be getting home.'

Jonathan lived on his own. It would be lonely going back to an empty flat after what had happened. 'I'm not meeting her for a couple of hours,' she said. 'Why not come and have something to eat before you go back? We could walk along to Victoria Quays.'

There was a click and silence as the computer switched off. 'OK,' he said without enthusiasm. 'I'll get my coat.'

They left the gallery and crossed the bridge to the towpath. The air was frosty, and Eliza huddled into her coat, pulling her scarf more closely round her neck, and digging her hands deep into her pockets. They walked in silence for a while, then Jonathan said, 'What did they ask you about Cara?'

'Where I was, what I'd heard. They asked me what I knew about her. What did they ask you?'

He shrugged irritably. 'They wanted to know where I was. They wanted to know who I was with.'

'Well, you were in Leeds,' Eliza said. The police were bound to want alibis – something she hadn't been able to provide for herself, come to think of it.

'I had to prove it,' he said. 'I had to give them someone's name. It's very difficult.'

Aha! Jonathan had someone in Leeds. Something a bit clandestine by the sound of things. 'I'm sure they'll be discreet,' she said. 'All they want is to eliminate you.'

'Well, maybe.' He hunched his shoulders and pushed his hands into the pockets of his coat. 'They always make it sound as though you've done . . . something.'

Eliza nodded, though it hadn't been her experience particularly. She'd never had much to do with the police. She'd quite liked Roy Farnham on the couple of occasions – disconcerting ones, admittedly – that she'd talked to him. He'd seemed *simpatico*, interesting.

She felt a bit wary of this new Jonathan. She'd known him for almost fourteen years – oh, not well. He'd been her tutor at college – he'd arrived there in her final year. He had been a good tutor, if rather distant and impersonal. She'd had intermittent contact with him after that – the art world was a small one – and then he'd made her the surprise offer of her present job. Their relationship had always been an unequal, a professional one, with Jonathan in the position of power. She didn't want confidences from him that he might regret tomorrow.

They were at Victoria Quays now, and the dark of the towpath became the lights of the shop fronts and cafés, the hotel. The Parkway ran behind the canal basin, and the massive blocks of Park Hill and Hyde Park stood against the night sky in the distance.

They went into the café, and ordered food. Jonathan ordered a bottle of wine as well. Eliza shook her head when he offered her some. 'I'm drinking later with Laura,' she said. He poured himself a glass and drained it. Then he poured another.

'Are you all right?' she said.

He hunched over the table. 'It's just beginning to hit me.'

'I know.' There wasn't much else to say.

'My father wanted me to join the police,' Jonathan said suddenly, surprising her. 'It was what he always wanted to do. He didn't understand about art. It was my mother who could see I had the talent.'

'It's a macho kind of business,' Eliza said.

He looked surprised. 'Art? No, of course, you mean the police. It is. And I'm not into that kind of macho.' He drank more wine, frowning. 'It's all a power thing, intimidating people, pretending . . .' He stopped. 'I used to get bullied at school, you know.' She realized that he'd already been drinking. Was, in fact, a bit drunk. 'I got into karate after that,' he said. 'Worked like fuck at it for months. Then I beat them to a pulp.' He frowned. 'There was hell to pay. I thought my father would be pleased.' He shrugged.

Jonathan would hate the recollection of this talk tomorrow, especially if it got more personal. She hunted around for a response, but their food arrived then, providing a useful distraction, and she took the opportunity to change the subject. 'How's your own work going?' she said. Jonathan's photographic study of socially excluded children.

He shrugged, carefully scraping oil off his fish. He watched his figure like a hawk. 'It isn't. It isn't possible to be creative and get bogged down in all this paperwork. It's death to the artist.'

This hadn't been Eliza's experience. For her, working closely with other people's art acted as a stimulus.

'Flynn's not that good,' Jonathan said suddenly. 'He's derivative. He's just a good self-publicist.' He drank some more wine. 'I've got someone I'd like to exhibit, but he isn't really a gallery artist. He's a conceptual artist. He got really excited about Meadowhall.' The vast shopping mall on the outskirts of the city that had sucked some of the life out of the city centre, a vast temple to consumerism. 'He said it was created by an artist, a genius. It's a parasite, you see, in the city's guts and it keeps on growing.'

Eliza laughed. It was a clever comparison. Meadowhall stood beside the sewage works.

Jonathan gave a reluctant smile. 'He was serious,' he said.

'OK, but it's wonderful.' Eliza was entertained by the idea.

Jonathan had finished the wine now. 'I need to get home,' he said. 'I'll leave the car. Get a taxi.' He got out his phone and squinted at the numbers. He seemed hardly aware that she was there.

She checked the time. She needed to get going to be in time for Laura. 'I'll be off then,' she said.

He nodded absently, keying numbers into his phone.

By the time Kerry had done Stacy's hair and they'd tried on clothes and listened to CDs, Stacy's mum had come back and made tea.

'How are you, Kerry?' Stacy's mum said as she scooped chips on to Kerry's plate. 'You hungry?'

Kerry nodded. She was starving.

'You'll get fat,' Stacy said, looking at the piled-up plate.

Kerry was too hungry to care.

'Oh, lay off, Stacy.' Stacy's mum put her plate in front of her. 'Kerry's not a big lump like you. You've got a lovely figure, Kerry.'

Stacy sat at the table and nibbled a chip. She was frowning. She didn't like her mum paying Kerry compliments, but her mum only did that because she was sorry for Kerry.

So she nudged Stacy. 'Shall I put those sequins on your T-shirt?' she said.

Stacy stopped frowning. 'Like the ones you've got on yours?' she said.

Stacy's mum looked at Kerry's tiger T-shirt that she'd jazzed up to look like the one Samantha Mumba was wearing in *Bliss*. 'Aren't you clever, Kerry?' she said. 'I wish Stacy could sew like that.' What she meant was, *Poor little Kerry. Your mum drinks and your dad's in prison.* But Stacy didn't see what her mum meant. She thought her mum was always saying that Kerry was better at everything. She was frowning again. If Kerry wasn't careful, they'd fall out. Kerry needed to be friends with Stacy now, she needed her in a good mood, so she said quickly, 'It's Stacy's idea. Stacy thought of it.' And she pulled her magazine out of her school bag and started showing Stacy pictures, so that Stacy's mum began to look a bit fed up, and then she left them alone.

Stacy gave Kerry a quick look, and they both started giggling. It was going to be all right.

Later, they sat in Stacy's room watching the telly. Kerry was sewing sequins on to Stacy's T-shirt, and they were talking. Stacy had the window open so that they could smoke without her mum knowing. 'She says it's you makes me smoke,' she said, getting back at Kerry for the things her mum had said earlier.

'It's you makes me smoke,' Kerry said, and tried to blow a smoke ring. They started giggling again.

'Don't get ash on my top,' Stacy said, pushing Kerry's cig away from the T-shirt she was working on. 'Let's have a look at *Bliss*, then.' She sat cross-legged on the bed, turning the pages of Kerry's magazine. 'Mum says you shouldn't be able to afford this,' she said.

Kerry felt her face start to flush. She didn't want Stacy to know she'd nicked it. 'My mum gets it for me,' she said.

'No she doesn't.' Stacy went on turning the pages, looking at the clothes and the make-up. 'I really want one of them,' she said, pointing at a leather jacket that one of the models was wearing. 'She's taller than I am. She's got nice hair.' She glanced sideways at Kerry. 'That blue one'd look nice on you. It's only £65. I'm going to ask my dad to get me one like that, only cerise.'

Stacy knew that Kerry couldn't have a leather jacket that cost £65, and she couldn't make one, either. Then she looked fed up. 'They'll say I can have Mandy's.' Mandy was Stacy's sister. 'It's not fair. Mandy always gets new things and I get hand-me-downs. You're lucky. You haven't got a sister.'

Stacy didn't know about Lyn. But Lyn was only Kerry's half-sister. Her dad had gone away before Kerry was born. 'He wanted me to go with him,' Lyn used to say to Kerry when they were upstairs together and Mum and Dad were downstairs. 'But I said I'd stay and look after Mum. Because of *him*.' Lyn blamed Dad. 'We were all right until *he* came along,' she'd said to Kerry. And another time, shaking her: 'Say you hate him!' But Kerry wouldn't, and Lyn had been mad at her for ages.

Kerry tried to remember how it had been when Lyn left home. Mum had made her go, that's what Lyn said. Home had been all rows, Kerry could remember that. Dad had looked tired and worried, but that was the time when there had been Maggie and Ellie. On Saturdays, Dad and Maggie used to take them out, Kerry and Ellie, or sometimes Dad took them on his own. He liked Ellie – Kerry had been jealous sometimes.

Then it had been the last day, the day they went on the picnic, the day something had happened. And then Ellie was dead and they came and took Dad away, and Kerry could remember the eyes as her friends had walked past the house, still in a group. *You coming, Kizz?* But no one said that any more. Lyn. . . . its abut yor dad meet u at the cafy 7 dont b l8 . . . And *FDAY SAME PLACE 5.00.* Stacy

128

had said something, and she'd missed it. 'What?' she said.

Stacy rolled her eyes. 'What've we got tomorrow? In the afternoon?'

'It's English and then it's French,' Kerry said.

Stacy yawned and went back to her magazine. 'I really love Dermot O'Leary,' she said.

Kerry's idea began to form. 'He's not as cute as Martin,' she said, slowly.

Stacy thumped Kerry's arm. 'Shut up!' But she looked pleased.

'I think he fancies you,' Kerry said.

'Shut up!' Stacy's face was red now.

'I know something about Martin Smith,' Kerry said. She was stitching the last sequins on to the T-shirt. 'There. You can wear it now.' Stacy was watching her. Kerry smoothed out the T-shirt, making sure the sequins were lying flat. She held it up against Stacy's plump chest. The black would make her look thinner. And the sequins would show that Stacy had boobs, which was more than Kerry did. 'You'll look fab. I saw him in the market last Friday,' she added. Friday afternoons, the Year 12 students had study time.

'Who?' Stacy knew perfectly well who.

'Martin. He's got a job. He was loading stuff on one of the stalls.' That was true enough, Kerry had seen him on her way home. 'I saw Hog-face Susie talking to him.' Stacy was frowning. Susan Hogg was in Year 11, and she was pretty and slim and she knew it. Stacy hated her.

'You're making it up,' she accused.

'I'm not! I'm just telling you because you're my mate.'

Stacy looked at her. 'D'you really think he fancies me?' she said. Her face was all bright and hopeful.

'Course he does. But I suppose if he doesn't know you like him, he might as well go out with Hog-face.'

Stacy was biting her lip and looking uncertain. 'I know!' she said.

'What?'

'Why don't we go down the market Friday afternoon?' Stacy said. 'We could go after school.'

'I can't,' Kerry said. 'I've got detention and I'll get suspended. I want to meet someone too, and I can't go.'

'Who?' Stacy's eyes were round with interest.

'No one,' Kerry said. 'It's a secret.'

'I tell you my secrets,' Stacy said. 'You've got a boyfriend, haven't you? Go on, you can tell me.'

'I might, after,' Kerry said. 'But I can't go. You could, though. You don't need me.'

'Please, Kerry,' Stacy said. 'I daren't, on my own.'

Kerry knew that was true. Stacy didn't dare do anything. 'What if we get caught?' she said.

'I'll say it was me, I'll say I felt ill and asked you to take me home,' Stacy said. 'I'll say you didn't want to.'

'We'll have to miss the last class,' Kerry said. 'Or I'll be late.' She kept her eyes on her sewing.

Stacy was quiet for a minute. She didn't bunk off. Then she said, 'OK, if it's just the last class. And we go to the market first.'

Kerry wanted Stacy to say something like that, but now Stacy had, she felt uneasy, as though she was doing something wrong. It was all getting muddled in her mind. But there was only one thing that was important. Lyn had said *its about your dad.* And Dad saying, *Prison changes people, Kizz.* The last day, and then Ellie was gone, and Lyn was gone, and Dad was . . .

And Mum . . . Kerry hadn't thought about it before, not like this, but really, Mum had gone too.

'I'll say I was ill. I promise.' Stacy was leaning forward, her face urgent.

Kerry kept her eyes on the sequins that she was smoothing under her fingers. 'OK,' she said slowly. 'OK.'

Eliza pulled her scarf more tightly round her neck and quickened her pace as she walked up the hill towards the pub.

The pub was quiet, a few people at the tables and a couple of people standing at the bar. Eliza looked round. Laura was at one of the tables, and waved as Eliza came through the door.

The man behind the bar was reading the paper. Eliza wondered if he was reading about Cara's death, ten minutes' walk down the road. She caught his eye and gave him a smile. Eliza came here often enough to know most of the staff. She ordered a glass of wine and went across to the table. Laura jumped up to kiss her. 'Eliza,' she said. 'Sit down. Why did you buy a glass? I've got a bottle. Oh, it won't go to waste.' She crossed her legs, the epitome of casual chic in linen trousers and a loose, chunky sweater.

Eliza thought about the jeans-wearing, paint-bespattered student who had been the third member of the group with whom she had spent most of her student days. Eliza, Maggie and Laura. This pub had been one of their haunts. It always gave Eliza an odd sense of *déjà vu* now it had become, effectively, her local.

Laura looked at her in silence, then she said, 'You look awful. Or as awful as you ever do. Do you want to talk about it?'

Eliza had planned to tell Laura about Cara, about the police, about the man who seemed to be in charge of the investigation. But she wanted to get away from it. She shook her head.

'OK,' Laura said, 'let's forget about it for the moment. Tell me about the gallery. How's Jonathan?' Jonathan had been Laura's tutor as well, but they had established a friendship outside of the college environment, and had kept in touch over the years. For a while, their relationship had been close though Eliza was never sure exactly what the nature of that relationship had been. Laura always adopted a slightly protective attitude towards him.

'Oh, he's fine.' Eliza found Jonathan an easy

person to work for, on the whole. He let her shoulder rather more of the responsibility for the gallery than he should, but it was all useful experience. 'Jonathan's OK,' Eliza went on. That brief, rather revealing conversation stayed with her. 'I think he had problems when he was a child.'

'Did he tell you about that?' Laura's mouth twisted. 'The damage these macho men can do, trying to make their sons conform to their ideals.'

'He didn't say much,' Eliza said quickly. 'It's the first I've heard of it.' OK, she was curious. 'You mean Jonathan's gay?' She'd often wondered. It would explain the failure of his marriage. But why the secrecy?

'No.' Laura said, lighting a cigarette. 'OK,' she said in response to Eliza's look. 'I started again. I'll stop once I've got this next project out of the way. No, he isn't gay. But he does have his problems with women. Anyway,' she said, in an obvious attempt to change the subject, 'you've managed to entice the divine Daniel Flynn into exhibiting with you. How did you manage that, as if I needed to ask.'

'Well . . .' Eliza wasn't sure if she wanted to tell Laura about her situation with Daniel – not until she had a clearer idea herself of what it was. She'd told Laura about the Madrid days, the heady relationship that had gone so well, but she hadn't told her about its sudden end, the way Daniel had vanished behind a barricade of polite indifference.

She gave her a slightly edited version of events. 'I thought I'd got it right with Daniel,' she said. Eliza had a history of unsuccessful relationships behind her. 'But I didn't. I don't really know what happened. Every day, I'd be determined that we were going to sit down and talk about it, and somehow . . .' Somehow, Daniel had evaded that. And as time had gone on, talking became less and less possible. 'I gave up in the end. But now he's here, it's different . . .'

'He sounds like a game player,' Laura said. 'Don't waste your time. Believe me, it's not worth it.' She took a drag of her cigarette, narrowing her eyes against the smoke. 'Now, tell me about this canal thing,' she said.

Laura was a good drinking companion. They finished the bottle and had another glass each. Drinking made them hungry. Eliza had only had a sandwich with Jonathan earlier, and Laura hadn't eaten at all, so they went across the road to the Indian café. Their talk became more general as they sat at the Formica tables over dishes of spiced chicken and saffron rice. Laura was disparaging about Zak, her current – and apparently soon to be ex – boyfriend. In return, Eliza shared some more about her time with Daniel in Madrid. 'I don't think he's playing games,' she said. 'Not now. He might have thought I was.' Which was why he had avoided talking about it.

'Look,' Laura said, lighting a cigarette, 'you take it all too seriously. Most people do. Be honest.

Take me. Sometimes, all I want is sex. Most men don't understand that. They go all defensive, expecting me to start looking for commitment and declarations, and I want to say to them, "From you? You *are* joking? All I wanted was a shag."'

Eliza laughed. Maybe that was the attitude she needed to cultivate towards Daniel.

She and Laura arranged to meet on Saturday, the evening after Daniel's opening, and walked some of the way back into town together before Eliza turned off to the canal basin. It was a longer route back to the gallery, but she preferred it to the shortcut via the footpath and the canal bank. Even before the murder, Cara's murder, she wouldn't have dreamed of walking the towpath at night. And when she got back, instead of going through the yard to the steps, where the dark mouth of Cadman Street Bridge might still be visible along the canal in the night, she went in through the gallery, going through the rigmarole of alarms and security locks. She walked through the silence of the gallery and up the stairs to her flat, turning her music on as soon as she got in and leaving it to play as she made herself some cocoa and got herself ready for bed. She preferred silence to relax her at the end of the day, but the silence from Cara's flat spoke to her, and what it said, she didn't want to hear.

She fell asleep as soon as her head hit the pillow, but she woke late in the night, sitting up suddenly in the darkness. Something . . . she sat there in the chill silence. Nothing. There was nothing. She must have been dreaming. And after that her sleep was restless as she dreamt about footsteps and the sound of a child crying on the other side of the wall.

CHAPTER 7

Thursday morning, Eliza was up early and working on the exhibition. One more day. She was disappointed that Daniel wouldn't be here for this final putting together to collaborate with her in the fine-tuning that this last bit of the process required, but at any rate he'd be back for the opening.

She remembered suddenly that she had promised to send Tina Barraclough an invitation to the private view. She scribbled a note on a post-it and stuck it on the door where she couldn't miss it. If it went first class, Tina should get it tomorrow. She wondered what Jonathan would think about one of the detectives investigating Cara's death coming to the do – he talked, some of the time, as though Cara had got herself killed on purpose to inconvenience him.

She straightened up, pressing her hands into the small of her back. She was supposed to be concentrating on the exhibition, but her mind kept wandering. She looked out of the window. It was a bright, clear day, frozen and still. The sky was blue and the light reflected off the water in a dazzling glow. It was so different from the heavy water that flowed through the Brueghel, so different from the 'canal of death' of the newspaper article. Suddenly she wanted to be away from the claustrophobic atmosphere of Flynn's exhibition and out enjoying the fine winter morning. A walk would help to clear her mind. She headed down the stairs to the lower gallery, taking the steps two at a time in her sudden urgency to get out.

Mel, who was dealing with some outstanding clerical work in a rather desultory way, pulled a face when Eliza told her she was going out for a while. 'That means I'll be on my own,' she said. She hit the print button on her word processor and sat watching the paper run through the printer.

'Jonathan's here,' Eliza said.

'He's in his office,' Mel objected. 'People keep phoning.'

'Who?' Eliza said. She didn't want Mel talking to the press.

'Oh, it's just, "Are you open? When can we come down?"' Mel gave an exaggerated sigh.

Curiosity and sensation seekers, Eliza translated. 'Don't tell them anything,' she said.

'You mean I can't tell them when we're open?' Mel's obtuseness had to be deliberate.

'Of course you can,' Eliza said. 'You know what I mean.' She ignored Mel's raised eyes and had a quick glance through her post. It seemed to be all routine. 'Can you deal with this before lunch?' she said. Mel had hardly made great inroads into the work Eliza had left for her that morning.

'Jonathan says I've got to do art work,' Mel said, 'not typing and things.'

Eliza kept her tone even. 'This is art work,' she said. 'Art administration. It's essential.' She flicked through the last of the letters. Nothing important. She separated the junk and binned it. 'I think we need to keep the door to the upper gallery locked as well,' she said. It was inconvenient and restricted access, but, in fairness to Mel, no one could expect someone working downstairs to monitor any comings and goings. It would be different once the exhibition was open.

'Look, I'm going out,' she said. 'If there are any calls you can't deal with, tell them I'll call them back in an hour. I'll be back before then,' she said, picking up her jacket.

The day was still fine. Despite the cold, the clear skies gave a promise of spring. It was a deceptive promise this early in the year, but Eliza was glad of the respite from the winter gloom. She wondered which way to go. She could walk back towards Victoria Quays, get some coffee and sit in the sun watching the activity in the canal basin, or she could walk the other way, stay with the part of the canal she preferred, the part where the gentrification hadn't reached.

She remembered the canal the way she had first seen it, last summer when she had come to start work, disorientated by the sudden changes in her life, not sure, now that she had made her decision, that she had done the right thing.

She remembered the way the reflections rippled when the water lapped against the bank, suddenly, disconcertingly alive. She'd walked the canal often those first weeks, past the old warehouse with the corrugated roof, and buddleia growing from the cracked pipes. The summer had blazed in Mediterranean splendour, blue skies, hot pavements, and the canal had blossomed, the leaves and flowers flourishing among the rubbish. Butterflies had danced in the buddleia, tortoiseshells and red admirals, and she remembered that then, she had found the canal beautiful.

She wanted to paint it, not as the 'canal of death', not as a relic of industrial decay, but as it was, all its contradictions: pollution and danger and decay, yes, but also the regeneration of nature, in the way the crumbling industrial remains had become incorporated into the natural world – the purple flowers growing out of the cracks in the rusting fall-pipes, the small trees that colonized the guttering of the warehouses, the birds and the animals that exploited this relative seclusion so close to the city centre.

She noticed that the light she was passing was broken, shattered as though it had been the target of an air-gun pellet. As if on cue, two youths passed her, their eyes ahead almost as if they hadn't registered her. They were carrying air rifles and had a dog that looked, to her admittedly untutored eye, like a pit bull. Their wool hats were pulled low down around their heads.

She stopped and watched them walking ahead of her. They were coming to a bridge now, and they stopped and talked to an angler who was sitting by the towpath, aimlessly dipping his line in and out of the water. The towpath looked empty ahead, the weekdays not attracting the walkers that the weekend did. The isolation that had drawn her seemed less attractive suddenly, and she turned back towards the canal basin.

Five minutes of brisk walking brought her back to the gallery, and five minutes more and she was at Cadman Street Bridge. There were flowers against the base of the arch, where the path ran into the darkness of the tunnel, still in their Cellophane, left by the canal side. Flowers for Cara? Eliza paused to look at the label which had been faded by the rain. But Cara hadn't inspired much sympathy. People who mourned for strangers didn't mourn dead prostitutes. One bouquet, with a teddy bear attached, had been placed as a talisman for the recovery of Cara's baby. It was addressed to Briony Rose. *God will keep you safe.*

The flowers, decaying in their wrappings, seemed morbid. Someone else must have thought so too, because there was a second bouquet, but this one had been torn open. The flower heads had been ripped off. Maybe the youths with the air rifles had paused on their way past. Something in the water caught her eye, and she saw that whoever had torn the flowers apart had thrown the discarded heads into the water. They were red – roses? No, carnations – and they lay on the thin ice where the surface was still frozen in the shadows under the bridge and floated in the water. There was a card lying in the mud. She picked it up. It remembered an older tragedy: *For little Ellie*.

Ellie . . . *Raed azile* . . . Morbid. She needed some coffee.

She was about to move on when she realized that there was someone coming along the towpath in the other direction. He was approaching the archway of the bridge, where the path was too narrow for two people to pass. She stood back to let him by, and he gave her a nod of greeting as he came through. 'Eliza . . .' he said. He didn't seem surprised to see her.

She looked at him. A tall man with dark hair. His features suddenly resolved themselves and she realized it was Daniel.

'Daniel!' she said, surprised. 'I thought . . .'

'I was going to give you a ring,' he said. 'But I was on my way by then, so . . .' He shrugged. 'I wanted to come back,' he said. 'Do a bit more work with you on the set-up – get something out of it before the punters move in.' He jerked his head in the direction of the water. It was an oddly dismissive gesture. 'Nature seems to be anticipating art,' he said.

Cara. The triumph of death. 'She lived in the flats. I knew her,' Eliza said. She felt a bit bewildered by his sudden volte-face, by his casual reference to the canal death. The canal murder.

'It made it into the national papers,' he said. He looked down into the water, watching the flowers on the still surface. 'Why do people do that?' He sounded irritated.

'I don't know.' Eliza had wondered herself. 'They've left something for the children, but nothing for Cara,' she said, voicing the thought that had been in her mind when she read the labels.

'Well, toms,' he said. 'Who cares?' She looked at him in surprise. She hadn't expected him to say something like that. Then she saw that he looked angry. 'Just stupid kids,' he said. 'Stupid kids.'

She looked across the water. A boat was moored at the other side of the canal, but otherwise it was empty. It mostly carried leisure traffic these days.

'You know the canal well?' she said. He came from Sheffield originally, she knew.

He nodded. 'They've done it up along there,' he said. 'But it hasn't changed.' The sky was clouding over now, and the water looked leaden and dull. 'It's probably as good as anywhere to have an exhibition about death.' He looked down at her again. 'It's not a good place, this, Eliza.'

More 'canal of death' stuff. She checked her watch. If she wanted that coffee, she needed to get moving. 'I'm going along to the canal basin for coffee,' she said. 'Do you want to join me?' It would be a bit like Madrid, drinking coffee together, talking about art.

His eyes held hers for a moment, then he said, 'Aren't you working today?'

'I'm playing hooky,' Eliza admitted.

His eyes creased in that slight smile she remembered well. 'I won't say anything if you don't,' he said.

Eliza laughed. 'Jonathan owes me about six months in unpaid overtime. He won't mind.'

He frowned, looking at the water again. 'Massey's there today?' he said.

'Yes – he's in all day today.'

'Right. I'll get along there. I'll see you if I'm still there when you get back, OK?' He turned to go.

'OK,' Eliza said. 'I'll see you in half an hour or so.'

She thought over their exchange as she sat at a table in the café, stirring sugar into her coffee and watching the water in the canal basin changing colour in the winter light. She'd wanted to sit here with Daniel, pretend they were back in the Madrid days before things went so suddenly wrong. How had it happened? It had begun with the exhibition, with Ivan Bakst, with Africa.

Madrid

Eliza had never thought about going to Africa, or not until Ivan Bakst came back to Madrid. It was May. Her funding would soon be coming to an end, and she needed to start making some decisions. Madrid was so good for her – Daniel, the work, the people – that she'd been lotus-eating for months.

The night was warm. She was walking up the hill into Old Madrid, to the bar at the Puerta del Sol where she and Daniel customarily met. Madrid evenings started late, and the streetlights cast an orange glow across the uneven pavements and the tables that were starting to appear outside the cafés at night, now that spring was well under way.

She was early. She sat at one of the tables where she could watch down the narrow street and ordered some wine, the rioja they both drank. The bar wasn't busy yet, it was still too early, at nine, for the Madrileños to be out in force. It was colder now she was sitting, and she pulled her wrap round her shoulders. Maybe she should move inside before the bar got too busy and the tables got taken.

She moved into the shadows of the interior. The lights glowed a dim orange, glittering off the glasses and the polished taps, leaving the further recesses of the room in darkness. She looked round. The tables closest to the bar were taken, and the air was hazy with smoke. Further back, away from the light, it was quieter. She chose a table that gave her a view of the door, and sat down.

She was alone in this part of the bar, apart from a man at a table in the corner. He was sitting in the shadows. She could see the glow from the tip of his cigarette. There was something . . . The shadows . . . chiaroscuro, the planes of his face emphasized in light and shade, the eyes pools of shadow. It was as if he was wearing dark glasses . . . a fair-haired man in dark glasses . . . And she recognized him. Ivan Bakst, the man who had come to Madrid with Daniel.

He'd left a few days after she'd met them in the Prado, heading for Tangier, as he had told her. She hadn't been sorry to see him go. He'd been rather distant, cold and unfriendly. She'd wondered if he'd been jealous of the growing closeness between her and Daniel. And now he was back. She wished she'd stayed outside, but she hadn't. If she left now, he'd see her, if he hadn't already.

He had. He seemed to notice her looking at him, but the light still obscured his eyes. 'Ivan,' she said.

He pushed the chair next to him away from the table in invitation, and she went across. 'You're back,' she said, which was bloody obvious, come to think of it. 'Did you make it to Tangier?'

'Among other places,' he said. 'It was good,' he added, after a pause.

Eliza tried to think of something to say. 'What did you do there?'

He shrugged. 'It was an art thing,' he said. 'I need to think about it.' She had experienced this before, a reluctance to talk about his work. He was a conceptual artist. Eliza found this genre problematic. Conceptual art was the ultimate in abstraction. It focused on ideas rather than concrete form, was often transient, was often without a clear place. A conceptual artist might float hundreds of oranges in a swimming pool, but you couldn't take it home with you and hang it on the wall. The paintings she was working with had been crafted to endure. *The Triumph of Death* looked now probably much as it had when Brueghel finished it.

'It's part of something I've been working on,' he said. 'Your line of country, really.' He blew a smoke ring up towards the ceiling. 'Death, change, decay.' He nodded at the smoke, watching it as it wavered and dispersed in the turbulence. 'Like that. Everything changes. Everything moves towards degradation.'

There was something familiar about this conversation. 'Have you been talking to Daniel?' she said.

He ignored her, leaned forward and picked something up off the ground. He held it out towards her. 'Look,' he said.

Eliza recoiled. He was holding a cockroach between his thumb and forefinger. He turned it in the light, studying it. Its legs and antennae waved madly. '*La cucaracha*,' he said. 'Just the sort of nasty thing you get if you leave your evolutionary algorithm running for too long. The flying monsters in your painting . . .' He looked at her. 'Brueghel was probably familiar with the winged vermin.'

'Oh, get rid of it,' she said. She lifted her feet nervously, looking to see if the darkness had brought any more of the creatures out. He drew on his cigarette until the tip glowed, then applied it delicately to the beetle's shell. Eliza heard the *pop* of it cracking.

'Christsake, Ivan!' she said.

He dropped it, and crushed it under his boot. 'Gone,' he said. 'You can freeze the moment, but that's all you can do. That isn't art, it's record-keeping.'

And then Daniel arrived. The two men talked easily for a few minutes, then Bakst said he had to go. 'Nice talking to you, Eliza,' he said.

She nodded but didn't say anything.

'What's wrong?' Daniel asked as he poured himself a glass of wine.

She told him about the cockroach, and he laughed. 'Oh, come on,' he said. 'You asked him to get rid of it. Look, Ivan lives on a boat, he's used to catching and killing things. He's just come back from Africa. They don't have time to be sentimental about animals.'

'He told me he'd been to Tangier,' she said. Maybe she was being over-sensitive.

'He's been as far as Tanzania,' Daniel said. He sounded envious. She remembered that he and Bakst had originally planned to go to Africa together. 'He's got some plans for a show.' As he had told her. She wanted to know more about his work. Many conceptual artists were original thinkers, but there was a lot of space for charlatans, and it was often the charlatans who ran away with the publicity, and sometimes the awards. She wondered which category Bakst fitted into.

'What's he got in mind?'

There was silence for a moment. 'He wants to do something about the triumph of death. Something about putting it into a modern setting.'

Eliza remembered the sense of familiarity Bakst's words had given her. She looked at him. 'That's what you're doing.'

He shrugged. 'There's no copyright on ideas. If I shoot my mouth off . . . It'll be different from what I do, anyway.'

'Different how?'

'I don't know,' he admitted. She started to say something, but he shook his head. 'Forget it,' he said. 'What I do will be mine. What he does will be his. Did he tell you about those pots he made?'

'He never talks about his work to me,' she said.

He laughed. 'He probably sees you as too much of a gallery person. You can't get more gallery than the Prado. But this was brilliant.' His face clouded. 'I wish I'd thought of it. I don't know why he didn't get more publicity – but Ivan never goes for that kind of thing. Anyway, what he did was he got cremains, ashes from people who had died. He kept some and the relatives buried the rest, you know, in those little caskets. Then Ivan dug clay from the graveyards where they'd been buried and made it into pots. And he used the ashes in the glaze, and people had pots that were made out of their dear departed. He took photographs of them together. He called it *Soulmates*.' He grinned suddenly. 'Ivan said one woman – her husband had been having an affair. He made her a goblet. She drinks wine out of it.'

Eliza laughed, and found herself warming a bit to Bakst. Daniel's next words surprised her. 'Listen, have you ever been to Africa?'

She'd heard the frustration in his voice when he'd talked about Bakst's African trip. He'd been in Madrid for long enough. He wanted to move on. He began to outline his plans as they sat in penumbral light. He was going to go. She'd known – known from the start – that their paths would diverge eventually, but she would miss him.

'Come with me,' he said. 'When you finish here. You could paint. And then you could come back to your old masters, if you still wanted to.'

She felt a sudden lift of happiness. She was so convinced there could be no future in this relationship. It was too good. It couldn't last. But it didn't have to end now. It didn't have to end with Madrid. They could go to Africa together. She closed her eyes, thinking of the skies and the light and the vast African plains.

They could do that.

Tina just made it to the briefing on time that morning. Farnham was in the incident room as she flew through the door, and raised an admonitory eyebrow at her as she found herself a space to sit on one of the desks. The information was in from the house-to-house inquiries – no one

150

had any recollection of seeing anything suspicious around the canal or on the towpath, but there was one thing, a puzzling anomaly. 'There were one or two people out on the canal that night,' Farnham said. 'We've found two boats that went down the canal towards Tinsley from Victoria Quays, and one of them came back later in the evening.' A boat that did charters had taken a party up and down the canal. There had been a bar, a band and food, and it appeared that no one on board had noticed the existence of the canal at all, let alone a struggle on the canal bank.

The owner, who had taken the party out, had been more observant, but had had little to report. It had been a bad night and by the time they were coming back – they were back at the canal basin by about ten-thirty – the canal had started to freeze. He'd seen one other boat on the canal that night – its lights had been some way behind him as he headed towards the canal basin. He said it looked like a small boat, a cabin cruiser or something.

A second person had come forward who had taken his boat from the canal basin on to Rotherham and moored up there. Again, he hadn't noticed anything unusual on the canal, though he, too, had mentioned another boat. 'This man, Douglas Lovell, says he passed a cabin cruiser going towards the canal basin at around ten that evening. He said it was probably about half an hour from Cadman Street Bridge when he saw it. He didn't recognize it, and he says he knows most of the boats that use the canal.' He looked round the room. 'We're checking the boats moored on the canal between Tinsley and Victoria Quays. There aren't many – and there's only a couple of cabin cruisers. Those will need checking – who the owners are, where they were, who has access to the boat.'

West put his hand up. 'It could have come from further up the canal,' he said. The South Yorkshire Navigation went east to Keadby, forty-three miles, where it joined the River Trent. You could, using the inland waterways, get to the Thames, to Liverpool, to Hull from Victoria Quays.

Farnham shook his head. 'Tinsley locks is the stopper,' he said. This was a flight of eleven locks, rising 96 feet in one and a half miles, about three miles from the city centre. 'There's staff on duty all the time and it's assisted-passage only. They're locked. Anyone wanting to go through has to give twenty-four hours' notice. There's over a mile of locks there, and it takes between two and a half and three hours to get through. Only one boat went through the locks that night, up towards Rotherham, and we've talked to him.'

There was a stir of interest. 'So that boat is still on this stretch of the canal somewhere?'

Farnham nodded. That same murmur ran round the room, that awareness of having sight maybe, however briefly, of their quarry. 'We're looking, but we need to check those cabin cruisers. OK, next thing. Are we any nearer getting some background on her?' His eyes ran quickly over the team assembled in the room. 'DC Barraclough,' he said.

Tina reported back on her search through Cara's possessions, and her search through the records. On a hunch, she'd looked for the baby's birth certificate. 'She had the baby locally,' Tina said. 'I've still got to go and see them at the hospital, but she didn't seem to have a GP or anything like that. But they might have a previous address.' She hadn't been able to track down any recent contacts, or any indication of how Cara had arrived at the flat in the first place.

'Check it out,' Farnham said. He allocated tasks and the briefing was over for that morning. He seemed to be giving Tina a second chance. She found herself with the job of tracking down the missing cabin cruiser – which was fine by her. Tracking boats sounded like more fun than chasing Cara through the records. There had been enough publicity around the canal to make boat owners aware of the inquiries that were going on. Whoever had been on the canal in that unknown boat had chosen not to come forward. There were several reasons why this could be, but there was one that was clear and pressing.

Tina thought about the report that had come back from the laboratory after the post-mortem. It confirmed that the damage to Cara's hands hadn't happened in the course of a struggle to remove the cord that was pulling her under the water. Those injuries had happened a good hour before she died. Someone had broken her fingers, deliberately and brutally. Punishment? Had she got on the wrong side of one of the pimps? Maybe one of them was trying to move in. But if so, why kill her? The other option, a punter with a kink for pain, looked like a better bet. But again, why kill her? Sex killings, in Tina's experience, involved a perverted intimacy or, sometimes, frenzy – hands, ropes, knives . . . Tying a weight round someone's neck and dumping them in the water seemed strangely impersonal. It was the way you disposed of rubbish, the way some people disposed of unwanted animals.

Tina found herself wondering what it would feel like, that moment of falling into the water, knowing that a weight was going to pull you under, that no amount of struggling was going to keep your head above water, allow you to breathe. She could remember a time when she was a child. Her father had taken her to the baths and, when his attention was on something else, she'd pulled on all the floats and rubber rings she could find, and swum about, high in the water. Then they'd slipped, and suddenly her head was plunged under, and the floats had held her so that she couldn't lift her head. She could remember the seconds of choking panic, thrashing about, trying to find a way to breathe, before someone grabbed her and pulled her back up. Tina had had a horror of drowning ever since.

She wondered what she was going to find, once she had managed to trace Cara's background, the family and friends who had failed to come forward in response to the reports of her death. How had the girl ended up alone with a child, poor, working the streets, and then dead at – what? Nineteen? It was a terrible waste of a life, of a person, and Tina felt again that sense of baffled anger that murder always roused in her. How could someone – if they truly knew what they were doing – how could someone believe they had the right?

Daniel was still at the gallery when Eliza got back. They spent a couple of hours on the exhibition, and he hadn't been in a hurry to rush off. It had seemed quite natural to sit together on one of the deep window sills watching the canal. She told him about her plans to paint it, all the contradictions and contrasts that it represented. He had sketched intermittently as they talked, his attention on the water flowing by below them.

He talked to her about her time in Italy. He'd always been fascinated by her interest in the Renaissance masters, the changing attitudes to art over the centuries, the role of the artist today. He told her about his plans to travel once the exhibition was well under way.

'Africa?' she said. She remembered the plans they had made. He shook his head, not picking up her reference. 'I want to go back to New York,' he said. 'You know it?' Eliza had never been.

'Go,' he said. 'It's the most exciting city in the world.'

'I will,' Eliza said. 'But there's still so much of Europe. I've only been to Amsterdam once, and I've only been to Germany as a student. We went on a trip down the Rhine.' She smiled and then remembered. Maggie had been there. That was before Ellie was born. She watched a small boat heading up the canal towards the locks at Tinsley. She could hear the cracking sound of ice breaking under its bows.

'What are you thinking?' he said.

She didn't want to talk about Maggie. 'That I spent three years in Italy, but I never went to Naples.'

He turned his attention to the sketchbook again, frowning slightly as he worked. She watched him, the quick, sharp looks at the canal, then down, concentrating on the paper where his pencil made swift lines, black on the heavy grain of the paper. 'I can think of worse crimes,' he said. He sat back, and she leaned forward to see what he had drawn. He was about to close the book, but after a slight hesitation, he passed it across to her.

They were all unfinished, a series of sketches, isolated bits that had caught his eye, but the water and the weeds at the canal edges, the crumbling walls and the tangle of dead undergrowth, the suggestion of things floating in the water – all the ideas that Eliza had had about the canal, the contrasts between decay and life, turned into pencil marks on the paper. Her ideas.

He was watching her. She handed the sketchbook back, aware that something of what she felt was showing on her face. 'That's what I meant,' she said. 'The canal.'

He nodded and slipped the book into his pocket. 'I need to go,' he said.

'OK,' she said. 'We're all finished here.'

'Yeah.' He looked round the room. 'You've done a great job,' he said. He seemed undecided about something. 'Look, Eliza, let me buy you dinner, OK? Tonight? It'll be crazy tomorrow, and I'll be off later anyway.'

'OK,' Eliza said. 'Yes, I'd like that.'

'Right.' He smiled down at her. 'I'll pick you up. Say, eight o'clock?'

Roy Farnham turned his car into the small parking area in front of the gallery. There were cars parked in both the spaces, but he managed to pull off the road on to the small strip of Tarmac behind them. He was blocking the exit, but if anyone needed to get out, they could ask him to move. He wanted to look the gallery over. The consensus among the team was that Cara Hobson's death could be linked to her activities as a prostitute. It was the most obvious reason, and Farnham had no problems with that. Occam's Razor – why make life difficult by looking for complications? It was impossible to tell, after her long immersion, whether she had had sex before she died, but if she had, there was no evidence of force. Yet someone had hurt Cara Hobson, deliberately and brutally. Sexual sadism was one obvious explanation, but Farnham wasn't convinced. There was something impersonal about the brutality.

He gave a mental shrug. It was all speculation. He wanted to look at the gallery again. Cara Hobson had spent a lot of time here, according to Jonathan Massey and Eliza Eliot. Eliot had put this down to a desire for company, but, if that were the case, what had she been doing sitting on her own in the dark when Eliot had found her the night she died? And then there was the timing. He felt angry as he thought about that. Such a crucial point so casually let slip. He was pretty confident that Eliot's amended timing was correct, but the first statement she'd made clouded the issue.

As he went towards the entrance, a man came out of the gallery, looked at him blankly for a minute as Farnham caught the door from him, then headed towards the road in the direction of the canal basin. Not one of the car owners then. He looked vaguely familiar, but Farnham couldn't place him. Not Massey. This man was taller, clean shaven. Farnham watched him, then went into the gallery. The door closed behind him, the lock catching as it shut.

There was a desk in the entrance, but no sign of anyone. Farnham looked round. He wasn't trying to keep his arrival quiet, but no one came to see who was there. Poor security. He went past the desk and through some double doors. As he pushed the doors open, a girl came out of a room at one side of the gallery. 'Yeah?'

He was familiar with this studied, gum-chewing indifference. He wondered how old she was as he showed her his ID, and she made a carefully un-impressed face. Her hair was very fair, and her face had an almost clownish pallor apart from her mouth, which was painted a deep purple. The vampire effect was negated by an odd mix of ethnicity – mirror shards and gold embroidery on her waistcoat – and militarism – trousers tucked into her boots, heavily buckled belt. She looked odd but stylish. She folded her arms. *So?* Farnham supplied the mental dialogue. He kept his voice neutral. 'And you are . . . ?'

'Mel.' He waited. 'Young.'

The trainee. 'You do the office work here, right, Mel?'

Her face went a bit pink. She wasn't quite as cool as she was trying to be. 'I'm an artist,' she said. 'I only do this because . . .' She shrugged.

He thought quickly. Avuncular or monster? Did he even want to spend time sparring with a sulky teenager? He made a quick decision. He already knew that she had been out with her friends on Monday night, clubbing until the small hours. She'd known Cara at the gallery, but claimed no other association. He had no reason to talk to her at the moment. 'OK, Mel.' He kept his voice neutral. 'I'm looking for Eliza Eliot.' He wanted to get more of an impression of Eliot, see how she reacted in a work situation. He wanted to know how much he could rely on her judgement.

Mel Young looked at him with a gleam of interest. 'She's upstairs,' she said. 'She's been up there with Daniel Flynn all morning.'

Daniel Flynn. That was the man who had come out of the gallery as Farnham came in. His picture had been all over the papers. Farnham looked round the gallery. 'Upstairs?' he queried, mildly. Mel jerked her head in the direction of the doors, and half turned to go back into what looked like the office. Farnham held her gaze, and she bit her lip and flushed. Then she said, 'Up the stairs and through the double doors at the top. She's in the upper gallery.'

He nodded. 'Thank you, Mel,' he said, and she turned back into the office, starting to shut the door behind her with angry force. He stopped it. 'You'll need to leave this open,' he said. 'Or you won't hear if anyone comes in.'

'They won't,' she said. 'The door's locked.' *Mr Clever.*

'I got in,' he pointed out. She looked as if she was going to say something, met his eye and stopped. She went across to the desk with the same angry vigour and sat down hard. He suppressed a smile, and went back towards the entrance and the stairway to the upper gallery.

The stairs and landing were dark, but when he

pushed open the doors to the upper gallery, he found himself in a long, airy room suffused with a clear light. One wall was windows, high and arched with one central window that reached from floor to ceiling and looked down on to the canal. His first impression was one of chaos – things propped against walls, display screens set out at random across the floor – but it gradually resolved itself into a pattern as if someone was in the process of setting out the room according to a carefully devised plan.

The images on the pictures began to impinge and he found himself in the middle of depictions of violence and death, familiar and unfamiliar. Then he heard feet on the wooden floor, and Eliza Eliot came into view, moving quickly, her face alight and welcoming. 'I didn't . . . Oh.'

He wasn't who she had been expecting. 'Miss Eliot,' he said, 'have you got a few minutes?'

'Eliza.' The room was cold, but her face was flushed and her eyes looked bright. 'I thought . . . Yes, of course. Is there any news?' She ran her fingers through her hair distractedly.

He kept his observation discreet, but this was interesting. He shook his head. 'Nothing new,' he said.

'The baby?' she said.

'Oh. Yes, she's out of hospital. They've put her with foster parents for now.'

He looked round the room again, and she followed his eyes. 'I'm setting it up for the opening,' she said.

'It's Daniel Flynn's exhibition, *The* . . .' She broke off. 'Daniel Flynn's exhibition,' she said.

'The Triumph of Death.' Daniel Flynn. He remembered what Mel Young had said: *She's been up there with Daniel Flynn all morning.* That might also explain the bright eyes and rather flustered demeanour, very unlike the cool and serious persona he'd seen before.

'Yes . . .' She looked at him with a slight frown. 'Do you know Daniel's work?'

He looked round the gallery, at the few visible examples. 'Not my kind of thing,' he said. He caught her quick, assessing glance. 'Tell me about Cara,' he said. 'When did she first move in?'

'I can't give you an exact date,' she said. 'About three months ago. The baby was tiny. The Trust can tell you.'

He shook his head. 'The Trust didn't know she was there.'

Her eyes widened in genuine surprise, then comprehension dawned. 'Squatting,' she said. 'You know, that explains a lot. I couldn't understand why they'd let that flat – mine wasn't properly finished, and the staircase . . .' She saw his look of query. 'The staircase that runs past the gallery. They're supposed to put in an outside door so you can get out from the flats without coming through here. The other steps are OK, but they're a bit scruffy. And they're cold and wet in winter.'

'How might she have got a key?' Farnham said.

Eliza shook her head. 'I don't know. I got mine

from the Trust. I think we keep spares in the gallery. To the outside doors, anyway.'

Farnham ran this through his mind. The outside doors were the real problem. It probably wouldn't be too difficult to get access to an uncompleted flat, put a lock on the door.

'You found her in the gallery,' he said. 'How did she get in when it wasn't open?' He made a mental note to talk to her about security, remembering the ease with which he had wandered in.

She bit her lip and frowned. 'During the day she used the door from the stairs. It's supposed to be locked, but it gets left sometimes –' Her mouth twisted slightly. 'Almost all the time, actually. Before Cara moved in, there was no reason to lock it, really. But that evening – I don't know how she got the codes for the alarm.'

Farnham had a pretty good idea. What she was saying confirmed his suspicions. 'OK,' he said. 'But why didn't you keep the door locked once she started coming in?'

She shrugged. 'It's convenient for me. I keep a lot of my stuff upstairs – we're short of office space. And Cara wasn't a problem. She'd distract Mel sometimes, but, to be quite honest, that doesn't take a lot of doing.' He caught her eye and smiled slightly. He'd seen enough to know what she meant. She smiled back. 'And it was easier for her to come down the gallery stairs with the baby than use the outside steps. There was no point in being . . . It was only when Jonathan got a bit funny about it . . . it wasn't really much of a problem.'

He began to get the picture as they talked. Cara would come through the gallery on her way to wherever she was going in the day, and would stop to chat, look at the stuff that had come into the gallery, and then go on her way. Minor nuisance value. Until she'd started messing round with the alarms. And then she'd died.

'So what about that night you found her in here?' he said. 'Do you think she'd done that before? Let herself in when the gallery was empty?'

She shook her head. 'I don't know,' she said. 'I don't think so – we've done a lot of evenings here recently. Someone would have noticed, I'm sure.'

'What was she doing that night?' He stopped her as she began to speak. 'I know what she said she was doing. What was she actually doing?'

Eliza stood by the large window, her arms wrapped round her waist, looking down at the canal that glittered in the winter sun. 'She was sitting on the sill,' she said. 'Downstairs. She was looking out at the canal.'

He thought about what she'd said. 'She was looking out of the window. Was she looking out for something?'

She shook her head. 'I don't know. Just looking, I think.'

He looked round the gallery, struck again by the uncluttered lines, the arched windows, the clear light. The cruelty of Flynn's images seemed to offend the simple beauty of the room. 'Why this?' he said.

She looked up at him. 'What would you rather have?' she said, sharply. '*The Hay Wain?*'

He'd hit a nerve there. Interesting. He nodded slowly, thinking about what she'd said. 'Yes, probably,' he agreed.

She flushed slightly. 'Sorry, I didn't mean . . .' Though she clearly had.

'Well, thank you for your time,' he said. He looked round the room. 'Perhaps I ought to come and see this once it's up.'

'Yes,' she said. She stayed by the window, watching him as he went through the door. Something was bothering Eliza Eliot. He wondered what it was.

Madrid

The thought of Africa stayed with Eliza, but it seemed to stay in the realm of the abstract. Daniel fired his own enthusiasm for Africa spending time with Bakst, talking about Tanzania with him, but he was taking no practical steps to get there.

Her contract had only another two months to run the morning she and Daniel had paused to look at the bookstalls outside the botanical gardens, on their way to the Prado.

'Look,' she said. She'd found a book on Tanzania. She flicked through the pages, looking at plates of the Serengeti. 'We need to do something about this,' she said. They'd need visas or permits, presumably. And inoculations, malaria . . . they needed to do some research. This was all stuff that Daniel had said he would do. 'You haven't got the time,' he'd said. But that was as far as it had got. Eliza was a forward planner. She liked to have things organized and arranged well in advance. She liked things to happen smoothly, without the stresses and catches of last-minute planning.

'Shall I start asking around?' she said now. Flights, and they'd need somewhere to stay. What about transport – would they be able to get a car? What kind of car? A four-wheel drive?

'I'll do it,' he said. 'Don't worry.'

They were at the entrance to the Prado. Eliza looked up the steps, to the pillars and the portico that ushered visitors into this temple of art. As a member of staff, she got to go in by the lower entrance. Daniel came in with her. He wanted to spend more time studying *The Triumph of Death*. For someone who claimed to abhor gallery art, he had developed what was almost an obsession with the painting.

He waited while she checked her post. There were a couple of postcards from friends, a letter from her mother that she put in her bag to read later. The only other letter looked like business, a buff envelope, typed. She opened it, prepared to drop it in the bin.

'. . . lottery?'

She hadn't been paying attention. She blinked. 'Sorry?'

'I said, "Have you won the lottery?"' He gestured at the letter she had been staring at.

'No, it's . . .' Eliza read it again. It was from her ex-tutor at college, Jonathan Massey. He was offering her a job – or inviting her to apply for one – a newly funded post at one of the Arts Trust galleries . . .

> I'm looking for an exhibitions curator, someone with a wide range, not just 20th century. It seems to me that you would be ideal. It will be advertised at the end of this month. I've taken the liberty of enclosing a copy of the advert . . .
>
> I'd very much like you to apply for the post.

'It never rains,' she said slowly, showing the letter to Daniel. 'A job like that at one of the Arts Trust galleries. Even in Sheffield . . .' The northern city held few attractions for her. But a post like that would put her firmly on the ladder for the arts career she was trying to carve out for herself. Her name would be in the right circles. She would be able to paint, and people in the know, people of influence, would look at her work. She wouldn't be just another painter trying to struggle her way up from under the heap. She looked at Daniel, who was reading his way through to the end of the letter.

'Well,' he said. 'What a choice. Admin in South

Yorkshire or painting in Tanzania.' He grinned at her. 'How are you ever going to decide, Eliza?'

He didn't understand. It wasn't an issue for him. His career as an artist was burgeoning. The name 'Daniel Flynn' was appearing in the arts magazines. Serious galleries were asking for his work. Important critics discussed him. She didn't say anything.

'Eliza?' He was watching her closely.

She could feel all the joy of Africa, all the satisfaction she'd felt at the recognition Jonathan's letter gave her, leaking out of her, leaving her blank and empty. This was the irony of it. Two of the things she most wanted – and they had arrived together, and she had to make a choice. Her emotions were urging her towards one choice, but the practical voice that lived inside Eliza had a different counsel. There was no choice. An opportunity like this would only come her way once.

He could see her decision in her face. 'You're going to go for it, aren't you?' His voice was suddenly neutral.

'I'd be mad not to,' she said. 'I may not get it – the competition will be fierce. But I'd be stupid not to try. If I don't, we can still . . .'

He slid off the desk where he had been sitting waiting for her to finish with the post, and picked up his jacket, which he slung over one shoulder. 'Perhaps,' he said. 'I might have other plans.'

They never talked about it again. They never talked about Africa again. Daniel became elusive, taking long trips away from Madrid, spending more time with Ivan Bakst. He still came to the Prado, still engaged her in discussions about the Brueghel. He said he was starting to get absorbed in his new work, though he wouldn't discuss its progress with her. He was amiable yet distant.

Nevertheless he seemed genuinely pleased for her when she interviewed successfully and was offered the job. 'I knew you'd get it,' he said, kissing her lightly. But in his eyes, she'd chosen the job over him, and he didn't seem prepared to forgive that.

Tina was trying to redeem herself. She could have shrugged off Farnham's complaints about her timekeeping, even about her attitude – a couple of days when she was late in, a bit of inattention at briefings – OK, it wasn't great, but it wasn't a hanging offence. But messing up an important witness statement – she couldn't forgive herself for that. And Farnham wasn't going to forgive her either, unless she could do some really good work.

Her chances seemed limited, though. Tracking down the missing boat had looked interesting, but, at the moment, she was having no luck. And looking into Cara Hobson's background – which was what she was doing now – was routine. If Cara had been killed by one of her clients, then details of her early background wouldn't offer much to the investigation. But Farnham had set her the task, and she was following it up, being good, being conscientious.

She checked the street sign. OK, third road on the left, fifth house up. She pulled up outside a thirties semi and focused her mind on the interview. Her search in the records had produced Briony Rose's birth certificate. It hadn't been too hard to check back after that. She now had the basic information about Cara Hobson's life. She'd been in local-authority care from before her fifteenth birthday. She'd come from a broken home and had cut off all contact with her family. Tina was having trouble tracking them down.

She was on her way to talk to a woman who had worked in the hostel where Cara had lived for a few months after leaving care. She might be able to give Tina some leads towards Cara's friends and contacts in those last years.

Denise Greene was in her late forties, a tall, rather brusque woman. She invited Tina in, having given her identification card a desultory glance. She had been a care worker for years, working in a children's home in the Firth Park area of Sheffield. She was disparaging about the system with the evangelism of one who has seen an organization from the inside.

'It's never satisfactory,' she said in response to Tina's question about the way the care system dealt with the children entrusted to it. 'I mean, take me. I left. Can you imagine, as a kid, having a mother who can hand her notice in?' She laughed out loud. 'There's plenty might want to,' she said.

She'd worked in the hostel for six months, before leaving the care system altogether. 'It wasn't a bad place,' she said. 'It's closed now. It gave them a kind of halfway house – it's hard to go straight from care into a place of your own, specially if you haven't got any family to go to.'

'Yes,' she said when Tina asked her if she remembered Cara. 'It's going back a bit, mind. Nearly five years now. She was a nice kid, Cara, but she was one of those who was made for trouble. A bit of a Dilly Daydream, a bit slow. She was on the game by the time she arrived at the hostel. There's nothing you can do, you know. They wait outside the homes – the men, the pimps. There's a fortune to be made. Well, the girls, they don't know any better.' She looked at Tina. 'There's nothing you can do,' she said again. 'I left. I couldn't stand it. I got another job, moved away.'

'When did you come back?' Tina found the woman's defeatism depressing.

'Six months ago. I missed Sheffield. I work in an office now.' She looked at Tina. 'You can't beat it. At five o'clock, I leave, and I don't think about it again until I walk through the office door at half past eight.'

'Do you remember if Cara was friendly with anyone in particular?' Tina said.

'She had a friend used to come and see her. They'd been in the same care home. They used to go out together. And she got friendly with one

171

or two of the girls who came in around the same time she did. But I left soon after that.'

'This friend she went out with, was she another one who was on the game? Can you remember . . . ?' Tina had her pen poised.

'Her name? Yes, I can. Sheryl, Sheryl Hewitt. And yes, she was.'

Two young girls cementing their friendship over prostitution. No wonder Cara had ended up the way she did. But Tina could try to track Sheryl Hewitt down. It seemed likely that Cara would have kept up the contact, at least for a while.

Nearly five years. Any trail would have gone cold by now. Maybe Sheryl Hewitt, if she could be found, would be able to fill in the gaps in Denise Greene's story. 'OK. I'll need to talk to this Sheryl. Do you have any idea . . . ?'

The other woman shook her head again. 'No. I don't know where she went. She ought to have done OK for herself. She was bright. But I don't know.' And Tina had to leave it at that. At least she had a name now. It would give her something to take back to Farnham.

CHAPTER 8

The restaurant was quiet, only three tables occupied when Eliza and Daniel arrived. The waiter showed them to a table by the window, and Eliza leant back in the cushioned chair as Daniel ordered some wine. 'There's a rioja.' He smiled at her. Rioja had always been her choice. 'That suit you?'

'Fine.' Eliza smiled back, letting the memories show on her face. She watched the comings and goings in the street outside. On the corner a bit further up, there was a barber's shop, bright green with a large window. It was open, even this late in the evening, and a fair-haired woman stood behind the barber's chair, brilliantly illuminated as though she was on a stage. It was like a painting by Edward Hopper, one of those late-night cafés, all hard light and bright colours.

Daniel was sitting opposite her and his eyes followed hers. 'Hopper,' he said.

Eliza nodded, pleased that he'd seen what she had seen. There was a moment of silence as they adjusted to the new context, then Eliza said, 'What are you doing once the exhibition's opened?'

The waiter arrived with the wine, and Daniel didn't answer until they were alone again. He swirled the wine round in his glass, and said, 'I don't know. I've got some ideas – I wanted to get to Bamiyan.'

'Bamiyan?' She was blank, then she realized. 'The Buddhas,' she said. The ancient statues destroyed by the Taliban.

'I want to do some work – put together a show – about what exists after something is gone. It's more than just nothing,' he said. 'That emptiness represents something. But it'll have to wait for now.' He rubbed his hand over his face. He looked tired. His hair was untidy and he hadn't shaved. His eyes were unfocused. 'It was that poor little cow that got killed,' he said. 'It got me thinking – how is the world different now that some teenage hooker isn't here any more? We don't even notice the gap – no books of remembrance for her,' he said. 'Or any of the others – the junkies, the runaways. No one notices. Yet they noticed the Buddhas. So . . .' He swirled the wine round his glass but didn't say any more.

'Or New York?' she said. *What exists when something is gone . . .*

'Yeah. Maybe.' He was looking out on to the road, and he moved his shoulders irritably when she spoke.

'Do you never want to stay on in Sheffield?' she said after a while. 'I mean, do you have family here still? Friends?' He'd never talked to her about his background, his family. He shook his head. There was silence again. When they'd talked in the gallery, it was as if there had been no lapse of time – they were together again, the words flowing, the ideas sparking between them. 'I'm sorry,' she said. 'That's none of my business.'

'No, it's not that. I'm tired.' He seemed to make a conscious effort and smiled at her. 'I've told you my ideas for what I'm doing next. Your turn.'

'OK. But I'm not sure what plans Jonathan . . .'

'Not the gallery. Your own work.' He filled her glass and the waiter came over to take their order.

Eliza made a pattern on the tablecloth with her fork. She wasn't sure, now, that she wanted to talk to Daniel about her work. 'I've got something . . .' she said.

'The canal? Paintings of the canal?' He too was thinking about their conversation earlier that day.

'Something like that,' she said. Why didn't she want to tell him about her Madrid painting, and the ideas that were beginning to form in her mind around it?

'So it's still in the ideas stage,' he said. She nodded.

The silence was more comfortable now, and she waited to see what he would say next. 'I don't have family in Sheffield any more,' he said, going back to her earlier question. 'And if I did, I don't think I'd want to stay.'

'Are your parents still alive?' Eliza's mother lived

on the south coast. Her father had died six years ago.

He shook his head. 'My father might be, but, as I've never met him, it's not an issue. My mother died three years ago.'

'I'm sorry,' she said, with conventional regret.

'Don't be. I'm not.' He refilled their glasses. 'We're going to need another bottle at this rate.'

Eliza could feel the wine going to her head, but she was enjoying the slight recklessness that it created. 'What about sisters? Brothers?'

'I had a sister,' he said. 'A half-sister. She died when she was in her teens.'

Eliza felt a twist of sadness. 'I'm sorry,' she said again.

'Yeah. Well . . .' He shrugged, but then the waiter arrived with their order, and they didn't go back to the subject.

Later, they shared a taxi back. Eliza, relaxed by the wine and the good food, was in a mood to take risks, but when they got to her flat, he helped her out of the taxi, put his hands on her arms, kissed her lightly on the mouth and said, 'I'll see you at the do tomorrow, Eliza.'

And the taxi pulled away, leaving her standing there on her own.

Kerry's diary

Thursday, 17 January
There was a letter today. I dont now who

sent it. I thought it was about dad but it wasnt. I'm going Friday afternoon like she said. I'm taking Stacy up the market. I got it wrong last time but it wasn't my fault I got lost. I wrote a letter to Dad tonight. I can't tell him about Lyn yet. He might get dissapointed but I said I'm doing something so he'll now. Mum was on the sofa again tonight . . .

There had been a letter addressed to Kerry on the mat that morning. Miss Kerry Fraser, typed. No one wrote to her, only Dad. She had stuffed it in her bag, and opened it when she was at the bus stop. It was a piece from a newspaper. She unfolded it and looked at it. THIRD DEATH AT SUICIDE JAIL.

She could still remember the tight feeling in her chest as she'd read the article. But it wasn't about her dad, it was just about some kid who had hanged himself in prison. Still the tight feeling didn't go away. She could remember Dad's last letter. He'd sounded so sad. He'd said, 'Prison changes you, Kizz.'

She huddled up on her bed, crouched over the paper in front of her. She didn't know what to say to Dad. She wanted to tell him it would be all right, and she wanted to tell him that she wasn't all right, that she was lonely and unhappy, that Mum didn't care any more, but people in prison got depressed. THIRD DEATH AT SUICIDE JAIL.

Her dad wouldn't do that. It had said in the article about a kid who'd killed himself because he'd been bullied. And no one cared. He'd torn up his sheets and hanged himself. And another one, about a kid who set his prison cell on fire . . . Kerry couldn't stop herself. She'd shown it to Mum when she got home. Mum had pulled a face, screwed it up and dropped it in the bin. 'What do you want to read that for? You don't want to read this rubbish.'

I'm fine, Kerry wrote. Then: *Mum's fine. She sends her love.* She bit the top of her pen. *It'll be all right, youll see. School is OK. I made my world wildlife T-shirt into a sequin one. It looks fab.* She couldn't think of anything else to say. *I hope your OK too. Lots of love. Kizzy. xxxxx.*

Her eyes felt heavy with sleep. She addressed the envelope carefully, with Dad's number, and the wing, and then the address that said 'prison' as clear as anything. The prison address was Love Lane. She put her own name and address on the back of the envelope. If she didn't do that, then Dad wouldn't get it. She tucked the envelope deep into her school bag, and turned out the light.

The next day, the day of the opening, should have been hectic. Eliza was in the gallery early, going over the preparations, checking the exhibition to make sure that everything she and Daniel had discussed was now in place. And the gallery had to be ready for a massive influx of visitors the following week.

The Triumph of Death was moving to London after five days.

But by half past nine, Eliza felt as though she had put her foot on a step that wasn't there. There was nothing for her to do. She'd hired a caterer to deal with the opening, a temporary receptionist was demonstrating her efficiency in the office, even Mel seemed hyped up by the coming event.

'For Christ's sake, Eliza . . . !' Jonathan said after she'd wandered into his office for the third time to see if there was anything she could help him with.

She went to see if the temp needed any help with the last of the admin. 'I'm fine, thank you,' she said. 'Why don't you leave this to me?'

'I could . . .' Eliza looked round. The gallery was quiet. Jonathan was talking to someone on the phone. 'All the details for tonight are . . .' He put his hand over the mouthpiece and looked at Eliza. 'For Christ's sake, Eliza,' he said again, 'take the rest of the morning off.'

'Someone might call from the paper . . .'

'I can deal with that.'

Eliza was surplus to requirements. 'OK,' she said. The idea of a morning off was starting to appeal. She could go shopping, buy a new dress for the party. 'OK, I'll go.'

An hour later, she was sitting in the winter sun in a coffee bar, her new dress in a bag beside her, and the shoes that she hadn't intended buying but hadn't been able to resist. She tried not to think about her credit-card bill. The new dress and the thought of Daniel Flynn were mixed together in her mind and she felt a frisson that was both exciting and dangerous. It was only ten-thirty, and she had the rest of the morning free. She remembered her conversation with Maggie's landlord a few days ago. She'd told him she wouldn't be able to do anything until after the opening, but now she had a bit of time. She could sort the stuff at Maggie's in a couple of visits. She could spend the rest of the morning there, and then she would know what kind of task she was facing.

The roads were congested, and it took her half an hour to get from the town centre to the suburb where Maggie used to live. Maggie had spent the last year of her life in a small flat in Walkley, about half an hour's walk from the graveyard where Ellie had been buried, and where she now lay. It occupied the ground floor of a house that was strangely isolated, set back on a steep side road. Access was through a small gennel and up a flight of stone steps, then through a gate into what must once have been a beautiful garden, private and enclosed, only it was long overgrown, the shrubs encroaching on the path and hanging over the neglected patch of lawn.

Eliza had been there a couple of times when Maggie was still alive. The second time Maggie had invited her round for a drink. The evening had been uncomfortable, Eliza remembered. Maggie had tried hard not to talk about Ellie or about Mark

180

Fraser, the man she had wanted to be part of her future – the man who had been, irretrievably and devastatingly part of her future and who was now serving a life sentence for killing her daughter. Eliza wouldn't have minded. At least the talk would have been real. But Maggie pushed the conversation on to Eliza's work at the gallery, their shared interest in art, anything other than the topic that must have been at the front of both of their minds.

'So, he must think you're hot stuff – Massey,' Maggie had said with that odd combination of belligerence and approval that she used back then to talk about Eliza.

She refilled her own glass and waved the bottle at Eliza, who shook her head. They had each provided wine for the evening. Eliza had only had a couple of glasses, but both bottles were nearly empty. 'I may as well finish this,' Maggie said, upending the second bottle over her glass. She stood up and went into the kitchen. There was a slight uncertainty to her walk, but no other indication that she'd drunk so much. She brought more wine with her.

'Not for me,' Eliza said quickly.

Maggie looked at her. 'You saint,' she said. She picked up her glass. 'He'd done it before, you know,' she said suddenly. 'Fraser. Mark Fraser.' Her voice caught on the name as though it choked her to say it. 'His daughter. His stepdaughter. He'd been up to stuff with her. He was a paedophile and they must have known, but nobody did anything.'

'I know.' Poor Ellie. Poor Maggie, left with the guilt.

'And he was teaching, for God's sake. And he saw Ellie . . .' Maggie's head drooped. 'And there I was, all ready for a new relationship. You know, I discussed Ellie with him. I talked about how it was bad for her not to have a father. And he listened and he said all the right things. I thought he was wonderful.' Eliza could remember Maggie's letters, suddenly full of this amazing man she'd met. She didn't know what to say. 'And you know why I was asking him?' Maggie's voice was rising to a shout. 'It was because I fancied him, because I . . .' She broke off and drank some more wine. She looked at Eliza. 'His wife, you know what she did? She threw the girl out. That's what she did. So Ellie . . .' She emptied her glass and began to take the cork out of the new bottle.

'Let me.' Eliza took it off her and busied herself with the bottle opener. If she took her time, maybe Maggie would forget about having another drink.

'They never said sorry,' Maggie said. Her voice was bewildered. 'You know, that's what I want. I want to know that he knows. That he knows what he did. If I thought he knew, really knew, I might . . .' She looked at Eliza. 'Give it here,' she said impatiently, taking the bottle and corkscrew from her. She opened the bottle and poured herself another glass. 'If he just knew,' she said.

That had been the last time Eliza had seen

Maggie. They'd talked on the phone a couple of times, but, somehow, Eliza had been busy, and then Maggie had been involved in her campaign, galvanized by the news that Mark Fraser's lawyers were talking about flaws in police procedure and an appeal.

And now she was dead.

Eliza picked up the post from the doormat as she let herself in and checked through it. Junk. She looked round the flat, remembering. There was very little here. The furniture wasn't her problem. A clearance firm was disposing of it. There were no photographs on the walls or the shelves, no ornaments, though Maggie, as a student, had been a collector of pots, things she picked up from junk shops and charity shops.

There was a card pinned to the cork board on the kitchen wall. She looked at it, and felt a slight chill running down her back. It was a postcard reproduction, so small that the detail was crowded to the point of incoherence, but she knew it so well. *The Triumph of Death*. Then she remembered. She'd given it to Maggie the last time she'd seen her, when she'd told her about Daniel's exhibition. Maggie had seemed indifferent, but she'd kept the card.

Even though she remembered now why it was there, she felt cold, uneasy. Brueghel's dark masterpiece seemed to be escaping from the gallery, creeping into the world outside – just the way she'd imagined in her plans for the exhibition.

She shook her head. Morbid fancies. She needed to start sorting things out here so that she could tell the clearance people to come and take the rest away. The flat was tiny. It could have been charming, if Maggie had ever bothered with it. There was a living room at the front, a bedroom and a bathroom at the back. The kitchen was in an off-shot.

She checked the bedroom, rummaging through the clothes that had been carelessly crammed into drawers or on to hangers. There was a faintly stale smell that suggested the sheets piled on a shelf hadn't been properly aired, that the clothes themselves were perhaps a day too far from a wash. In those last few years, Maggie really hadn't cared.

There was nothing there. She went to the living room. There was a small bureau, empty apart from some folders. Eliza flicked through the first. It contained bank statements, business letters, certificates, a passport – unused for years – all the expected paraphernalia of daily life.

The next folder contained letters: copies of letters that Maggie had written, and replies. Eliza checked through them quickly. These were part of Maggie's campaign to keep Mark Fraser behind bars. She had written to newspapers, to MPs, to her solicitor, to various pressure groups. She'd had sheaves of replies. There were address lists – people who, presumably, were happy to assist in her campaign. There were also letters that had no salutation, handwritten rather than typed. Had these been sent? If so, had Maggie written out copies? She looked at one and then pushed the pile back into the folder. Maggie had written these letters to Mark Fraser, and the grief and rage that burned off the page was more than Eliza could stand. She didn't want to share this . . . *Every breath you take was stolen from my child and I will make sure each one is a burden to you that . . .*

There were also yellowing newspaper cuttings that looked as if they had lain in the folder undisturbed, apart from a couple of more recent ones that lay at the top. Eliza unfolded one of the older ones. It was a story about Ellie's disappearance: FEARS GROW FOR MISSING SOUTH YORKSHIRE CHILD. The recent ones related to Mark Fraser's appeal: CHILD-KILLER FRASER IN NEW APPEAL.

She looked in the bureau drawers next. Here was the more personal stuff. Boxes of photographs: Maggie through childhood and her teenage years, as a student. Eliza found one of herself with Maggie. She couldn't remember the occasion, but it looked as if they were at a party, dramatically dressed and made up, making a big thing of being art students, no doubt.

And then photographs of Ellie – as a baby, as a little girl, growing up, smiling, beautiful. These photographs looked as though they hadn't been touched for a long time. Eliza could feel the dry contamination of dust on her fingers. All of these photographs, to go – where? Maggie had had no family, or no close family.

And in the next drawer – memorabilia. A child's drawings, a first shoe, a tiny box containing what Eliza first thought was a shell, then realized was a tooth, a milk tooth. A lock of hair, fair, curling round the blue ribbon that held it. And another lock, this one tied with black ribbon. The hair looked dull and stiff. Eliza pushed the drawer shut abruptly.

She stood up and stretched, pressing her hands into the small of her back to relieve the crick that had developed. *You're getting old, Eliot.* She needed to sort through the photographs, decide who might want them. Or maybe they should all be destroyed. Eliza would like to keep a few – one or two of Maggie, some of Ellie.

And the personal stuff, the milk tooth, the locks of hair. Maybe Eliza could buy a plant, a small shrub, a rose, maybe, and plant it on Ellie's grave with those last things buried in the roots. And the pictures and the shoe – those could be burned and the ashes scattered at the same time.

But now wasn't the time to look through this stuff, now wasn't the time for reflection. She packed the papers into folders, discarding obvious junk – magazines, coupons, old receipts. She put the folders of letters and the boxes of photographs on to the back seat of her car. She could sort through them at her leisure back at the flat. She left the cuttings and the other papers for later.

She didn't want the story of Ellie's death, of Fraser's trial, any closer to her life than it already was. She checked her watch. It was gone one. It hadn't taken her much time at all. She'd missed lunch, so she drove down into Broomhill and stopped for a sandwich at the small coffee bar. She would be back at the gallery in plenty of time for any last-minute crises.

Tina Barraclough was on the trail of the missing cabin cruiser. Her luck was in. The canal patrol officer, Michael Riley, was on the Sheffield stretch of the canal and free to talk to her. She drove through town and parked by the side of the canal below the flight of eleven locks that had, with luck, trapped the mystery boat. It was a clear, cold day. The water gleamed in the sunlight, and a couple of men sat on the opposite bank, fishing rods extended into the water. An arched bridge with white railings stretched across the canal and bare trees lifted their branches to the sky. The canal looked gentle and benign here, not a place of torture and violent death.

Michael Riley was a tall, weather-beaten man who knew the canal in all its aspects. 'It's shocking, this,' he said to Tina. 'Poor lass.' He was the first person who'd expressed much regret about Cara's death.

She explained what she wanted, and he nodded. 'Yes, I've talked to someone from your place,' he said. 'They wanted to know about traffic through the locks.' He went over the records again with Tina. One boat had gone through the locks the night of Cara's death, and there had been very little traffic since then.

'Could someone get through here without anyone knowing about it?' she said.

He shook his head. 'It's assisted-passage only. You'd need a key – and anyway, it takes almost three hours to get through all the locks.' He grinned at her, his teeth surprisingly white in his tanned face. 'It's not quick get-away country.'

Tina thought about a canal chase, two narrow boats in hot pursuit, drifting up the canal at three miles an hour.

'How many boats are moored below Tinsley locks?' she said.

'Twenty-eight,' he said immediately. 'It's pretty static at this time of year. There's a few come into the moorings at the canal basin, but most of the boats are regulars. I'll talk you through them.'

'Have any left since Monday?' The night of Cara's death.

'Not that I'm aware of,' he said. 'We get visitors in the summer, but not at the moment.'

Tina began to get a picture of the working of the canal as he talked. There was very little commercial traffic. A lot of money had been spent in the 1970s to widen the canal so that steel could be moved along the Don Valley. The completion of the works had coincided with the ravages that the Thatcher Government had inflicted on the steel industry, and the scheme had never come to anything. 'There's the one barge that runs scrap up to the Humber,' he said. 'But that's about it.' The rest of the commercial traffic was leisure. And then there was the holiday and recreational trade, and the residents. 'There's almost no holiday traffic on the canal at this time of year,' he said again.

Some owners took their boats out in the winter, but most had them moored up or even out of the water for maintenance. The residents lived on the canal all year, occasionally moving on if they could afford to change moorings. 'A boat's got to have a permanent mooring, see?' he said. 'Then there's visitors' moorings that they can use when they're moving around.'

'So any boat on the canal will have a permanent mooring somewhere?' Tina said.

'That's right, unless it's a trailer boat that's out of the water when it's not being used. Or unless it's someone who moves around all the time.'

Tina made some notes. This didn't bring her any nearer the missing boat. 'I'm looking for a cabin cruiser, or something that could be mistaken for a cabin cruiser after dark.'

'I can get you the name of every cabin cruiser with a mooring between here and Keadby,' he said. 'Who told you it was a cabin cruiser on the canal that night?'

Tina told him, and he nodded. 'You can rely on that,' he said. 'If Doug said it was a cabin cruiser he saw, then that's what it was.' He thought for a while. 'If I'd seen it, I'd likely be able to tell you which one it was. But I didn't. I wasn't on the canal that night.' He patrolled the canal regularly, covering its full length once a fortnight. Anyone who knew the system would have known when he was likely to be around.

'Could it still be on the canal?' she said.

'You can get a list of everything that's been through Tinsley locks,' he said. 'And that'll not be a lot at this time of year. Of course, someone could have brought a trailer in, taken a boat off up a slipway.' If they had, then the cabin cruiser could be anywhere. Tina felt depressed. 'But you couldn't do that without someone noticing. There's not so many places you can take them off.'

The house-to-house had included the boats. Tina made a note to check the statements. Maybe she needed to go back to some of them, ask them specifically. 'If that cabin cruiser is still on the canal,' she said, 'then where is it?'

'Moored up,' he said. 'There's only four cabin cruisers moored on this stretch of the canal, and I can tell you about all of them. Right. There's the *Lady Grey*. She's moored up below Tinsley. She belongs to a Mick Hughes. I haven't seen her out on the canal for a couple of months – he might be away. I've got a contact number. There's the *Mary May*. She's moored near Don Valley Stadium. Let's see . . .' He checked his list. 'Calloway. Steven Calloway. He lives in York. He doesn't take her out – she's been up for sale for a few months.'

'OK,' Tina wrote the details down.

'Then there's the *Eleanor* – she's only been on the canal six months. That's the Stricklands. They've had boats on the canal for years. They're around a lot. The *Eleanor*'s at Tinsley as well. And then there's the *Lucy*, she's nearer the canal basin at Shirland Lane . . .' He checked his notes again, frowning. 'I'm not sure who the owner is – I'll need to get back to you on that.'

When she left, Tina had a list of all the boats that were moored on the canal, the moorings, and the names of the owners. This, surely, shouldn't be too difficult. She checked the time. Her shift was nearly over. She just had time to get back to the incident room and type this up. She could put it through for Farnham to include in the briefing tomorrow. She needed to have a few early nights, lay off the sex-and-drugs-and-rock-and-roll.

But tonight she wanted to get away as early as she could. She was going to the private view at the Second Site Gallery. She'd made the mistake of mentioning it to her colleagues. Even Tina, inured to the laddish culture of the canteen, hadn't realized exactly how many double entendres could be made from the phrase 'private view'. The joke had kept everyone happy for the day.

As she came back into the office, Dave West said on cue, 'Viewed any good privates lately, Tina?'

'Well, if I have, they certainly weren't yours,' she

said, resigning herself to the hilarity around her. Now, how to word the report to Farnham quickly and succinctly . . . ? She ran the information she had through her mind, and also any possible follow-up she should have done. She didn't want to be wrong-footed at the briefing by a question she couldn't answer.

'It'd stunt your growth,' she riposted to yet another half-heard private view joke. She typed the report quickly. She was pretty sure she'd covered all the options Farnham could reasonably have expected her to cover. OK, that was it, she was done. She grabbed her coat and headed for the door, amid a barrage of comment.

Kerry watched Stacy at the mirror. She was fidgeting with impatience. She wanted to grab Stacy by the arm and drag her out of the toilets. They'd got into town late. They'd skipped the last class, but Stacy had insisted on going in for registration and the first class. And now they were in town, Stacy had insisted on going into the toilets in the big store and changing into her new top and doing all her make-up again. 'Do my hair, Kerry,' she said now.

'There isn't time. It looks fab,' Kerry said.

'Is my face OK?' Stacy could never believe she looked all right.

'Yes!' They needed to get to the market in time for Kerry to go and meet Lyn. There'd been another letter that morning. Another newspaper article. JAIL SUICIDES UP. She'd sent a message to Lyn: *ok 4 2nite?* And Lyn had replied: *OK. DONT B L8.*

As Kerry thought about it now, she felt prickles of tension running up and down her back. She checked her watch. It was after four. She thought about her dad hanging from his bed frame, the sheets tight round his neck. She thought about her dad, trapped in a burning cell, and she grabbed Stacy's arm. 'Come on. You look fab. Come on.'

Stacy shook her off. 'I'm nearly ready,' she said. But it was twenty past four before they were running down the hill towards the market.

'Slow down.' Stacy was panting behind her. 'I can't run as fast as you can.'

But Kerry pelted on down the hill, and then they were at the market. Stacy gasped for air and looked accusingly at Kerry. 'I wanted to get here before he'd gone,' Kerry said, before Stacy could speak. 'Come on.' She threaded her way past the stalls until she saw the one where Martin was working. She pulled Stacy back behind the next stall and said, 'There he is.'

Stacy giggled with excitement. She kept looking at Martin and then ducking back. 'He's seen me,' she said. 'What shall I do?' Her face, normally rather heavy and plain, looked pink and pretty. She was loving all the hiding and the whispering and the giggling, and it gave Kerry that feeling of mean wrongness inside her again. It was for

Dad, that was what was important. 'Tell him I'm here,' Stacy said. 'Tell him we'll meet him in the coffee bar.'

It was obvious to Kerry that Martin had seen them and blanked them, probably because he didn't even recognize them. But Stacy was deep into the game. It might be OK. Kerry thought quickly. Stacy would be OK if Martin didn't actually talk to her, didn't ask her out. Stacy was really shy with boys. She just wanted to think that he would, that he liked her. She felt a bit better.

'OK,' she said. 'Shall I tell him you fancy him?'

'Kerry!' Stacy was thrilled and outraged.

It was easy to play the game. 'I'll say, "My mate fancies you. Look, she's over there." And he'll . . .'

'Shut up!' Stacy shoved her and collapsed into giggles. Kerry tried to laugh too, but it sounded awkward and false. Her heart was beating fast and she wanted this to be over.

'I'll say we'll meet him in the coffee bar,' she said. 'Shall I?'

'Go on! But you're not to say I like him. Don't say that. Promise.' Stacy's eyes were bright.

'OK.' Kerry smiled her reassurance and went over to the stall, looking back at Stacy, who gestured her forward, *Go on. Go on.*

He was calling as she walked towards the stall: 'Bananas, two pound for eighty pence, get them here, two pound . . .' A kind of litany to pull in the passers-by. When people stopped to buy, he put the bananas in a bag, took the money, quick as anything, his eyes already hunting for the next customer. But Stacy had to see her *talk* to him. She took a breath.

'How much are those?' She pointed at a tray of odd, wrinkly things. She didn't know what they were.

'Passions?' he said, oddly. 'Fifteen pee each.' His eyes were roaming round for more customers.

'And those?' she said.

He looked at her this time. 'It's on the ticket.'

'I haven't got my glasses,' she said.

'Twenty,' he said. Kerry couldn't buy anything. She didn't have any money.

In desperation, she said, 'You go to our school, don't you?'

He looked at her again. 'How should I know?' he said. 'Look, you want to buy something? I'm working here.'

Kerry backed away as he began calling about bananas again. Her face felt hot. She hurried back to Stacy, who was half-concealing herself behind the next stall. 'He says he's working,' she reported. 'He said he can't. You'll have to talk to him at school on Monday.' Her voice sounded odd and strained. 'I'll help you,' she said.

Stacy looked at her. 'We can't go now. We've only just got here. We can wait for him.'

There was a heavy feeling in Kerry's chest. She looked at her watch again. It was five o'clock. 'I can't,' she said. 'I've got to meet someone.'

'Kerry!' Stacy's eyes were accusing. 'You said!'

'I told you to hurry! I'm late!' Kerry was moving away through the early evening crowds.

Stacy followed her. 'You can't go,' she said. 'Let me come too.'

'It's a secret,' Kerry said. 'I'll tell you tomorrow, promise I will, I've got to go . . .' If she took Stacy, Lyn might be mad. She wouldn't talk about Dad. She turned away from Stacy, from her panicky face. She had to get down to the canal basin and it was after five already. She wove her way through the people and tore down the hill to the tram tracks. The streetlights were already lit, and the lights were on in some of the offices as she hurried past. She ran up the steps and across the bridge, then down the other side to Victoria Quays.

It was almost quarter past. She was late again. There was the bench outside the café, the place where Lyn waited for her. *Same place.* But there was no one there. She looked round. There was no sign of Lyn, and the canal basin was deserted in the cold evening. There were one or two people in the café, but she couldn't see Lyn. She stood by the bridge. There was a shadow on the water ahead, a boat drifting in towards the canal basin, its engine silent, its lights off.

But Lyn must have been here, must have waited for a few minutes. She must just have left. Kerry thought quickly. She hadn't passed Lyn, so maybe she'd walked back along the towpath. She wouldn't be far ahead.

Kerry ran across the bridge and along the

path, under the railway where the canal turned, and under the arch of Cadman Street Bridge. The lights made dim pools all along once she was through, and the towpath stretched away ahead empty. If Lyn had gone five minutes before, she would have been on the path, moving in that brisk way.

She pulled out the phone and looked again. FDAY SAME PLACE 5.00? She'd only been a bit late. It wasn't fair. There were steps up to the road a bit further on. Maybe Lyn had walked along here and gone up the steps. Kerry ran, her feet slipping in the towpath mud. She got to the steps, where there was a sign about taking bikes on Furnace Lane, and ran up them, stopping at the top as a stitch in her side doubled her over. But there was no Lyn. Maybe Lyn couldn't make it. Maybe that was it.

She got the phone out of her bag again and switched it on, but there were no messages. The light had almost gone now. She had to get back. She tried to key in a message as she hurried towards the bridge: *whr ru?* But her fingers slipped on the keys. Later, she'd do it later. She ran down the steps and back along the path to the canal basin.

She'd look in the café again. Maybe Lyn was waiting there. Maybe Kerry had missed her. But when she got there, the tables outside were still deserted. Kerry peered through the windows. It wasn't very busy. Lyn wasn't there. She turned away.

She was close to the water here, and her foot caught on something on the ground. She frowned. It was a mirror, a little hand mirror like the one Stacy used, but it was broken. It couldn't be Stacy's. Kerry looked back along the canal at the dark towpath.

She stood at the side of the canal, indecisive. Something in the water caught her eye, a momentary glint of red. She looked down, where the brightness from the café window spilled over on to the surface of the canal. Something matted, something . . . She recoiled. A dead cat floated in the water below her, bobbing slightly with the ripples, its eye gleaming red as the light caught it.

CHAPTER 9

Tina had never been to a private view before. She hadn't expected Eliza Eliot to remember her casual promise to send an invitation, and had been pleased when it arrived. It would be a distraction from work, from bad dreams, from her awareness of Roy Farnham's eyes watching her with cool judgement. Then she realized she didn't know what to wear for something like this. In the end, she'd compromised: smart trousers, glitzy top with a jacket, and boots that she'd picked up in the sales, that were designed for looking elegant rather than for walking around in. If she was over-dressed, she could keep the jacket on and be businesslike. If she was under-dressed, the top was glam enough for party wear. She put on her warm coat, which rather let the side down – it was the only weatherproof coat she owned and it took a lot of hammer when she went walking or rambling.

Keys, bag, cash, cigs . . . She couldn't decide whether to take the car. Bus. She'd opt for the bus. There would be wine – better not to risk it. Anyway, she didn't fancy leaving her car down by the canal basin.

The invitation said six-thirty. She got there at twenty to seven. The gallery was lit up and she could see the shadows of people moving in the windows upstairs, the gallery where the exhibition was, the place where she'd first talked to Eliza. A young woman with a sulky face was sitting at a reception desk downstairs, dressed in a style that seemed to owe a lot to studs and spikiness. She greeted Tina, gave her outfit a disapproving once-over, took her invitation and offered her a glass of wine in a perfunctory way. She looked very young. She must have drawn the short straw to be sitting at this desk downstairs while the party went on above her. No wonder she was looking sulky.

She went into the gallery, and was faced with a room full of strangers, some of them wandering around and looking at the exhibits, most standing in small groups, talking, laughing. It was a slightly daunting sight, but Tina knew how to work a room. She hung up her coat and looked round. Then she took off her jacket. She tried to get a sense of the exhibition. The – she wasn't sure what you would call them; she wanted to say 'paintings', but there were photo-montages, collages, prints – exhibits formed images of death and darkness that seemed to flicker round her, and she found herself looking for images of falling, for things smashed on the merciless ground. She switched her focus and concentrated on the people. There were familiar faces now. She could see Eliza at the far side of the room, acting as hostess beside a small man with close-cropped hair and a goatee beard – Jonathan Massey, the director. Standing next to them was a tall man with dark hair. He was chatting, or rather listening, to a man who was talking earnestly, gesticulating to emphasize the points he was making. He nodded occasionally, but his eyes kept wandering to the window behind his interlocutor, the window that looked out over the canal.

She worked her way through the crowd. There were so many people here, it was difficult to look at the exhibition anyway. Tina's plan was to make contact with Eliza Eliot, who had probably forgotten inviting her, pick up at least one introduction and work her way round the room from there. Eliza saw her as she came across, and smiled in recognition. 'DC – I mean . . . I'm sorry, I don't know your first name.'

'It's Tina.' Eliza Eliot looked beautiful in a dreamy, pre-Raphaelite way.

'Tina. You know Jonathan Massey, of course . . .' Tina saw a slight flicker cross Eliza's face as she remembered the circumstances of her and Jonathan's meeting. 'And you must meet Daniel Flynn.' The dark-haired man. Of course. He had 'artist' written all over him. Eliza interrupted the conversation, sending a carefully measured apologetic smile to the earnest man. 'Daniel, this is Tina Barraclough.' She glanced behind him, where the earnest man was moving away, looking a bit put out. 'Sorry,' she said. 'I couldn't think of a way to rescue you before.'

He touched Eliza's arm lightly and gave her a quick smile. *Aha!* Tina wondered if anyone else had noticed. She was aware of Massey frowning as he looked at her. 'Are you here in an official capacity?' he said.

'Just as a guest.' She smiled at him, making herself unthreatening.

'I need to talk to . . .' He walked off.

Tina raised her eyebrows at Eliza, who shrugged. 'Jonathan's a bit edgy tonight,' she said.

Daniel Flynn had detached himself from Eliza, suddenly looking interested. 'Official capacity?' he said. 'Don't tell me you're from the Ministry of Outraged Opinion.'

Moo. Tina caught his eye and smiled.

'Tina's involved in the investigation into . . .' Eliza couldn't find a socially appropriate word for murder.

'There was a death on the canal,' Tina explained.

'I know,' he said. He seemed restless, as if he wanted to be somewhere else. He dug his hands into his pockets and looked at her again. 'You're a police officer?' he said.

'Yes.' In Tina's experience, this was a conversation-stopper in most circles.

There was a flurry of activity over by the door. Eliza smiled at Tina. 'Excuse me. Look round, won't you. I'll talk to you later.'

She moved off, and Tina expected Daniel Flynn to go with her. Instead, he stayed where he was, looking past her at the room with the circulating crowd. 'I'll walk you round the exhibition,' he said.

'That's OK. You've got people to talk to.' She was surprised. Maybe he thought that a police officer, a *thick plod*, needed it all explaining. Then she told herself she was being paranoid.

He looked over to where Eliza was greeting a group of people. 'With a bit of luck, I might get away with it,' he said. 'Come on.' He took her arm and led her through the display stands, away from the door.

It was gone seven by the time Kerry got home. She'd waited for Lyn – she'd waited half an hour in case Lyn was late, but no one came. When Kerry got in, Mum was sitting in front of the television. It was on, but she wasn't really watching it. Her eyes wandered as she tried to focus on Kerry. 'Oh. You're back. Good day?' There was that smell again. She hadn't been in to work, Kerry could tell. She'd spent the day on the sofa. Drinking.

'What's for tea?' she said.

'Oh, I don't know.' Mum groped around the side of her chair. 'I've got a headache, Kerry. Can you run down to . . .' She was looking in her purse as she spoke. Kerry thought about Stacy's mum making chips. Kerry did the shopping when she came back from school and she cooked when Mum was poorly and she never had any clothes because Mum couldn't afford to buy her anything and now she was cold and wet and scared and there wasn't any *tea!*

Mum put her bag down on the floor again. She seemed to have forgotten about tea. Kerry noticed there were two cups on the table in front of Mum. One of them was full of cold, scummy tea. 'Did someone come round?' she said.

Mum frowned and picked up her bag again, pulling out her purse. 'Stacy's mum,' she said, just as Kerry was about to ask again.

'What did she want?' Had she come to complain about Kerry making Stacy bunk off? Would Mum notice? *I can't cope with this* . . . Mum's voice.

'*I* don't know . . . Something about . . .' Mum was reaching into her bag. She got her cigarettes out and lit one. She put her bag down on the floor. The cigarette slipped in her fingers.

'*Mum!*' Kerry grabbed at the cigarette before it dropped. Mum's eyes looked bleary and wandering. 'What did she want?'

'Oh, something about . . . was Stacy here. Something like.' Her eyes focused on Kerry. 'Why don't you bring Stacy here? You never bring your friends . . . We could . . . I could . . .' She pulled on her cigarette and slumped back in the chair.

So Stacy hadn't managed to get home on time. There was a sick feeling in Kerry's stomach. She was worried about school, that was all. 'What did you tell her?' she said.

'What?' Mum's voice had that blurry sound.

Kerry knew what it meant. Mum had put her purse away again. She hadn't even looked. She'd forgotten about tea. Kerry didn't want to go out again. If Stacy's mum was mad with Stacy, Stacy might tell her, then Stacy's mum would be mad with Kerry. Suddenly, she had a picture of Maggie's face in her mind, all twisted and blotchy, Maggie saying, *Get away from me* . . . But it wasn't like that, not now. It was just that Stacy's mum might tell the school. That was what was making Kerry feel sick and frightened. She wanted to tell someone. She wanted to tell her dad. But she didn't want to talk to Stacy's mum.

She went into the kitchen. The dishes were still in the sink from this morning. She looked in the cupboard, and then in the fridge. There wasn't anything much. She washed the dishes, then she made some beans on toast. She didn't feel hungry any more, but when she'd eaten them, the sick feeling went away a bit. Then she went to her room. There was someone she could talk to.

She tried calling Lyn, but she got the answering service. She sat on her bed and keyed the message into her phone: *whr r u?* She pressed 'send', and left the phone on the small table beside her bed. She left it switched on. She had pushed a chair under the door handle, though she didn't think Mum would come in to see her. Then she got out her notepaper.

Dear Dad
How are you? I'm fine . . .

It was the same as she'd written last time and the time before. She tore the paper up. What if Stacy still wasn't home? The thought popped into her mind, chill and unwelcome. What if Stacy didn't go home? That wasn't anything to do with Kerry. It wasn't her fault if Stacy went off somewhere. If they started asking questions, if they found out that she and Stacy had bunked off together, they might ask some more questions. They would stop her. Then there wouldn't be anyone to help Dad. Stacy must be at home by now.

The phone beeped. There was a message. She grabbed it and pressed 'read'. She looked at it. It didn't make sense. It was a mistake. It must be a mistake.

WHO R U?

Eliza closed the door of her flat behind her, kicked off her shoes and went across to the kitchen area. Her hand hovered over the wine bottle, then she switched on the kettle. She'd had enough wine at the party. It had been a success, she told herself. There was no doubt about that. The media people had turned out – several journalists from the nationals, someone from Channel 4 wanting to include the gallery in a documentary on the revival of arts in the regions, and the people from the Arts

Trust had been delighted. Even Daniel's sudden exit hadn't caused problems. It had been a typically eccentric thing for him to have done, and the local dignitaries who had missed their introduction to the VIP were sufficiently small scale, and sufficiently in awe of his reputation, not to take offence.

So why was she feeling so flat and so let down? She spooned coffee into the cafetiere as she waited for the kettle to come to the boil. Daniel had told her he would have to rush off. That was why he'd taken her to dinner the night before. She hadn't been expecting . . . Was it because she seemed to be the only one to have noticed that he'd left with Tina Barraclough? Tina who had been looking witchily sexy in trousers and a revealing top that had made Eliza feel dowdy in her new dress.

She poured coffee into a mug and wandered across the room to the windows overlooking the canal. She slumped into a chair. She was tired, that was the problem. It had been a long day. She thought about her visit to Maggie's. Maybe that was why she was feeling so low. Looking through the scant remains of Maggie's and Ellie's lives had brought back to her those days after the news of Ellie's death had reached her.

It was almost eleven. She and Jonathan had gone out to celebrate the success of the exhibition. It had been an evening Eliza had been looking forward to for weeks, the launch of the first major exhibition she had organized, the vindication of the faith Jonathan had shown in her when he gave her the job. And then she had let Daniel – or her response to Daniel – take all the gloss off it.

Her fault for letting it upset her. She tried to analyse her reactions. OK, part of it was the release of tension. And part of it was that she had thought, she had expected, even after the other evening, that she and Daniel had a future. The dinner last night – she thought they'd re-established something. She remembered Laura's comment: *Game player. Don't waste your time.* She was beginning to think that Laura was right. She had to make her mind up. Either she wanted a friendship with him – they shared an understanding of art, she liked him and he liked her – or she needed to cut him out of her life as a social contact altogether, keep any future contacts purely business.

There was something moving on the canal. She looked out of the window. A small boat was drifting towards the canal basin. Its engine must be switched off, because it was moving silently. Her imagination peopled the deck with skeletons, soldiers of the army of death wrapped in winding sheets, a living man, his hands tied, being thrown into the water, a millstone round his neck. *It were better for him that a millstone were hanged about his neck and he cast into the sea than that he should offend one of these little ones.* She thought about Ellie. If anyone had lived with the millstone of her death, it had been Maggie, and in the end, it had dragged her under.

She sat in the window, watching the moonlight on the canal as midnight came and went, then she switched the phone off, took a sleeping pill and went to bed. Something woke her in the small hours. She sat up, listening. But there was nothing. She'd been dreaming.

Saturday morning, and Tina had a headache. Let's be honest here, she had a hangover. And she had to go to work today. She groaned. Her first mistake had been to start drinking at six-thirty. Her second mistake had been to accept Daniel Flynn's invitation to dinner, and her third mistake – admittedly, made after her judgement had been completely wrecked by too much excellent wine and the last of her supply of coke that they'd shared in the taxi on the way to the restaurant – had been accepting Daniel's invitation back to his hotel.

She tried to sit up and her head thumped, laying her back on the mattress. At least she'd made it back home. She didn't normally go from 'Nice to meet you' to an all-out fuck in the stretch of a few hours, not these days, but the wine had seriously addled her judgement. *Barraclough, you're a slag.*

She rolled off the bed cautiously, keeping her head still. Her stomach felt awful and her recollections of the later parts of the evening were a bit vague. She felt stiff and sore, so they were probably recollections that would be worth having. Christ! She was old enough to know better. She hadn't managed to get her clothes off before she'd gone to bed. She was still wearing her trousers and her glam top. Her jacket was on the floor. Her bra and her pants hadn't made it home unless she'd stuffed them in her handbag.

He'd been good company. She could remember that. She'd been surprised, and rather disarmed, by his air of keyed-up tension, as though even now that he was a well-known and celebrated artist – someone like Tina had heard of him – he was still excited by an event like this. He'd walked her round the exhibition, telling her what he'd had in mind when he was planning it and when he was working on it. It wasn't the patronizing, thick plod thing she'd half expected. He'd been interested in what she had to say. She remembered the shock of recognition she'd felt, standing in front of a photo-montage in which a small boy, his hand gripped trustingly in the hand of an older child, walked away into an incandescent sea while Death played a hurdy-gurdy. 'I can't see that as art,' she'd said.

'But you know what it is,' he said. 'What about that one?'

It was a photograph of a young woman, fair-haired, heavily made up. Skeletal hands reached to embrace her. She looked at Flynn and shook her head. 'I don't know,' she said.

'She was a prostitute,' he said. 'Found dead. No one cared much.'

Tina looked at the photograph again. The woman

looked very young, except for her eyes, which looked haunted and dead. 'OK.' Tina acknowledged the point. 'But there is a difference, you've got to admit that.'

'Maybe,' he said.

People had kept coming over and engaging him in conversation, and Tina had twice moved away, aware that she had had more than her fair share of the star of the evening, but each time he'd sought her out again.

As the crowds began to thin, Tina had been aware of Eliza Eliot watching them. 'I think you're meant to be circulating,' she said.

He shrugged. 'It's more or less finished. I've done all my thanks to the gallery people here.' He looked across at Eliza, who was busy talking to a group of late arrivals, people who looked as though they were expecting the VIP treatment. 'Oh, shit. I can't face it,' he'd said. 'Not the local arty types. I've already seen anyone I want to see. Eliza can deal with them. I need to get out of here.' He looked down at her. 'Come with me. I'll buy you dinner. Or take you for a drink. Anything. You know everything you need to about the madness of artists.'

That was when they'd shared the coke, and they'd stopped off at Tina's favourite club so she could score some more. They'd ended up at a restaurant in Crosspool, one she hadn't been to before and one that was distinctly out of her income bracket. She'd enjoyed his company. He'd been interested in her work, in the demands it made on her. They'd talked in a very general way about the current case – he hadn't tried to pump her about it, but he was interested in the attitude it demonstrated to the deaths of prostitutes. 'We don't send the mobs out to avenge them,' he'd said.

'Or drug addicts,' Tina said, remembering her recent case.

He'd told her about flowers he'd seen by the canal, flowers that had been left, not for Cara, but in memory of Ellie Chapman, dead these four years past.

She could feel the wine relaxing her as they talked. He was interested in what she was saying, asking questions occasionally, but his signals – a smile, a look, a touch – promised more. 'What do they think about prostitute killings? Your colleagues?' he'd said.

Tina thought about it. 'Some of them' – some of her colleagues – 'think getting murdered is an occupational hazard for a prostitute. You know, that it doesn't matter, not so much.' He nodded as if that was easy enough to believe.

She found herself talking about the Ellie Chapman killing. 'Is that what you call it?' he said. 'The Ellie Chapman killing. He's appealing against the conviction, isn't he?' He poured more wine into her glass. 'Fraser? Has he got any chance?'

She shook her head. 'I don't know. The guys who worked on the case, it really pisses them off. If someone like Fraser gets off on a technicality – you

212

know, if the conviction is "unsafe" – that doesn't mean it was wrong, you know . . .' Her sentences were beginning to ramble as she spoke. She needed to be careful. *It doesn't mean it was right, either.* The thought popped into her head from nowhere.

'Was it unsafe? Fraser's conviction?'

She waved her hand to indicate she didn't know, catching her glass and nearly knocking it over. He grabbed it before it fell. 'Steady,' he said.

'There was a lot of strong feeling. Someone told me the SIO –' she met his inquiring gaze – 'the Senior Investigating Officer, wasn't sure they'd got enough to make a case, a cast-iron case.' She drank some more wine. 'But they knew it was him.'

He nodded. 'How did they get on to him?'

Tina tried to remember. Her brain wasn't functioning too well. 'I wasn't on that case,' she said. 'But we all kept an eye on it – you do when it's a kid. It was because he was there, you know? That was the first thing.' Her thoughts wandered. 'That's what it's like with murder cases. It's usually the person on the scene. They haven't planned it, it just happens.'

'And Mark Fraser?' he said, topping her glass up.

'He'd been abusing one of his kids. Ellie was friends with his daughter.'

He nodded. He didn't seem surprised.

'You aren't drinking,' she said.

He smiled, but his face looked tired and worn. 'I had too much at the gallery. I hate those things.

I get drunk. It's the only way.' There was silence for a moment. 'Wasn't there another death?' he said.

'The canal thing? Yes, a few days ago.'

'No. When Ellie Chapman was found. Wasn't there another death, someone else killed?'

The waiter came and cleared their plates away. 'Would you like to see the menu again?' he asked.

Daniel looked at Tina, who shook her head. 'Just coffee,' she said. She tried to smile at him. Her head was spinning. 'I need it. I'm pissed.'

'Coffee doesn't sober you up. I'll have an alert drunk on my hands.'

She squinted at him, trying to focus, and then laughed. 'There was,' she said, suddenly remembering his question. 'But it was an overdose. A smack-head overdosed down by the canal. There was a really pure batch on the streets. About four people died of it after that. There was a case a few months ago . . .' She made a face and picked up her wine glass. 'May as well go for it,' she said, and drained the glass.

He looked at her. 'Come back for a while,' he said. 'I've got wine, coffee. And you've got . . .' He smiled and she smiled back. She didn't need to say anything. He asked the waiter to call a taxi.

His room at the hotel seemed anonymous, as if he was careful to leave as little record as possible of his passing, to mark any stay, in any place, as transitory, temporary. There was none of his stuff scattered about the room, nothing in the wardrobe, she noticed as she hung up her jacket. The only sign of occupancy was the toothbrush and the soap in the bathroom. The drive in the taxi had sobered her up a bit, and now she had some misgivings, but when she came out of the bathroom and he started kissing her, the optimism of the coke they had taken, and the effects of the alcohol, made her reckless, and she surfaced from blackness in the small hours stretched out on the bed with her clothes scattered around her and the beginnings of a hangover.

The other side of the bed was empty. She sat up holding her head, and saw him. He was sitting by the window that looked out over the canal basin. She didn't want to talk to him. She needed to be alone. She wanted to limit the intimacy of what was after all just an encounter with a stranger. He called a taxi for her. 'I'll phone you,' he said, politely.

She laughed at him. 'Maybe,' she said.

Now, in the cold morning light, she was starting to feel bad about the way she'd behaved. She'd gone to a party – well, a kind of party – that she had been invited to at the last minute. She'd more or less ignored the woman who'd invited her. She'd drunk too much and made off with the guest of honour. She sent up a silent prayer that nothing new would turn up that would necessitate her going back to the gallery in her official role. If any of her colleagues got to hear about this one . . . Private view! She'd never live it down.

★　　★　　★

Eliza woke up feeling strangely alert. She had expected the combination of wine and a sleeping pill to leave her sluggish and woolly headed the next morning, but she felt rested and a lot more positive than she had the night before. Yes, the long-anticipated opening had been a letdown, but that was to be expected – it was bound to leave her feeling a bit lost and empty at the end of it. The important thing was, it had been successful.

She sat up, stretching. The sun wasn't up, but the night was fading and the sky was clear and bright. She looked out of the window. The canal was gleaming in the early light, and she could see the shimmer of ice on the water. She checked the time. It was almost seven. The gallery didn't open until ten. She had plenty of time.

When she came out of the shower half an hour later, she noticed that the message light on her answer-phone was blinking. Two messages. She pressed the button, towelling her hair as she listened. The first one was from Laura: she was going away for the weekend – work – so their planned meeting would have to be rearranged. The other one was from Daniel Flynn. His voice sounded cautious, as though he wasn't sure what her reaction would be.

'Eliza? Daniel. Sorry about last night. I got a bit freaked. Look, I'm in Sheffield for a few more days. I'll be coming in to the gallery – can we have lunch? A drink? Sometime? Give me a ring. I'm at the same hotel.'

So, some kind of an apology from Daniel for running out on her last night. Sincere, or just another game? She needed to think about this. The night before, she had been plagued by an irrational need to see him again. Morning reminded her of the need for caution.

It was gone eight by the time she was dressed. With a sense of anticipation, she hurried down the stairs to see if Jonathan had brought the papers in. The closed door of Cara's flat dampened her optimism, but she pushed it determinedly to the back of her mind. Mel was in the office, un-characteristically early. She was wearing trousers cut very low on the hips revealing the mandatory tattoo in the small of her back, and a short waistcoat. Her hair, still blonde, was pulled back from her face. The effect was stylish and striking. For the past couple of days, since Cara's death, in fact, Mel had been pale and subdued. Today, she looked better.

'That's a nice outfit,' Eliza said.

Mel gave her an assessing look as she examined the remark for underlying barbs. 'I made it.'

'You ought to go into design. You've got the flair – you should have finished that course.' Mel had dropped out of the design course at the local college.

'They were all losers,' Mel said dismissively. Then in a rare moment of confidence, she added, 'I want to go to that college in London – you know, St Martin's. It's hard to get into, but Jonathan thinks I should go.'

Jonathan was a St Martin's graduate, and had worked there for a while. That would explain why Mel was prepared to hang on at the gallery and at least try to charm Jonathan – she wanted a reference that would carry some weight. In Mel's eyes, Jonathan, with his one successful exhibition, and his name on a new and – for the locality – important gallery, was a big name in the art and design world. It was almost refreshing to find a chink of naivety in Mel's armour, and Eliza felt more kindly towards her as they began the day's work.

'Is Jonathan in yet?' she said.

Mel was downloading e-mails. 'Dunno.' She checked her make-up as she waited.

There didn't seem to be anything interesting in the post. 'Daniel Flynn said he might drop by. Let me know if he does.'

Mel gave her a sidelong look. 'He left early last night. I think he went off with that detective woman.'

Eliza kept her face down, pretending to be absorbed in the letter she was skimming. 'Did he?'

'She looks like Angelina Jolie,' Mel said. 'I wonder where they went?'

'I've no idea,' Eliza said, more sharply than she meant. She left Mel with instructions to check the papers and make copies of the early reviews to send to various organizations that she hoped would be prepared to support the gallery in the future. She went upstairs. She wanted to spend an hour going round the exhibition before they opened.

The day was as busy as Eliza could have hoped for. The gallery thronged with casual visitors, groups from the art colleges, people from the Trust coming to look at the way their investment was dealing with its first major foray into the place where the art world and hard commerce met.

Even Mel, looking very much the part, was animated and enthused by the sudden change of atmosphere the influx of new people brought. Only Jonathan seemed unhappy. 'It's a one-off,' he'd said to Eliza in a brief hiatus. 'It's the combination of a fashionable name and a murder. We need something longer term than this.'

'Which we'll get.' He was probably right about the murder. Eliza had talked to two journalists already who had come with a view to writing 'canal of death' features. 'Most of these people are here for the show.'

He shook his head. Eliza left him to it. She was finding his relentless pessimism wearing. Her mind was buzzing with plans for ways they could build on the success of the exhibition, and she wanted to get them into more concrete form before they died under the weight of Jonathan's gloom.

By the time they closed, she was exhausted. The evening was drawing in and she hadn't seen daylight at all. She made herself a cup of camomile tea – a taste she had acquired in Madrid, the ubiquitous *manzanilla* – and sank into her chair. Silence.

Mel appeared in the doorway. 'Can I go now? There's nothing else to do.'

There was probably plenty to do, but Eliza didn't have the energy to argue. Anyway, it was after five. 'OK. Is Jonathan still here?'

'He's in his office. He's got someone with him.'

'Who?' He hadn't said anything to her about any appointments.

Mel shrugged. 'Dunno. Some art guy.'

'About the exhibition?' If it was anything to do with the exhibition, then she wanted to be involved.

'Yeah. Or something.' Mel extracted a piece of chewing gum from her bag and folded it into her mouth. She began to chew it noisily, something that never failed to irritate Eliza.

'Christsake, Mel,' she said.

'What?' Mel knew perfectly well what Eliza meant. 'Daniel Flynn phoned. I told him you were busy.' There was a moment's silence. 'Well, you were. He said it wasn't important.' Defensiveness. Eliza must have managed to get under her skin.

'OK,' she said. She didn't much want to talk to him anyway. She waited while Mel collected her bag. Coats were, apparently, not worn this season.

After Mel had gone, she went quickly downstairs to Jonathan's office to see who the visitor was. His door was shut, but as she lifted her hand to knock, it opened. 'Eliza.' Jonathan looked taken aback to see her. 'I thought you would have left by now.'

'Mel said there was someone here about the exhibition.'

'No.' He seemed uneasy. She waited. He glanced behind him and looked back at her. 'Have you locked up upstairs?'

'No need. The gallery's closed now.'

'Hello, Eliza.' A man had come up behind Jonathan and was observing their exchange. She looked at him for a moment before she realized who it was. Ivan. Ivan Bakst. His fair hair was longer than she remembered it. His eyes, revealed without the dark glasses he customarily wore, were a strange light colour. Maybe the glasses were a necessity rather that the affectation she had assumed. He looked casual, relaxed, entertained by the interaction he was observing. It was a contrast to Jonathan's edginess.

'What are you doing here?' she said.

He laughed. 'That's what you said last time you saw me.'

Jonathan was looking from one to the other in nervous irritation. 'Ivan was just going,' he said.

Ivan bowed his head in agreement. 'But that was before I realized Eliza was here,' he said. 'As you can tell, she's delighted to see me and we have catching up to do.'

'I didn't know you knew each other. But I do have a lot to get on with . . .'

'I won't keep you.' Ivan was still watching

Eliza, still smiling. 'Eliza and I have a lot in common.'

Eliza didn't like the air of intimacy that Bakst was weaving around the two of them, isolating Jonathan. She explained quickly, 'I met Ivan in Madrid, with Daniel Flynn.'

'Daniel. Yes, of course. Now . . .' Jonathan made shooing gestures with his hands. 'We really . . .'

Ivan kept his attention on Eliza. 'That's what we have in common, Eliza and I. *The Triumph of Death*. And Daniel Flynn, of course.' He kept his eyes on her, as if he was trying to tell her something. 'I wonder, if you wrote a genesis of this . . .' he gestured at one of the posters advertising the exhibition, '. . . from conception to birth, what would you say?'

Odd question. Her mind played with it. *Conceived in Madrid, born . . . where?*

'Genesis?' Jonathan's gaze moved quickly between them, nervous, uncertain.

'*The Triumph of Death*,' Bakst said, catching Eliza's eye with a quick smile.

'It's good,' Jonathan said. 'But I . . .'

'It isn't finished yet.' Bakst said this to Jonathan, then returned to Eliza. 'Jonathan thinks this might be a good place for me to exhibit,' he said, looking round the gallery. 'We've been talking about it.'

He must mean his own *Triumph*. The idea he'd lifted from Daniel and had been unable to complete. This was what Jonathan was being so shifty about. He was negotiating some kind of deal

222

with Bakst. The exhibitions programme was Eliza's responsibility. He shouldn't be discussing anything without letting her know, and he must have realized at once how closely linked the concepts of the two pieces of work were, no matter how differently they may be executed. Now he caught her eye over Bakst's shoulder and shook his head. 'Daniel Flynn suggested it,' he said.

Bakst was looking at the poster again. He flicked it dismissively with his finger. 'Ideas have their time,' he said. 'One or two people latch on to something at the same time. Then everyone else jumps on the bandwagon. The trick is, getting on the bandwagon early enough.' His smile was almost mischievous. 'Some of us are very good at that.' He turned to Jonathan. 'But I'm keeping you. I'll be in touch. Soon.' He raised his hand in farewell, and headed towards the entrance. His canvas jacket didn't look as though it offered much protection against the cold.

Jonathan waited until he'd gone, then blew out his breath. 'Don't ask,' he said.

'You aren't seriously planning to –?' Eliza wanted this settled now.

Jonathan shook his head. 'Bakst isn't a gallery artist,' he said.

'You know of him?'

'Someone suggested him.' He seemed to think she needed more explanation. 'Flynn thinks highly of him so I said I'd talk to him. We won't be able to offer him anything. I don't want to offend anyone. I was worried you were going to say something.'

In Madrid, Daniel had seemed resigned to the fact that Bakst was prepared to lift his ideas. He hadn't shown much sign, either then or more recently, of rating him as an artist. But they were friends. Daniel said he knew Bakst from college days. Maybe it was some kind of loyalty thing. Odd.

Jonathan was on his way home. He left Eliza to lock up the gallery and set the alarms. She looked at the time. It was almost six. She was quite glad that her evening with Laura had been postponed. She was tired after the night before, and all the upheaval of the day. Her flat beckoned. She was going to have a bath, make herself . . . what? A bacon sandwich. A bacon and egg sandwich. She needed comfort food. OK, a bath, a sandwich in front of the television, and an early night. And just at the moment, that seemed like the best thing in the world.

Kerry hated Saturdays. Saturday used to be the best day of the week when she got her money and she and Ellie used to go into town. Sometimes Dad would come too, and he'd get them burgers from McDonald's. *Don't tell Maggie!* It was one of their secrets. Mum always had a headache on Saturdays, so it was good to go out for the day. It had been a Saturday when she and Ellie and Dad had gone to Conisbrough.

Kerry hated Saturdays.

She sat in her room running a comb through her hair. She'd been going to do it like that photograph she'd seen, Buffy wearing loose trousers and one of those short tops with her hair up, but she couldn't be bothered. There wasn't any point really.

She pulled her school bag from under the bed. Maybe she could do some homework. She was sick of getting into trouble. And if they found out she'd bunked off on Friday . . . But Stacy would say it was because she was ill and Kerry had taken her home. They'd believe Stacy, Stacy was always a favourite. She looked at the phone. She could call Stacy. She'd feel better once she'd talked to Stacy. Because then she'd know that Stacy was going to stick with the agreement and wasn't mad with her. But . . . Later. She'd phone later.

She picked up her bag and went downstairs. They were doing *Romeo and Juliet* at school, and she had to write about if it was different for Juliet than it was for people now. Kerry liked the play, even if it did have a sad ending. But when she got downstairs, the room smelled of Mum's cigarettes and everything looked dirty where the sun was shining through the glass. Mum was sitting at the table in her dressing gown, smoking. Her green mug was on the table in front of her. 'It's twelve o'clock,' Kerry said.

'Oh, don't nag, Kerry,' she said. 'It's Saturday. I've earned a rest.' She was looking out of the window. *From what?* Kerry wanted to say, but she didn't. Mum's face looked creased and sad, and she'd tied her hair back with a bit of blue ribbon that looked odd against the tangle of grey. 'It reminds me,' she said, looking at the sky. She turned away from the window. 'What are you doing?'

'I was going to do my homework,' Kerry said.

'Oh, take it upstairs,' Mum said. 'I don't want you under my feet all day. Why don't you go out? It'll do you good to get out.'

'Were there any letters?' Maybe there was a letter from Dad. Mum shook her head.

There was a knock at the door. Kerry looked at Mum, who was staring out of the window again, and went to see who it was. She didn't think before she opened it, and she was suddenly back four years when she saw two coppers on the doorstep, a man and a woman. She began to push the door shut, but the man kept his arm against it and the woman said, 'Kerry? Kerry Fraser? Is your mum in?'

'What have you done now?' Mum had come through from the front room and was standing in the hall.

'DS Martin,' the woman said to Mum. 'Judith Martin. It's nothing that Kerry's done. We're a bit concerned about one of her friends. Can we talk to you?'

Mum shrugged and stepped back. 'You'd better come in,' she said.

Kerry looked at the open door, but the man was standing there. He looked at her and shook his head slightly. *Don't even think about it.* She followed Mum into the room. Her stomach had gone tight when the woman had said that about a friend. She thought about the canal side, and the mirror broken on the ground. Mum was getting a cigarette out of the packet, ignoring the one that was still burning in the ashtray. Her hands shook, and a cigarette fell on to the floor. The woman picked it up. Mum took it in silence and stood with her back to the room, trying to light it. Kerry could hear the *flick, flick* of the lighter as the copper, the woman, spoke.

'We're a bit worried about Stacy, Kerry. Can I talk to you?'

Kerry didn't want her mum there. She had seen the way the coppers looked at each other when Mum came through from the kitchen. Mum's dressing gown was scruffy because she never bothered to wash it, and her feet were bare and they were dirty too. Her face looked creased and grey with angry red blotches on her cheeks, and her hair looked stupid with the blue ribbon tied round it. Mum's hair used to be blonde like Kerry's, but now it was a sort of grey colour too. And there was that smell again, and her voice was all . . . so you couldn't understand what she said.

There was a smell in the house, of all the things that hadn't been washed and the kitchen bin that needed emptying, and it made her feel ashamed.

She saw the expressions on their faces, like Mum was nothing, and like she was nothing, and she felt cold and angry inside.

Detective Sergeant Judith Martin looked at the fair-haired girl sitting in front of her, and wondered if the defensiveness she saw coming off her, the closed face and the stiff, defiant shoulders, meant that Kerry had something to hide, or just that she was hostile to the police. It could well be the latter, she knew. Kerry Fraser, Mark Fraser's daughter. She wouldn't have made the connection if the boss hadn't tipped her off. 'You may not find Kerry or her mum too receptive,' he'd said, and explained quickly about the girl's background. Now, she was racking her brains, trying to remember the details of Fraser's family, his arrest. It was a case that most of the officers at Sheffield HQ remembered well.

Fraser had been accused of abusing his daughter – no, his stepdaughter, that was right. Had he been convicted of it? She couldn't remember. But this girl was his natural child. Had her father abused her as well? She smiled at Kerry, trying to reassure her. 'There's nothing to worry about, Kerry,' she said. The girl was silent. She probably knew that there was always something to worry about once the police hove into view. She sought round for a way to get through to the girl. She noticed that she was wearing a sweat-shirt that had been jazzed up with beads and sequins to look like one of the shirts that all the kids were wearing at the moment. She remembered Stacy's mother, Christine, saying, 'And then that Kerry goes and encourages her, sews sequins all over it.'

'Kerry, I'm here about Stacy, Stacy McDonald,' she said again. 'You're her friend, aren't you?' She watched Kerry carefully, trying not to make her observation too noticeable.

'Kind of.' Kerry shrugged. 'Sometimes.'

'She's there all the time.' This was the mother, an overweight, rather sluttish woman who was slumped in a chair, smoking, her gaze vague and incurious. She smelt of acetone, and the dressing gown she was wearing was soiled and creased. Odd that such a heavy, ungainly woman should have such a pretty, delicate child.

'Stacy didn't go home last night,' she said. Now Kerry did react. Her eyes widened in surprise and – was it? – alarm. The mother didn't react, stolid in her chair. 'So I wondered,' she went on, 'if you might be able to help us. Stacy's mum's really worried about her. And so am I. Did you see Stacy yesterday after school?'

Kerry was looking down at her hands. She shook her head.

'Did you see her at all yesterday?'

A pause. A nod.

'Did she say where she was going after school?'

A pause. A shake.

'She didn't say anything?' She was finding Kerry

very hard to read. 'Listen, Kerry, no one is going to get into trouble over this. We want to know that Stacy is safe, get her home again. Is it a secret? No one will say that you told.'

Kerry shook her head again. She looked up this time. 'She didn't say anything. She wanted me to do her hair.'

More interest in her appearance. The top, the make-up – and now a request for a hair-do. 'Yesterday?' she said. 'She wanted you to do her hair yesterday?'

Kerry shook her head. 'Just sometime,' she said.

Martin couldn't tell if Kerry was lying or not. 'Does Stacy have a boyfriend?' she asked.

Kerry shrugged. 'She didn't say.'

She felt on more secure ground now. 'Oh, come on, Kerry. You and Stacy must have talked about boyfriends. What did Stacy say?'

Kerry looked at her under her lashes, assessing. 'She likes, you know, music guys and TV guys and things. She doesn't have a boyfriend.'

There was a wrong note here. She was hiding something. 'But is there anyone she likes?'

Kerry's eyes slid sideways. 'She likes Andrew,' she said. 'In our French group.'

'Do they go out? Has Andrew asked her out?'

Kerry shook her head. 'I told you. Anyway, her mum won't let her.'

Everything Kerry was telling her fitted in with what she'd already been told. Stacy was shy and young for her age. There was just that slight wrong note. Adolescent secrets, and Stacy had been up to something on Friday. Would she have kept it secret from her friend? 'Listen, Kerry, Stacy could be in serious trouble,' she said. 'I mean, something bad could have happened to her. If you've any idea at all where she might be, you must tell me. It could make all the difference.'

This time, Kerry met her eyes. 'I told you,' she said. 'I don't know.'

CHAPTER 10

Sunday was the first free day Eliza had had for weeks. It was disorientating, having time to decide what to do. She planned to spend the morning going through the stuff she'd brought back from Maggie's flat. It was still in the car, so she had to go out into the winter morning.

The sun was pouring into her flat when she returned. She slanted the blinds to keep it out of her eyes. She dumped the folders on to the table, next to the paperwork for the exhibition, some of which had been there since the evening Cara came to the flat. She remembered the small figure leaning over the chair as she tucked the infant in, the rather helpless way she dumped the bags and baggage she'd been hauling around with her.

She pushed the thought out of her mind and made herself a cup of coffee while she devised her strategy. She'd go through the papers – letters and Ellie memorabilia – first. And then she'd try and make some decisions about the photographs.

An hour later, she was beginning to wish she had never started. Her hands felt dry from the dust that seemed to have accumulated round the papers. She had sorted them into piles: letters, mostly relating to Fraser's forthcoming appeal, Ellie memorabilia, cards and drawings and some school work. A story about a dragon called Albert: *meanwhile, Albert was enjoying a nice meal of roast damsel in distress and chips* . . . Birthday cards and Mother's Day cards, some clearly school-made, some bought. It looked as though Maggie had kept them all. *Roses are red, violets are blue, best mum in the world, I love you!*

Eliza ran a grimy hand through her hair. Mixed up among the letters, she'd found an article written after the conclusion of the court case, after Fraser's life sentence. The judge had said, 'In your case, I recommend that life means life.' Looking at the cards and the old school work, no penalty seemed to Eliza to be adequate response to the loss of Ellie. *Roses are red . . . I love you!*

Maggie had loved Mark Fraser. She had believed in him, at first.

'They've had Mark at the police station all night,' she'd told Eliza. 'They're wasting time with Mark when Ellie could be . . . could be . . .'

'Why Mark?' Eliza didn't know him. He was a name that had appeared more and more in Maggie's letters and phone calls, an involvement that seemed genuine, but fraught with the problem of another relationship, other children.

'They were with him,' Maggie said. 'I had a load of marking, so he took them out for the day . . .'

'They?'

'The girls, Ellie and Kerry. Kerry's his daughter.

He loves taking them out. He's always taking them places . . .' Her voice faded slightly as she spoke, then rallied. 'I made them a picnic. It was cold last night. Ellie was lost in the woods. She'll have been cold. She left her jumper on the boat . . .' Maggie was crying now. 'Lize, Mark wouldn't hurt Ellie. He loves her.'

Roses are red . . . Had Maggie been whistling in the dark even then? Had she begun to realize how she, apparently sophisticated and streetwise, had been deceived by the man who had come to her door bearing gifts? The knowledge had come brutally enough, not long before the canal side gave up its secret and destroyed any last vestige of hope that Maggie might have had.

But by then, she had known. Fraser's stepdaughter had come to Maggie with her story.

'Kerry?' Eliza said.

'No, the other one. Lyn. She told me about him.' Mark Fraser had been trying to abuse his step-daughter. It had begun with charm. He had bought her presents, tried to take her to the places she liked to go to. 'Ring any bells?' Maggie said, and her laugh was bitter. Then he had started watching her, coming into the room when she was bathing, when she was getting dressed. 'And touching her, she said. She told me he'd started touching her. She wouldn't have anything to do with him, and she was scared he'd go after Kerry. She told me. She said, "He's a pervert!" She told her mother, but the mother didn't want to know. Do you know what she did? She threw the kid out. Weeks ago. So she came to me. It was too late, but she came to me.' The hate in Maggie's voice was chilling. 'And that child must have known. Kerry must have known. And she pulled Ellie into it. She must have known.'

A fortnight after that call, Ellie's body had been found. Fibres wrapped round the skeletonized remains 'could have come' from Fraser's sweater, the sweater he claimed he'd lost. He might still have got away with it – the fibres alone were not conclusive proof, though the evidence that had built up was damning. Fraser had sent Ellie into the woods. Fraser had gone after her. He had tried to assault his stepdaughter. But the clinching detail came from hairs caught in the fibres. They were Mark Fraser's. The DNA profile convicted him.

And the circumstances had convicted Maggie, both in her own eyes and in those of the tabloid press. Maggie was a single parent. She described herself as an artist. She'd had several relationships during Ellie's childhood, one or two that had over-lapped – all details that the press ferreted out. And then she'd got involved with a married man, a man with a wife and two children. A man who was a paedophile. And in the pursuit of her own gratification, she'd given this man all the access he'd needed to her daughter. The sympathy that Maggie had evoked in the press when she was 'Ellie's heartbroken mum' and 'courageous mum Maggie' evaporated.

And Maggie had accepted this picture. It was as if demonizing herself was the only way she could cope with her grief for Ellie. Nothing Eliza could say or do seemed to dent her determination. And eventually, Eliza had stopped trying.

There were just the photographs now, Maggie's life in a few slim wallets. She opened each one and flicked through the contents. These seemed to be early pictures. The more recent ones must still be at the house. College pictures. Photographs from Maggie's childhood, student days, her degree show – Eliza could remember that. Ellie as a baby. More Ellie photographs. She looked at these more closely. They were from the summer she had spent with Maggie, what? Eight years ago. Eliza and Ellie in the park, Ellie in the pool with Eliza helping her to swim, a picnic on the grass.

She ran her fingers through her hair again. She didn't know what to do with these. She pushed the pile of stuff away from her, and the exhibition papers, followed by some of the photographs, cascaded on to the floor. *Shit!* She went round the table to pick them up. A couple of photographs had fallen out and got mixed up with the papers. She looked at them.

These were later. Ellie was older. It was like a shot through a window on to a balcony, or . . . She suddenly realized what she was seeing. They were taken on a boat, from the cabin, as though the photographer had been focusing through the window into the bright sunlight. In the first one, Ellie hung over the side of the boat. She was wearing a bright yellow jumper and blue shorts. Her hair shone in the sunlight. It looked as though she was trailing her fingers in the water. Spray made a halo of colour round her head. She was laughing. In the second one, there were two girls leaning on the side, looking up at something that was beyond the camera's view. Ellie was pointing, her face solemn. The prints were dated, 20.6.98. The day Ellie died.

Eliza stuffed them into one of the wallets. She didn't want to look at them. As if in tune with her thoughts, the shadows were creeping into the room. The afternoon was drawing in and the winter sun was almost below the horizon. The last rays were lighting up her window, illuminating the Madrid painting that was on her easel. She went across the room and looked at it, the blocks of hot light, the hard lines of the shadow contrasting with the tones and shadows of the canal side. She looked at the way the colour changed as her eye was drawn towards the edges, from brilliance, to a dull orange, to the monochrome of a Yorkshire winter. The painting was becoming a fusion of her experiences, the light of Madrid, its slow fading into winter darkness.

She picked up her brush, put a blank canvas on the easel, and began to sketch in the outlines of something that had been in her mind for weeks. Her hand was deft and sure, and she became absorbed in the work and the daylight faded and the moon rose over the canal.

Madrid

The moon faded in the dancing lights of the Madrid night. Eliza walked up the cobbled hill towards the Plaza Mayor, towards her last evening in Madrid. The people she was leaving behind, the friends she had made, had wanted to make a night of it, meeting up at a café for tapas, moving on later to a restaurant. But her plane left at eight the next day, so she arranged an early rendezvous – by Madrid standards – so she could get some sleep.

Her address book was stuffed with cards. She had invitations to keep her travelling for the next ten years. She truly didn't want to leave. She hated goodbyes. She had wanted this last evening to be like so many others she remembered – sitting outside a café in the summer warmth, listening to the chat, joining in one of the endless arguments about the merits of this medium or that medium, this artist or that artist. But it was different in one crucial way. Daniel wasn't there.

He'd decided to take an opportunity to visit Seville. A friend was going, he said. He'd left the day before.

'I was going to ask you to see me off,' she said.

'I know. It can't be helped.' He'd been uneasy, keeping up that unacknowledged distance that had existed between them ever since the news of her successful interview had come through.

'We don't have to . . .' she said.

'I haven't got much time,' he said. 'I just wanted to say goodbye.' And they'd wasted their last few minutes in that awkward space of unacknowledged emotions.

And that last encounter had cast a blight over the evening. By ten, as the streets were getting busy, she felt the need to get away. She made her excuses. The last hugs and goodbyes exchanged, she left. 'Don't walk me back,' she protested as some of them rose. 'I've had enough goodbyes.' She edged her way through the crowds and left the plaza by one of the arched alleyways that led back on to the streets. She wanted to be home.

She wasn't sure where home was. Her apartment? But that had no welcome now with its empty cupboards and packed cases waiting in the hallway for the taxi. The workshops in the Prado? She had finished everything she had to do there. Her table was empty. The galleries of the museum? But all the light and colour that the galleries had been to her in those early days had changed. Home had to be in England. Home would be that dark northern city she had chosen. Chosen over Spain, over light, over Daniel.

The lights in the alleyway seemed to flicker, the stone of the archway and the cobbled street gleaming faintly in the lamplight. This was Old Madrid. This was the city of the Inquisition, of tortures and burnings. This was the Madrid of Brueghel's dark triumph: the inevitability of death.

The air was breathless with heat. She wanted one last moment. One glass of wine – her own farewell. She would see her friends again, or most of them, in the itinerant world of the artist. She would see Daniel again. But Madrid – maybe she would never come back, and if she did, it wouldn't be this Madrid she returned to. It is not what is seen, it is the eyes that are seeing it. Madrid was changing as she watched, because she was changing.

There was a bar in the alleyway, still quiet as the busy time of the evening built up. She went in and sat at a table. The waiter brought her a plate of olives, and she ordered a glass of wine. 'I'm leaving tomorrow,' she said in her halting Spanish. 'I'm saying goodbye.'

He nodded in half-comprehension, and smiled.

The bar was almost empty. There was a man reading a newspaper at a table near Eliza, and at the back of the room, in the shadows, two men were talking, huddled across the table. She could hear their voices and occasional laughter. Something about the voices . . . She looked more closely. One of them, sitting in profile to her, was . . . she squinted through the shadow – it was Ivan Bakst. He was leaning forward, listening to his companion, then he leaned back and laughed as the other man gestured. Her attention focused on the second man as he joined in the laughter.

It was Daniel. He'd said . . .

The door opened, and the first surge of people arrived. Suddenly, the bar was lively, a Madrid evening was beginning. More people piled in through the door. She couldn't see the two men any more through the sudden crowd.

It didn't matter. She and Daniel had said everything they had to say. So he couldn't face saying goodbye, seeing her off? That wasn't such a crime.

She paid for the wine and threaded her way out of the bar. She didn't look back.

Saturday night, Tina Barraclough had tried to cure her hangover with wine and a couple of lines of coke. It had been a bad idea. It was still with her the next day, and the Sunday morning drive to York with Dave West exacerbated her headache. Dave was in exuberant good form and sang and joked his way up the M62. Her head was throbbing and her stomach felt uneasy as she shook hands with Steven Calloway, the owner of the *Mary May*, one of the cabin cruisers that was moored on the canal. He was a man in his thirties, a financial adviser, confident and successful. His house was spacious, overlooking the river, furnished with comfortable leather chairs, minimalist side tables and floor lamps. He was dressed informally in jeans and a sweater, and his large frame, his slightly weathered skin and bright blue eyes suggested to Tina someone who was happier outdoors and active than sitting inside, even on a cold winter's afternoon. 'Officer Barraclough. Officer West,' he said. 'Sit down. Do you want anything? Coffee?' He had a glass of water in front of him.

Tina shook her head to the coffee. 'Just some water, thanks,' she said, and thought she caught an amused gleam in his eye as he looked at her.

Dave stepped in as Tina remained silent, and ran through the situation they were investigating.

Calloway's face lit up. 'A mystery boat on the canal? It's like *Boy's Own*.' He caught Tina's eye and smiled, then made a conscious effort to look serious. 'The *Mary May*?' he said. 'I've already talked to someone. I haven't been near her for months.'

Through her hangover, Tina found she was rather drawn to Calloway's outdoor looks and easy-going manner – a total contrast to Daniel Flynn's evasive complexity. She was aware of Dave giving her a quick glance, slightly puzzled, slightly impatient. She pulled herself back to the interview and tried to concentrate. Her head gave a thump. 'Why is that, Mr Calloway?' she said.

He smiled at her. 'Because she's a wreck, a canal-going wreck. She isn't good for much else. She belonged to my father and I inherited her. I'm trying to sell her – I fork out for mooring, and maintenance, for something I don't use. If she was worth it, I'd move her. The South Yorkshire canal isn't where . . .' He looked at the two officers. 'I prefer something ocean going. I keep my boat at Hull.'

'Has anyone taken the *Mary May* out recently?'

Calloway had been asked to account for his time on the night of Cara's death. He'd been in York all evening, he said, in the pub. And then he'd gone home.

He shook his head, then said, 'You'd need to ask the broker. It's the place behind the stadium in Sheffield. They're dealing with it. They've got the keys.'

'Yes, I've got that,' Tina said. 'So as far as you know . . .'

'I've no idea. They'll call me if they make a sale. People come and look – but no one's bitten so far.' His face went serious. 'After the call I got from your colleagues, I gave the broker a ring and he went across to have a look. She's locked up, the tank's full, everything shipshape. Or as shipshape as that old boat ever gets.' He looked at Tina. 'I don't want her, but my father thought the world of that old girl. I wouldn't like to think she'd been used for . . . anything like that. So I got them to check.'

'You don't have keys to the boat?' Dave said after a pause. Tina realized she should have checked that.

'I've got a key to give me access,' Calloway said. 'But both the ignition keys are with the broker.'

West nodded. 'How long is it since you saw that key, Mr Calloway?'

'I . . .' He looked discomfited for a moment. 'I don't know.'

'Could you check it, please?'

Calloway went to the desk and rummaged round in one of the drawers. 'It's . . . somewhere here, I'm sure . . . Yes.' Tina met Dave's eyes. For a minute, she'd thought they had something.

Calloway was holding up a key. 'This is the one,' he said.

'Can you confirm that?' Dave wasn't giving up so quickly.

Calloway didn't seem to find the question odd. He held the key up to the light and squinted at it. He nodded. 'Yes. See?' He leaned across and showed it to Tina. At the top of the key, the letters *MM* had been scratched. 'My dad used to mark his keys,' he said. 'Save them from getting muddled.'

'If we wanted to have a look,' Tina said, 'we could get the keys from the broker?'

'Oh, yes, any time.' He looked at Tina again. 'Or give me a ring and I'll come across and show you round her – not that there's much to see.'

'Well, thank you, Mr Calloway, you've been very helpful.' Tina shook his hand.

'Let me have your number, Officer,' he said. 'In case I think of anything else.'

She had to put up with West's barracking about smooth bastards all the way back to Sheffield.

Eliza worked on her picture until well into the evening. It was her first painting of the canal. What had been almost random blocks of colour were starting to form a complex pattern of inter-dependencies that built up the relationship between the reds and the greens and the blacks that made up the walls and the water and the undergrowth that thrived in the abandoned places of the canal side. Eliza breathed in the smell of the paint as she mixed the colours on her palette. She had spent so much time thinking about someone else's work that she had lost sight of her own.

She worked until the fading light sent shadows over the canvas, then shook herself out of her concentration and became aware of her surroundings again. She switched on the local news and listened with half an ear as she looked in the fridge, trying to decide what to eat . . . *further closures at* . . . She hadn't been shopping with all the work for the opening and then sorting out Maggie's stuff. Eggs, bread . . . *retailers who had expressed concern about the disruption* . . . She wanted something more interesting than that. She straightened up and stretched. She could go out . . . *is growing about missing Sheffield school girl Stacy McDonald* . . . She could go into town. She thought about calling Daniel. After all, he'd left a message asking her to contact him. Bad idea. For a moment, she wondered about contacting the enigmatic Roy Farnham – but she didn't have his number. And anyway, things were different now. That was a contact that would have to keep.

She cleaned her brushes and had a quick shower to get rid of the smell of turpentine. She pinned her hair up and put on her black dress with the close-fitting top and loose, calf-length skirt. She

245

was tall enough for flat shoes – more comfortable for the walk up the hill into the town centre. She scooped up Maggie's papers and put them into a drawer. She left the photos on the table. She needed to decide what to do with them.

The corridor outside her flat looked bleak and functional in the glare of the light. She looked at Cara's door. She felt cold. She pulled her collar up round her neck as she opened the door on to the outside steps.

As she locked the door at the bottom, she noticed that there was a light on in the gallery, in Jonathan's office. He must have come in after all, to catch up on the work he'd missed on Saturday. He used to do that a lot when Eliza first started at the gallery, often staying away during the day, then coming in and working late into the night.

The towpath or the road? She looked along the canal side. The towpath was the quicker route, and several people were hurrying along it in both directions, bundled up against the cold. She pushed her hands deep into her pockets and walked briskly towards the canal basin. It was far colder than she'd realized; the puddles of water on the ground were sparkling with frost, and she could see the gleam of ice on the water of the canal. If she'd known how cold it was, maybe eggs on toast would have seemed more attractive.

She was at the arch now, where the canal curved slightly. The water gleamed in the darkness, and then vanished as the light was cut off by the bridge.

She quickened her pace as she went through the tunnel, slowing again as she reached the other end and the moonlight faded as the lights of the canal basin came into view.

Dear Dad
~~I am very worried and I need~~
Something has happened and
I don't know what to

Dear Dad
I hope you are well. I am well. Mum is well. School is really boring right now. I am going to see Westlife when they come to the Arena. I got a new skirt and I altered it and it looks really good like the one I saw in J17.

Kerry sucked her pen and read what she'd written. It was dark outside and her room felt cold. The draught came in round the windows in this house. In the other house, Dad used to get that sealer stuff and put it round the windows where the wood was loose. When Mum said, 'Mark, this place is falling to pieces,' Dad had laughed and said, 'No it isn't. You just want to move.' Mum had never liked the old house. It was big and draughty with lots of rooms. Lyn said that she and Mum wanted to live somewhere new and modern.

'Like where we used to live, before she met *him*,' Lyn had said. Lyn always called Dad *him*, never

'Mark' and never, ever 'Dad'. 'He's not my father,' she used to say to Kerry when Kerry asked her why. 'I'm going to go and live with my father when I'm old enough. He wants me to.' But Kerry knew that Lyn's dad didn't keep in touch, never came round, never wrote to Lyn or sent her cards or presents. Lyn didn't even know where he was, though she never admitted it. Dad always said, 'Leave her, Kizz, she'll come round.' Only she never did.

Maybe she should phone Stacy's house and see if Stacy had come home. She looked at her watch. It was ten o'clock. It was too late to phone, but Stacy would surely be back by now. She had to be. Kerry ignored the cold feeling inside her. She'd been right not to tell the copper. She didn't know where Stacy had gone. If she knew, she would have told, but she couldn't tell them she'd been down the market, down the canal basin. She'd get excluded for sure, and then Mum would do what she'd done to Lyn. *Beyond control*, that was what Mum had said, and then Lyn had gone. Mum always said that Lyn had been born to trouble.

She could hear shouting outside, and someone was screaming, the kids messing around on the estate again. Kerry peered round the curtain. Sometimes she wanted to go out, meet up with the kids out there who were hanging out and having a good time while Kerry was sitting upstairs in her room on her own. But they might . . . She could remember them shouting at the old house, before she and Mum moved, *Paedo! Paedo!*, and they'd chucked stones at the windows. It would be different when Dad came home.

Kerry bit her nail. She was remembering the day in Conisbrough, the last day, the day Ellie went away. They'd gone on the water-bus. Kerry rocked herself gently on the bed. And it was like the way the water-bus had rocked as it puttered slowly up the river. She closed her eyes. Dad had shown Ellie the wave foaming up the side of the boat, and Ellie had leant over, trying to trail her fingers in it, while Kerry looked over her shoulder. And Dad was standing up watching the river bank and the trees. There was hardly anyone else on board that day, and she and Ellie had run along the inside of the boat that was long and narrow with seats like a pub, and it *was* like a pub because there was a bar, only it was closed, and a door that said *Toilet* and a door that said *Kitchen*. And then they were at the landing and they could see the castle on the hill, all broken and falling down.

Her eyes snapped open. She reached for her bag and searched around inside it. She pulled out the phone and switched it on. She waited in suspense as it registered, then she heard the faint beep, and allowed herself to look at the display. But there was nothing there. She checked her messages anyway, in case something had gone wrong, in case a new message had come. She let the messages run across the display, weeks of messages: *c u @ caff usual time don't b l8*; *dont b a div kizz bunk off*; *c u fday same time caff*; *dont let the cow get u down*; *2sday 7 caff*. Kerry's eyes skimmed them. And then the special one. *its abut yor dad meet u at the cafy 7 dont b l8* . . . But she had been late, and she had missed Lyn, and she hadn't seen her since. And she didn't know what to do.

She could hear Mum's feet on the stairs, slow, uneven. *Step, creak. Step. Step.* She slipped the phone under her pillow, watching the door. Mum's feet moved along the corridor, hesitated outside Kerry's room, moved on and past. Kerry heard the bedroom door open and shut. That was it. Mum wouldn't get up again now. She turned off the light, and lay back against her pillow, watching the shadows on the wall.

She used to be scared of the dark when she was a little kid. Mum wouldn't let her sleep with the light on, and she'd wake up sometimes and it was all black except where the curtain was she could see a faint light and the curtain would move and bulge, and she'd lie there trying not to call out. Dad used to say, *That's my brave Kizzy,* but there was nothing to be brave about, not then.

The night was cold and clear. Frost glittered on the pavements, and the moon shone with an icy brightness. Eliza walked home via the road, past the hotel – she wondered if Daniel was there – under the old bridge towards the gallery. The steps looked dark and uninviting. Once or twice, Cara had forgotten to lock the door at the bottom and Eliza had found evidence of people using the stairs for shelter at night – the remains of a cardboard box, an old blanket and once, more worryingly, a discarded syringe.

She let herself in through the gallery entrance, resetting the alarm once she was inside. She hesitated, then switched off the alarms. She wasn't tired, and she felt like wandering around the exhibition in the empty silence of the night. She remembered the light in Jonathan's office earlier, and opened his door to check if he was still there, but his room was dark and empty. She switched the light on. His desk was clear, apart from a small picture propped against his desk lamp. She looked at it. A reproduction from Daniel's exhibition. She picked it up. It was the Vietnamese children running down the road in the napalm blaze, naked and screaming in terror. She turned the light off again – she didn't want anyone coming to investigate what was going on in the building so late – and wandered into the moonlit gallery.

She walked slowly through the empty space, her feet echoing on the floor, *tap-tap, tap-tap*. The moon was high in the sky now, and the light made patterns on the floor between pools of shadow. *Tap-tap, tap-tap* as Eliza walked past the pictures, and she remembered that strange echo she'd heard that night, almost like a disturbance in the air of something soft and heavy moving through the rooms behind her. She looked out of the window at the water that lay still and silent below her in the moonlight.

Dark and still. The silence of the gallery lay around her and she closed her eyes, listening. The call of a night bird. A siren fading away into the distance. She could hear the sound of the water washing against the canal side, and there was a cracking noise. She looked out of the window, and saw the shape of a boat coming down the canal. It was in darkness, almost invisible in the night. Wasn't that illegal? Weren't they supposed to show lights? Its engine must be off, that was why she hadn't heard it before. It was only the disturbance in the water and the sound of ice cracking under its bows that had warned her of its coming. She listened as it went past.

She stretched and went towards the stairs, switching on the gallery alarm as she left. The light in the corridor outside the flats was harsh, illuminating the scratches on the paintwork, the patches of damp on the walls. Common areas. Neglected. Outside Cara's flat, her feet crunched in some debris. The corridor needed cleaning. It was cold. The heating didn't extend to the common areas, and a flow of icy air seemed to wrap itself round her bones. She let herself into the flat, feeling the residual warmth from the heating. She turned on the floor light, relaxing in its softer glow.

She kicked off her shoes and wandered through

the flat. She was aware of the empty gallery below her and the empty flat next door. She was walking on the boards now, rather than the rug, *tap-tap* like the sound of her feet across the floor of the gallery. She pulled off her dress, her stockings, her pants, then wrapped herself in the towelling bathrobe that had been her treat to herself at Christmas and headed towards the bathroom. A shower would relax her.

Once she was in bed, the warmth began to creep over her. She picked up her book, but after less than a page, the print began to swim in front of her eyes. She put the bookmark in, and dropped the book on to the floor. She turned over and pulled the quilt up round her neck, resting her face on her hand, feeling her thoughts start to disintegrate into dreams as she drifted off to sleep.

And she was swimming in the canal in the sunshine, except she was caught in an icy current, and Daniel Flynn was standing on the bank and they were supposed to be having a picnic together, but he was walking off down the towpath with someone, and the current was so cold her legs were too stiff to swim fast to keep up with them. The dark water under Cadman Street Bridge lay ahead of her, and the bridge was creaking, creaking, and it was going to fall on them. She tried to call out, to warn them, but her voice would only make a whisper.

She tried again, and then, suddenly, she was awake in the still of the night, and the icy current was there, and the creaking, faint but clear in the silence.

She sat up, shivering. Her head felt muddled and she was still half in her dream. Cara had left the fire door open again and the freezing night air was blowing into Eliza's flat. She shuffled her slippers on and went across the room. She was standing in her front door in the stream of cold from the open fire escape when her mind began to work. Cara wasn't responsible. Cara was dead. Cara had been killed. But the door was wide open, and the creaking, it wasn't in her dream, it came from . . . Her head turned slowly. From the dark lobby in front of Cara's door. *Creak* and silence. *Creak* and silence. Like the ropes of her swing when she was a child as she sat on the old wooden seat before she began to push it up to swing among the low branches of the trees. As she sat there absently, letting the swing rock her, the ropes had made that sound: *creak* and silence, *creak* and silence. Her hand reached for the light switch, but the corridor remained dark. The bulb must have blown.

And there was a smell like . . . like drains or garbage, like something left too long to rot.

And it drew her like a magnet. The awake Eliza, the day-time Eliza was starting to come alert in her head, starting to say things like *Wait!* and *Stop!* But the night-time Eliza, the Eliza who was still half in a dream, walked towards the darkness of the lobby, her hands reaching out, feeling for whatever it was

254

that made that strange noise like rope moving slightly, pulled tight by a heavy weight.

There was something moving in front of her face. She ran into a soft and heavy weight that moved and then swung back against her, engulfing her in the darkness where things rotted and a dream voice sang in the night. There was fabric against her face and something cold and her brain couldn't interpret what she was touching. A person, a person who was so cold, who was standing in mid-air, the legs dangling free . . .

Her knees hit the floor with a thump, her hands sliding numbly down the legs and feet of the figure that dangled loosely in front of her face, barely visible in the darkness, spinning slightly as the rope creaked.

And then the moon came out and shone with a cold clarity on the thing that swung gently above her.

CHAPTER 11

The corridor was harshly lit by the arc lamps that the scenes-of-crime team had rigged up. The call had come in the small hours, and Farnham felt spaced out by fatigue. He looked up at the bedraggled figure. The dangling legs looked sturdy. The toenails were painted pink, but the polish was chipped. It was hard to tell what she was wearing, because the body had been draped in a blanket, but he could just make out a grey skirt and a dark top. He could see something glitter as the light caught it. He moved closer.

Shadows fell on the lobby walls from the differently angled lights. As people came and went on the stairs, the air currents moved and the body swung slightly, making the shadows dance. The effect was oddly stroboscopic and he found himself thinking of film, of photographs, of paintings and designs. He shook his head to clear it and pulled his eyes away from the shadows. The noose had been tied so that the knot was at the front of the neck, forcing the head back towards the ceiling. The legs dangled, but the arms ... at first he couldn't see them, then he realized that they were tied, pulled behind the body and bent up. There was something wrong about the head, but the way the lights were angled left it partly in shadow and he couldn't make out the details from where he stood.

A door opened somewhere and the dangling figure swayed. The rope creaked. Dancing bones. *Where did that come from?* Maybe this was too much like Halloween. He dragged his mind back to the job. Tired. He was tired. The pathologist spoke quietly to him. 'I'll need to have a closer look before I can tell you any more, but she didn't die here. She's been dead . . . I don't know.'

'She was dead when someone strung her up?' Farnham said. 'Are you sure?'

The pathologist looked at him. 'A hanging can be a messy death,' she said. 'Forget all that stuff about the drop and instant death – in the days of public hangings, they used to talk about victims dancing at the end of the rope. Their friends used to try to get to them and pull on their feet to speed things up. It *can* be quick. Sometimes the pressure on the neck stops the heart, but if the victim asphyxiates as the rope tightens, you get the build up of pressure, oxygen deprivation, incontinence, the lot. I don't know how she died, but if it was hanging, she wasn't hanged here.'

Farnham looked up at the oddly positioned noose. He wanted a close look at that knot. 'I thought it snapped the neck, hanging,' he said. 'Bang. Gone.'

She looked at him over her glasses. 'I used to know someone who worked for the prison service when we executed people in this country,' she said. 'They'd leave the body hanging for a certain length of time before they cut it down. It made the job much worse for the prison staff who attended. They would talk about the body trembling, and facial contortions, but they were always told it was post-mortem reaction. Well, I've seen a lot of dead bodies, and I never saw one that pulled faces at me. Spinal-cord severance at the neck isn't always fatal. People survive it. You don't get to dance, that's all.' Her voice was sharp. She turned back to the body, ending the discussion.

Farnham watched her in mild surprise. *What rattled* her *cage?* He turned his attention back to the scene in front of him. They were lowering the body now, laying it out carefully on the body bag so that it could be transported to the morgue. The light shone on the head and face, and he closed his eyes. He remembered the post-mortem report on Cara Hobson, the evidence of torture. They were dealing with madness here.

'She's young,' he said to the pathologist, who was kneeling beside the body.

The woman nodded. 'Early teens, I'd say.' She looked up. 'That's a guess,' she added. She had a reputation for never committing herself until she was certain. 'Have we got a description of the missing school girl?'

Farnham looked at the body, then at the pathologist. 'It fits,' he said. He'd been following the case. Now it looked as though it was going to be his. 'Can you do something with her before we get the family in to identify her? Or are we going to have to . . . ?'

She shrugged. 'I'll see what I can do,' she said.

Someone came up the stairs behind him. He moved quickly to stand between whoever it was and the body. It wouldn't be the first time reporters had managed to talk their way in. Then he saw it was Tina Barraclough, looking anxious and jumpy. He watched her, and saw her eyes look past him, down, then jerk quickly away.

There was something he needed Barraclough to do . . . for a moment, he had trouble sorting out the myriad tasks that needed allocating, then his mind cleared. Eliza Eliot.

She'd called it in. When Farnham had arrived, he'd found her with the officers who had responded to the call, huddled on the floor in the office clutching a bottle of vodka. Apparently she'd walked into the hanging figure in the dark – enough to get anyone started on the vodka, in Farnham's book. But he needed to know what had happened – what she'd seen, what she'd heard and what she'd been doing in the lobby of the Hobson flat at that time anyway, and he needed to know before she drank herself into a stupor. He'd gently detached her from the vodka bottle, but he'd needed to get up here fast.

'DC Barraclough,' he said. 'The gallery woman, Eliot. She's downstairs. Go and see how she is, see if she's fit to talk. She's pretty shocked. Make sure they're looking after her – I'll be down to talk to her as soon as I can. I want it while it's fresh, OK?'

Barraclough nodded and turned back down the stairs towards the gallery. Farnham looked up at the ceiling again. A pulley wheel had been screwed into the joist, and the scenes-of-crime team had found plaster and sawdust on the floor. The rope, threaded through the wheel, looked new – no evidence of fraying or abrasion marks. He'd need to check the photographs taken when they were investigating Cara's death, but he was pretty sure the pulley wheel was recent – very recent. He could remember putting one in once, in a garage. It had been fairly simple once he'd located the joist.

He looked down at the draggled figure lying on the floor. A thirteen-year-old girl with her whole life ahead of her, transformed into this cadaver. It would have been dark along here when Eliza had made her find. Would it have been worse to stumble into the figure in the blackness, or to see it with the clarity that he had now? He couldn't decide.

As Tina went down the stairs, she couldn't get the image out of her mind: the body lying on the floor, the blanket that had been draped round the shoulders falling back, revealing the small, chunky figure. And then Farnham had moved slightly and she had seen the face, starkly illuminated by the arc lights. The girl's hair – what was left of it showed that she had been fair-haired – had been roughly shaved off, leaving wisps and strands. The eyes were gone. There were raw wounds on either side of the head, where the ears had been severed and the blood had run down the face and neck, staining the top the girl had been wearing that glittered with incongruous sequins. A skull. The head had been reduced to a featureless skull.

Her mind came abruptly back to the moment. She was at the bottom of the stairs, in the entrance hall to the gallery, and she could see someone talking urgently to one of the officers who was controlling access. It was Daniel. Daniel Flynn. She thought he'd gone, left Sheffield the day after the private view. The morning after that disastrous encounter, she had hoped there would be no further involvement of the gallery. But that had been her fear of embarrassment at seeing Eliza Eliot again, Eliza who had watched her leaving with Daniel, an unreadable expression on her face.

She hadn't thought about the possibility of Daniel himself being pulled into the investigation. If he was, if she had to tell Farnham what had happened . . . She thought about the coke, about what Daniel could tell Farnham, if he chose. *Oh, Christ, you stupid cow!* She hesitated. Daniel had moved out of sight. She could see Eliza Eliot sitting on a bench at the far side of the gallery. She had a blanket wrapped round her shoulders and her hair hung in tangles round her face. This wasn't the elegant, arty woman of Tina's memory. She looked a wreck. Tina dithered for a moment. Farnham wanted her to make sure Eliza Eliot was OK, but she needed to talk to Daniel urgently, before he disappeared again. She needed to get some idea of what he was doing here. She made her decision and moved towards the entrance.

But then she heard feet on the stairs behind her, and she moved back quickly from the door and pretended to be engrossed in one of the posters advertising the exhibition. It was the only reason she could think of for being close to the outside door. Farnham looked at her as he came past. 'You're not here to admire the pictures,' he said. 'I want to find out what the Eliot woman knows. Now, please.' He was looking through the doors to where Daniel Flynn had been and his face looked set and angry.

'Sorry, sir.' Tina cursed her luck, took a deep breath and crossed the room to where Eliza was sitting.

Eliza watched the moon set over the canal, the water changing from the blackness of shadow to the steel gleam of a mirror as the light caught the surface, the air still with the clarity of frost. Someone had put a blanket round her shoulders, someone had pressed a hot drink into her hands. She could hear feet on the stairs, voices around her. It was like a party, like the private view. People came and went through the gallery, doors opened and closed, but she felt shut away from it, not part of the purposeful activity that must, surely, be able to explain that . . . Her mind switched away. She pulled the blanket more closely around her. She didn't know if she felt cold or not. The tea slopped over her fingers and down her arm. She looked at the drops that had spilled on to the blanket as they soaked in, leaving a dark stain.

'Eliza . . .'

She looked up. It was Tina Barraclough, but she'd changed from the party, was wearing a dark suit, had her hair pulled back off her face. She must have . . . But it wasn't the party. Eliza's head swam, and she remembered how she had walked down the stairs into the gallery. She hadn't gone to the flat. She didn't want to take the touch of the thing that swung in the hallway into her home. She'd walked down the stairs past the alarms that had wailed an electronic cacophony around her as she spoke on the phone in Jonathan's office, her voice sounding calm and distant. Then, and it had seemed the logical thing to do at the time, she had taken the bottle of vodka he kept in his desk, unscrewed the top, and choked down mouthfuls of the pungent liquid. Then she had sat down on the floor, wrapped her arms round her legs and waited, small and unnoticeable in the dark. With the noise of the alarms and the flashing lights, they might not see her. They might just leave her alone in the corner, in the shadows of the gallery, and maybe she could creep back upstairs and sleep until the dream went away.

'Eliza.' And Roy Farnham was there again. He was crouched down in front of her, looking at her. He took her hand and rubbed it between his own. 'You're freezing,' he said, and looked up at Tina Barraclough. 'Has the doctor seen her?'

'Yes.' Eliza could talk for herself. 'Yes, I'm OK. I think I'm . . .'

He let go of her hand as he stood up again. 'You need to tell us what happened. What was it, Eliza? What made you go out and look?'

And she was in the darkness again, and the smell was there. Someone needed to get into Cara's flat and clear out whatever was in there, rotting, decaying . . . She felt herself begin to shake and the voices went on over her head. *She can't . . . in shock . . . seen the medic? . . . need this as soon as . . . Stacy's mother before the papers . . . need to find out what she . . .*

She was in the gallery. There were police officers all round. She was with people she knew. Tina Barraclough was there, and Roy Farnham. She was safe. 'It's OK,' she said. Her voice sounded odd, flat and distant, and her tongue felt too big for her mouth. 'I can remember it all.' And she closed her eyes and the evening scrolled against her eyelids as she told them. She told them about going out, about the light in Jonathan's office, about the restaurant just round the corner from the library. 'It was quiet,' she said. What had she had to eat? That was Farnham wanting to know. For a moment she thought he was making small talk, then she remembered that she'd been sick, thrown up on the floor like some hopeless drunk. She felt embarrassed, then angry with herself for minding.

And now she could feel the cold welling up from somewhere deep inside her and she wrapped the blanket more closely round her, but that seemed to be keeping the cold in, and she told him about waking up with the draught from the fire door blowing round her, and that creaking noise in the silence of the night.

'Listen, Eliza.' Farnham was sitting beside her now, trying to get her to focus. 'Eliza?' She had a sense that time had passed, and realized that he had finished asking questions. She tried to remember what she'd said, tried to get a grip of her thoughts, but they drifted again. She tried to concentrate on what he was saying. 'You can't go back to your flat tonight. Is there someone we can call? Or I can take you to a hotel. I can get someone to bring you some stuff.'

Maggie, they could call Maggie. Maggie would know. The thought drifted oddly through her mind. Who to call? Laura? But Laura was away. Jonathan? She couldn't go to Jonathan's. Where were all her friends? She had no friends, not in this city. She shook her head again, trying to clear it.

She could hear voices now, and someone was coming towards her. Tina Barraclough. Farnham stood up, and Tina spoke quickly to him. Farnham seemed to demur, then nodded abruptly, said something to Tina that Eliza didn't catch, then walked away across the room. Tina looked at Eliza and said, 'There's someone here – Daniel Flynn.' She waited for Eliza's nod. 'He says you can use his hotel room – he's coming down to the incident room to talk to us.' *To help us with our inquiries* . . . 'He'll take you to the hotel, if that's what you want . . .' Tina sounded uncertain.

The hotel. Just up the road. That would be fine. 'That's . . . fine,' she said.

'I'll drop some stuff off for you,' Tina said. 'Some clothes for tomorrow, stuff like that. What do you need?'

Eliza realized she was in her dressing gown. 'Some jeans, you know, and wash stuff . . .' It all seemed too hard to think about.

Tina had her coat from somewhere, and a pair of shoes and she was in the entrance to the gallery where Daniel was waiting by the receptionist's desk. Eliza found herself passed from one to the other as though she had no will of her own. And a strange passivity was holding her. Shock, or the alcohol? She wasn't sure.

'Are you all right?' Daniel was looking over her

shoulder as he spoke, to where Tina was disappearing behind the closing gallery door, and then
he put his arms round her, pressing her head against
his shoulder. For a moment, he reminded her of
the Madrid Daniel, the companion in the cafés, the
lover in the night, the man who shared and understood her ideas about art. But this was Sheffield
and it was cold and dark. And Daniel was changed.

He had his car parked outside the door, in the
restricted area. Jonathan wouldn't . . . 'I'm a bit
woozy.' She couldn't begin to explain what she
felt.

'They said you put away a fair bit of vodka,'
he said. 'You look a bit spaced out – best thing,
probably.' Then they were driving fast along the
road and the hotel lights were in front of her.
He swung the car round into the car park.

Except it was stopping her from being in control
of her thoughts, and Eliza needed, really needed,
to be in control of her thoughts. 'What time is it?'
she said.

'Almost five.' He opened the car door and helped
her out.

'How did you . . . ? What were you doing at the
gallery?' *Helping the police with their inquiries.*

'I heard the alarm go off. I wasn't asleep. I
guessed where it was coming from so I thought
I'd better have a look.' She felt his arm move in
a shrug. 'The police were swarming round by the
time I got there. Anyway, they'd have wanted to
talk to me even if I hadn't turned up.'

'Why . . . ?' Eliza was having trouble following what he was saying.

'It's obvious, isn't it?' he said. They were in the hotel lobby now and he was guiding her into the lift.

She remembered a line from a joke or a cartoon: *It sure is disobvious to me.* 'Obvious?' she said.

The lift stopped. 'Don't worry about it now, Eliza.' He opened the door of his room. She blinked as the light snapped on. 'OK, no one will disturb you. I'll ring when I get back – see what's happening.'

She looked at him. She hadn't realized he was leaving straight away. 'Stay,' she said.

He shook his head. 'Bad idea, Eliza.' He ran his finger down her cheek. 'You'll be OK.'

She hadn't meant that. She just didn't want to be alone.

The bed looked undisturbed. The room was as neat as if it was unoccupied. The only sign of habitation was a bag stowed in one corner. 'Go to bed,' he said. 'You're out on your feet.' He pulled the curtains across the window and went to the door. 'I'll see you later,' he said. He hesitated, then closed the door behind him, leaving her alone in the room.

Farnham leaned back in his chair, listening to Daniel Flynn accounting for his evening, for his sudden arrival at the gallery. A child had been killed, and yet Flynn seemed to be treating this as some kind of game of wits between them. He seemed to be choosing his words carefully, skirting around the edges of the trap he was waiting for them to spring. He had been carefully evasive, only offering information he seemed sure they already had and waiting for questions before he offered anything else. He behaved, in fact, like a man with something to hide, a man who had been coached by a solicitor who knew his job. He had no firm alibi for the evening, not from around nine the previous night, after he'd eaten. He'd gone back to his room.

Had anyone been with him? No. Had anyone seen him? The reception staff would have seen him come in. Would they remember? Ask them. He had no idea. What had he done then? Watched television, read, had a beer from the mini-bar. He'd ordered a sandwich from room service a bit before midnight. What time had he gone to bed? He hadn't.

And how come he'd been at the gallery shortly after the police had arrived?

He'd heard the alarms going off and had gone along to check.

Why? Why not phone the police?

He hadn't been sure it was the gallery, but he had a valuable exhibition there. That was what he'd been thinking about. He had his mobile, he would have phoned if there was any sign of a break-in. He knew Eliza was there.

He'd *heard* the alarms?

269

Yes.

And he'd known . . . ?

He hadn't *known* but he'd thought they might be from the gallery.

He'd been in his room at the other side of the hotel and he'd heard the alarms from the gallery? All that way?

No, he hadn't meant that. Sorry. He hadn't been able to sleep, so he'd gone out for a walk.

Where?

Along the towpath. And that was when he'd heard the alarms. He hadn't made the connection at first. By the time he'd got to the gallery – he'd made his way back to the hotel, picked up his car – by the time he'd got to the gallery, the police were there. He'd hung around trying to find out what had happened. Then he'd realized that Eliza needed help so he'd offered his room.

So what time had he left the hotel?

About ten minutes before the alarms went off.

Could anyone corroborate that?

The night porter had seen him.

Did he know a girl called Stacy McDonald?

No.

Did he know the McDonald girl had been missing?

No.

Where had he been the night that Cara Hobson had died?

In Whitby.

Could anyone confirm that?

Probably not. He'd spent the early evening in the pub, talked to a few people, had a game of darts.

And then?

He'd gone for a walk, got some fish and chips. And no, he hadn't met anyone. He doubted they'd remember him in the chip shop. It was the first time he'd been there.

When had he got back?

Half nine? Ten?

And Friday, the day of the opening?

He'd spent the afternoon in his hotel room.

Alone?

Alone. He'd got to the gallery just after half past six. He'd left there about eight-thirty, gone for something to eat.

And then?

He'd gone back to his hotel, probably got in around midnight.

Could anyone corroborate that?

The staff at the restaurant? The hotel staff?

Flynn was hiding something, but if the hotel staff could corroborate his story, Farnham had no reason to hold him. It didn't prove anything, but whoever had strung Stacy McDonald up had spent some time in the lobby of Cara Hobson's flat, if Farnham was right, and the pulley wheel had been put in the ceiling that night. Flynn told them he had no plans to go anywhere, that he might return to Whitby, but he would let them know if he did. In the end, Farnham let him go, pending confirmation of his story.

It was well into the morning by then. Farnham left the interview room and went to his office. He was looking out of the window, watching the first glimmer of light to the east, when he saw Tina Barraclough leaving the building, walking briskly towards a car parked on the other side of the road, as Flynn came into view. She stopped when she saw him, and her face was tense and anxious. Flynn smiled at her and shook his head before he turned back towards the town centre. Barraclough stayed by the car, her hand on the door, her eyes on the retreating figure.

CHAPTER 12

The day had started early. The team, gathered for the briefing, were showing signs of fatigue. They were under-staffed, Farnham knew. He needed at least two more senior officers and he wouldn't get those for another couple of days – and he needed more people on the ground. Someone gave him a cup of coffee – black, bitter, from the machine. The plastic cup was almost too hot to hold, the liquid slopping over the sides, scalding his fingers. He ignored that and took a swallow, feeling the effect of the caffeine almost immediately. The briefing was coming to an end. The mood was sombre. Almost no progress on the first killing, and now they had a second. Cara Hobson had been nineteen and a prostitute. But Stacy McDonald had been a child.

'OK,' he said, summing up. 'You all know what's happened.' He looked round the team. 'We've got a firm ID. Ligature mark round the neck, cause of death: asphyxiation. There's no evidence of sexual assault. But there's something else.' He described the mutilations to the head and face. He paused, giving time for questions, then introduced the woman who had been waiting quietly by the door. 'This is Judith Martin,' he said. 'DS Martin is joining the team. She was working on Stacy McDonald's disappearance.'

Martin came to the front of the room. 'I talked to Stacy's friends and to her teachers after she was reported missing. We haven't got very far. Stacy doesn't seem to have had many friends at school. She seems to have led quite a sheltered life for a thirteen-year-old. I got the impression she was young for her age. Her best friend claimed that she was interested in a lad in her year. We've brought him in, but, to be quite honest . . .' She gestured. Farnham knew what she meant. The murder looked too elaborate, too carefully planned, to be the work of another thirteen-year-old. 'The other interesting thing,' Martin said, 'is that several people, including Stacy's mum and her friend, say that Stacy took particular care with her appearance that day. We're going to the school again later today to talk to the kids again.'

After the briefing, Farnham returned to his office. He went back to the sheets of paper on the desk in front of him: the statements from the gallery staff about Cara Hobson, about the night that she died. Eliza had found Cara in the gallery when she finished work. The gallery had been locked up and the alarms set, but, somehow, Cara had managed to switch them off. He skimmed the statement. She'd claimed to have got the

274

codes from Massey, from watching Massey set the alarms – something Massey vehemently denied.

Cara Hobson and her baby had been living in the flat unofficially. The Trust knew nothing about her. The gallery wasn't the kind of property to attract squatters – commercial premises that were used every day. To gain access, Cara would've had to have keys to the outside doors. Farnham had a pretty good idea of how she had got them, but he needed some supporting evidence.

He went back to the statements. According to Eliza Eliot, and corroborated by Mel Young, Cara Hobson had spent a disproportionate amount of time at the gallery. Eliza's statement said: *I thought she was probably lonely, but I didn't have much time to talk to her.* Young's statement said: *She was there a lot. She was interested in the paintings and she liked to talk about them.* But the information he wanted wasn't there – who did Cara talk to and what times did she come to the gallery? He pinched the bridge of his nose, trying to focus his mind. Had he let something slip past him? He looked at Massey's statement again. He mentioned Cara's presence in the gallery, but nothing about what she did when she was there. *She was in the gallery too much. It got in the way of work.*

What did they know about Massey? Farnham pulled another sheet of paper towards him. Massey was thirty-eight, came from Birmingham originally. He'd worked in London, supporting himself by teaching. He'd had a successful exhibition and then moved to Sheffield Art School. After that, he seemed to have gone into art administration, and finally got involved in the setting up of this new gallery. No criminal record. One marriage that had ended in divorce in 1992.

There was one thing in the three statements that puzzled Farnham. Eliza and Mel Young had both talked about Cara spending a lot of time in the gallery, but neither of them had sounded unduly hostile towards her. Massey, on the other hand, hadn't had a good word for her. Farnham looked at the photograph he had pinned to the board above his desk. He always kept a photograph of the victim in sight, to remind him that he was dealing with a person, and that person's life had been taken away from them. No matter what the provocation, Farnham could never find it in himself to forgive that.

Cara Hobson had been lovely with her slight build, long hair and wide-eyed prettiness, looks she had, apparently, turned to good commercial use. And yet, in a way, he'd been seduced by it himself – he found the idea of the violence inflicted on her abhorrent, found the idea of her prostituting herself distasteful. She seemed too young and too vulnerable – which was exactly what so many prostitutes were. He was getting sentimental in his middle years.

He wasn't drawn to women like Cara – he preferred strong-minded, independent women.

He wasn't attracted to fragility, either physical or mental – he preferred adults. But a lot of men were, and most men would not have found the presence of an attractive young woman like Cara onerous. He looked at Massey's statement again. Indifferent irritation was one thing, but this read like something closer to hostility. Was Massey protesting too much? He had an alibi for the night of Cara's death, but there was something in the statement that didn't ring true, something that jarred.

He narrowed his eyes. Eliza. Massey was her employer, had, apparently, given her a real career break. She wouldn't be willing to gossip about Massey, and, if Farnham's suspicions were right, gossip was all that would support them. But he needed to ask Massey the right questions. He checked his watch. Eliza had had enough time to sleep it off by now, and she might still be a bit disorientated, a bit incautious. He'd go and see how she was. She could talk him through the exhibition – he needed that information anyway.

Eliza lay in the darkened room, trying to get her mind to keep still. She couldn't sleep, but she couldn't manage to wake up properly, as if the combination of the alcohol and the shock had put her into a trance state and every time she relaxed her vigilance, she was feeling her way along that darkened corridor, breathing in that tainted air. In the end she sat up and turned the light on, squinting at the digital display on the bedside radio.

She must have slept after all. It was after ten. She pushed back the quilt and stood up, feeling leaden with fatigue. A shower might bring her round. She wondered when she could go home, and what Daniel had done for the rest of the night. He'd gone to talk to the police. Maybe he was still there. She didn't want to think about that.

The bathroom was luxurious, warm, spacious, with an abundance of soft, thick towels. Eliza stood under the shower for a long time, letting the hot water wash away the feel of the night. She felt a bit better as she dried herself and she began to plan her way through the next stages of the day. She phoned down to reception and found that a bag had been left for her. Someone would bring it up straight away.

She began drying her hair, listening out for the door over the noise of the drier. Her bag, when it arrived, contained wash things, clean underwear, jeans, a top and some shoes. She was getting dressed when the phone rang. She hesitated, then picked it up. 'Daniel?' she said.

But it was Roy Farnham. 'Sorry to disturb you,' he said. It was no more than a conventional apology.

'It's OK. I was up,' she said.

'I'm downstairs,' he said. 'I saw them take your bag up, so I thought you must be awake. I need to talk to you. Are you up to it?'

'Now?' What else was there to talk about? She'd told him all of it last night. She didn't want to go over it again. The cold feeling was starting to come back.

'Eliza? Are you all right?'

'Yes. Sorry, I was just thinking. Yes, I'm OK. I mean, you know . . .' She felt strangely detached, and seemed to have lost her ability to form a coherent thought.

'Are you ready now?' he said. 'I need to see you at the gallery.'

She stalled. 'I'm just getting dressed.'

'Have you had anything to eat?'

'No. I'd better get something.' That would postpone her return. Maybe he'd leave it, whatever it was, until later.

'There's a café in the hotel,' he said. 'I'll meet you there, if that's OK. I haven't been home yet. I need something to eat too.'

His night had probably been worse than hers. He'd looked drawn with fatigue when she'd left the gallery. 'All right.' She preferred the idea of talking to him in the café anyway. She checked the bag again. Whoever had packed it hadn't put in any make-up, but her brush was there. She ran it through her hair and glanced in the mirror. She'd have to do.

She went through the hotel lobby and past the health club to the café. Roy Farnham was sitting at a table reading a newspaper. 'You look like I feel,' she said as she joined him.

He gave her his quick smile, but didn't relax into social mode. Business then. 'But you're OK for this?' he said, folding his paper.

'For breakfast? Fine. It's a long time since I had breakfast with a strange man.' She smiled at him.

Briefly, he smiled back, and she thought about leisurely breakfasts on the balcony in the Madrid sun. Only now, the man sitting opposite her wasn't Daniel but this rather reserved man with the warm smile. It was an attractive idea. He was watching her, and she hoped her stray thought wasn't clear on her face. But all he said was, 'And about going back to the gallery?'

'You mean the flat?'

He shook his head. 'No, we're not finished on that corridor yet. I want you to show me the exhibition, Daniel Flynn's exhibition.'

That surprised her. 'The exhibition? OK, if you want. I mean, it's there, go and look at it.'

'I want you to talk me through it, tell me about the picture, the one that it's all based on.'

'*The Triumph of Death*?' Eliza's cappuccino and croissant arrived then, and she stirred the white foam of the milk, letting the coffee colour it. She licked the chocolate off her spoon as she thought. 'I can tell you a bit about it now, but wouldn't it be better to ask Daniel?' Maybe he would tell her what had happened to him.

He picked up his coffee. 'I'm asking you,' he said.

'Is he OK?' she persisted, 'Daniel? He said he was coming in to talk to you.'

His face was neutral. 'He's giving us a hand with something,' he said, which was presumably a more friendly way of saying *He's helping us with our inquiries.* He raised his eyebrows. 'The painting? You were going to tell me about it.'

Eliza thought for a moment. 'It's a bit difficult. It'd help if you told me what you wanted to know.' His shrug suggested that he wasn't sure himself. 'It's medieval,' she said. 'Not the dates, but what it's about, the dance of death.' She told him about the hierarchical systems of medieval society, the inequalities that were levelled in the face of death. 'I suppose it made it easier to cope with the system if you thought it was all going to be balanced out in the end. You can see it in the painting. The powerful – cardinals and kings – are struck down with all the rest. Only Brueghel makes death an army, and there is only one escape route: the grave. It's quite merciless. They take them all, men, women, children.'

A group of women came into the café from the health club, laughing and talking.

'How long have you known Flynn? Do you know him well?' Farnham said. He was listening to her, leaning forward slightly to keep their talk private.

'About a year. I met him when I was working in Madrid, at the Prado. The art gallery,' she added.

281

He looked at her. 'I know,' he said.

'I'm sorry. I wasn't sure if you . . .' He'd wrong-footed her, and she acknowledged it with a resigned smile. *Fifteen-love.*

'I met him when he came to look at the Brueghel,' she said. '*The Triumph of Death*. He was with another artist, Ivan Bakst.'

'Bakst?'

She looked at him. He'd recognized the name. 'Do you know him? He's in Sheffield. I saw him the other day.'

'Has he been to the gallery?' Farnham seemed distracted from the line of thought he'd been pursuing.

She nodded. 'He came to see Jonathan about an exhibition. Daniel's a friend of his – I think he's been pushing Bakst. '

Farnham was silent for a moment. 'Is he still around?'

'I think so. I'm not sure, to be honest. Daniel might know,' she said.

'OK.' He looked at her. 'I'd like to get back to this exhibition. Why did Flynn choose that painting?'

'I think it was partly something I said to him.' She thought about the morning she and Daniel had met in front of the painting and the repercussions of that meeting. 'I said that you couldn't understand it properly if you didn't have the background – it's very biblical. The sources are Revelation and Ecclesiastes, but if you don't know that, it looks like a splatter movie, really.' She could remember what she'd said to him: *I'd put it in a current setting. A cityscape, industrial ruins, show people a modern triumph of death.* Something . . .

'Someone who was religious would understand it?' His question pulled her back before she could complete the thought.

She nodded. 'If they knew their Bible,' she said.

'Spare me religious nuts,' he said. 'Sorry,' he added, in response to her inquiring look. 'Just thinking about another case.'

She told him about the fascination she and Daniel had shared with the beautiful, macabre panel. 'I left Madrid six months ago – it was only a temporary contract – to take the job here. So I haven't seen Daniel for a few months, not till he came here for the exhibition.' She hoped that careful explanation would skirt round the difficult areas.

'It's unusual, isn't it?' he said. 'An exhibition like this coming to a small gallery. Was that because of your friendship with Flynn?'

She looked at him, but he seemed to have used the word with no sense of irony. 'The Second Site put in a bid, same as all the rest. It was a good bid.' That sounded a bit defensive, so she added, 'Daniel's connections with Sheffield helped, of course. And he knew I'd understand his work. So it had something to do with it.' Luck, and connections always came into these things. Everyone knew that. But it was merit as well. If she hadn't been able to handle it, none of the rest would have mattered.

'He knows Massey as well, doesn't he?' Farnham tasted his coffee, pulled a face and tipped in some more sugar. 'Got to give this up,' he said.

'Not that well,' Eliza said. She'd always got the impression that Daniel and Jonathan didn't have a lot of time for each other.

Farnham rubbed his eyes with his thumb and forefinger. He looked exhausted. 'All I can get from Massey is what a pain Cara Hobson was,' he said.

His professional mask was slipping. Eliza smiled slightly, distracted by the thought of Jonathan's querulous lament against Cara. 'He never stopped complaining about her,' she said.

He raised his eyebrows. 'Was she that much of a nuisance?'

Eliza shook her head. She could see Cara's small figure standing in the gallery, the baby cuddled in her arms. Sometimes, Eliza had found her chatting to Mel, distracting her when she was supposed to be dealing with the clerical work. Mel found the clerical work dull, and was more than willing to be distracted, but it was usually Eliza who had to deal with that. 'No,' she said, 'not really. She hung around a lot, but she didn't get in the way – and she seemed to like the exhibits. She just got on Jonathan's nerves sometimes.'

He nodded, concentrating on his coffee. He stifled a yawn. 'Too much night work,' he said. 'Like your boss.'

'He doesn't do much night work,' Eliza said. 'Well, not recently. Last night was the first time for a while.'

'But he used to?'

Eliza was puzzled. Farnham seemed to be losing the thread of the conversation. 'Before the exhibition, yes, he was there late most evenings,' she said. 'But it's been quieter since.'

'Same for you, I suppose,' he said.

She shook her head. 'It's a blessing and a curse living over the shop. If I need to work late, at least I can do it in the comfort of the flat. Until I began work on Daniel's show. Then I needed to be in the gallery.'

He was silent, then seemed to shake himself back to the moment. 'OK,' he said. 'I'd like to see this exhibition.'

She had finished her coffee, and the croissant had suddenly become over-rich. 'I'm ready when you are,' she said.

He took her out of the café via the hotel, where his car was parked. They were back at the gallery in a couple of minutes. Eliza looked at the mellow brick and the hard concrete of the stairway, and suddenly felt cold and sick. Farnham seemed aware of something, because he said, 'OK?'

She swallowed and nodded. 'It's like getting back on a horse,' she said, and then wished she hadn't. It sounded flippant. He didn't seem to notice but held the door open for her. She was aware of activity around her, but she couldn't see anyone she knew – presumably these were all Farnham's people. Where was Jonathan? Or Mel, for that matter?

She led the way upstairs, and stood in the cool light that illuminated Daniel's vision of a modern apocalypse. Farnham went straight across to the Brueghel. She stood beside him, looking at it. She remembered the first time she had met Daniel. 'Tell me about this,' he said.

She looked at the reproduction of *The Triumph of Death*, the multitudes of the dead rising up from open graves, disembarking from ships, hunting down the living without mercy and without regret.

Farnham was pointing to the detail where a chorus sounded trumpets above still water with brick walls and arched bridges, and figures of death on a raised platform threw a man into the water, a man with a heavy weight tied round his neck. Decaying corpses floated in the stagnant pool below. A figure struggled in the water beneath an arched bridge. She had a sudden memory of Daniel standing by the window, looking down at the canal. *It's like the Brueghel landscape – you've even got the arched bridges and the dead trees.* She shook her head to clear the image. 'Libertines,' she said. 'Thrown into the water with millstones round their necks.'

She let her eyes wander over the familiar vision of a nightmare from centuries past. A man had fallen under the wheels of a cart that was being driven relentlessly forward. A supine figure exposed his throat passively to the knife. A dead woman lay on the ground, her baby in her arms, a starving dog sniffing hungrily at the infant. A fleeing woman was embraced by skeletal hands.

Farnham stood beside her, watching her as she looked at the panel. Then he drew her across the room to one of the free-standing displays. 'And this?' he said. He had stopped in front of the photo-montages, images from the 1939-45 war: Hitler's army in retreat, hanging a young girl, a suspected partisan, and a detail from the Brueghel that recurred throughout the exhibition, a figure, tortured and garrotted, hanging from a dead tree, the arms tied and pulled up. The head was forced back, the face almost skeletal, the skull naked, the eye sockets empty, a raw wound where the ear had been. She'd lived with this image for weeks.

Suddenly she understood why Daniel had said, 'It's obvious.' How could she not have realized? She was back in the lobby of Cara's flat, looking up as the moon came out, at the head wrenched back by the noose, the bloodstains black in the pale light, the shadows of the empty sockets. *And the raven of the valley shall pluck them out* . . . She couldn't swallow. She pressed her hand over her mouth as she thought of Cara in the water under Cadman Street Bridge, under the arch.

Her eyes met Roy Farnham's. He was watching her, observing her reaction. He'd wanted to know if she'd seen the connection before. He was checking her out. '*Christ!*' she said. '*Jesus Christ.*'

She could smell coffee and croissant. She was going to be sick. She stepped backwards, breathing deeply through her mouth, trying to get herself under control.

He took her arm, but she shook him off.

'Don't,' she managed to say. 'Don't.' Her breathing was slower. He watched her. 'I'm all right,' she said. 'I'm . . . It was . . . I saw it last night, but it didn't connect, not till now. It was a shock. I'm all right.' She took some more deep breaths. The sickness receded.

He was frowning slightly as he watched her. 'Are you sure?'

'That figure,' she said. Her voice sounded a bit shaky, a bit out of control. She tried again. 'What did you want to know?'

He was still watching her carefully as though he was afraid she was going to fall over. 'Anything. What do you know about it? Why did Flynn pick it out?'

Daniel. Daniel had known. How had he known? 'It's something Brueghel would have seen,' she said. 'Mutilated cadavers on display – to remind people of the price of sin, I suppose, or just to keep them afraid. Daniel picked it out because of the other hangings, the Nazi ones – it's the same thing.'

She was cold. She could feel herself shivering. 'Maybe you need to go back to the hotel,' he said.

Eliza shook her head. She didn't want to go back

to that luxurious, impersonal room. She could phone Laura, go and stay there overnight. 'It's OK,' she said. 'I can go to a friend's.' But Laura wouldn't be back until this evening. She couldn't face the gallery, not now. It would be closed all day anyway. Maybe longer. She didn't know. She still had the key to Maggie's. She could go there, make the day useful, finish off the sorting out she had started. 'I've got somewhere I can go,' she said.

'OK,' he said after a minute. 'If you need to get in touch, if you think of anything, or if anything happens . . .' She looked at him. 'Anything that worries you,' he said, 'anything at all, you can get me on this number –' He gave her a card. She looked at it and pushed it into her bag.

'You'll never find that,' he said. 'Put it in your phone.' He stood up. 'Remember,' he said. 'Anything.'

Kerry looked at the clock. Still half an hour of English to go. She was supposed to be writing an essay about *Romeo and Juliet*. She leant her head against her arm and let her pen doodle on the page of her notebook. *WHO R U?* That odd message that had turned up on her phone. But it had been a mistake. Another message had come. *WHR R U?* That was what Lyn had meant – Where are you? Kerry had tried calling, but Lyn wasn't answering, so she messaged back: *at home. I was 18. I need 2cu.* I was late. I need to see you. Nothing

289

had come back, and now she was in class and the phone was switched off.

She was impatient to see Stacy. They didn't have English together. Stacy was in the top set. Kerry used to be in the top set, in her old school, before Dad . . . Before she and Mum moved. Stacy was bound to be back by now. She'd be OK. She'd be all right. And Kerry had to talk to Stacy before she got the summons to go to the office. *If* she got the summons. Maybe no one had noticed she'd bunked off. She sighed and nudged Marie who was sitting next to her. 'What did we have in French? On Friday?'

'It was a test,' Marie said. 'She took it in at the end. It was for the assessment.' She looked smug.

Kerry felt cold. If there'd been a test, and an important one, then they'd have noticed she wasn't there. 'I was poorly,' she said. 'I was in the loo all through French. Did anyone say anything?'

'You bunked off,' Marie said.

'I never,' Kerry said. 'I was poorly.' Marie didn't believe her. She was going to get caught, and she didn't know if Stacy would still agree to the story. It didn't seem like such a good story now. If she got excluded . . .

'Yes you did.' Marie said coolly.

'Kerry! Marie! Perhaps you'd like to tell all of us what you think about Juliet's speech. You *are* talking about Juliet's speech, I assume?' Mrs Hall, the English teacher, was watching them from the other side of the classroom. She had eyes in the back of her head.

'Sorry, miss,' Marie said. She was quiet for a minute, writing in her notebook. Kerry drew a picture. She wasn't sure what it was going to be, but it was turning into a gravestone, like the one in the cemetery where . . . She stopped. Marie was whispering again. 'It's OK. We didn't have a test. I was winding you up. We had a supply teacher and they put us all together. She never did a register, so no one noticed.'

Kerry began to breathe again. And that meant they hadn't noticed Stacy either. Kerry and Stacy were in the same group for French. Stacy wasn't much good at French, or at maths. Kerry used to be, before . . . 'Kerry!' Mrs Hall was standing right behind her. Kerry jumped. Mrs Hall picked up Kerry's notebook and looked at it. 'So you think that the significance of Juliet's speech is *whr r u –*' She carefully pronounced the words as they were spelt. A giggle ran round the room, and Kerry felt her face going red. '– and a few scribbles.' She looked closely. 'A gravestone. Well, at least it's appropriate. Now, I want you to get on with your work, Kerry, and I want to see you at the end of the lesson.'

After Mrs Hall had gone, Marie nudged her. 'You can look at mine,' she said.

Kerry rolled her eyes to show that she didn't care about what the Hall had said, but she was grateful. Not so much for the offer of the work – Marie

291

really wasn't very good – but for the support. Kerry had felt the treacherous tears starting in her eyes, and now she could blink them back. 'Thanks,' she mouthed as Marie shifted her arm so that Kerry could read what she had written. The lesson dragged on.

When the bell went, Kerry headed for the door, hoping Mrs Hall would have forgotten that she wanted to talk to her, but no such luck. Kerry kept her face carefully blank as she listened to the usual . . . *need to apply yourself . . . intelligent girl . . . better attitude . . .* Didn't she understand? It didn't matter any more. But what did the Hall know about anything? What did any of them know?

She was late into the canteen, and there wasn't anything much left by the time she got to the front of the queue. She looked round the canteen. There were kids crowded round the tables, talking and shouting, and there was the noise from the football game in the yard. She could see Marie at one table and she took her plate – she'd got chips and beans, it was all they had left; she'd go on her diet again tomorrow – and went over. There was an empty seat at the next table. She could pretend she was going to sit there.

Marie called to her as she was walking over. 'Kerry! Kerry Fraser! Come on, then.' She moved across on her chair to make room for Kerry to perch on the edge.

Kerry put her tray down on the table and fitted herself in next to Marie. 'What's that then, Kerry?'

One of the girls, Ruth, prodded at Kerry's chips and beans.

'You'll want to pin the bed sheets down,' Marie said, 'after that lot. Give us a chip.'

'Look at her!' Ruth again. 'Cottage cheese salad and now she's eating all our chips.'

Kerry ate as the talk whirled round her. It was good to be in a group again. No one knew about her. No one knew about Dad. No one knew about Mum, except Stacy.

'Hey,' Marie said. 'What's happened with Stacy McDonald?'

Kerry was aware of the sudden silence round the table, the interest. '*I* don't know,' she said. She remembered the police and felt herself going red.

'She was on the telly.' One of the other girls. 'This morning. They've got the cops out looking for her.'

Kerry hadn't watched. She didn't watch the news anyway, nor did Mum, not since Dad . . .

'She got a boyfriend?' Ruth's eyes were bright with interest.

'She likes Martin Smith, doesn't she?' Marie said to Kerry.

'No!' It jumped out of Kerry, taking her by surprise.

Marie looked at her. 'Course she does. You were talking about him in the bogs.' Marie's eyes were sharp now, staring at Kerry.

'We were *not*!' Kerry pushed her plate away. 'Those chips are crap,' she said.

'You were talking about Martin Smith in the bogs,' Marie said again. 'And you bunked off, didn't you?'

'No I didn't,' Kerry said, but Marie wasn't listening.

'Look,' she said, nudging Kerry. There was a sound of something banging and a sharp voice calling for silence. Kerry was aware of the noise level in the room dropping, the scraping of chairs and the echoing voices fading away.

The head was standing at the front of the room with some of the teachers. There was something wrong. Kerry felt her stomach knot and she looked over to the windows where the fire door was. Maybe she could . . .

The head was saying something. '. . . all go to your base rooms, please. *Don't* go to your class. Your year tutor will meet you in your base room. Year 9 girls, Mrs Sandison's group, I want to talk to you.'

'That's us,' Marie whispered in Kerry's ear. She squeezed Kerry's arm. 'What's up?'

'*I* don't know,' Kerry said. 'How should I know?' She couldn't get out by the fire escape with Marie hanging on to her arm. And now the head had seen her and was coming over. She was smiling, kind of. She didn't like Kerry. *Excluded for a period of six weeks* . . . She'd said that in the letter.

'Kerry,' she said, 'I need to see you in my office. Come along.' Kerry was aware of Marie's eyes, round with interest, fixed on her. She looked back at the fire-escape door, but there were two teachers coming behind her, almost as if they knew she was going to run away. They looked serious. She followed the head along the corridor to her office. There was a woman waiting for her and there was a man and he was wearing a uniform. And she was back at the day they'd come for her dad. Mum was screaming and crying. *You bastard, you bastard!* she shouted at Dad, while Kerry huddled in the kitchen, waiting for him to come in and explain, for her mum to come in and explain. They took him away, all in their uniforms, shouting. They *hurt* him. Dad was staggering, and they pulled him around as though they hated him.

But that wasn't the worst. The woman was the cop who'd come to her house, who'd had a friendly smile and cold eyes and who'd come to talk to her about Stacy.

'Kerry,' the woman said, 'do you remember me? Judith?'

Kerry gave a quick, assenting jerk of her head. She didn't want to talk to the cops. 'Listen, Kerry, we want to talk to you about Stacy. I'm afraid we've got some bad news about her, and we need your help. Someone hurt her very badly . . .' Kerry felt a chill inside her. Blue skies and the river, and Dad coming into the bedroom. He used to come in when she was smaller, read her stories, play games. Dad saying, 'Something bad may have happened to Ellie, love.' *Someone hurt her very badly* . . . Her mind was racing. Stacy. She thought about Stacy's angry face as she watched Kerry leave. Her stomach felt tight. It wasn't her fault if Stacy hadn't gone home. She looked at the woman called Judith, and at the head. The woman's face was serious. 'We asked your mum if she'd like to be here while we talked to you, but she wasn't very well. We can go home and talk to you there, if you'd rather.'

Kerry didn't want to talk to them, but the question jerked out of her almost against her will. 'Is Stacy dead?'

It was Mrs Sandison, her year tutor, who answered. 'Yes. I'm sorry, Kerry.' Kerry liked Mrs Sandison, who was young, and fun. Like Maggie used to be.

'Are you OK, Kerry?' It was the woman copper. Kerry knew how this worked. They said things like, *Are you OK?* And the next thing, you were telling them things that were secrets and then suddenly there weren't any secrets any more and everything came apart and when it came back together there was nothing left, nothing right any more, nothing the same. She kept her face turned away. *Fuck off, Copper!*

'It's all right, Kerry,' the woman said. 'You aren't in trouble.' Her voice was still friendly, but Kerry could hear something underneath. They pretended to be nice, but they wanted something. They pretended to like you, but they didn't. She'd learned that. 'Kerry, I don't think you told me everything when I talked to you before. I understand that you didn't want to get Stacy into trouble, but it's different now. Isn't it?'

Kerry looked down at her hands. She didn't know what to think. They were saying that Stacy was dead, but it wasn't Stacy who was dead, it was Ellie. And soon they were going to start asking her all the questions and she'd say things that came out meaning something else, and then the more she tried to explain, the more they'd look at her as if they understood, only they didn't understand at all.

'Isn't it?' the woman said again.

Kerry nodded again, just once. If they found out she'd bunked off, gone down the canal – suppose they found out about Lyn, about getting Dad out of prison. They'd stop her. Someone else must have seen Stacy in the market. Someone must. Let them tell the police. She had to think about Dad.

'Listen, Kerry,' the woman said, 'we want to find the person who did this to Stacy. We want to stop whoever it was from doing it to someone else. Now, we know that Stacy was planning to do something on the day she disappeared – did she tell you about it?'

Kerry shook her head.

'But you fixed her new top for her, didn't you?' The woman smiled. 'You're very good at doing things up, aren't you? Did you do your own top?' She was looking at Kerry's Samantha Mumba T-shirt.

Kerry waited.

'Stacy's mum says it was your idea,' the woman said.

'It wasn't,' Kerry flashed back. Stacy's mum always blamed her. She remembered Maggie's face as she said, *Get away from me*. And now Stacy's mum would hate her too. Only Stacy's mum had never liked her, really, she just liked feeling sorry for her. Kerry used to think that Maggie liked her, that Maggie wanted her and Ellie to be sisters, but Maggie hadn't liked her either. *Get away from me, you . . .*

'Stacy asked you to do it?'

Kerry jumped as the woman spoke. She hadn't meant to say. They did that, they made you say things. She looked at the woman warily, then nodded her head.

'She must have wanted the top for a special reason,' the woman said. Kerry shrugged. 'Come on, Kerry,' the woman said. She didn't sound angry, but she sounded firm. She wasn't going to go away, leave Kerry alone until Kerry told.

Kerry's mind was working fast now. She had to tell them something that would make them go away. She could say she didn't know, but they wouldn't believe her. She'd tried that, and they knew she was lying. She had to think of something else. She gave the woman a quick assessing glance. The woman smiled encouragingly. Kerry bit her lip. She thought about Mum and how she'd be this evening, how she'd cry and say she was sorry, then she'd start saying things about Dad and Kerry would have to think of a reason not to be there so that she didn't have to listen. She thought about Stacy's voice: *You can't go!* She thought about the day they came and took Dad away. *I'm sorry, Kizzy!* She tried never to think about that, the way he'd looked as if they were hurting him and he didn't know what was happening . . . And she felt the tears coming into her eyes and looked at the woman again. 'Stacy . . .' The woman nodded encouragingly. 'She bunked off that day, in the afternoon. She wanted me to go with her, but I'll be excluded if I bunk off again, so I said I wouldn't.' She couldn't stop the pictures now. Her eyes were hurting and everything looked blurred and distorted. 'We had a fight,' she said. 'Stacy was fed up with me for not going.'

She was aware of the adults around her exchanging glances.

'Why did Stacy "bunk off"?' the woman said.

'She was going to meet someone in town, only she wouldn't tell me,' Kerry said. 'Because she was mad at me.' *And the man had put his hand on Dad's head and pushed him down into the car and Mum had been screaming . . .*

'A boyfriend?'

Kerry blinked and felt tears run down her cheeks.

'It's all right, Kerry. Tell me in your own time.' The woman's voice sounded soothing and kind.

Kerry had to remember who she was. 'Why didn't anyone notice that Stacy wasn't at school?'

'We had a supply teacher,' Kerry said. Her voice was wobbling out of control, and now she'd started thinking about that day she couldn't stop. She wanted to, but she couldn't. She tried to remember what Marie had said, but her mind wouldn't think. 'They put all the groups together and she . . .' Kerry stopped. She didn't know if the supply teacher had been a man or a woman. She swallowed and her voice felt firmer. 'I mean, the teacher didn't notice. That Stacy wasn't there.'

'Didn't she take a register, Kerry?' That was Mrs Sandison. Kerry shook her head.

The woman wrote something down. 'What did you do?' she said. 'Did Stacy miss anything important.'

'It was French.' What had Marie told her? She remembered her own panic. 'We had a test,' she said.

'And Stacy never said anything to you about this person she was going to meet?'

Kerry shook her head.

'OK, Kerry, thank you for telling me that. You should have told us as soon as we asked you – keeping it secret didn't help Stacy.' The woman paused. Kerry could feel her looking. 'Listen, Kerry, would you like us to take you home?'

Kerry kept her head down and shook her head again. Mum would think that was great, Kerry arriving home in a cop car.

'I'll take you, Kerry.' That was Mrs Sandison, and now Kerry was really crying. She was thinking about her dad, about Ellie and about Stacy, and suddenly she felt as though there wasn't anywhere in the world where she wanted to be any more, that somehow, something was broken and she couldn't see any way at all of mending it.

CHAPTER 13

T he chance encounter with Daniel Flynn nagged at Tina's mind as she drove through the city centre. She should have said something to Farnham. As soon as the possibility of a connection between the images in Flynn's exhibition and the deaths associated with the gallery had been identified, she should have told him. Why hadn't she? She knew why she hadn't. The coke. OK, there was no proof, and Flynn would be admitting as much as she was if he told anyone, but somehow, that wasn't a comforting thought. She got the impression that he wouldn't give a damn about it, that whatever he might have to lose by making such an admission, he didn't care about. But she – she wasn't sure what the implications would be. Some SIOs might be prepared to turn a blind eye, but that wasn't Farnham, she felt pretty sure. She shouldn't have gone anywhere near the gallery at all, not in a social capacity. But people did get involved, did get personally entangled during an investigation. It happened. That wasn't the point, though. It was the coke . . .

She should have said something straight away, got her retaliation in first. If Farnham found out and she hadn't told him . . . he'd know why, if Flynn mentioned the drugs. But even if he didn't . . . things like this got out. *Private views.* And even though there had been no reason why she shouldn't have got involved with Flynn at the time it happened, it would still reflect badly on her judgement because it would muddy the waters of the case. Maybe Farnham would want her off it. She couldn't investigate Flynn. Her usefulness to the team would be compromised. *DC Barraclough? Oh, she got taken off that case because she shagged a suspect.* Because she shagged a killer . . .

A car horn sounded behind her and she realized the lights had changed. *Oh, very bright, Barraclough. So busy sorting out your personal life – your personal mess – that you cause a crash. Good move.* She moved off and forced herself to concentrate on what she was doing. She could decide what to do about Flynn after the briefing.

She turned off the Parkway towards the lower Don Valley. She was still checking on the mystery boat. So far, she'd drawn a blank. Of the four cabin cruisers that had been moored on the canal – the *Eleanor*, the *Lady Grey*, the *Lucy* and the *Mary May* – only the *Mary May* and the *Lucy* remained as viable possibilities. The *Eleanor* was disabled with a broken steering mechanism, and the people moored next to the *Lady Grey* were residents who confirmed that she'd been at her mooring until at least midnight the night Cara died. The owners of the *Lucy* were away and hadn't yet responded to her attempts to contact them.

She was here to check Steven Calloway's story and take a look round the *Mary May*, the cabin cruiser that was moored below Tinsley locks with a *For Sale* sign in the cabin window.

The boatyard office was small and cluttered. There was nowhere to sit, apart from a cracked stacking chair in front of the desk that had a pile of folders on the seat. 'We can't get the staff,' the broker explained vaguely as he moved stuff round on his desk. 'Charlie Norton. How can I help?'

Tina explained about the sighting of a cabin cruiser, and the problem of identifying which one had been out on the canal that night. He grinned at her. 'If no one's come forward, they'll have been up to no good,' he said.

Which, Tina thought, was rather the point.

'Someone after a bit of leg-over, something like that,' Charlie Norton went on.

Tina ignored that. 'I've got to check the *Mary May*,' she said. 'I've talked to the owner.'

'Well, she weren't out that night,' he said, with some emphasis. 'We don't take people out in the middle of the night in winter.'

'Is that how it works?' Tina said. 'If someone wants to look at a boat, you take them over there?'

He shifted some piles of paper round. 'Yeah, something like that.' He sat on the edge of the desk. 'Anyone can go and look. The boat's there.

But if someone's interested, they get in touch. I arrange for them to view the boat, then one of us'll take them across to it.'

'What if they want to take it out?' Tina said.

'No problem. We go with them – let them run it around a bit, check it out. Then take it back to the mooring and set it up again.'

'OK.' Tina thought. 'Would you let anyone take a boat out on their own?'

'No. Well, I might if I knew them, but not in the general run, no.'

'Who's taken the *Mary May* out recently?' Tina said.

'There's not been . . .' He opened a drawer in the filing cabinet and took out a large notebook. 'It's . . .' He flicked through the pages. 'Someone had a look a couple of months ago – and then they came back, a week later, took her out on the canal. Bill dealt with that. Apart from that, nothing.' He shook his head. 'She's old, the *Mary May*. Not been properly maintained. He'd be better scrapping her. Might get a bit for her that way.'

There had been no potential buyers taking the *Mary May* out the night of Cara's death – but anyone at the broker's office could have got the key. 'Who has access to these?' she said.

'Me,' he said, 'and Bill. There's no one else. And we keep the keys in the safe. There's some valuable boats on our books. Do you know how much a classic narrow boat would set you back?'

Tina shook her head. She had no idea.

'You'd be looking at fifty grand at least. We keep these keys secure.'

'Could you tell me where you were on the night of the fourteenth?' The night Cara Hobson had died. If the keys were secure, then maybe the brokers weren't.

He gave her a flat stare, but he seemed less offended by her question than he had by her suggestion that someone could have helped themselves to the keys. 'Am I a suspect now, then?' he said.

'No,' Tina said with honesty. There was nothing she knew of to link this man with Cara Hobson. 'But I need to account for those keys.'

He nodded. 'The fourteenth's our wedding anniversary. Me and the wife and Bill and his wife went out to eat, then we went on to their place till late. OK?'

It sounded convincing. She'd need to check it, but if he was telling her the truth – and it had the ring of authenticity to Tina – then neither of the partners at the brokerage had been on the canal on the night in question.

'I'll need to have a look at the boat,' Tina said. The *Mary May* sounded like a dead loss as far as the mystery cabin cruiser went, but she had to tell Farnham she'd checked it out.

'I know. Steve Calloway phoned, said it'd be OK,' he said. He went to the safe and got out the keys. Tina noticed that he kept the safe locked. 'I'll need to lock up,' he said.

'That's OK. I know where she's moored. You don't need to come with me if you're busy.' Tina reached for the key ring in his hand.

He held it away. 'No, she's my responsibility, the *Mary May*. I'll take you up there.'

Tina waited, hiding her impatience as he locked up and set the alarms. The security system seemed excellent. He noticed her watching as he was securing the door behind him. 'I told you,' he said. 'There's valuable stuff we're responsible for. We take our work seriously.' He was clearly still offended by her question about the keys.

'We can go in my car,' she said. She didn't want the hassle of following him through the heavy traffic.

He seemed about to object, then nodded. 'As long as you drop me off back here,' he said.

They drove out towards the moorings in silence. He whistled quietly through his teeth as she negotiated her way through the traffic, as though he was thinking something over. She left him to it, and as they approached the signs for the big cinema and entertainment complex where she hoped to be able to park, he said suddenly, 'Why all this interest in the boats? The lass was drowned – you don't need a boat for that.'

'We need to eliminate something from our inquiries,' Tina said. The rote response, and it didn't convince him.

'The boat people,' he said, 'they don't cause trouble, you know, just because they live on the river, on the canal.'

'I know,' Tina said as she swung the car into the concrete acreage that was Valley Centertainment. The bright colours and the lights seemed to emphasize its windswept bleakness. *Eating, dancing, cavorting!* the lights flashed. Well, she'd done her share of that, she supposed. She parked near the tramline, and they walked towards the bridge that would take them to the canal.

'You could have parked closer,' he said. 'On the other side.'

Tina nodded. 'I knew there'd be space here,' she said.

The sky had the leaden dullness of a winter afternoon, and the lights on the towpath were already lit. The air was chill now, and Tina hunched herself into her jacket, wishing she'd put an extra jumper on.

The mooring was quiet. There were three boats: two narrow boats that looked abandoned, and a small cabin cruiser with faded paint and dirty curtains in the cabin window. 'Here she is,' Charlie Norton said. 'The *Mary May.*' He offered the keys to Tina. 'That's for the padlock, and those two are for the engine. One of them's faulty,' he said.

She stood and looked at the boat for a minute. It was old and shabby. 'Does it look OK to you?' she said.

He shrugged. 'She's still on top of the water,' he said. 'What do you mean?'

'Does it look as if anyone's been on board since you were last here?'

He shook his head. 'Go and check,' he said. 'But she's locked up tight.'

She looked round it from the water's edge, then stepped carefully on to the deck. A plunge into the canal was exactly what she didn't want. These waters were dangerous and deceptive. They looked still, but there were underwater sluices and machinery, the unpredictable currents caused by passing boats. The *Mary May* was secured by a heavy-duty padlock. She checked it carefully. There were no scratches or distortions to suggest that anyone had tampered with it. The hasp was solid, the screws rusted into the wood.

The deck vibrated slightly under her feet as the broker jumped aboard beside her. He didn't say anything as she unlocked the padlock and went down the steps into the cabin.

But there was nothing there. It was exactly as the broker had told Steven Calloway. The cabin was spartan and clean, though it smelled faintly of damp – unavoidable in a boat, Tina supposed. She checked the locks on the windows. They were closed tight. It would be no serious challenge to break into the *Mary May*, but not without doing some damage. The boat was secure.

She looked at the engine and the controls. Again, you'd need a key, and those were in the possession of the broker and, presumably, Steven Calloway. 'Could you hot-wire the engine?' she said.

He laughed. 'It's diesel, love.'

'So how would you start it without a key?'

'You wouldn't.' She waited. 'Well, you'd have to use the handle, and . . . You could do it, but it'd make a hell of a mess.'

She looked round the pristine cabin and shook her head, puzzled. The only candidate that seemed possible for the mystery third boat now was the *Lucy*. She'd have to step up her attempts to track down the owners.

Eliza parked her car outside the narrow gennel that led to Maggie's front door. She left the car in gear – the hill was steep – and opened the back to get the shopping that she'd picked up on the way. She noticed a small box that had slid half under a seat. She pulled back the lid – more photographs. She must have left this in the car from her last trip to Maggie's. She could check through them today. She tucked the box under her arm and locked the car door.

The gennel smelt damp and no one had cleared away the autumn leaves. She struggled up the steps and pushed open the gate into the garden, almost dropping the box. The branches of the shrubs slapped wetly against her as she walked up the path to the door. She dumped the box on the front step as she fished in her bag for the key. When she unlocked the front door, a draught blew round her and the dank chill of an empty house enveloped her.

Her mind had equipped her with a picture of careful order: the remaining files to be sorted placed neatly on the table, the stuff she'd already been through arranged into piles – things to be discarded, things to forward to Maggie's solicitor, things Eliza wanted to keep. But one pile of folders had fallen over, disturbing the carefully organized papers. Some of them had slid to the floor.

She checked her annoyance – she should have been more careful, but she'd been in a hurry before. She put the stuff she'd brought back with her on to a chair, and stretched. The draught was still blowing, and she went through the flat looking for the source to see if she could block it off.

The small bedroom at the back of the flat was just as she remembered, but the draught was worse here. It seemed to blow straight on to the bed. Eliza went through to the off-shot kitchen. She found the source of the draught here. The window, an old sash-cord frame, was slightly open at the bottom. It was jammed at an angle, as though it hadn't slid shut evenly. She was surprised she hadn't noticed it before. She wrestled with it, shaking the window to free it. She had to open it, and then have two goes at closing it before it slid shut. It needed some serious renovation work, which she doubted it was going to get. The latch was clogged with paint so she couldn't lock it. She made a mental note to let the landlord know. She checked the back door. It was firmly bolted.

She went to the front room and sat at the table, trying to decide where to begin. She was reluctant to get started. Her eyes felt heavy, and the temptation to sink into one of the armchairs and sleep was almost irresistible, but she didn't want to sleep now, and then find herself awake in the small hours going over and over the events of the night before. The business of getting to Maggie's, planning what she was going to do, trying to remember what she had done last time, had helped to distract her, but now she was alone, they came crowding back. She took a deep breath and made herself focus on the here and now.

She picked up the folders that had fallen off the table, checked through the papers and made sure that everything was still more or less in the right place. Now she could get on with what she had come here to do.

Her visit to the shops ensured that she had coffee and bread and cheese to keep her going. She'd forgotten about heating, though. The electricity was still on, but she had instructed the landlord to turn off the gas, and the only source of heat in the small flat was a gas fire in the front room, unless you counted an infrared ceiling heater in the bathroom. For a minute, Eliza toyed with the idea of working in the bathroom under that meagre heat source, but dismissed the idea. She could keep her coat on.

She made coffee and sat down at the table, holding the mug between her hands to warm them. She spent a few minutes familiarizing herself with the papers – where had she got to? – then set herself a work schedule. Most of the papers were sorted.

The business papers – insurance, bank statements, invoices, would need closer attention.

She picked up one of the letters: . . . *would be grateful if you could add your support* . . . She looked at the next one. . . . *for your donation of £5* . . . They all seemed to be copies of letters either soliciting support or thanking people for contributions. Was there any need to keep them? Any need to even read them? Probably. People had given money, and now the campaign was halted. Eliza couldn't think of anyone who was likely to carry it on.

She began skimming them, putting the ones that gave any useful information to one side. There were letters from people offering support, letters from people who thought that Maggie might support their own causes: . . . *more severe forms of justice.* The Bible tells us . . .; . . . *only answer is to bring back the rope* . . . The dark hallway was in front of her again, and the moonlight shone, briefly, illuminating the lobby where the figure swung in the shadows, only now it was the figure from the Brueghel, transported from the painting into her life . . .

Maybe letters from cranks weren't the best things to be looking at now. She decided to take a break and made herself more coffee, then, realizing she was hungry, she cut a slice of bread and a piece of cheese. Her diet was going to pot – croissants for breakfast, bread and cheese for lunch.

She wandered round the flat as she ate, trying

to bring back the memory of the younger Maggie, not the woman she'd known in the last year of her life, old before her time and defeated – no, not defeated, still fighting, but burning with a flame of anger and hatred that had consumed her in the end. Maggie.

She wandered into the bedroom. This room was lighter, it got the afternoon sun, unlike the front room that was shaded by foliage. She wondered if Maggie had had any real companions in the last years, apart from Ellie's shade; any lovers who might have given her another reason for going on, apart from avenging her daughter's death. There had been nothing, or nothing Eliza was aware of. Suppose the wishes of the letter writer had been realized. Suppose Mark Fraser had hanged for his crime. Would Maggie have been any more able to come to terms with what had happened? Somehow, Eliza doubted it.

She looked at her watch. She needed to get back to work, get this lot finished and out of the way today. She had finished the pile of letters. She turned to the box of photographs, which were arranged in date order, each envelope carefully labelled. *Cornwall, '96; Christmas concert '96; Ellie, summer '97*. From winter '97, the writing had been partly erased, scratched out with heavy lines of ink. *Ellie, K—, —k, Ellie, Ke—*. Names that Maggie no longer wanted near her daughter's name. The last wallet was unlabelled. She opened it and looked at the top one. A man with two girls. The picture suddenly resolved and she recognized Ellie. The man standing behind her – that must be Mark Fraser. In the newspaper photographs, his eyes were shadowed, he looked surly and unshaven. Here, he looked ordinary, a bit tired. He was smiling, one hand on Ellie's shoulder. A second photograph was of Ellie again, this time with another girl. They had their arms round each other and were pulling faces at the camera. The river was in the background, the water shining in the sun. The day on the river.

She remembered the two photographs she'd found among the stuff she'd taken to her flat. Part of the same set. She ought to keep them together. She put them with the things she planned to take back with her, when she got access to her flat again . . .

Once more she shut the thoughts of the previous night out of her mind. There was nothing she could do about it. That was the last of the photographs. She pulled the file of press cuttings across. What to do with these? Was there any point in keeping the cuttings? Eliza had a feeling that Mark Fraser's appeal was coming up soon. She hesitated, undecided. She could probably junk the lot. But if anyone did want to pursue the campaign against Mark Fraser's release, then they might need these painstakingly collected cuttings.

She flicked through them to make sure that there was nothing other than cuttings here. There were copies of the earlier ones she'd looked at already, the stories from Ellie's disappearance, the reporting of the arrest and trial. She paused over these. Fraser had had a wife and daughter living with him. Maggie had talked about that when she first met – or when she first became aware of – Mark Fraser. Eliza wondered what had happened to them. Fraser's daughter and Ellie had been like sisters, Maggie had said. But maybe that was wishful thinking. Maggie had wanted Fraser to leave his wife, start again with her and Ellie. And after Ellie's death, Maggie's anger and hatred had seemed to encompass the child as well as the man. Presumably the friendship had made Ellie – always an intelligent and quick-witted child – lower her guard. But if the child had been abused by her father . . .

She looked at the headlines.

ELLIE KILLER 'ABUSE' ALLEGATION
FRASER DAUGHTER BREAKS DOWN ON STAND
JUDGE CONDEMNS 'MONSTROUS CRIME'

She skimmed the articles. Mark Fraser's step-daughter hadn't been called to give evidence, she realized. The stepdaughter – *who cannot be named for legal reasons* – had gone into care before Ellie's murder, termed 'out of control', and subsequently accused her stepfather of abuse. Eliza remembered Maggie's story, that the girl's mother had thrown her out. She checked the dates. Fraser's arrest had followed shortly after. Fraser's own daughter had been a witness to Ellie's disappearance. Eliza frowned as she read on. The child was nine, apparently, and had been unable to give evidence in court that might help to convict her father. What child would?

FRASER DAUGHTER BREAKS DOWN ON STAND. Abused children didn't stop loving their parents, not always. Maybe the child had drawn Ellie in somehow . . .

It wasn't something she wanted to think about. She went on through the cuttings, to the more recent ones about Fraser's lawyers preparing to take his case to the Criminal Review Board. And there was a separate pile, clipped together. These were smaller cuttings, apparently unconnected, but dated around the time of Ellie's disappearance. They were from the local paper, and seemed to be about some kind of drugs problem. She looked through them. There were photocopies of articles about overdose deaths. POLICE WARN OF HEROIN DANGER ON STREET . . . THIRD DRUG DEATH IN SOUTH YORKSHIRE; and there were some cuttings about a police operation: FIVE HELD IN DRUGS RAID.

She read through the articles, but nothing jumped off the page at her. She didn't recognize any of the names or any of the places. But how would she know who Maggie knew, after all these years? She put the cuttings with the discards.

Her phone rang. She checked the number. It was from the gallery. She felt her heart beat a bit faster as she answered it. 'Hello?'

It was Jonathan. 'Where are you, Eliza?' His voice was anxious. 'I thought you'd phone me. What's happening?'

She'd meant to contact him. But surely the police had told him by now. 'You know about . . .' she began.

'Yes. I thought you'd phone me as well.' He sounded panicky and uncertain.

'I just couldn't,' she said, her voice sounding sharp in her own ears. Surely Jonathan could understand how she must be feeling? There was silence. 'Where are you?' she said.

'I'm at the gallery. They needed someone here while they searched it. Again. When are you coming back?'

Eliza closed her eyes. 'Tomorrow,' she said. 'I'm coming back tomorrow. We can open the gallery again when the police have finished.'

'Oh . . .' She could hear the sound of voices, activity on his end of the line.

'I'm at Maggie Chapman's,' she said. 'I thought I might as well use the time to finish off the stuff.'

'I need you here!' Jonathan said. 'He wants me to go down and make a statement. They've searched my office, Eliza. And they've taken my computer.'

He. That would be Farnham. 'It's routine,' she said wearily. Though taking Jonathan's computer didn't sound like routine to her. She remembered Roy Farnham talking to her in the café, his apparently inconsequential chat about working late that suddenly didn't seem so inconsequential. He'd found out from her that Jonathan often worked late in the gallery, on his own. Suddenly, the police action took on a sinister slant. 'But you've got an alibi for the night Cara was killed.'

'Of course I have,' he said.

Eliza still felt uneasy. 'It might be an idea to get some legal advice,' she said.

'Why should I?' he said. 'I haven't done anything. It makes me look . . .'

'Well, it's up to you,' she said.

'And you're not coming back today?'

So that was why he'd phoned. He wanted to get away from the gallery, have someone else deal with the police search. She closed her eyes. Not today. She couldn't deal with it today. Let Jonathan cope. 'No,' she said. 'I'll see you tomorrow.'

Eliza stared at the phone after he had rung off. Her flat wasn't going to be available, nor did she want to go there. She wondered if Laura would be back yet. She tried the number again, but it was still the answering service. It was getting late and she was starting to flag. The light was fading outside. Her eyes were suddenly heavy from the lack of sleep. If she could get her head down for an hour . . . She could lie down on the stripped bed, rest for a while. The thought of lying in that empty room seemed morbid, but she couldn't drive in this condition. There was still some bedding in the cupboard. She found a pillow, spread a sheet over the mattress and wrapped herself in a blanket. She lay down, telling herself that she would sleep for half an hour. Her eyes closed as soon as her head touched the pillow.

Jonathan Massey's carefully cultivated image was beginning to slip. He hadn't shaved that morning, and his small beard was looking unkempt. The studied casualness had become the rumpledness of haste and tension. Farnham didn't want to make snap judgements. Massey had just had the big opening of his gallery come down around his ears in the aftermath of sordid, sadistic murder, months of careful and expensive planning gone up in smoke. But he was nervous. Remembering what had turned up in the search of his office, Farnham wasn't surprised.

He'd started off as though he was confirming minor details. He'd checked Eliza's story about the visit Ivan Bakst had made to the gallery. Massey confirmed what Eliza had told him. He'd checked Massey's whereabouts on the night Stacy McDonald went missing. It was when the initial interview had moved beyond these details that Massey began to show signs of nerves.

'Mr Massey,' Farnham had said, when Massey accused him of harassment, 'you aren't under arrest. You're free to leave at any time.' Massey had weighed this up, and for a moment, Farnham thought he had overplayed his hand and that Massey would go, but he stayed, looking uncomfortable and edgy.

Farnham took him again through the evening

before Cara Hobson's death, his visit to Leeds, the location of the gallery staff, stuff he already knew. And he noticed, as they talked, that Massey relaxed. He didn't mind talking about the evening of Cara's death. Farnham circled round again. 'Tell me about the problems you had with Cara in the gallery.'

'I've already told you.' That wary hostility again.

'I just need to get it clear in my mind,' Farnham said.

Massey shrugged slightly. 'She was in the gallery too often. It was as simple as that.' His hands were fidgeting with a pen.

'OK.' Farnham moved closer. 'Was that during the day, or when you were working late?'

He could see the reaction on Massey's face. 'Well, any time. Really, I don't see . . .' Massey shut up and looked at Farnham, waiting.

'So she came to the gallery when you were working late?' Farnham kept his voice neutral.

'No.' Massey's hesitation was almost imperceptible.

'But you did work late?' Farnham persisted. He watched to see if Massey would now try and deny it.

'Maybe. Sometimes. A bit,' he said. 'An art gallery isn't like a supermarket. It isn't a nine-to-five operation, you know.'

'Of course,' Farnham said politely. 'Now, my problem is, Mr Massey, that you say you had all these problems with Cara, but you never made any complaint to the Trust.'

321

Massey was silent, then, 'I told you,' he said. 'There wasn't anything they could do.'

'But according to Eliza Eliot and Mel Young, you found her a serious problem,' Farnham said. 'And on the morning she died – before you knew, of course – you found out she'd interfered with the alarm system in the gallery. But you still didn't contact the Trust. I would have done, long before it got to that stage.' He made his voice sympathetic. Massey had had a problem.

Massey studied the pen in his hand. 'Well, I didn't get round to it,' he said.

'That's a pity, really,' Farnham said. 'It would have alerted them to the fact that she was there.'

Massey nodded, then reacted. 'I didn't . . .' he said. Then, a bit too late, 'What do you mean?'

'She was occupying the premises illegally,' Farnham said. 'But someone must have given her access.'

'I don't know anything about it!' Massey said.

'OK.' Farnham was always interested in denials of accusations that hadn't yet been made. 'Someone gave Cara Hobson access to that flat, someone who knew the system, and who would have had all the exterior keys.' He saw Massey's hands become motionless. 'Her visits to the gallery constituted a security problem, especially if she was coming in out of hours, and yet the person who was responsible for the security of the gallery never drew official attention to her presence.'

Massey didn't say anything.

'And when we searched your office, Mr Massey, we found keys in your desk. One of those keys was for the flat that Cara Hobson was living in.'

Massey swallowed. 'I'd forgotten,' he said. 'She gave me a key, a spare.'

'Why did she do that?' Farnham said, leaning back in his chair.

'She kept locking herself out. She asked us to keep a spare in the gallery.'

Farnham nodded. 'When did she ask you to do that?' he said.

Massey looked at the sheaf of notes in front of Farnham. He'd forgotten his lines and wanted a prompt. Farnham kept his gaze on Massey, kept his smile polite and inquiring. 'I don't really remember,' Massey said after a moment.

'You said in your first statement,' Farnham reminded him, 'that you had nothing to do with Cara – that you'd barely spoken to her. But then she comes and asks you to keep a spare key to her flat?'

'It was just . . . she asked me. So I said I would. I expect she asked me because I'm the one in charge. I don't know. I didn't ask her. She just . . .' He trailed into silence.

'Was that when you showed her how to set the alarm?' Farnham said.

Massey was silent for a bit too long. 'No,' he said.

'So when was that?'

'I didn't show her . . .' Massey was struggling

323

now. He was lying, and he knew that Farnham knew he was lying. 'She might have needed to get in the gallery,' he said. 'If she locked herself out and I wasn't there.'

Farnham waited, letting his scepticism show. 'I didn't kill her!' Massey said, suddenly.

'No one is saying you did,' Farnham said. 'So, tell me about this key.'

He wouldn't meet Farnham's eye. He shifted uncomfortably in his chair and addressed the wall above Farnham's head. 'I kind of knew her,' he said. 'I thought she needed looking after. And the flat was empty. It wasn't going to be let for months.'

'You "kind of" knew her, Jonathan. What does that mean? How long have you "kind of" known her?'

'I can't . . .' Massey caught Farnham's eye and stopped. 'About five years,' he said. Farnham waited. 'I've got . . . I was working on something. Only I was teaching, I'm still . . . it still isn't finished. Things get in the way. I got interested in these photographs of children in care. You know, "Will you be my parent?" – that kind of thing. So I was taking pictures of the real children, the kids out on the streets, the ones who sell themselves and take drugs and die young mostly. I was going to call it "Will you be my parent?" That's how I met Cara. She was with this other girl, Sheryl. They were kids, really. Just kids. Sheryl was in trouble already, but Cara wasn't. She posed for me and I gave her money. So she wouldn't need to.'

'How old was she?' Farnham said.

'Fifteen,' Massey said. Then, defensively, 'They weren't like that. It wasn't that kind of photograph. I'll show you if . . .'

'And when she needed somewhere to live?' Farnham prompted.

Massey nodded. 'What was the harm?' he said.

Farnham picked up one of the sketchbooks they'd found in the search of Massey's office. He opened the book at a page with drawings: a naked female torso, the breasts barely formed, the body thin and childlike. 'Let me get this clear,' he said. 'You were having sex with Cara Hobson?'

Massey went white. '*No!* Is that all you can think of?'

Farnham shrugged. 'She was a prostitute, Mr Massey.'

Massey seemed to be struggling for words. 'She was just . . . I didn't know that. I didn't want . . . she was so . . . beautiful. She posed for me. That's all. I did sketches. You've seen them. I took some pictures. You can see those if you want. She came to the gallery. It wasn't often. Now and then.' Farnham could see beads of sweat on his forehead. 'That's all. I wasn't there the night she was killed. You know that. I was in Leeds.'

He had been. That was one of the first things they'd checked. And the murders of Cara Hobson and Stacy McDonald carried the mark of the same killer. But the picture that was forming in Farnham's head was an unpleasant one. The small, childlike figure of Cara Hobson, the meticulous detail of the drawing as though every line of the girl's body had been devotedly recorded.

Alibi or no, Farnham wanted to look at Jonathan Massey very closely.

CHAPTER 14

Something woke Eliza. She sat up, throwing off a dream of soft footsteps and someone singing in the night. It was dark. She reached out automatically for the bedside light, but her hand encountered emptiness. The room was cold, and the air flowed across her in a stream of ice. Cara had left the door open . . . No! She was suddenly wide awake. She was at Maggie's, she'd fallen asleep. She sat up, her eyes straining in the dark. There was silence.

She could remember waking up in her flat the night before. She shook her head to clear the images, and listened again. She was at Maggie's. She could remember now, sorting through the cuttings and the letters, the sudden tiredness and lying down on the bed. It was probably a good thing something had woken her up, or she might have stayed here all night. Something in the street? The house was set too far back from the road. Noises from the street wouldn't have disturbed her, especially not here round the back where there was just the dark yard and the gennel behind it.

She got her bearings, and reached behind her for the switch to turn on the light. She tugged it, but nothing happened. She tried again, and again. Nothing. She couldn't remember if it had been working earlier. She sat up, disentangling herself from the blanket that was wrapped round her and swung her feet on to the floor. She needed to know what time it was, but it was too dark to see her watch. She hadn't contacted Laura. It might be too late to phone.

She couldn't stay here. The cold was seeping into her bones. She became more aware of the flow of chill air that seemed to be coming from the bedroom door. She hunted round with her feet until she found her shoes and slipped them on. She used the blanket as a shawl, and groped her way across the room. She tried the light switch by the door, in case the one over the bed was faulty, but it didn't work.

Neither did the switch in the corridor. She pressed it, but again, nothing happened. She stood for a moment, puzzled. This light had been working earlier, she was sure. Was there a power cut? Maybe she should try and get her stuff together and go.

But she could feel the cold drifting down the corridor from the small kitchen. She felt her way along the corridor and into the off-shot. The cold was intense. Her eyes were becoming accustomed to the darkness now, and she could see a lighter rectangle that was the open door.

It was a second before her mind took it in. The open door. The back door was open.

She hadn't locked it. Her mind seized on that. The door must have blown open in the night. But she'd checked it. She could remember doing that. It had been firmly bolted. She pressed the light switch again and again, but nothing happened. She felt around on the worktop and found the box of matches that she had seen earlier by the cooker. She let the pale light of the flame illuminate the door. The match dropped from her fingers and flickered on the lino before it went out.

The bolts had been pulled back.

Everything was still and quiet, but now the silence had a waiting, watching feel. The implications of what had happened were starting to sink in. The door had been unbolted from the inside. Someone had been here while she slept, someone had . . . Her hands were shaking. She had to get out. Her phone? Where had she left her phone?

Back in the bedroom, it was back in the bedroom. She took a deep breath and went into the blackness of the corridor and the bedroom. The bedside table was at the far side. She could remember putting her phone down there. She crawled across the bed and ran her hands over the table. The phone was there.

There was a crash from the back of the flat, from the kitchen where the door opened on to the silent yard and the gennel in the night. She gave up any pretence of calm and ran for the front door, ricocheting off the walls of the corridor, her hands scrabbling with the lock, and then she was outside, slamming the door shut behind her. Her breath was coming fast as she tried to get her bearings. The high walls cut off the light, and the moon was hidden. The garden was black night.

She oriented herself. The door was behind her. She was facing down the path. The steps would be over there, to her right. She began to walk, quickly but carefully, away from the house.

Everything was silent, and then, clear as anything in the still night, from the house behind her, the *click* of a latch, and she was running again, half-falling down the steps, her hands scrabbling against the rough bricks of the wall and then she was back on the road, her feet slipping on the ice, her breath coming in shallow gasps as the cold air attacked her throat. Her car, she needed to get to her car. But she'd left her bag, her keys – they were back in the flat.

She made herself stop, listen again. The road was dark and silent. An owl called in the distance. The pavement shone with ice. There was no one in sight. But she had her phone. She pressed the button to make the display light up. The battery was low – she'd left it on as she slept. One call. If she phoned the police . . . an open door, nothing missing, things going bump in the night – they had their priorities. The flat had been standing empty, was known to be empty. They wouldn't pull the stops out to catch an opportunist thief who would be long gone by now. She'd put the number of Roy Farnham's mobile into her phone that morning. 'If there's anything else . . .'

She was moving again, a ragged stumble down the icy pavement as her feet slipped. She pressed the 'call' button. For a horrible moment, she thought she was going to get the message service, then he answered. 'Farnham.' He sounded as if he might have been asleep, and she realized she had no idea what time it was.

'It's Eliza,' she said. 'There's been . . .' She didn't know where to start.

'Where are you? Are you OK?' He sounded awake and alert now.

'Yes, I'm at Walkley, I . . .' She told him as coherently as she could what had happened. It sounded garbled and melodramatic as she spoke, but he responded to the urgency in her voice.

'Are you out of there?' he said.

'Yes, I'm outside, I'm trying to get down to the main road.' She listened again. Feet on the steps behind her? *Imagination!* 'Roy!'

'Get away from there. Keep your phone switched on and keep your finger on the SOS button, right?'

'Roy, listen, the battery's low.'

'OK. Get away, get to the road. There'll be someone with you in –' The phone beeped and was silent. The power had gone. She was very alone now. She had to get down the hill, get to lights, to people. She could see the streetlights below her, but there was no traffic, no life, just the empty pavements gleaming in the frozen night. She listened again. Nothing. She tried to quicken her pace, but her feet were slipping on the ice, sending her sideways into the road. Her shoes had no grip.

And now she could hear the sound of a car coming down the hill behind her, the crackle of the wheels on the Tarmac as the car freewheeled closer. She began to run. She had to get to somewhere where there might be passing traffic, people, anything. Her feet slid out from underneath her, and she fell half into the road, aware of the head-lights of the car illuminating her, aware of the sharp sting of the Tarmac where it had cut her knees. She was trying to get to her feet – he could see her now and she had to get away – as she heard the sound of a car door slamming shut and feet moving fast on the pavement towards her.

Two uniformed officers were helping her to her feet, and Eliza felt her breathing begin to slow down, and the road was just the steep hill where Maggie's house was, and the night was a still winter's night, with knives of frost in the air that stabbed at her chest as she tried to get her breath. 'Are you all right, love?' one of them said. He was a thickset man, solid and reassuring.

She took a deep breath. 'I'm OK,' she said. 'I think I panicked.' She told them about the flat, and the sound of the door in the night.

'You were lucky. We were just round the corner

when the call came through. Let's have a look then.'

His partner had already disappeared up the steps towards Maggie's. She followed his bulk, watching the play of light from his torch as it illuminated the walls, the steps with the dead leaves of autumn still lying. It must be close to dawn, she thought as she reached the top of the steps. There was a faint light illuminating the garden, instead of the impenetrable blackness she remembered. Then one of the officers was snapping instructions into his radio, and she came back to the reality of the crackle of flames and the smell of burning.

The front room, the room where she'd sat the night before, sorting the papers, was ablaze.

'Are you sure about that, Eliza? Do you need to go over it again?' Farnham watched Eliza carefully as she shook her head. She'd had a shock on top of the shock of finding Stacy McDonald's body; she'd had two broken nights and she had been cold and panicked when she'd called him. But she looked calm now, seemed very certain about what she was saying. He sent his mind back to his attempts to get her to clarify the time she had heard footsteps from the flat next door the night that Cara died, and decided that she was well able to differentiate between what she knew, and what she was uncertain about.

He'd given instructions for the patrol car to bring her in when he heard about the fire. Strictly speaking, this was nothing to do with him, but there were some coincidences that he wasn't happy with, and he wasn't prepared to leave it. Twice now, someone had been up to no good close to Eliza Eliot – once near her flat at the gallery, once at Maggie Chapman's. He'd stepped back and let the official systems take over, but he wanted Eliza's story on his own record, in the kind of detail he doubted any investigation into the break-in would get.

She clasped her hands round the cup of canteen coffee he'd been able to rustle up, as if she still couldn't get warm. 'I dropped one match on to the kitchen floor. It went out. I didn't have a lit match anywhere else in the flat. I'm sure.'

'OK.' Farnham was satisfied. The fire had taken hold very quickly, far more quickly than a dropped match on to a tiled floor would account for, and it had been focused in the front room of the flat, away from the kitchen where Eliza had been using lit matches to find her way. By the time the fire had been put out, the front room had been a mess of smoke-blackened walls dripping with water. Someone had set that fire.

And his investigation was tripping over the threads of an earlier death. Cara's body had been found very close to the place where Ellie Chapman had been found. Maggie Chapman had been buried the day before Cara was killed. And now there had been a break-in at Maggie Chapman's flat.

Child killings tended to stick in the mind. Most

serving officers prayed that they would never have to investigate one. And now he had a dead thirteen-year-old on his hands. Was there a connection? He couldn't see one. There were things he needed to look up and people he needed to talk to. But it was after four and he'd managed – what? – two hours' sleep before he'd been woken by Eliza's call. He had a briefing to conduct in a few hours. Eliza looked as bad as he felt. She was slumped wearily in her chair, fighting to keep her eyes open. 'Where are you going to go?' he said. She couldn't go back to her flat.

'A friend's. But I need to get some stuff.'

'We've finished up at the flats,' he said. 'Can you get in? You didn't leave your key back there?'

She shook her head. 'It was in my bag.' They'd managed to retrieve Eliza's bag from the flat, but her car keys and her other things were buried somewhere among the ashes.

'OK. I'll take you back.' He needed to get out before the working day proper began. 'There's an all-night café not too far out of our way. Do you know it?'

She nodded. 'Near the station?' she said.

He remembered their last meeting in a café. 'How do you feel about breakfast with a strange man again?'

He surprised her into a smile. 'OK,' she said. 'But we can get something at the flat. I've got coffee and stuff.'

Her flat was five minutes' drive away at this quiet

time of the morning. The sky was clear and the moon was full as he pulled up in front of the gallery. She took him up the outside staircase.

He looked at the concrete stairwell as they went up. It was poorly lit with dark landings. It seemed secure enough, the bottom door had a good lock on it, but he still didn't like the idea of Eliza coming up and down here by herself at night. 'Why don't you use the gallery entrance?'

'I do usually,' she said. 'But this is quicker when the gallery is closed.'

'Use the other entrance,' he said. 'Until this is sorted.'

She unlocked the door at the top of the staircase. 'I wasn't too bothered before,' she said. 'I mean, it's secure enough.' She was opening the door. He moved quickly beside her and went through ahead of her, blocking her view of the empty corridor, the shadows in the dark of the winter morning. She looked at him assessingly for a second. 'I've got to get used to it,' she said, 'if I'm going to stay here.'

'Now may not be the best time,' he said.

She didn't say anything, just unlocked the door to her flat.

He hadn't been here before. His first impression was one of space and shadows. A window at the far end of the long room gleamed faintly with the reflection of the moon on the canal. Eliza pressed a wall switch, and the window went black, as pools of light illuminated the room, the kitchen area with its red

336

tiles, the groups of chairs with throws in vivid greens and deep reds, scatter cushions lying randomly across them. An easel stood at the far end of the room in front of the window.

Eliza checked the answering machine and went over to the kitchen. After a while, the smell of coffee began to drift through the flat. He wandered across the room, his policeman's eye checking the light on the machine: 0. No messages. He looked at the canvas on the easel, one that she was, presumably, working on. At first, it looked a mess, then his eye began to pick out bits of the canal, the arched bridge, a broken fall-pipe with a dead shrub, a mat of weed and rubbish on the water. He frowned. He couldn't understand why she didn't paint what she could see out of the window, if she wanted to paint the canal.

'Sugar?' she said.

'One, please.'

She brought two cups of coffee across to where he was standing. She gave him one, and stood beside him, looking at the painting. 'I started that the day . . . the day before yesterday,' she said.

The day they'd found Stacy McDonald. He didn't want to get on to that topic. 'Why don't you paint that?' He gestured towards the black square of the window.

She glanced up at him. 'I have.'

He shook his head, baffled.

'It's . . .' She was searching for the words. 'Look, you've got this idea in your head that's the canal.

To you it's a place where you're investigating something, where a murder happened. To me, it's – well, it *is* that, but it's a lot of different things as well. I'm trying to paint *that* canal. It isn't just a line of water under a line of sky. Think about it. You never see it like that and you never think about it like that, unless you're thinking about a picture of it, right?'

This was all a bit arty-farty for him. 'A canal is a canal,' he said. 'That suits me.'

She looked at him for a minute as she thought about this, then she smiled. '*The Hay Wain*,' she said. 'Fair enough.' There were shadows under her eyes. She pushed her hair back off her face as she kept her gaze on him. He raised his eyebrows in query, and she said, 'I probably wouldn't do this if I wasn't too tired to think straight,' and she reached up and put her hands on his shoulders, and kissed him lightly.

His first reaction was surprise, then he put his arms round her and pulled her closer. She kissed him again, a warmer, longer kiss. In his fatigue-drugged state, he wasn't prepared to listen to the voice of reason and common sense that told him it was mad to let this happen with someone who was so closely tied in with an investigation. He was happy to go with it, to let her take this as far as she wanted to, and she seemed to want to take it all the way. She pulled his jacket open and pressed herself closer to him and he kissed her again.

He tightened his arms round her and lifted her off her feet. He walked her over to the bed, let her drop, and she fell back on to the covers, pulling him down with her. He slipped his hands under her jersey and eased it over her head. She was wearing a thin blouse, but no bra, and he could see the shadow of her breasts. He ran his fingers across them, feeling the nipples harden under his touch. He kissed them through the fabric, catching them gently with his teeth, and he heard her breath quicken. He unbuttoned the blouse and peeled it off her shoulders and down her arms. Her breasts were small. He could cup them in his hand.

'They aren't very big,' she said, ruefully.

'They're beautiful,' he said.

She kicked off her shoes, and he undid the fastenings on her trousers, slipping them down her legs. 'Wait,' she said. 'I'd better . . .' She gestured towards a door that was, presumably, the bathroom. She stood up, the whiteness of her skin glimmering in the half-light. 'I won't be long,' she said.

He felt dizzy with the mixture of excitement, confusion and fatigue. He lay back against the pillows, aware of a faint perfume that said 'Eliza' to him. She had come on to him so strongly and he couldn't understand where that had come from, didn't want to think about it. He was too tired to think. His thought processes seemed to be breaking up. He had to be back in the incident room in a couple of hours and he had to . . .

Her painting. The pieces and parts of the canal that shifted and coalesced, the beauty and the decay, and the discarded remains, the dark hair floating like weeds on the surface of the water. Like the painting, the swollen body floating in a sea of putrescence, the tortured figure, mutilated and eyeless, decaying at the end of a rope. And so many more, the flames and the knives and the pikes and spears, and it wouldn't make a pattern, not a pattern he could read, just a pattern that said madness, and torture, and death, and then there was darkness and after darkness . . . It all drifted away into chaos.

Farnham was coming back from a long way away. There was something wrong. This wasn't his bed, he was lying on top of a quilt with something light covering him. He could smell coffee. He lay there in the blankness of first waking, then his memory began to work. He reached out, and he breathed again when he found the space on the bed beside him was empty. The images from the night before were coming back to him. Eliza kissing him, Eliza lying on the bed, Eliza, naked, fading into the shadows. *Shit!*

He pushed himself up on to his elbow, rubbing his eyes with his thumb and forefinger. 'Eliza?' he said. Someone had taken his shoes off, and pulled a red throw over him. Christ, what time was it? He looked at his watch and relaxed a bit. Seven-thirty.

'I was just going to wake you.' Eliza came into

view wearing a dressing gown. Her feet were bare and her hair was wrapped in a towel. She looked a bit wary, a bit defensive.

'I'm sorry, Eliza.' He'd fallen asleep. She'd been naked on the bed with him and he'd fallen asleep. It would be funny if it wasn't so . . . Though it was probably for the best. Now he could think straight, it would have been crazy to let a complication like that get in the way of the investigation.

She relaxed a bit. 'I don't usually have that effect.'

'You didn't,' he said. 'It was me.' He couldn't leave it there. 'Listen, Eliza. Last night . . .'

'I know. It's OK. It's a bad idea at the moment. We were both a bit looped.' She unwrapped the towel and shook her head. Damp hair fell round her shoulders. 'It's OK,' she said. 'But you need to get to work. Look, I've got stuff here. You can have a shower and I'll do us breakfast.'

'You still get breakfast with a strange man,' he said.

'Not so strange,' she said. 'Not so strange.'

She was setting the table when he came out of the shower, feeling more rested and awake than he had for days.

'I've done some eggs and some toast,' she said. 'Want to eat?' Her hair, as it dried, was curling in tendrils round her face.

She put plates and the coffee pot on the table, pushing aside a pile of folders that lay there. 'All that stuff,' she said.

He looked a query at her.

'Maggie's stuff – her papers. I was going to decide what to do with it all, and now it's destroyed, most of it. I should have burned it in the first place.' Her laugh was without humour. 'And I should have listened to her landlord.'

Suddenly he was working again. 'Her landlord? Why?'

'He phoned – he was worried about Maggie's stuff. He said that there'd been kids or something hanging round the flat.'

Farnham made a note to check. An empty flat, a bit of publicity – it could easily have attracted vandals or cranks. But he still wasn't happy. 'These papers, this stuff that got burned, what was it?'

'Oh, letters and newspaper cuttings.' She frowned. 'And photographs. But I saved some of those. I brought a pile of them over a few days ago. Look –' She pushed a photograph across the table to him. Eliza sat on a patch of grass, her long legs tucked underneath her. Beside her, smiling a gap-toothed smile at the camera, was a little girl – five? six? 'Ellie,' she said.

He nodded. There didn't seem much to say. But he needed to know more about this fire. 'Whereabouts in the flat were they, these papers and things?' He'd left instructions for as much as possible to be preserved, but he had a feeling that there wouldn't be much, not of the kind of ephemera Eliza was describing.

'On the table in the front room,' she said. She

was looking at the photograph, running her finger across its surface.

Where the fire had been. 'What were they about, the letters, the cuttings?' She'd remember now, while her mind was focused on something else.

'Mark Fraser. The court case. The appeal.' She shrugged. 'What you'd expect.'

'Nothing else?' He noticed that she was frowning, looking puzzled. 'What?' he said.

'There was something about drugs,' she said. 'About people dying, overdoses, something like that.'

One of the overdose victims had led them to Ellie's body. 'And the letters?' he said.

'Mostly about the appeal,' she said. 'The campaign, trying to get support, you know.'

So what would anyone want to destroy in that lot? Names? Addresses? Would any of it be duplicated in the stuff Eliza had here? Who would know she had it?

The coffee was rich and strong, and he could feel the caffeine starting to work. 'And the photographs?' he said.

'They were all Ellie. I've got some of them here, like I said. The ones at the flat were more recent, Ellie when she was a bit older.' She was looking at the photograph she'd shown him, turning it round in her hands. 'And there were the ones from that day. The day on the river.'

The day Ellie Chapman disappeared. Anything?

But the original investigation would have gone through those. There would be copies with the case files. Where would be the mileage in destroying those? 'Good coffee,' he said, to lighten the atmosphere. He needed to think.

She refilled their cups. 'Bad coffee is a crime against nature. I think we've both got a day ahead that needs a caffeine jolt.' She got up from the table and went across to a small chest of drawers. 'I just remembered something,' she said. She was checking through the top drawer as she spoke. 'Here –' She had something in her hand as she came back across the room. She held it out to him. 'These,' she said.

She gave him two photographs. He looked at them. In the first one, a fair-haired child was leaning over the side of a boat in a fine rainbow spray of water. The second one showed two girls standing on a boat. They were studies in colour, the blue of the water and the sky, the heavy shadows of the woods on the bank, the brightness of the children, the yellow of their hair, the flushed gold of their skin, the crushed-raspberry pink of their mouths.

'Those must have got separated from the others,' Eliza said. 'I brought them across here on my first visit.'

'And they're . . . ?' The scene made it clear what they were, the boat, the river.

'From that day.' The camera had been set in date mode: *20.6.98*. The day of Ellie Chapman's disappearance. 'There's Ellie, look, and the other one must be Fraser's daughter.'

Kerry Fraser. It looked as though being Kerry Fraser's friend was not a good long-term option.

She was still looking at the pictures. 'There's something . . .' she said. He waited. She shook her head. 'I don't know.'

'Can I take these?' He wasn't sure why he wanted them. It was the same feeling that she had expressed: there was 'something'. He wanted time to think about it. But now he'd spent enough time on this. He hesitated. This was going to be a tricky moment to negotiate. 'Look, I have to go. What are you going to do? You can't stay here.'

The flat had a warm and welcoming feel, but beyond the door, someone had left the relics of violent death, and below her, in the gallery where she spent her days, images of those deaths occurred and recurred on the walls around her. She couldn't stay here.

She bit her lip and looked away. 'I think . . . No, I'm going to stay with a friend. She would have put me up last night, only I fell asleep at Maggie's.' She shook herself. 'I can't believe what happened. It's just – it isn't real somehow.'

'What about now?' he said. 'Can I take you anywhere?' Not that he really had the time. He needed to be back at the incident room.

She shook her head. 'I've got to go down to the gallery.' She forestalled his objection. 'I know we can't open today, but there are things I've got to do. I don't know where Jonathan is . . .' She looked at him and he shook his head. 'If Jonathan doesn't come in, then I'm in charge. So . . .' She shrugged.

He wasn't happy about it, but the gallery would be safe enough. His own people would be in and out for most of the day. 'OK. But you won't be here on your own at night?'

'No. I'm going to Laura's. Do you think . . . ?' She tried to frame the question, then left it open.

'I don't know what to think, Eliza,' he said. 'I think you shouldn't be here on your own.' It was time he was leaving. He needed to be careful now. He wanted to cool things back to – it couldn't go back to investigating officer and witness, but away from the raw excitement that had caught them both in the sleep-deprived aftermath of the night.

She walked to the fire-escape door with him. 'I'll need to lock it behind you once you've gone,' she said. 'Roy . . .' He looked at her. 'Thank you.' She gave him a quick hug and stood back.

'Eliza,' he said. 'Look, I'm sorry.'

'It's OK,' she said again, but he had a feeling it wasn't. As he went down the stairs, he reflected on the curse of professionalism.

Tina sat at the back of the briefing room, keeping away from Farnham's direct gaze. She didn't know what to do. The look that Daniel Flynn had directed at her as she unlocked her car had been redolent with a meaning she had been unable to interpret. She wanted to go and see him, find out what he meant, what his plans were. But that would be the stupidest thing of all. Sense would send her to Farnham – a confession of the liaison, no need to mention the drugs – but it was too late for that. He wouldn't forgive her silence.

'. . . other contacts of Cara Hobson's? DC Barraclough?'

West nudged her and she jumped. Farnham had asked her a question. Cursing herself, she tried to reconstruct what he'd said. Cara Hobson, the interview with Denise Greene . . . Cara's friend. 'Sheryl,' she said. 'Sheryl Hewitt.'

'Have you managed to track her yet?'

Tina gathered her thoughts quickly. Sheryl Hewitt. 'No, sir. I've been looking at the boats.' Was she in the shit again?

'OK,' Farnham said, and Tina released the breath she had been holding. 'But we need to give this priority now. We're looking for a connection between Stacy McDonald and Cara Hobson. On the surface, there isn't a lot. Stacy lived at home with her parents and her two sisters. She wasn't one for going out, clubbing, anything like that. She seems to have been a pretty average thirteen-year-old. One other thing that may or may not be relevant: Stacy's best friend was Kerry Fraser – Mark Fraser's daughter. DS Martin . . . ?'

Tina watched the smart and efficient Judith Martin as she stood up. Martin was younger than she was, and she was a sergeant already. 'I talked to Kerry Fraser yesterday,' she said. 'Kerry says that Stacy played truant on Friday to meet a boyfriend in town. She claimed she didn't know who the boyfriend was. She got upset when I pressed her . . .' A murmur ran round the group. 'She was genuinely upset,' Martin said, 'but I'm not sure exactly what was upsetting her. Kerry's very hostile towards the police.'

Tina had heard about the arrest of Mark Fraser. It had been botched. It had been violent and high key, reflecting the tabloid-fuelled rage the community felt about Ellie's death. Nine-year-old Kerry had been in the house and had tried to fight the officers who were taking her father away.

Farnham was speaking again. Now he was talking about the Ellie Chapman case. There'd been a fire at Maggie Chapman's flat, and Eliza Eliot had been involved. Past cases, past deaths. Tina saw it again, that fleeting image, that glimpse that her eye couldn't interpret until it was over, the shadow, falling like a bird from high above her . . . She shook herself back to the moment, and saw Farnham looking at her. 'It's on the canal,' she said abruptly.

'Barraclough?' Farnham said.

'Sorry, sir. I was thinking about the Chapman case. Conisbrough is on the canal – it just seemed like another connection.' She felt her face flush. She hadn't been concentrating, and now it was obvious.

But Farnham took her comment seriously. 'Yes. Don't forget that. As DC Barraclough pointed out, the Chapman case is linked to the canal. You're actually on the river at Conisbrough, but it's part of the same waterway, the Sheffield and South Yorkshire Navigation. And it's a long way from these recent cases – about seventeen miles from here. But Ellie's body was found close to where Cara Hobson was found. Like DC Barraclough says, it's a link. OK . . .' He allocated the tasks for the day.

Tina tried to concentrate, but her mind kept drifting back to the Chapman case. She could vaguely remember the newspaper coverage. Maggie Chapman hadn't attracted the usual amount of sympathy. She had been a bit too arty, a bit too bohemian, a potential home wrecker as well, given her relationship with Mark Fraser – there had been a subtext of suspicion to the early newspaper reports. It looked as though the investigating team, too, had had their doubts about her.

Farnham's voice interrupted her. 'DC Barraclough?'

She tensed, but he seemed unconcerned. 'Sir?'

'I want you to check something at the library.' She relaxed. He told her about the cuttings Eliza Eliot had seen at Maggie Chapman's house. 'Apparently she was interested in the overdose cases as well. I've had the fire people on,' he said. 'There's nothing left of those papers. I want you to try and sort out those newspaper reports, OK? I want the reports from the Chapman case, but I want those drug stories as well. Eli—, the Eliot woman said that they were from the local paper. I want to find out what Maggie Chapman's interest was.'

'Yes, sir.'

He was still looking at her with a slight frown. 'Are you all right, Tina?'

'Yes, I'm fine.'

He kept looking at her, and she could feel herself starting to go red, then he said, 'OK. Get on with it.'

CHAPTER 15

Eliza watched Roy disappear down the stairway, feeling strangely empty. She didn't know what she wanted from Roy Farnham. Last night, he had seemed like a haven in a world that was proving increasingly unpredictable and dangerous. Fatigue and fear had left her spaced out, and she had wanted, needed, the surcease of sex, yes, but also the warmth and the closeness. But making a move – that had been a bad mistake. And now, she wondered if she was reacting to Daniel's rejection, coming on to the nearest attractive man. What did she and Roy Farnham have in common?

They were both involved in murder, that was what they had in common. But for a brief time, she had felt like she hadn't felt since Madrid, had just wanted to abandon herself to his mouth, to his hands . . . She shook herself out of that reverie. Now, when she saw him, she was going to be tense with embarrassment. She remembered how she'd felt when she'd come back to the bed and found him sprawled out asleep. For a moment, she'd been angry, wanted to shake him awake, but she'd been aware earlier of his grey-faced exhaustion, and as she stood there looking at him, at the lines of tension on his face even when he was asleep, he'd seemed suddenly vulnerable, and her anger had vanished. She'd taken his shoes off, careful not to disturb him, and unbuttoned his shirt before covering him with one of the throws off the chairs. She'd slept for a short time herself, curled up in one of the chairs, but it had been a fitful, unrefreshing sleep.

More than anything now, she wanted to lie down. Her body ached with fatigue, and she felt cold, a chill in the bone that radiators and warm clothes couldn't touch. But she had the gallery to deal with. It was almost eight. She picked up the phone and keyed in Jonathan's number. He answered after ten rings, as she was about to hang up. His voice sounded dull. No, he wasn't coming in. There was no point. The gallery wasn't going to be open. The exhibition was moving on in a few days. They'd missed the boat. He listened to her arguments for a minute, then said, 'Do what you like, Eliza,' and put the phone down.

She sank into the chair. It wasn't fair, she was too tired, she couldn't cope. The thought of lying down for half an hour was almost irresistible, but she knew if she gave in to her tiredness now, she would sleep the clock round. She needed to get dressed. She noticed, with the detachment of fatigue, her clothes from yesterday lying on the floor by the bed where Roy had discarded them. She picked them up, noting the faint smell of musty dampness that had infused Maggie's. She shoved them into the washer and went into the bathroom, dumping her dressing gown on the floor. Then she turned on the shower again, and stood underneath it for ten minutes, letting the cool water wake her up a bit.

She needed to think, to make some decisions about the gallery. If everything got sorted today, there was no reason why they shouldn't open tomorrow. People would want to see the exhibition, especially now. Eliza hadn't seen the papers, but the link between Daniel's exhibition and Stacy McDonald's death would surely have been widely reported. She got dressed. Jeans would be fine for today. Her hair had dried in a tangle. She pulled the brush through it and tied it back. She was in the gallery by eight-thirty, to find a message from the agency that was supplying extra staff for the week of the exhibition. Suddenly, they had no one available. She wasn't surprised, but it was something else that she needed to deal with urgently. It didn't matter for today, but she couldn't open the gallery tomorrow without the staff. She tried phoning Mel, but there was no reply.

Farnham's team were already at work in the exhibition gallery when she came downstairs from her flat. She watched through the door, letting the now familiar images draw her eye. The death armies, the fleeing children, the young girl with the haunted eyes, the hanging . . . She stopped. She needed to get to work. She walked briskly down the stairs, aware of the empty silence around her. Then she heard the sound of the entrance doors, and footsteps across the floor.

Mel came in. She stopped when she saw Eliza. 'What's going on?' she said. She looked wary. 'Are you all right?' she added after a moment.

Eliza didn't want to talk about it, particularly not to Mel. 'Yes, thank you, I'm fine. We've got a lot to do. There's only the two of us. We can't open today. But we need to make contact with the people who are coming on Friday to move the exhibition, and there's been a lot of press interest, and some TV, I think, so we need to let them know we're available. I want you to check the e-mails and the messages, and sort them out for me to answer before lunch.'

'Where's Jonathan?' Mel said after a pause.

'He isn't coming in. He's ill.' Eliza could hear her voice sounding abrupt, but she made no attempt to modify it. She was angry with Jonathan for folding, for leaving her to carry the can. 'We just need to get through the essentials and then get off.'

'Ill, how?' Mel waited, then, when Eliza didn't reply, made a face. 'Is Daniel coming in?'

'I don't know. Come on, we need to get this lot sorted. I don't want to be here any longer than necessary.' She didn't need Roy Farnham's warning to feel uneasy in the gallery now. She left Mel sullenly sorting through the post and went to her office, where she began to go through the proposed list of exhibitions for their next season. Having got

The Triumph of Death, Eliza had ambitious plans for the artists they would be exhibiting in the future, unless their new notoriety would . . . but she didn't need to worry about that. Whatever happened, the profile of the gallery was now raised. The artists would come. So she might as well make the most of it.

Kerry spent the day in dread. Every class, every time the door opened, every time she saw a teacher coming towards her, she expected the words: *Kerry Fraser, the police want to see you.* She didn't know why she hadn't bunked off, except she didn't want to be at home. Mum hadn't even got up – it was going to be a bad day.

But as the morning went on, no one came for her and she began to relax. When the maths teacher wasn't looking, she reached into her bag and checked her phone. She'd turned the 'audible alert' off. But there was no message. She'd tried and tried to phone Lyn, but she wasn't answering.

There was something else in her bag, something she'd picked up off the mat this morning as she left for school. She hadn't opened the letter. She didn't want to, because she knew what it would be. It would be another piece of paper all about what happened to you in prison and people killing themselves. She'd look at it later.

At lunch-time, she went and sat on the ground in the sun, her back against the wall. Out of the wind, it was warm.

She could remember another sunny day.

The castle had been boring. It was on top of a green hill and it was all falling down. But the water had been as blue as anything and Ellie had run up the green hill and Kerry had followed her, and they had slid down, rolling to the bottom, and they were both screaming, and Dad had called them a couple of big kids.

And they'd had a picnic. Ellie's mum did good picnics. 'I can't come with you.' Kerry could remember her saying that. 'I've got to get this finished.' And Dad had said, 'Don't worry. We'll be fine.' And they'd smiled at each other. Kerry and Ellie had a game where they pretended to be sisters together, pretended that they lived in the same house and that Ellie's mum was Kerry's mum.

It had been so hot that day. And they'd sat down by the river. Then Ellie wanted the toilet, and Dad said, 'Go in the bushes, Ellie,' but Ellie didn't like that. She always waited until there was a proper toilet. Only Dad didn't know that. And Ellie went off into the bushes, and then Dad had gone off. 'Wait here,' he'd said to Kerry, and she hadn't minded because there were strawberries with the picnic and she'd sat there eating them and the sun had been so warm on her back, and the sky was blue and the water was blue. And then, ages after, Dad had come back. But Ellie never did.

The last day.

'Move over.' She blinked and she was back in the

playground. Marie was standing there, watching her with some of the others. She moved up to make room and they talked about boys and clothes and music and things that didn't really matter, and it was nice. She told Marie she would do her hair, and Marie asked if she would put some sequins on a T-shirt, and it was almost like having friends again. Until they knew. Until they found out.

She went to the toilet before they went in for afternoon registration. She locked the cubicle door and took the letter out of her bag. She didn't want to open it. She sat there staring at it. She could throw it away – but she had to know. She slipped her finger under the flap and pulled it open. Inside, there was a newspaper cutting: SEX SLAYER BLINDED IN JAIL ATTACK. She read the article. A man had been attacked in prison, a man who'd done things to kids, who'd done what they said Dad had done. And now he was blind. Her hand shook as she screwed the piece of paper up, screwed it up and threw it down the toilet. She flushed it, and flushed it again. Gone.

'Are you there, Kerry? You are so going to be late.' Marie, waiting for her, impatient. 'News flash! The bell went five minutes ago.'

She didn't know what she was going to do.

Tina had no problems tracking down the newspaper articles about Ellie Chapman's death. She skimmed the headlines, but nothing leapt off the page at her, nothing to connect these with Cara or

Stacy. She wondered if Farnham was going down a blind alley here. The drug stories were harder to find. They hadn't made the national press. Using Ellie Chapman's disappearance as a starting point, she began searching the archives of the local paper. That took most of the morning, but by the end, she had the picture. A batch of pure heroin had hit the streets around the time of Ellie's disappearance, and several addicts had died.

The stories appeared as unrelated incidents at first – a dead man, a known addict, found in a squat, two women treated for overdoses, just three-line paragraphs. Then the stories gained a little prominence as the deaths were linked: POLICE WARN OF HEROIN DANGER ON STREET . . . THIRD DRUG DEATH IN SOUTH YORKSHIRE . . .

She almost missed the last story. Like the others, it wasn't front page. It was a couple of short columns tucked away at the bottom of a page, in the newspaper dated a week after the 'guilty' verdict had been passed on Mark Fraser. FORGOTTEN VICTIM IN ELLIE MURDER. She read through the article and realized that she, too, had forgotten. It was another drug death.

A girl had been found in a boat moored on the canal, a known haunt of the local junkie community. The dead girl had not at that stage been identified. A vicar who worked with the young homeless, with the young drug addicts, had castigated the authorities for their lack of interest in this death. 'We can't even give this dead child a name,' he'd said. A police spokesman had said that the matter was in hand and they were investigating a series of overdose deaths in young addicts that had occurred recently, but that they weren't looking for anyone else in connection with the teenager's death.

Tina frowned. Too many parallels. She thought about the recent deaths she had come across – those had been overdose deaths. She wondered if the dead girl had ever been identified. Her eyes were feeling heavy, and she shook her head to clear it. *Concentrate!*

She went back to the newspaper reports. She wanted to see if there had been any follow-up. The girl's death had been overshadowed by the tragic discovery on the towpath. Ellie's body had lain undiscovered in the bushes for months. But that wasn't where she'd been killed. The body had been moved. Tina remembered Farnham talking about that at the briefing. It had been concealed somewhere, sealed away somewhere warm and damp, the pathologist had speculated, and moved after three or four weeks.

Tina sat with the pile of papers. The still waters of the canal threaded their way through these killings – a boat that vanished from the water, a gallery that overlooked the canal, an exhibition that had some connection, a child abducted from the river side. She thought about Daniel Flynn talking to her at the private view. 'The processes of death and decay . . .' he'd said, leading her around the paintings and photo-montages. Art and death – the obsession wasn't new, Tina reminded herself. Brueghel demonstrated exactly the same fascination. Art and death and water. She went back to the articles.

Suspicion had fallen on Mark Fraser as a matter of course – he had been with the child when she vanished and witness evidence, supported initially by the evidence of his own daughter, said that he'd gone after Ellie, to look for her, according to his statement. To rape her and kill her, according to the prosecution. The evidence linking Fraser to the killing had been ambivalent. Fraser had been a teacher. He had had a relationship with Maggie Chapman – the perfect way of gaining access to Ellie, and gaining her trust. His wife was an alcoholic. She had had a young daughter when Fraser married her – another young child exposed to his perversion, another victim left unprotected. His stepdaughter had accused him of sexually abusing her, Fraser had denied it. Which he would. And the child-care team said that it was possible that Kerry, the younger child, had been abused as well. The interviews were inconclusive, but the child had talked about the secret and had then clammed up.

Where was his stepdaughter now? Tina made a note to check.

She went on through the newspapers. There was no mystery boat attached to Ellie's disappearance – all the traffic on the river that day

360

had been accounted for. A local man had reported screams in the woods near Conisbrough around the time of Ellie's disappearance, but he hadn't done anything about it. 'There's always kids screaming in those woods,' he'd said to a journalist. He hadn't known that a child was missing. The screams may have been nothing to do with Ellie anyway.

It was all tenuous. She made notes on what she'd found. Maybe someone else had uncovered a closer link – maybe Farnham was barking up the wrong tree entirely and she had wasted her morning.

And the dead girl, the addict whose end had been overshadowed by the finding of Ellie's body. Had anyone ever identified her? Was there a name on her grave? More trawling through the records. It was time to go back to the incident room. If the information she wanted wasn't in the Ellie Chapman file, then it would be in the records somewhere, if it was anywhere. Maybe the dead girl had never been identified – it wouldn't be the first time.

She collected up her photocopies and walked back through town. The fine morning had deteriorated, the sky was heavy with clouds, making the day dim, as though the sun had barely risen. It was starting to rain and the pavements were wet and slippery, the cobbles in the precinct making her ankles turn. They were designed for appearance, not for walking on, like a pair of fashion shoes.

The rain was getting heavier. She hadn't brought her umbrella, and by the time she got back, hurrying down the hill as she left the redeveloped part of the centre and began passing shop windows that were empty, or were piled high with the cheap and the tacky, her hair was wet and dripping down her neck, and the rain had started to penetrate her jacket.

She felt the familiar weight of depression descend as she came through the entrance, nodding a hello to the man on the reception desk and letting herself through into the main part of the building. It seemed such a short time ago that she had come into work every day with a sense of excitement and challenge, a sense of being involved in something important. Now, she felt a sense of dark apprehension as though she, by her actions, could push the case down the route she could remember so well, the route that led to the tower block and the death in the night that still haunted her dreams. *That wasn't your fault. That wasn't anything to do with you.* But the mantra didn't work, had never worked.

She looked back through the door as it closed behind her, back into the reception area, dull and functional with its grey lino and painted walls. Someone had left the building as she went through the door, someone who had caught her eye for some reason. She squinted back to see who it was, and her stomach lurched. Daniel Flynn.

★   ★   ★

Farnham had sent for the records relating to the Ellie Chapman case. He couldn't ignore the way this current investigation kept tripping over the threads from four years ago. He wasn't sure what he was looking for. He wanted to go through everything, try to pin down that nagging feeling of 'something', the 'something' that Eliza had felt as she looked at those photographs.

But he didn't have the resources to spare for a full review of the evidence. He'd already sent Barraclough on what was almost certainly a wild-goose chase to track down some press cuttings, and he'd told one of the uniformed officers to go through the files and find any photographs of the river trip. There was just the one set, apparently, developed from the film in Mark Fraser's camera, and these he now had on the desk in front of him.

He'd glanced at them, but he didn't have time to do any more. He was waiting for Daniel Flynn. He tapped his pen on his desk as he thought. Massey or Flynn? They were both disturbingly close to the killings. Flynn claimed to have been in Whitby the night that Cara died, but there was very little to substantiate that. Massey had been in Leeds. What about Stacy? They'd both been in the gallery the evening she vanished. Massey had gone on to a restaurant with Eliza Eliot, but after that, after about ten-thirty, he'd been alone. Daniel Flynn's story was even thinner. One of the waiters at the restaurant where he said he'd been had recognized his photograph, but said this man had been there with a woman. Flynn said he'd gone there alone.

Massey claimed his relationship with Cara Hobson had been 'innocent', whatever that may mean. In Farnham's book, there were more ways than one of having a sexual relationship. He said he'd moved her into the flat because she needed accommodation urgently, and she had repaid him by posing.

He read through Massey's statement again – the story depended on the woman who was alibiing Massey telling the truth. If she knew how serious the case was, if she knew the consequences of providing a false alibi, she might back down. They needed to put some pressure on her. He'd arranged for a search of Massey's flat. He needed to see what, if anything, turned up there.

He was thinking it through, when his phone rang. Daniel Flynn was downstairs, waiting to see him. 'OK, take him to the interview room,' he said. There was no reason, or none that he could find, for Flynn to harm Cara Hobson – there was no evidence he even knew her – but his exhibition, his *Triumph of Death*, was linked to the killings in some way. Farnham needed that link.

He'd gone through Flynn's previous statement earlier. He checked his notes, and tried to clear his mind as he went down the stairs. He was distracted, trying to work through the connections, two children by the river, an exhibition, a dead prostitute, a dead teenager . . . Eliza.

He brought his mind back to the moment as he sat down opposite Flynn. He thanked him for coming in, and flicked through the file on the desk in front of him. 'Mr Flynn,' he said. 'One thing that has been puzzling me – why did you bring your exhibition to a small gallery in the north of England? Why not go straight to London?'

Flynn shrugged. 'I come from Sheffield,' he said. 'It was a homage to my roots.' He said it with a light irony, but Farnham could detect a bitter note underlying the words.

'I see,' he said. 'OK, why this gallery?'

Flynn stared at the ceiling, thinking. 'Why not?' he said. Farnham waited. Flynn looked at him and acknowledged the inadequacy of his reply with a slight smile. Farnham almost responded – against his better judgement, he quite liked the man – but he raised an interrogative eyebrow.

'Well,' Flynn said slowly, 'I know the people, I know Jonathan Massey – and I know Eliza Eliot.' He was quiet for a moment, then he went on: 'I needed someone who could work with all the pieces, pull them together for the final exhibition. I knew Eliza could do that.'

Farnham nodded. He wasn't convinced by that one, but let's see where Flynn was going with it. 'So there were people you could trust with your work?' he said. Flynn remained silent, waiting. 'Was that it?' Farnham said.

'And I liked the setting,' Flynn said.

Farnham thought about it. 'OK,' he said. 'Tell

me about your Sheffield roots. How long were you in Sheffield? Where did you live?'

Flynn wasn't smiling now. He was still leaning back in his chair, but he no longer looked relaxed. 'I was born here,' he said.

'And your parents were . . . ?'

'Local people? My mother was.'

'Your father?'

Flynn shook his head. 'I've never met my father,' he said.

'And is your mother still in Sheffield?'

'In a manner of speaking.' Flynn shrugged. 'She's scattered around the crematorium somewhere.'

'I see.' But Farnham didn't, yet. This didn't sound like deep-rooted devotion to a place. It sounded like a mix of hostility and indifference.

'When did you leave?'

'Fifteen years ago.' The answer was prompt. Flynn hadn't had to think about it.

'And you come back much?'

'I came back in 1998,' Flynn said. His eyes were unfocused now, looking into the distance.

Four years ago, the year Ellie Chapman had died. 'Why then?' Farnham said, keeping his voice neutral.

'I'd just got my first big exhibition,' he said. 'I realized I was going to go places. I wanted to come back, look at where I'd come from, I suppose.' He sounded distracted, as though he was thinking about something else.

'When did you start planning this exhibition,

this *Triumph* thing?' The killings had all the marks of being carefully planned. The links with the painting, that bit of glorification of violent death that would have had the tabloids jumping up and down if it had been produced today, were too carefully organized to be the result of impulse. An image he didn't want, a passive figure exposing its throat to the knife, flashed into his mind. He had to stop this before the next one – and there would be a next one, he was sure.

Flynn stared at the ceiling. 'About a year ago,' he said. 'I started work on it about that time.'

'And how many people knew about it?'

'Not many,' Flynn said. 'My agent knew.'

'Eliza Eliot?' Farnham tried to ignore the slight tension he felt inside him as he waited for Flynn's answer. He didn't want to find that Eliza had lied to him.

Flynn nodded. 'It was talking to Eliza that gave me the idea in the first place, but she didn't know the details, not until it was finished.'

Twelve months. 'That was when you were first planning it? So you wouldn't have said anything to her earlier than that?'

'That was the first time I met her,' Flynn said.

'You said she was one of the reasons you wanted the exhibition to come to Sheffield,' Farnham pointed out.

Flynn frowned. 'Well, she was an added incentive, let's say.'

Farnham rubbed his hand over his face. He

was feeling the lack of sleep now. He could do with another shot of caffeine. Eliza's coffee had rather spoiled him for the stuff that came out of the machine. 'Mr Flynn, I'm investigating the murder of a woman and a child. This exhibition of yours seems to have brought some lunatic out of the undergrowth. I need to know who knew what was in the exhibition, and how early on they knew. I need to know everything you can tell me.'

'That's a tall order,' Flynn said. 'OK, who knew? I talked about the ideas in Madrid, but no one knew the details. I didn't know them, not until I started working on it. When I started it, no one, only me. Then, when I could see it was going somewhere, I discussed it with my agent, with Eliza. But once it was finished, about three months ago, lots of people knew. There was a buzz in the press, it was everywhere. Specially as it was coming to this gallery first. Good publicity gimmick.' His tone was light, but there was something underlying it that Farnham couldn't quite interpret.

'Was that the reason you let it come here?'

Flynn grinned. 'That, and Eliza.' He looked at Farnham. 'Eliza and I have a history,' he said.

Farnham hoped that nothing showed on his face. That wasn't something he'd wanted to hear, and it was something Eliza had kept quiet about. He wasn't surprised, now he thought about it. 'The night of the party, the night the exhibition opened, no one seems to remember seeing you at the restaurant.'

Flynn shrugged. 'I was there,' he said.

'On your own?'

Flynn looked at the ceiling. 'I was with someone,' he said after a slight pause.

'At the restaurant?' Farnham said.

The same slight hesitation. 'She came back to the hotel with me.'

'Until when?'

'Not sure . . .' Flynn caught Farnham's look and grinned. 'It wasn't a watch-the-clock sort of night,' he said. 'But she left around three, something like that.'

Farnham didn't like the way this was heading. 'Eliza Eliot?' He liked Eliza. But she'd provided a partial alibi for Massey. If she had, in fact, been with Flynn, then she'd lied, and he needed to know why she'd lied. It also left Massey wide open.

But Flynn was shaking his head. 'No. Eliza and I – that's been over for a while.'

'I need to know who you were with, Mr Flynn,' Farnham said.

Flynn looked at Farnham. 'It's nothing sinister,' he said. 'I just don't want to embarrass anyone.'

'I understand that,' Farnham said. 'But this is a murder inquiry. You say that someone can confirm where you were on Friday night. I'll need to get that confirmation.'

'I spent part of the evening at the gallery – you

know about that. Then I took . . . we went to get something to eat.'

Farnham waited.

'Then . . .' Flynn was thinking. He seemed to come to a decision. 'I went back to the hotel with the person I'd taken to dinner and, like I said, she left at around three. A bit after. Then I slept until about nine the next day.'

Farnham shook his head. 'I need a name,' he said.

'OK.' Flynn gave a rueful smile. There was a gleam of – what? – amusement? Regret? in his eyes. 'Actually, it was one of your officers. The one with the long black hair. Tina. Sorry.'

Farnham kept his face expressionless. Barraclough! What the *fuck* – ill-advised choice of word – what the *hell* was Barraclough playing at? 'OK,' he said. 'Thank you, Mr Flynn. You should have told me this last time I talked to you.'

Flynn stood up, looking uncertain. 'Is that it?' he said.

Farnham nodded. 'For now.'

He waited until Flynn had left the room, then he picked up the phone. 'Send DC Barraclough in to see me,' he said. 'OK, as soon as she comes back, then? Immediately.' He hung up and took a deep breath. He couldn't remember the last time he'd felt so angry.

Eliza worked quickly. She wanted to get through all the important stuff and get away from the gallery. She'd phoned Laura and arranged to spend the night over there. Laura had tried to persuade her to leave at once. 'Can't all that wait?' she'd said.

But it couldn't, and as the day wore on, more and more work piled up on her desk – phone calls, letters, e-mails, all of which required urgent responses if the gallery was to capitalize in any way on the prestige of *The Triumph of Death*. And if it didn't, then Eliza was out of a job and with a notable failure on her CV. She knew there had been some speculation when she got the job, speculation about her lack of experience, her suitability – there were people who would be happy to see her fail. Even with that pressure on her, she hadn't found the energy to do more than compile lists, things to be dealt with tomorrow, and bite Mel's head off when she came asking if she could have the afternoon off.

She came into the office now, tapping on the door with ostentatious care. Eliza curbed an instinct to snap. 'Yes?' she said. Her voice sounded terse.

'I've got some more people who want to talk to you about the exhibition,' Mel said. 'And one or two other things I can't deal with. And what shall I do with Jonathan's e-mails?'

'I'll check those in case there's anything urgent. Is everything else OK?' She shouldn't have taken it out on Mel – it was Jonathan she was angry with.

'There's a list of people to phone,' Mel said.

Eliza took it and ran her eyes over it. Some of these should have been followed up at once. Her head swam with fatigue. It would have to wait until tomorrow. They'd understand.

Mel hovered. 'Yes?' Eliza said, letting her impatience show.

'Where's Daniel Flynn?'

Eliza looked at her in surprise. 'I've no idea,' she said. 'Why do you want to know?'

'Well . . .' Mel was looking at her with an expression that Eliza found hard to classify; a bit anxious, a bit calculating. She seemed to come to a decision. 'The police took him in,' she said.

Eliza looked at her. 'Daniel gave a statement. So did I.'

'Do you think they know . . .' Mel was fiddling with the pens in Eliza's desk tidy. She gave Eliza a sidelong glance and said, 'Maybe I shouldn't say anything.'

'About what?' Eliza said. She was uneasily aware that she'd concealed her relationship with Daniel from Roy Farnham.

Mel shook her head. 'Jonathan's probably told them,' she said. She wandered over to the window, looking down at the canal, where the light was starting to fade. 'Oh, look, there's a boat,' she said.

Eliza waited impatiently. 'About what?' she said again.

Mel's glance was almost sly. 'You know,' she said. 'About Daniel. His arrangement with Jonathan.'

'Arrangement . . . ?' She didn't know what Mel was talking about.

Mel was looking at her and smiling. 'Didn't you know?' she said. 'I thought you knew. With you being the curator.'

What was Mel talking about? 'Just tell me,' she said.

'Daniel arranged with Jonathan to have the exhibition here nearly a year ago,' Mel said. 'Jonathan didn't want it, but he couldn't really turn it down.'

'Mel, that's a load of rubbish.' Eliza couldn't understand what had put that idea in Mel's mind. 'You can't go round saying things like that.'

'Oh, it's true,' Mel said. 'Cara told me.' Her eyes were bright. 'So I wondered,' she said.

Eliza could remember Daniel's voice as they stood in front of the Brueghel together: *I like the idea of a cityscape. Industrial ruins.* He could almost have been describing the canal. She shook herself back to the present. 'What would Cara have known?' she said briskly. 'That's ridiculous.' Before Mel could say anything, she went on: 'You might as well go. But be in first thing tomorrow. We might be able to open.' The police team had left at lunch-time. She needed to check with Roy, but they seemed to be finished with the gallery. For now.

It was after three, and suddenly she wanted to be on her own to make these last few phone calls, and then she could be off herself. She waited until Mel left, pulling on her jacket against the cold

373

evening air, then she went into the small kitchen and filled the kettle. Instant coffee might be foul, but she needed the caffeine.

She was sitting back at her desk when she heard the sound of footsteps across the gallery floor. Mel must have come back for something. 'What is it?' she said, irritably.

'Coffee.' Daniel's voice behind her, and a hand holding a carton appeared in front of her. 'From down the road. Hot, sweet, sinful. A bit like you.'

'Daniel!' She spun her chair round and looked at him. He was unshaven and rumpled – he looked as if he'd spent the night on a park bench, not in a four-star hotel. 'You look awful.'

He yawned. 'So do you, beautiful. With more reason. Are you OK?' He ran his hand over her hair. 'Poor Eliza.'

She turned her chair slightly to move away. 'I'm OK,' she said. 'How did you get in?' Mel's words nagged at her mind.

There was a moment's silence before he said, 'I bumped into your resident dysfunctional adolescent on her way out. I was on my way back, and she told me you were still here. So I persuaded her to wait for me while I got coffee for my good friend Eliza who will boost my flagging morale before I go and catch up on my sleep.'

'Good friend? Convenient friend.' Eliza opened the top of the carton. The rich smell of coffee filled the room.

'I got her to do it extra strength. They don't

understand coffee here,' he said. 'What do you mean, "convenient friend"?'

'I mean, I'm your good friend if you need me. Out of sight, out of mind if you don't.' She wondered what he wanted, what had brought him here.

'That upsets me. Convenient friend. How have I made you convenient?' he said. He sounded hurt. He had always responded badly to criticism, even as a joke.

'OK,' she said. 'I meant . . . You more or less ignored me for months, but now you've got the exhibition at the gallery, there are things I can do for you.' If she hadn't been so tired, she never would have said it. It was over and done with and not worth rehashing. She was too tired to get into the discussion. 'Let's not go over that now.' Of all the times to start talking seriously . . .

'I've always thought about you,' he said. 'From the time I first met you.'

'Look, forget it.' Eliza said.

'As your "convenient friend" I put your name forward for this job,' he said. 'Massey would have gone for some boring administrator with more experience otherwise.'

Eliza felt her fatigue fall away. 'What do you mean?'

'I mean, I phoned Massey a few weeks after we met in Madrid. I told him you were available.'

'Wait a minute!' Nothing was making sense any more. Or it was all making far too much sense.

'What about Africa? Tanzania? You threw me over because I went for this job rather than go to Africa with you, remember.'

'Not so,' he said. 'It wasn't any big thing. We weren't pretending it was any big thing, were we, Eliza? You were going to be at a loose end when your contract finished. Africa was just another option, that's all.'

She closed her eyes. Daniel hated conflict, he hated criticism. Had he got bored, taken the easy way of drifting out of the relationship by using something she had done as the lever? His defensive expression told her she was probably right. 'You could have told me,' she said. 'Instead of leaving me to think . . .' The hours she'd spent agonizing over her decision! But why go to all that trouble . . . and why would Jonathan listen to Daniel's recommendation anyway? OK, they'd been students together, but that didn't count for much. There was something else. 'The exhibition,' she said, slowly.

He was looking a bit uneasy now. 'You were the right person to put it together,' he said.

'But it wasn't even coming here,' Eliza said. 'Not then.' She remembered the letter that had come out of the blue, asking her to apply for the post as curator for the new gallery, and she could hear Mel's voice: *Daniel arranged with Jonathan to have the exhibition here nearly a year ago.*

He suddenly looked away. 'It was on the cards,' he said.

I like the idea of a cityscape. Industrial ruins. She remembered how interested he'd been when he realized she shared his ideas about the Brueghel, more so when she told him she had roots in this city. 'On the cards?' she said. 'You planned for it to come here all along, didn't you?'

He looked evasive for a moment, then nodded. 'Yes, I did. I asked Massey to keep it quiet. I had – have – some good reasons, Eliza.'

'And you let me think . . . I thought I'd got this job on merit. But you'd offered Jonathan *The Triumph of Death*. He'd do anything you asked, wouldn't he?'

'I told you.' His voice was carefully neutral. 'I wanted you to curate the exhibition. What's wrong with that?'

'Nothing, if you'd told me.' Eliza put her head in her hands, then looked at him. 'I've been working here on the assumption I got the job through merit. I thought that we got *The Triumph of Death* because I put in the best bid. Now you're telling me that it was all arranged behind my back, and I've been congratulating myself for something that was nothing to do with me. Can't you see . . . ?' He was looking at her blankly. She was angry, but she was too tired to articulate her anger clearly.

'OK,' he said. 'I should have told you. I'm sorry.'

'What good is sorry?' The damage was done. 'Have you told the police?' And now Roy would have to know what a fool they'd made of her.

He started to say something, then stopped. 'No,' he said. 'Not yet. I wanted to tell you first.'

'Look,' she said, 'you'd better go and do whatever it was you came to the gallery to do. I'm busy.'

He raised his eyebrows at her tone. 'For what it's worth, I was going to ask if you wanted to go for a drink. Tonight,' he said.

She shook her head. 'Daniel, that's the last thing I want to do,' she said.

CHAPTER 16

'The DCI wants to see you,' the officer on the desk said to Tina with relish as she came into the main offices. 'As soon as you come in, he said. He's on the war path.'

Daniel. Tina had been waiting for it, and, now it had come, she felt more resigned than worried. She should have told Farnham at once. It had been inexcusable. She could lose her job for this. 'OK,' she said.

'I'll tell him you're on your way, shall I?' He picked up the phone.

'No, I'll be there before you get through,' Tina said. He put the phone down with a look of disappointment – probably missing out on the vicarious glory of convicting the snotty DC Barraclough of whatever crime she had been guilty of. Tina let herself through the door, and headed up the stairs. She might as well get it over. She could hear feet coming down towards her, and Dave West swung round the corner, moving fast. He brought himself to a halt. 'Tina, the DCI . . .'

'I know,' she said.

He looked worried. 'What's wrong? Why's he after you? Do you need any back-up?'

She was touched by Dave's concern. They'd worked together a lot, and they'd always watched each other's backs, but she shook her head. 'No. Thanks. I've dropped myself in it – best you don't get involved.' She made a throat-cutting gesture.

'OK.' He sounded reluctant. 'Listen, did you find anything? The news stories?'

'There's something, not much,' she said.

She told him what she'd found. He nodded without enthusiasm. 'Give Farnham something to get his teeth into,' he advised. He checked his watch. 'Look, I've got to go.' He looked at her for a minute. 'Good luck,' he said.

She nodded thanks at his retreating back, and began her climb up the next flight towards the incident room. *Goodbye, career, it was nice knowing you!* What had happened to the bright, efficient DC Barraclough with her quick mind and her clear ambitions? Barraclough who enjoyed her work, would do what was required of her with meticulous ease, who knew when to use her initiative? Barraclough who enjoyed her life, who *had* a life, and, OK, a slightly risky taste for the milder mind-altering substances, but who would never, never have got involved with a witness and lied about it, would never have risked class-A drugs, would never have missed important things in a witness statement.

OK, maybe it was the sloppy, inefficient, unprofessional Barraclough who was going to lose her job, but she would give the other Barraclough, the real Barraclough, one more chance. There was a piece of the picture she had been putting together from the records that was missing. The real Barraclough wouldn't have dreamt of coming back to the incident room without that information until she'd checked all possible sources. She wanted the name of the dead addict. Someone would have dealt with that case. If there was a name, it would be in the records in this building. She turned and went back down the stairs.

She knew that records of cases over the past five years were kept in the basement. Without a name or a case number, she wasn't sure where to start, but it was possible that the recent drugs investigation she'd been involved in might refer back to this older case. There were some parallels. Also, no one would wonder why she was looking at those files.

It took her half an hour to find the information she wanted, and then another half-hour to track down the files relating to the dead addict. Farnham would be breathing fire by now. But she was determined to get the information, present it to him, and then, if he wanted her off the case, at least she'd have one credit against her name to balance out the black mark on her record.

She skimmed through the reports from the finding of the body. It wasn't quite as straightforward as she'd assumed. There had been an anonymous call in the early hours of the morning – the caller had never been found. Most probably it had been another junkie – one with a conscience, but one who didn't want any involvement with the police.

The dead junkie had been young – under twenty, the post-mortem said. The cause of death was an overdose of heroin. No one else was being looked for in relation to the death, apart from the suppliers. There was no indication of force or physical violence. The dead woman had apparently shot the means of her own death into her veins. But then, weren't all drug users seeking a kind of oblivion? *And what kind of oblivion are you looking for?* The thought was unwelcome and she dismissed it. The only circumstance that was slightly unusual was the lack of any form of identification on or near the body.

Tina went on through the file. Most of it related to the drugs investigation, the supply of pure heroin that was killing addicts. It hadn't made a big splash in the papers – who cared if a few junkies were killing themselves sooner rather than later? And then it had stopped. As though the supplies had dried up or been adulterated by the street dealers, and the problem had drifted away.

She stared into space, thinking. The person who had dumped Ellie's body – she realized she was no longer thinking 'Mark Fraser' automatically – had chosen a good place. It was overgrown and secluded.

It had been months before the body was found and, even then, only in relation to another investigation. How had the person – Fraser? Who? – known about the place? Was it someone who had been familiar with that part of the towpath, someone who knew it and knew that the thick undergrowth there was rarely disturbed, that the only people who came there were walkers who didn't linger on that part of the towpath, or junkies on their way for a fix? Was Ellie's killer one of the heroin-using fraternity?

Why hadn't the original investigation team looked at this? Had they looked at it and dismissed it because . . . The details of the case came back to her: because Fraser's stepdaughter had made her accusation against him. The investigation had focused on Fraser as the prime suspect, on Ellie as the route to Fraser, and the dead woman in the boat had become, as the headline said, the forgotten victim.

Tina realized she hadn't thought about her impending interview with Farnham for the past hour. She looked at her watch. He must know she was in the building now. She was aware of the tension building up as she turned the pages. She was in flagrant breach of instructions. Suppose they'd never discovered the identity of the dead woman? Suppose they had, and it was nothing to do with the case? She could feel her shoulders start to tighten and the first throb of a headache in her temples. She was beginning to realize she'd made a mistake – it would have been better to have taken her hunch about the dead addict to Farnham, let him know what she was doing. Unless she could bring something useful back, he'd see this as another excuse.

She was skimming the pages now, turning them fast, missing things. She either had to do this properly or not at all, but it was too late to go upstairs with nothing. She was past the date of Fraser's trial and conviction now – a parallel case brought to a satisfactory conclusion and closed. They didn't seem to have searched too hard to find the identity of the dead addict and she was near the end of the file.

Then she found it. It was there, a grainy photograph of a girl with fair hair and shadowed eyes. She looked at the caption, and a sense of vindication flooded through her. She had a name for the dead woman – the dead girl, she amended. And she had her connection as well. The dead girl had been just fifteen, a runaway from local-authority care who had, somehow, slipped though the net of the original searches – not that it would have made much difference at the time. A girl who had drifted through the inadequacies of the care system until something had made her abscond, drift on to the streets, into prostitution, into drugs and into early death, a death that had been overshadowed by the high-profile tragedy of Ellie Chapman.

But Tina had heard her name before, heard it when she talked to Cara Hobson's ex-care worker,

Denise Greene. The girl who had become friendly with Cara Hobson because they had shared the experience of coming into care, had shared the casual drift into prostitution, a drift that had taken this girl into the coils of addiction as well. The name of the dead addict was Sheryl Hewitt.

And as she looked at the photograph, she realized something else. She felt the jump of excitement as an important connection slipped into place, but she also felt a lurch of apprehension. If she had been in trouble before, she was in worse trouble now. The face that looked at her from the newspaper cutting was the same face that had looked back at her from the photo-montage in Daniel's exhibition. He'd said it: *She was a prostitute. Found dead. No one cared much.*

She did.

It wasn't sunny any more. The sky was heavy with clouds, and the light was starting to fade. Kerry didn't want to go home. She lingered in the school entrance. The police might be waiting for her at home. That was why they hadn't come to get her at school – they were going to get her at home, and Mum too, probably. She needed to see Lyn, she needed to get the stuff about Dad, whatever it was. But even if she did get it, maybe no one would listen. Who'd care? She was Kerry Fraser, Kerry Fraser whose dad was a pervert, Kerry Fraser who told lies, Kerry Fraser who bunked off school, Kerry Fraser whose mum so much couldn't cope with her that she was pissed out of her face all the time.

She got out her phone again. She'd have to be careful – she'd kept it switched off most of the day, but it would run out eventually. She switched it on. She felt a jump in her stomach as the message icon flashed at her. She pressed the buttons, but nothing appeared on the screen. She looked again – it was voice-mail. She called the answering service.

It was Lyn. Lyn hardly ever sent voice-mail. Kerry could hardly hear what she was saying – she was whispering, and the crackle of interference obscured the words. *Hi, Kizz. Sorry I've not called. Too busy. I'm like 'Get me out of here!' I'll call soon.* But nothing about Dad. Kerry wanted to throw the phone down in frustration, beat it against the wall to make it say what she wanted to hear. It wasn't fair, Lyn wasn't being fair.

Then there was a flurry of talk and laughing and Marie and her group came down the steps with their arms linked, their bags on their backs or hooked over their shoulders. Marie saw her and stopped. 'You coming, Kerry?' she said.

Kerry looked at her and shrugged. 'Might do,' she said. 'Where you going?'

'We're going to Meadowhall, we're going to the movies.'

Kerry's heart jumped, then she felt the letdown. She couldn't go anywhere. She didn't have any money. She shook her head.

'Come on, Marie.' The others were tugging at Marie's arm, wanting to get going.

'Oh, go on,' Marie said. 'If you do my T-shirt for the weekend, I'll treat you.' She said it like it was no big deal.

'OK,' Kerry said. She could feel her face brighten. 'All right. I'll do it tomorrow.'

'Come on.' And Kerry was incorporated into the group as they linked arms and headed for the bus stop into town. Kerry was part of the group and she wasn't part of the group. A bit of her as talking and laughing and listening, and another bit of her was thinking about Lyn, and about Dad, and about how she didn't know what she was going to do next because she couldn't go home.

Snow was starting to fall as they got into town. No one was in any hurry. It was nice wandering round the shops, looking in the windows. It was cold and wet, but somehow, in a crowd, it didn't seem to matter. They bought burgers and Coke. Kerry didn't have money for a burger, so she pretended she wasn't hungry, but she had a Coke.

'I so don't need this,' Marie said, patting her stomach. 'Look at me.' She offered Kerry some chips. Kerry helped her out. It was after six by the time they walked up the hill to the tram stop at the cathedral, just as a tram was gliding up to the stop and they all piled on. It pulled away smoothly, and Kerry let her mind wander. The tram swooped over the flyover, swayed round a corner and pulled in to the next stop. More people piled on to the tram and Kerry got separated from the others. She peered through the crowd and saw Marie looking for her. She waved and smiled. It was OK, she was going to the movies. The windows of the tram were black. It was night outside, now, but she knew the canal basin was down there, behind some buildings . . . Her eyes snapped open. She didn't want to think about it.

The tram picked up speed. It was racing along now. Kerry, standing, was squashed against the side. Then she heard the beep of her phone. She eased her hand into her bag and slipped it out to check. The icon was flashing. *New message.* Soon. Lyn had said she'd call soon. She almost dropped it as she pressed the buttons, and had a sudden vision of it crushed under the feet of all the people with Lyn's message unread and lost. She pressed 'read', and the words scrolled across the screen: *WHR R U?*

She looked down the tram quickly. Marie and the others were talking. The tram was just pulling away from the stadium. She keyed the words in quickly. *Don vlly stdm. Trm.* Don Valley Stadium. On the tram.

She waited, tense. The phone beeped almost at once. *MT U ON TOPATH RLY BR 7.30 RGNT DNT B L8.* Meet you on the towpath, railway bridge. Urgent. Don't be late.

The railway bridge. The railway crossed the

canal just a bit back into town. She had to get off the tram and go back down the towpath. The next stop was the Centertainment. She could go over the footbridge and walk back along the towpath. She keyed the message in, quick, keeping herself close to the door. *Cu @ 7.30 rly br.*

Then the tram was slowing. She was by the door and out as soon as the doors opened. She stepped back into the shadows as the tram waited, watching through the bright yellow of the windows. Marie and the others were still there, still talking. They hadn't noticed. She backed away. She didn't want anyone seeing her going towards the canal.

The tram didn't move away from the stop at once, and she backed away from the lights, round the cinema complex, into the car park. She looked round. It was all burger places and bowling and . . . She read the flashing neon. *Eating, dancing, cavorting!* The high, bright lights flooded the car park, and the signs on the cafés and the bars flashed in greens and reds and blues, but there was nobody there. There were cars in the car parks, there were people in the cinema and in the restaurants, but the car park was a deserted stretch of concrete. From a distance – Kerry had seen it often enough from the tram or the bus – it looked lively and fun, but now she was here, it was lonely and dead.

She was cold, and it was still snowing. She could see into the cinema foyer. There were people there, queuing for tickets, buying ice cream and sweets in the shop. The smell of popcorn drifted out through the doors and it made her want to cry. Mum used to make popcorn, years ago, when Kerry was small. Kerry and Lyn used to like watching. Lyn would tell Mum to make it in the pan with the glass lid, and Mum would drop the golden bits of corn into the hot oil and put the lid on, and soon the corn would start to jump and explode into white clouds, and Mum would put some butter on and some salt, and Kerry and Lyn would sit in front of the telly eating it. 'It's like at the movies,' Lyn used to say.

'You know what giants do,' Lyn said once, holding up a piece of the corn. 'They drop little kids like you in hot oil and all your insides explode and they eat you while you're still alive.'

'Do not,' Kerry had said, uneasily.

'It's true,' Lyn said. 'Your dad's a giant. He'll do it to you one day, when you're asleep.'

'He'll do it to your dad,' Kerry had said. 'Your dad's a . . .' She tried to remember what Dad said. 'Your dad's a *shit*.' She giggled. 'That's why you smell!'

Lyn had smacked her face and Kerry had started crying, then Mum had come in and shouted, and Lyn had shouted back and then Dad had come and it had been everybody shouting, and Mum said, 'Oh, I can't cope with all of this. Why can't you all get on? I'm going to have a drink,' and she'd poured out drinks for her and for Dad, and Dad looked worried and puzzled. And Lyn had smiled.

She needed to get to the bridge. The tram would have gone by now. She ran back to the stop, then over the footbridge. There was a pathway leading to the canal side, overgrown with bushes, dark, shadowed. She stopped. It was quiet. There was no one there. She ran lightly along the path, then she was by the canal, a wide, flat pool gleaming in the lamp light, boats moored on the far side, quiet, still.

The boats were painted: red, green, blue. They reminded her of the water-bus on the sunny day, the last day. They had names that were homely and happy: *Carol, Spider, Trent Lady, Mary May*, but they looked ramshackle and abandoned, the cabin windows dark and empty, the decks deserted.

She didn't want to be on the towpath, but she didn't want to go back through that narrow, over-grown footpath. She hesitated, but the towpath lights were working, and it wasn't so very late. If she started walking now, she'd be at the bridge in plenty of time. She tucked her hair inside her coat as the rain began to fall more heavily, and started walking back towards town.

The problem of Tina Barraclough nagged at Farnham, distracted his mind from the important details of the investigation. He was tired and he'd been wrong-footed by Flynn. Was that influencing him? He tested his anger and it felt solid.

Barraclough had got herself involved with a witness – OK, it happened. He didn't approve, but it wasn't a hanging . . . his mind edited the thought. It wasn't a capital offence. She'd got herself involved with a suspect – that was worse, but in fairness to Barraclough, Flynn hadn't been a suspect at the time of the opening. She'd kept the information concealed. That was the stopper. That was the killer. And he was going to take her apart for that.

He picked up the phone and called through to the incident room. 'She did come back,' a voice said in response to his query, 'but I don't know where she is now.'

'Page her.' Farnham had had enough of Barraclough for the moment. He had a killer out there, and two people who were disturbingly close to both the killings and the gallery – and to Eliza Eliot, who was, thank Christ, safely out of the picture, staying with her friend.

He remembered the photographs from the Ellie Chapman case. He might as well have a look at them before Barraclough gave him the material she'd collected from the archives. He spread the photos across his desk, along with the two he'd taken from Eliza's flat. He was curious as to why they'd been separated from the rest.

That was interesting. They weren't there. Either the photos Eliza had given him were not part of the same batch, or the set in the Chapman file was incomplete. Had there been a second film? Unlikely.

Fraser had not used up one film on these. He looked at the pictures, trying to sequence them.

There were three taken on the boat, one of the two girls sitting on benches smiling especially for the camera, one of Ellie pretending to fish over the side of the boat. There was one of a man with Ellie – Mark Fraser, he recognized the face from the newspaper reports. They were typical holiday snaps, with feet cut off, posts sprouting out of the tops of heads – family, fun . . . The word *innocent* drifted through his mind.

It must have been chilly on the river as both girls were wearing jumpers. Ellie's was yellow, Kerry's was red. And Mark Fraser's was beige, the beige wool jumper that had been wound around Ellie's body when she was seen again, six months after these pictures had been taken. There was nothing innocent here.

Then there were a couple of pictures taken on the bank. The two girls posing with their arms round each other, the two of them climbing up the grassy slope that surrounded the castle. They were wearing T-shirts this time. And shortly after that picture was taken . . .

But the pictures Eliza had given him had been taken from the middle of the sequence. The girls were on the boat. They were wearing the red and yellow jumpers. Farnham looked again. These pictures were different. The ones he'd been looking at had been taken on the deck. These were taken from inside the boat, through a window. And the camera that took these pictures had been set in date mode. There was no date across the bottom of the other prints.

Christ. The implications of what he was seeing hit him. There had been someone else on the boat that day who was interested in Ellie. Someone inside the boat, someone who'd taken pictures. Someone who'd . . .

His phone rang, breaking his train of thought. It was his secretary. 'DC Barraclough is here to see you,' she said.

'OK,' he said. 'No calls, please.' This wasn't something he was particularly looking forward to, and he had other things he needed to deal with now. There was a knock on his door. 'Come in,' he called, and Tina Barraclough came in. He'd expected nervousness or sullen defensiveness, but this was a Barraclough he hadn't seen before, quick, keen, who started speaking before he had a chance to say anything.

'I'm sorry, sir, I know you want to talk to me about Daniel Flynn, but I've found something important, look –'

Farnham listened as she took him through the story of the dead addict and the unrecognized link between Cara Hobson and the Ellie Chapman killing. Sheryl Hewitt, the dead junkie. Sheryl Hewitt, Cara Hobson's friend.

Those photographs. Eliza had assumed they'd come from Maggie's, that she'd brought them across with all the other stuff she'd collected. But Cara Hobson had been in Eliza's flat that night. He remembered Eliza's description of her, laden with baby paraphernalia and bags, struggling out of her chair. How easily could a couple of photographs slip out of a bag or a pocket, unnoticed by either woman?

Barraclough was putting a cutting in front of him. 'That photograph's in the exhibition,' she said, showing him the grainy picture of a young girl. 'Sheryl. I remember seeing it.' Flynn! *Shit!* And he'd let the man walk out of there. 'Wait,' he said as he got on the phone. He wanted Flynn bringing in now. And he wanted all the files on the Chapman case. 'OK,' he said as he put the phone down. 'That was good work, Barraclough.' She flushed and looked pleased.

But it made no difference. 'You know what this means?' he said, pushing the cutting across the desk at her. 'This puts Flynn in the frame. And anything you do in relation to Flynn is contaminated now. Why the . . . why didn't you tell me at the time?' He could feel a headache starting behind his eyes. Not enough sleep and too much to do. And it had to be Daniel Flynn she'd got herself involved with. Fucking maniac with his sick paintings and his sick mind. At the same time, he was aware of the glaring anomaly of his position, the fact that his own attitude towards Flynn could hardly be impartial now. Well, that was his business, his decision. 'You know I should take you off this investigation, don't you?' he said.

She bit her lip, and nodded. 'Yes, sir.'

She kept her eyes down. Her face looked pink. He hoped to Christ she wasn't going to start crying. He couldn't cope with a crying woman just now. 'Why didn't you tell me at the time?' he repeated.

'I don't know,' she said after a moment.

'Well, you'd better find out, Barraclough. Now.' If she'd told him, then the damage would have been minimal. There was no reason to have kept it quiet, unless . . . There had to have been something else, and he wasn't going to let himself be blindsided again.

She shook her head. 'It was . . . I was embarrassed, I suppose.'

He wasn't buying that. Barraclough was no shrinking violet. You didn't work in this job for any time and stay thin-skinned. Or you didn't survive in it. 'Come off it, Barraclough. You'll have to do better than that. What was it? You told him something you shouldn't?'

She flushed again. 'No, sir,' she said.

She could still resent a slur on her professionalism. What the fuck had gone wrong with her? At least she hadn't been shooting her mouth off about the investigation to a suspect.

So what had been the big secret? Orgies? He found himself confronting the rather disturbing mental image of a naked Tina Barraclough entwined in a heap of bodies. 'Threesomes?' She looked at him indignantly. 'Pills?'

He saw the expression on her face and realized he'd got it. *Shit!* An officer – and someone on his team – using drugs with a civilian. He was going to have to hang her out to dry. 'All right . . .' His phone rang. He swore under his breath and picked it up. 'I said, no calls,' he snapped at his long-suffering secretary.

She was impervious to his moods. 'I think you'll want to hear this,' she said.

It was Judith Martin. 'The Fraser child,' she said, without any introduction. 'She *wasn't* at school the afternoon Stacy went missing. I've found something you need to see, sir.'

It was after six. Tina Barraclough sat at her desk. She could feel the eyes of other members of the team on her, knew that they knew she was in trouble, wondered if they knew why. She was aware of the buzz of activity, of action around her. She tried to tell herself that she had, at last, achieved some credit. Farnham had actually told her that she had done a good piece of work – but he wasn't going to let it drop. She closed her eyes, sending her mind back to the interview. Farnham had got so close to the drugs – then the phone call had stopped him. Something was happening and she was being sidelined, might be off the case, might even find herself back in uniform, back dealing with traffic, back with paperwork and

Saturday-night drunks and . . . Wasn't that better than . . . ? The tower block. The falling shape. The *thump* of the impact and then the silence before the voices started shouting, the running feet, the impetus to action as she stood there frozen, looking but not wanting to see what lay on the ground almost at her feet.

'Tina?' It was Dave West, looking at her with concern. She jumped and shook herself. 'Is it right?' Dave said. 'They're saying you're in the shit with Farnham.'

She nodded, not trusting her voice.

'Look, things seem to be moving.' His voice was low and urgent. 'But I've got half an hour – let's get a coffee, tell me about it.'

'What's happening?'

Dave cast a quick glance around the room and spoke quietly to her. 'The Fraser kid – it looks as though she might know something about the McDonald girl's movements on Friday. They're trying to track her down.'

'She's gone missing?' Tina felt cold. She had been involved in this investigation – she had done the bare minimum of everything she'd been asked to do. The one time she'd pulled the stops out and done a decent job, she'd come up with some-thing. If she'd found it sooner, maybe they'd have their killer in the bag.

'No. She went off with her friends after school. Her mate's dad is picking them up at nine,' Dave said. 'Come on, let's get a coffee.'

'No.' Tina put the last of her stuff into her bag. 'Thanks, Dave, but I'm tired. I want to get home. And I'm not exactly flavour of the month with the boss, so . . .' *Better stay away from me.*

'OK,' he said reluctantly. 'Look, I'll . . . you know . . .'

'It's OK, Dave,' she said. She smiled. 'I'll give you a ring. Go on, get a break. You'll need it.' She kept the smile on her face until he'd left the room. It was almost empty now, just someone inputting data, someone else answering the phones. She looked round at the cluttered desks, the flip chart with the notes from the morning's briefing, the photographs – Cara Hobson smiling bewilderedly over her baby's head. What would happen to the child? Was there any family? Cara in the water, a bundle of rags caught in the weeds and the litter by the side of the canal. A close-up of Cara's neck, the twine round it, digging deep into the flesh.

Stacy McDonald, a child, her face plump under the carefully applied make-up. The mutilated cadaver hanging from the ceiling, harshly illuminated from below, the shadows hard across the ceiling, the head mercifully in darkness. A reproduction of the Brueghel dominated the wall, a celebration of death from centuries before, a celebration of murder, of mutilation, of torture and cruelty. The madness of artists.

This was crunch time for Tina. She had decisions to make, and she couldn't put them off much longer. If she resigned, would her nightmare of the falling figure, the sense of blame, of inevitability, finally leave her? Would it be worth giving up the years she had put into this job to start again, doing – what? Yesterday, the confrontation with Farnham would have given her the incentive she thought she needed to leave, but now . . . she had experienced that sense of triumph when she had followed up her idea and tracked down what might prove to be a vital link in the case they were investigating. Could she give that up? Would she be allowed to keep it?

Her phone rang, making her jump. She checked the number, aware of the covert observation from the other side of the room. It wasn't anyone she knew. She was tempted to let her message service take the call, but she answered. 'Tina Barraclough.'

'DC Barraclough,' a voice said. 'You probably don't remember me. We met at the weekend. Steven Calloway.'

For a moment her mind was blank, then she made the connections. Steven Calloway, the owner of the *Mary May*. She remembered the slight frisson that had passed between them. 'Mr Calloway,' she said. 'How can I help you?'

'Well,' he said, 'you could call me Steven, for a start. I'm in Sheffield for the evening, and I wondered if you were free. I know it's short notice, but if you are – we could get something to eat, have a drink, maybe? What do you think?'

Tina blinked. She had been expecting some revelation, something to tell her that *again*, she'd screwed up, but it was just a come-on – and one that would have been welcome a few days ago. Would probably be welcome again tomorrow, but now . . . 'That sounds like fun,' she said after a short pause.

'But?' he said. 'There's a *but* coming, right?'

'It's been a long day – I need to get home, get some sleep.' *Don't try and talk me into it!*

'Well, that's a pity. I'm only in Sheffield for one night,' he said. 'But I'll be around again in a week or two. Would it be worth my while phoning you then?'

She laughed, her mood lifting for a second. 'Yes, why not?' she said.

'That makes me feel better about it,' he said. 'I might forgive you.'

'Forgive me? For what?' For turning him down?

'Locking me out of my own boat,' he said.

It took a second for what he had said to register. 'What?'

'Locking me out of the *Mary May*,' he said. 'Is she some kind of crime scene?'

Tina felt her breath stop in her throat. 'I don't know what you're talking about.'

'It wasn't your lot? It'll be the broker then. He'll have lost the keys. I'll get . . .'

'No, wait.' Tina felt a sense of urgency. The mystery cabin cruiser had to be on the canal – all the boats that had gone through the locks were accounted for. This was another part of the investigation she'd been responsible for. And though she had looked, she'd left it as an unsolved problem. 'Tell me exactly what happened.'

'Is it important? OK . . .' He responded to the impatient catch in her breath. 'I thought I'd take a look at her as I was over that way. I don't usually bother, but I'm thinking about scrapping her. Anyway, when I got there, my key wouldn't open the padlock. I tried for ages. I thought it was just stiff. But no joy. My key wouldn't work. So I thought you lot must have locked the old girl up – might have let me know. But it wasn't you. I don't think it's much of a mystery. It's probably Charlie.'

'Charlie?' Tina said.

'The broker. He'll have put a new padlock on for some reason. Anyway, it was a good excuse to phone you.' Charlie Norton. She remembered her visit to the boatyard.

'So – let me get this clear – your key isn't the right one for the lock on the *Mary May*?'

'Got it in one,' he said.

Tina checked her watch. 'What time does the broker's close?' she said.

'They're usually there until quite late,' he said.

'Could you go there, Mr Calloway? Someone will be there to meet you.'

'This sounds like business . . . DC Barraclough, I'll see you soon.'

Tina was on the phone to the broker as soon as Calloway had rung off. She spoke to the man she had seen before, Charlie Norton. He sounded impatient and irritable. No, he hadn't changed the locks on the *Mary May*. The key was the same one as always. Yes, he'd check it now. There was silence for a few minutes and then he was back, his voice sounding more impatient. It was exactly the same key. No, no one had been to look at the boat since the last time he'd spoken to her. There was no interest in it at all. Yes – this said with a heavy sigh – he would wait until someone came to the office.

Steven Calloway was already at the broker's when Tina pulled up. She could see him in the office, talking to the man she recognized as Charlie Norton. Problem? She should have made sure she got here first. They looked up as she came through the door, and for a second, she wondered if she was looking at men who were capable of torturing a thirteen-year-old girl before they killed her, of stringing her up as some kind of joke or warped homage to an exhibition that celebrated the cruelty and depravity of humanity.

But Calloway didn't seem worried. 'Officer Barraclough.' His eyes were alight with interest. 'The plot thickens.'

The broker, looking impatient, interrupted. 'It's a wild-goose chase, Steve,' he said. He looked at Tina. 'He's brought the wrong keys with him, that's all.'

'Tell me what's happened,' Tina said. She wanted clarification of Calloway's story. She looked at

him. 'You went to get access to the *Mary May*.'
He nodded. 'When?'

'Yesterday,' he said. 'I came across to see friends,
and I thought I'd take a look at the old girl.' He
shook his head. 'She's past it, really. I ought to . . .'

Yesterday! 'And what happened?' Tina tried to
hide her impatience.

'Oh, well, I tried to unlock the padlock, and the
key wouldn't turn. I told you.'

'Of course it wouldn't,' the broker said. 'You
were using the wrong key. Look.' He held up a
bunch of keys. Tina reached out for them. 'That
one,' he said. 'That's the key for the *Mary May*.'

Tina compared it with the one that Calloway
was holding. They were the same size, very similar,
but the blades were different. She felt a sense of
anti-climax. It was nothing important, after all.
Calloway had made a mistake.

'Bull— Rubbish,' Calloway said. 'Think I don't
know my own keys? This is . . .'

'Just a minute,' Tina said. 'Mr Calloway, are you
sure the key you used is the one for the boat? You
didn't pick up the wrong key by mistake?'

The broker shifted, but Tina shut him up with
a look. 'Yes,' Calloway said.

'Could anyone have taken the key?' she said.
'Switched keys on you somehow?' It seemed like
a lot of effort to find out who the owner of the
Mary May was, find out where he kept his keys,
perform the switch.

He shrugged. 'I never thought . . .' He looked at

the key closely. 'No,' he said. 'This is the right key. Look.' He was holding the key up against the light and Tina could see, scratched into the end, the letters *MM* that she remembered from the day she had talked to him in York.

The broker was looking uneasy now. 'I don't know anything about this,' he said. 'This is the key you gave me, and this is the one we've always used.'

'Let's see.' Calloway took the other key and studied it closely. He shook his head. 'Dad marked all his keys,' he said. 'So unless you got another cut, this isn't the key I gave you.'

Tina was thinking. If someone had been playing games with the keys, then that meant they would have access to the boat. But that still left the engine key. Getting a spare key for a padlock wasn't such a big deal, but getting a key for an engine, that was much more of a problem. 'What about starting the boat?' she said, voicing part of her thought out loud.

'Oh, I couldn't have done that,' Calloway said. 'Charlie here's got both the keys for that. Or he's supposed to have them.'

The broker held up the key ring. There were three keys – two for the engine and one for the padlock. He was looking more uneasy now. 'It didn't mean anything at the time,' he said, 'but when I took someone out, I found one of these was faulty.' He looked at Tina and Calloway. 'I meant to check it out sometime, but it didn't seem urgent, not unless the boat sold.'

Tina was beginning to see how it had been done.

'Run through exactly what you do when you show people round a boat, Mr Norton.' She could remember what he'd done when he'd taken her to the *Mary May*.

'I just show them . . .' he said.

'In detail. Exactly what do you do when you get there?'

'I unlock the boat and let them have a bit of a look, then I take them for a quick run, if that's what they want.'

'You do it?' Tina said.

'If they're interested, they take her out. But I'm there with them,' he said.

'But no one was interested in the *Mary May*?'

'There was one person came back,' the broker said. 'But that was it.'

That was it. That had to be it. 'So he came once and had a look round, then came back . . .'

'Something like that,' the broker said. 'Bill's the one dealing with the *Mary May*. I only remember because there was no one else showed an interest.' He looked at Calloway. 'Bill did his best for you, said you didn't use the boat, you were looking for a quick sale.'

'Well, that's true enough,' Calloway said.

Tina tried to keep her patience. 'Where's Bill? Is he here?'

'Not till tomorrow,' the broker said. 'He's gone to look over a barge going for a song.' He was talking to Calloway now. 'Sailing barge on the Medway, at Upnor. Beauty. Only £110,000.'

Calloway whistled. 'What's wrong with her?'

'That's what . . .'

'Mr Norton.' Both men looked at her. 'What would Bill have done the second time he took this person to see the *Mary May*?'

The broker shrugged. 'Same as the first time, except they'd go on the canal.'

Tina felt the tension of frustration. 'Did Bill say anything – did anything unusual happen?'

'Not that . . . Now you mention it, that was when we found the faulty key. He couldn't get the engine to start. Bill tried, but he said the key wouldn't go in. That's why the spare's on the key ring. He had to use that.'

That was it! If the keys to the *Mary May* had been stolen, the broker would have contacted the police and secured the boat – unless he didn't realize the keys had been taken. And to get access to the boat, you didn't need to steal the key – you could steal the padlock. 'When someone's looking over a boat,' Tina said, 'what do you usually do?' She tried not to make the question confrontational.

'I wait,' the broker said. 'Talk to people, if there's some out, while I wait. Have a quick check round the boat, see if anything's in need of a fix. Just here and there.'

'And Bill?'

'He does the same.'

So it wouldn't have been difficult to perform the switch. Pocket the original padlock, substitute your own, switch keys on the key ring so the broker wouldn't notice the change. That solved the problem of access. Was access enough? A cabin cruiser, an unidentified cabin cruiser, had been seen on the canal the night Cara died. Whoever had been running her had to have a key to start the engine, and for the ignition, you would need to steal a key.

And one of the keys that Steve Calloway had given to the broker was suddenly faulty, the day the potential buyer had come back for a second time, a longer look around the boat, a boat he now knew a lot about. She looked at the ignition keys. They were close, they were not the same. Substitute a different key for the same kind of engine – pocket the original and claim the key you have been given is faulty. That way, both the broker and the thief had access to the boat. But the owner didn't. How much of a gamble would that have been? He already knew that the owner showed little interest in the boat. Calloway had only checked now idly, perhaps wouldn't have chased up the problem he'd had with access if he hadn't been interested in contacting Tina.

'Let's go and have a look, Mr Calloway,' she said.

Farnham skimmed the diary Judith Martin had found in Kerry Fraser's room. Martin spoke quickly and quietly, keeping her voice low for the benefit of the woman slumped in the chair in the inter-view room next door. Farnham thought she could probably have used a megaphone and not made much impression. 'It was late by the time I managed to sort out the mare's nest Kerry had given me,' Martin said.

'What does –' he gestured with his thumb to the woman – 'say?'

'She doesn't say anything much.' Martin's mouth was tight with disapproval.

Farnham thought. Kerry Fraser had been seen on the tram heading towards Meadowhall with a group of friends. He'd despatched a couple of cars to find her, but there was no report back yet. They could be anywhere in the vast mall's shops, cafés, cinema. He checked his watch. Almost half-past seven.

He looked at the diary again. Far from attending school on Friday afternoon, Kerry had truanted with Stacy McDonald. There seemed to have been some kind of rendezvous arranged – *I looked but she wasn't there and then Stacy went*. Stacy went where? Where was the meeting, what had happened?

'Who's this "Lyn"?' he said.

'The half-sister. You remember, in the Fraser case – the stepdaughter accused him of abusing her.'

'OK.' He drummed his fingers as he thought. 'What happened to her?'

'She went into care,' Martin said, 'before Fraser's arrest. The mother says she's had no contact with her for over a year.'

'And now?'

'I don't know, sir. We're looking.'

Farnham felt events running too fast ahead of him. The Chapman case again. He needed to have those facts at his fingertips, and they'd barely started looking at the old records. They needed to find the people who'd been on the boat that day, re-interview them, identify the mystery photographer. There was the link that Barraclough had found: Sheryl Hewitt, the dead junkie, Cara Hobson's friend. And now this 'Lyn', Mark Fraser's stepdaughter, a third girl who had been in care, a girl who was the same age as the other two. A picture was starting to form in his mind. Cara Hobson had gone into care around the time of Ellie Chapman's disappearance. She'd made a complete break with her family, according to the care worker Tina Barraclough had talked to. 'Cara', 'Lyn' – Carolyn? Could Cara Hobson be Mark Fraser's stepdaughter? But that didn't work – Kerry Fraser talked about communicating with 'Lyn' after Cara was dead.

He went back through the pages of the diary, aware of Judith Martin's eyes on him. Phones. There was no phone in Cara Hobson's flat – she'd probably had a mobile, but that had gone missing. The phone at the Fraser house had been cut off for months. The planned meetings had gone wrong. As far as he could tell from the diary, all the contact since Cara's death had been via text messages.

'I'll talk to the mother,' he said.

Mrs Fraser was still slumped over in the chair. She looked at him with dull eyes as he came into the room, taking a drag on her cigarette. The room smelt of smoke and acetone. Her face was puffy and her eyes were red. 'Mrs Fraser . . . ?' he said.

She looked at him. 'What do you want with Kerry? What's she done now?' She stubbed out her cigarette and lit another one.

'Mrs Fraser . . .' She seemed about to say something, but shook her head and waved her hand at him to go on. 'We've been looking at Kerry's diary . . .' He opened the book at the pages he'd marked. 'We know she spent the afternoon with Stacy, the day Stacy disappeared. We need to know who she's been seeing,' he said. 'Who's been contacting her. She keeps talking about Lyn, about meeting Lyn . . .' He looked at her to see if she was taking in what he was saying.

'She's nothing but trouble, takes after her father.' Her eyes, already bloodshot, looked redder.

'Who was that, Mrs Fraser?' Save him from drunks, particularly maudlin drunks.

'Lyn,' she said. 'We were fine, me and Mark and Kerry. It was always Lyn causing trouble.'

Farnham suppressed his impatience. 'Tell me about Lyn,' he said. 'Where is she now?'

'Always fighting, her and Kerry.' She lit another cigarette, ignoring the one that was burning in the ashtray.

'Kerry was meeting her,' Farnham said. 'She says so in her diary. Tell me about her.'

'I don't know.' The woman was fidgeting and looking towards the door. She seemed to make an effort to concentrate. 'She left. She wanted to go. She never liked Mark. She was always causing trouble. We never had a chance.' A tear ran down her cheek.

Maybe Lyn had had good reason not to like her stepfather, Farnham thought. The woman seemed to have forgotten that. 'Where did she go?' he said.

Her gaze moved away. 'She left home,' she said, after a pause. 'I couldn't cope. Not after *he* . . .'

'Mark Fraser?' Farnham prompted.

'Yes. Him. I couldn't cope with her.'

Fraser's stepdaughter had gone into care. Cara Hobson had been in care. 'Where is she now?' The Fraser woman sat looking out of the window. 'Mrs Fraser?' he said.

She shook her head. 'It isn't Fraser,' she said. She looked round the room. 'I need a drink,' she said.

Farnham needed a drink too, but after half an hour spent in this woman's company, half an hour of breathing in the acetone smell of her alcohol-damaged body, the sourness of her breath, he felt as though he didn't want to touch another drop as long as he lived.

Judith Martin tapped on the door. She looked at Farnham, and he made a quick apology to the Fraser woman. 'Kerry's friends,' Martin said. 'A couple of the dads are panicked now and have gone looking for them, but Meadowhall is crawling with kids of an evening, and without knowing where the girls were headed . . .'

Farnham checked the time. Half past seven. He didn't want the Fraser child on the streets for any longer than necessary. 'Tell them to keep looking,' he said. They'd need to be discreet. The Fraser child wasn't co-operative. If she got the idea the police were looking for her, she might well do a runner. There wasn't much to come home for that he could see.

Then he registered what the woman had said. He turned back to her. 'It isn't Fraser?'

'My name,' she said. 'I divorced him. Fraser. After . . .'

'I'm sorry,' he said. They should have got this sorted out. 'What . . . ?'

'It's Young,' she said. 'My maiden name. *When I was Young . . .*' She smiled vaguely at a distant joke and for a moment he caught an image of what she must have looked like before the alcohol took its toll. Then the significance of what she had said struck him. 'Young?' he said. He was aware of Martin looking across, puzzled. 'Mrs Young . . .'

'Ms . . .' she corrected him, still smiling.

Oh, for . . . 'Ms Young. Lyn's name – what's it short for? What's Lyn's full name?'

'Lyn. She didn't want Mark, didn't want Kerry. She was always on about *her* father. Her dad. She never saw him. He never came near her. It spoiled

413

things. We had a lovely relationship, me and Mark, until Madam got to work.' Her eyes filled with tears. 'And then Mark met *her* . . .'

'Lyn's name, Mrs – Ms Young.' Farnham was holding on to his patience with difficulty.

'No one cares about it,' she said. 'She's not a nice person. It's my own daughter, I know, but she's not a nice person.' Her eyes focused on Farnham. 'Melinda. It's a pretty name.'

Lyn. Melinda. Mel. Mark Fraser's stepdaughter, Mel Young.

Tina swung her car into the parking space. The restaurants and the bars and the cinemas were all lit up, and the lights were flashing: *Old Orleans . . . Bowling . . . Eating, dancing, cavorting!* The car park was busy, even in the snow. The concrete expanse gave a sense of bustle and life, until she got out of the car and looked around. There was music, loud music, coming from the bars. Behind the doors of the cinema, she could see the ticket booths, the steaming popcorn, the banks of sweets and drinks, but it was a world inhabited by sound and machines. It was like being abandoned in an electronic world that went about its business, entertainment, oblivious to the fact that the people were long dead, long gone.

And as the machines ran down, the lights would vanish, one by one, the doors and windows would be boarded up, leaving an abandoned tower in the night from which a figure plummeted down . . .

'Bit of a dump. Where's the mooring?' Steven Calloway had pulled up behind her. 'I didn't come this way yesterday.'

She blinked. Daydreaming in the middle of an investigation. *Pull yourself together, woman!* 'We can cross the tram tracks,' she said. 'It's easy to park here – that's why I use it.'

He was looking round as she led the way to the tram stop. 'Which circle of hell is this, do you think?'

She looked sideways at him. *Thick plod?* But he seemed to be talking half to himself, looking round almost in bewilderment. 'It's the one for people who watch too much television,' she said. He laughed, and followed her as she made her way across the tramlines and over the bridge to the towpath.

The snow was falling heavily now. The mooring was in shadow, the towpath lights dim in the winter night, the sky heavy with cloud. It looked very different from when she had been here in the daylight. She could see the shapes of the boats, but there were no cabin lights, no signs of any life. 'Where . . . ?' The darkness was confusing her, stopping her from getting her bearings.

'Along here,' he said, moving away from the light to a place where deep shadow lay across the canal. 'She's over here.'

Tina followed, her eyes squinting into the darkness, trying to ignore the flicker across her vision that was the snow, the sense of falling, of imbalance. The night was playing tricks with her eyes. She couldn't see any boat in the darkness. She stumbled as her foot caught on something on the path. She reached in her pocket for her torch. 'Here.' Calloway's voice out of the darkness again. Then, 'What the . . . ?'

'Mr Calloway?' Her foot slipped in the slush. The snow was starting to settle. 'Mr Calloway? Steven?'

'It's . . .' He was standing by the mooring, looking round. 'I've lost my bearings. It's . . .' He turned back.

'What is it?' She could see the faint gleam of the light on the water.

'The boat,' he said. 'My boat, the *Mary May* – she's gone.'

Tina looked at the dark water of the canal, the towpath vanishing into the night ahead. The mooring was empty. The *Mary May* was out on the canal.

The snow was settling on the towpath as Kerry trudged towards town, towards the railway bridge. She'd meet Lyn – she was going to be early this time – and she'd get the stuff, then she'd tell Lyn about Stacy, about Mum, and maybe Lyn would tell her what she should do. 'You're too soft,' Lyn would say. 'You want to stand up for yourself,

Kizz.' Lyn could stand up for herself. No one messed around with Lyn.

She'd pulled the hood of her jacket up, but the wet of the snow had soaked through. She was starting to shiver with the cold. She pulled the phone out of her pocket and looked at it again, afraid she might have read the message wrong, got the time and the place wrong. *MT U ON TOPATH RLY BR 7.30 RGNT DNT B L8*. She was passing the high walls of the factories and warehouses now, getting closer to the city centre. She could see the railway bridge ahead. The towpath lights wavered as the snow got thicker. Where was she going to go tonight? How could she go home? They'd know by now she'd been lying.

The path ran into the darkness under the bridge. The flat metal of the girders made a roof above her. She was briefly sheltered from the snow, and she paused to shake it off her jacket and her hood. The bridge funnelled the wind that seemed to cut through her – she was past shivering. A numbness was starting in her hands and feet that made her feel – almost – warm. She checked her watch. It wasn't half-past yet. She was going to get there in time. She was going to get there early. There was a singing in the metal, then a drumming, and the bridge thundered as a train ran towards the station. Kerry leant against the wall and let the noise and the vibration run through her, emptying her mind of everything except the one thing, the thing that mattered. She had to get to Lyn.

Her mind was flying ahead as she hurried the last quarter mile. Lyn would have to tell her now what she meant – *its abut yor dad meet u at the cafy 7 dont b l8 . . .,* why she'd been sending all those cuttings. Lyn must think that Dad was in danger, but Kerry knew that. And she knew that Dad hadn't done anything to Ellie. They'd said about Dad doing things to Lyn. Kerry felt something deep and ashamed inside her. He never. That was wrong. But she'd told them that already. They hadn't believed her. Maybe they'd believe Lyn.

She pulled the phone out of her bag and switched it on. The message icon flashed. *New message.* She pressed *Read new* and watched the letters running across the screen: WR R U? Lyn. Lyn was waiting somewhere near. She keyed it in quickly – *rlwy brij topath* – and hurried on. She could see it now in the darkness ahead, the low arch of the bridge.

She heard a noise behind her, a strange cracking sound. She looked back. A boat was coming along the canal towards her, the ice breaking under its bow. It drifted out of the darkness, appearing and disappearing through the snow. Kerry tucked her chin in against the flakes that landed wetly on her face. It would be nice to be on a boat, it would be sheltered and it might be warm. She remembered the times she'd seen orange light shining through the windows of the cabins on the houseboats at night; they'd always looked warm and welcoming. But this boat was dark and silent, drifting past her, slowly, slowly, and it bumped gently against the canal side, slowing, stopping. Kerry quickened her pace.

The boat was a darker shadow against the darkness of the canal. It was like a ghost boat, cutting through the water with no one there, coming out of the shadows and then vanishing into the shadows again . . . Like Ellie, walking into the woods, out of the bright sunlight of the last day as the darkness under the trees swallowed her up.

Then something came out of the darkness and hooked on to her arm. The pain shot into her shoulder, making her shout out as the thing that had gripped her jerked her back and she sprawled forward, towards the canal, towards the water. A white face with a sad mouth and a red, leering smile hung in the darkness in front of her. Something grabbed her hair as she fell and hauled her on to the boat, a hand covering her mouth as she gasped with the pain and shock. Then she was face down on the wood, in the slime of water and snow and muck, and the pain in her arm was throbbing and throbbing. Her arm felt wet, a warm wetness that made her feel weak and sick, and the hand that had caught her was twisted in her hair, forcing her head up, and there was a heavy weight on her back.

The weight pressed down and her head was pulled back further. A voice whispered in her ear: 'Not a sound, little one, or I'll snap your spine. But you'll still feel it when I cut your throat and you bleed to death like a dog. So, not a sound, please.' The voice was bored, cold, but she could feel the edge of the knife burning against her throat, and all of her went leaden as a surge of cold ran through her. She couldn't control the shaking and she realized she'd wet herself like a baby.

'Someone wants to *cavort* with you.'

CHAPTER 17

Kerry lay on the floor of the cabin. She had given up struggling against the tape that was wrapped round her arms and wrists, her legs and ankles, across her mouth. Her arm was stiff and sore, and stung where the boat hook had cut it. 'Keep you out of trouble, hey, Kizz?' the voice had whispered. The weight of the knee in her back lifted, but the voice was whispering in her ear now, close, tickling as the breath disturbed her hair. 'Like a crab. Tie up its pincers and put it on ice. I worked in a bar, Kizz, a year ago, on the seafront, in Greece. The tourists would come to eat – best seafood on the island, they said. And I'd take a crab, all its little legs trying to scuttle, and put it on to the fire, where the coals were red hot. They jump off, you know, Kizz, and they try to crawl away and you let them go a little bit, then you put them back. And they watch, the tourists, and they look away, and you ask yourself, will they eat it when you put it in front of them, all hot and melting and wonderful? They do, you know. They can't resist.' A waft of sour breath caught her. 'Oh, Kizz. Did you really think you could save your dad?'

Then she was alone. The blood from her arm felt sticky. She tried to struggle, but the tape wouldn't give. After a few minutes, she heard the sound of an engine and the floor underneath her began to vibrate. And the shapes of the buildings began to move past her. She struggled again, trying futilely to free her hands, but then the engine stopped, and she felt the slight thump of the boat drifting into the bank. They'd arrived.

She heard feet again, and twisted her head round, trying to see, but the cabin was dark. A light from the towpath shone through the window. She could feel the vibration under her as feet crossed the cabin, and then, in the dim light from the towpath, she could see a face. She would have screamed if the tape hadn't stopped her. It was a white face with a contorted red smile painted over a crying mouth, eyes like black holes. And then she realized. It was a mask, a clown mask like some of the kids wore to parties or for Halloween. Just a mask, just a clown-face. Then the figure became a shadow again and moved away.

She could see a dim glow, blue, and for a moment she could make out the figure crouched over, the blue light illuminating the mask. A phone display. It was a phone.

A phone. She turned her head quickly before the light went out. She could see her bag, a dark shape on the floor by the bench. She tried to roll on to her side, keeping her eyes on the place where her bag was. Her phone, it was inches away, it was switched on. She tried to push herself closer, get her bound hands nearer to the bag. Nearer.

She heard the *beep* of her phone as it received a message, and then a hand cracked across her face and her head thumped against the floor. 'Stupid, *stupid*.' The clown face smiled its painted smile. The clown mouth wept.

Kerry's voice struggled against the tape, but no sound came out. She felt something touch her face, her tight-shut eyes. Gloved hands. 'Look, Kizz.' She opened her eyes. A phone, her phone with the Buffy cover that Stacy had given her for Christmas, was in front of her. The message icon flashed.

'Look.' The letters were running across the display, but she screwed her eyes shut again. A hand covered hers and bent her little finger double, pressing the top joint back and up against the base. Kerry tried to shout, but the tape held her mouth. Another jolt of pain shot through her finger, and her teeth clamped shut against her tongue. The warm taste of blood filled her mouth. She wanted to be sick. 'Look.' The insistent whisper, the gloved hand threatening.

She opened her eyes and tried to read the words. *SO SORY KIZ DIDNT MEAN IT*. There was a soft laugh. 'So now you know.' Kerry's head was hurting, and her hand was throbbing. She tried to move to take her weight off it. She couldn't straighten her finger.

She was aware of the figure crouching down beside her, and she was pushed on to her back. 'I'll have to take some of this off, after.' And something cold touched her neck. It was so cold, it stung like a wasp on a hot day, and her neck felt sticky and warm. She began to struggle. 'Don't fight, Kizz. There's worse things than this, you know.'

She tucked her chin down against her chest and heard the soft laughter again. She could feel the tears of panic running down the sides of her face, clogging her nose. She could feel the warmth and the stickiness on her neck, on her hair. Dim in the moonlight, she could see the hand holding the knife, lifting a handful of her hair and letting it trail back to the floor. She could see the glints of gold and red as the light caught it.

'It's the fine detail they don't notice, Kizz. They'll see the whole picture, but they won't see the details.' The whisper was further away now and the warm stickiness was trickling down her neck, matting in her hair. 'In the water, the blood trails away in streamers, and it floats and curls around. But you won't bleed to death, Kizz, you'll drown. Don't worry. You can't struggle. You'll breathe in the water. The next bit won't be nice, Kizz. You'll choke and you'll shit yourself and you'll have convulsions. It won't last too long. Then you'll die.' The hand gripping her hair had tightened, the pull against her scalp making her eyes water. 'The canal's not so deep, Kizz. If they'd leave you, I'd come back. We could keep company, you and me. You'll lie in the mud on the bottom, and slowly, Kizz, slowly, you'll start to rot. Then you'll float, and your skin will be swollen with water. But they won't leave you, and this time, I can't be here.'

The cold seemed to be in her bones. She tried to roll over, and felt the blood start to run down her neck again. She heard feet moving across the cabin, felt the floor underneath shake slightly. Something banged, and then again, and she heard the sudden gush of water, water running fast under pressure.

Then feet crossed the cabin again, and her body lifted off the floor as she was kicked in the side and she could feel the crunch of her ribs and then the pain and she rolled back on to her injured hand and she thought she was going to be sick. She needed to breathe through her mouth and she couldn't. And then the feet were moving past her again. And she felt the cold water start to trickle round her as she heard the feet on the steps, on the deck and gone. And she curled around the pain, unable to move, unable to make a sound.

After Daniel had left, Eliza sat at her desk, trying to work, as her mind went over and over the information that he had given her. Had their relationship really been just a casual fling, fuelled more by proximity than anything else? Yet he'd stayed on in Madrid after meeting her, had resisted her own attempts to define the relationship as casual – though they had both known that circumstance might end it. She hadn't wanted to love him, hadn't wanted the concomitant pain, but in the end, she had allowed herself to relax her guard.

And it was like the end of the relationship all over again. In Madrid, it had never properly ended – it had evaporated in Daniel's evasions. And now it was, irretrievably, completely over, she realized how much she had been building on having it back. But it had gone, and it had taken everything else with it. It was as if her entire career was up for grabs again. She had thought she'd found her niche in the art world – she had an almost instinctive understanding of the work of other artists, she knew how to present it, how to interpret it, how to exhibit it in a way that allowed people to make their own interpretations. And she'd thought that skill had been recognized and valued. But it had all been a sham.

Daniel must have phoned Jonathan soon after they'd met at the Prado. He'd wanted her to curate the exhibition – that was true enough. They'd talked about it as Daniel was working on it. Her ideas had influenced what he'd done, she knew. She could still remember their meeting in front of *The Triumph of Death*:

I always think that this is in the wrong place for

it . . . It ought to be in the shadows . . . I'd put it in a current setting. A cityscape, industrial ruins, show people a modern triumph of death.

She'd said that, not Daniel. He'd called the painting a fifteenth-century video nasty. And it had been Ivan who had queried her desire to move it away from the other paintings: *Where else would it belong but among the Boschs?* Ivan who had recognized the words of Cennino Cennini: *Do not apply any pink at all, because a dead person has no colour . . .* Ivan who'd talked about modern attitudes to death and decay. Daniel had listened, as he'd listened to Eliza, encouraging her to talk again and again, returning to the Brueghel. Oh, he had come up with his own ideas – or had he? Daniel and Ivan had been travelling together, but they'd come to Madrid because Ivan had wanted to.

And Ivan was working on a modern *Triumph*, had shared his ideas with Daniel. He'd come to Sheffield to try and sell his work to Jonathan. And he'd said: *I wonder, if you wrote a genesis of this – from conception to birth, what would you say?* Ivan knew. *The Triumph of Death* wasn't Daniel Flynn's. It was Eliza Eliot's and Ivan Bakst's.

She gave up the pretence of working. She barely had the energy to get herself home. The thought of the drive to Laura's seemed overwhelming. Why did this have to happen when her flat – which looked more and more inviting – was effectively out of bounds? She wished she could just crawl upstairs, run herself a hot bath, fall into bed and forget this wretched day.

But she couldn't. It would be stupid. She hadn't needed Roy Farnham's caution – the events of the night before were warning enough. She needed to get away from here. She gradually became aware of the silence around her, and the fact that, away from the pool of light from her desk lamp, the gallery was dark. She checked her watch. It was after seven-thirty. She'd meant to leave before five, and she'd been sitting here staring into space, trying to come to terms with what Daniel had told her.

She began her routine for closing up. She locked the upper gallery and set the alarm. Something nagged at her as she came downstairs, something she'd forgotten. She couldn't bring it to mind. She collected her coat and her work bag from the office, checking that her phone was fully charged before she tucked it into the side pocket. If anyone needed to contact her, they could. One of Roy's team had dropped her car off. It was out the front. She'd meant to throw some overnight things into a bag, but it was late now and she didn't want to go up to her flat. Laura could lend her the basics. It was only till tomorrow. She dumped her work bag on the floor by the door, and began to lock up.

She'd kept herself numb all day with fatigue and with work, but her defences were crumbling now, and as she moved wearily round the empty gallery, her mind kept taking her back into the darkness outside Cara's door, back into Maggie's, listening in the night for feet moving softly behind her, back to the haven of her home, feeling the sudden urgency of Roy Farnham's mouth against hers. She didn't want to think about it. Tomorrow. Tomorrow would do.

She was exhausted. She felt angry with herself for losing control of her life. What had she done these past few days apart from let herself be pushed around by events? She was angry with Daniel, even more angry with Jonathan for his deceit and his desertion, leaving her to cope with what was, in the end, his responsibility.

She checked the downstairs gallery quickly. It was getting colder. The windows looked out over the canal. It was snowing. The water was dark and leaden, the towpath in shadows. A boat was moored near the bridge, but the path was deserted. Roy Farnham's warning echoed in her mind. She went to turn off the lights and set the alarm. Her feet echoed, *tap-tap*, as she crossed the wooden floor. She keyed in the alarm code and turned out the lights. The gallery faded into darkness, and, for a moment, she was back to the night she had seen Cara sitting on the window ledge, looking out along the canal.

And it was there again, that echo. The echo she'd heard the night that Cara died. She stopped and listened. Nothing. Silence. Her imagination? She'd set the alarm. If there was anyone in the gallery, it would go off – except . . . She realized then what had been worrying her earlier: she hadn't heard the long tone that told her the alarm was working. She hadn't heard it upstairs, either, but she'd missed it in her rush to get away. She keyed in the code again, but nothing happened.

There must be a fault, she told herself, trying to ignore the chill that was creeping down her spine. Her heart was starting to beat fast. She looked back. The security light was a dim glow in the ceiling, but the room itself was concealed in deep pools of shadow. If the alarm was faulty, she could phone the engineer and someone would be there soon. But what if the alarm wasn't faulty? What if someone . . . ? But no one knew the codes, apart from her and Jonathan. *And Cara. Cara knew.* Jonathan had changed the codes after that. No one knew those codes.

She needed to get out of there. Two people had been killed. She needed to get out of there, *now*. She turned towards the door, and heard the echo again, almost beyond audibility, *hush-hush*, soft shoes moving quietly across the floor behind her. Her eyes strained at the shadows. It was there again, coming from – not behind her, not from the gallery, but from the door. She spun round.

The sound – it was – where was it? The walls, the floors, the ceiling, all bounced the sound off them, making direction impossible to judge. The shadows danced as her gaze flew around the room seeing

430

movement where there was nothing, hearing other things now that the faint sound of footsteps had stopped. She waited, trying to calm her breathing. *OK. OK.* She just needed to walk quickly to the door, and get to her car. Then she needed to phone Roy. No, she needed to dial 999 first and then get Roy and . . .

Her heart thumped. There was someone standing between her and the exit, in the doorway to Jonathan's office. 'Who's there?' Her voice was high. *Don't let him know you're scared!*

'Eliza?' And the figure became Jonathan, standing uncertainly in the dim glow of the security light.

'Jonathan.' She could feel her heart hammering. 'You frightened the life out of me!'

He came towards her. 'Sorry. Sorry.' His voice sounded tired and dead. 'I didn't want to talk to anybody.'

'The alarm isn't working,' Eliza said.

'It's OK.' He was in the light from the entrance now and she could see his face. He looked terrible, white and exhausted with dark shadows under his eyes. He was at least two days away from a shave and his beard looked ragged. This disarray in the normally meticulous Jonathan unnerved her. 'I changed the settings,' he said.

'Why? Why didn't you tell me?'

He waved his hand vaguely, looking round the gallery as he spoke. 'I thought you might go before I did. I didn't want you to set the alarm while I was still in here,' he said after a moment.

'But that's . . .' He wasn't paying her any attention. 'You look awful. What's happened?'

He shook his head slowly. 'They think I did it,' he said. 'They think I killed those two girls.'

Eliza looked at him in bewilderment. 'They don't. They've let you go. Anyway, you were in Leeds.'

He shook his head. 'They don't believe me. *Us.* They don't believe us. They've pulled Patricia in. They'll put pressure on her. If she thinks she'll get into trouble . . .'

'But the night the girl disappeared – you were at the gallery, at Daniel's party. We all were.'

He shook his head again. 'No one knows exactly when she was taken. It doesn't mean anything. I'm an artist, see? That makes me a psycho in *his* eyes.' His? He must mean Farnham. 'And they think an artist did it – the painting, the Brueghel. The one your boyfriend brought here.' His tone was suddenly venomous.

'I didn't know you knew,' she said, keeping her voice calm. 'And Daniel isn't . . . We don't have a relationship any more.'

'A relationship,' he said. 'No one has a relationship with Flynn. He used you, Eliza.' His face seemed to crumple and he sank down into one of the chairs, burying his head in his hands.

Appalled, Eliza looked at him. She'd never managed to get close to Jonathan, never really got to know him. She remembered the conversation they'd had a couple of days before the party when he'd talked about his father, a deceptively light tone concealing deep bitterness. It had been one of the few personal conversations they'd had. And now he seemed to be having a breakdown. Under the stress of everything that was happening at the gallery, he was coming apart. 'Jonathan?' she said.

'I'm sorry.' His voice was muffled. 'I shouldn't have said that.'

'I know about the job,' she said. 'About the exhibition. Daniel told me.'

He nodded, his head turned away. He pulled a tissue out of his pocket and wiped it over his face. 'Don't worry,' he said. 'I wouldn't have thought of you if Flynn hadn't mentioned you – but you gave the best interview. And you've done very well. Really very well.'

His voice was detached. He sounded as though she was a student who'd handed in a piece of work, but they were talking about murder, about the death of a woman and a child, they were discussing the possibility of Jonathan being charged with those murders. He seemed to have lost his grip on reality. She was starting to feel more and more uneasy. Suddenly, she wanted to get away. 'I need to go,' she said. 'I'm staying with Laura tonight. We need to lock up here.' Her voice sounded artificial and nervous.

'Lock up,' he said. 'Yes.' His eyes searched around the gallery again. Eliza could see through the window behind him that the snow was still falling. 'Do you want a drink?' He'd taken off his glasses, and his eyes had a naked, unfocused look. 'I've got some whisky in the office – we could have a drink. We could go up to your flat. It's nice there, peaceful.'

'I haven't got time,' she said. 'Laura's expecting me.' She moved across towards the door, towards the exit, where her car was parked. She could see her bag where she had dumped it by the door. Her phone! So close, and just too far.

He moved in front of her. She stopped. 'Why won't you stay?' he said. 'Half an hour. Have a drink.'

She tried to keep her voice steady. She couldn't get past him to the exit, but there was another way out. 'OK,' she said. 'But in the office. Wait here. I need to get my stuff from the flat.' She waited a moment. 'I'll do that,' she said carefully, 'then we can have a drink before I go.' Her smile felt awkward and artificial as she backed away towards the stairs leading to the flats. He was watching her, but he was letting her go. 'See you in a minute,' she said.

Then she was through the door and on to the stairs. She began to run as soon as she was out of sight. Up the stairs, along the corridor and out through the other door – get away and get some . . . But he might think of that, might come up the outside staircase and cut off her escape route. It couldn't be Jonathan! Her rational mind knew the idea was ridiculous, but something was urging her up the stairs, *quick, quick, hurry, before it's too late*! The flat. She had to get to the flat, lock the door and phone. Get help. He might not realize what she was doing before the police arrived.

She heard a sound behind her and turned, but the stairs were empty. She remembered the night she had found Cara in the gallery, that sense of another presence, inimical, threatening. She remembered how she'd been half expecting the alarm to go off, she'd been so convinced that there was someone else in the gallery. She could remember the high note of the alarm as she and Cara had climbed the stairs.

She was through the connecting door. Something nagged at her as she fumbled in her handbag for her keys. Something she'd forgotten in the gallery? Her eyes were playing tricks, making movements in the shadows.

Her key, where was her key? That sense of something forgotten clamoured urgently at her mind, making her fingers clumsy, making her hands shake as she fitted the key into the lock. Because now her memory was working. She was walking up the stairs with Cara, a bit impatient with herself for getting involved, and the high tone of the alarm was sounding, letting her know that it was safely set. And it had stopped, and she'd tensed, expecting it to go off, only of course it hadn't because there was no one in the gallery. Except – the sound of the alarm hadn't just stopped. It had dropped a tone. She could hear it as clearly as if she was back there: Cara chattering nervously about Daniel's painting, her rather impatient rejoinder as she was distracted from something she *knew* was important – the different sound the alarm had made, the sound it made when she had set it by mistake and had had to punch the code in again to stop it.

There *had* been someone else in the gallery that night. Someone who had waited until she and Cara were out of sight, someone who knew how much time there was before the alarm set, someone who had punched the code in at the last minute to turn the alarm off.

The door of her flat swung open and she was through it in a moment, slamming it behind her, snapping on the light. She could hear the phone ringing in the gallery downstairs. That didn't matter now. She needed to lock the door and get to her own phone.

And then the lights went out. Without warning, she was in darkness. The key dropped from her fingers and hit the floor with a metallic sound. The sudden dark blinded her. All she could see was blackness and dancing colours. She reached out and touched the door, feeling across it for the handle. It was like the night in Maggie's kitchen, when the power . . . Power cuts at Maggie's, power cuts here? Now she could hear . . . could she? Or was it her imagination? Footsteps, slow and quiet in the corridor outside. The door!

She dropped on to her knees, feeling around. The key, she couldn't find the key! Her eyes were getting accustomed to the dark now, and she could see her hands feeling through the shadows, could see the door, a faint glimmer of light wood in the darkness.

She touched something cold and metallic and she grabbed it, nearly dropped it again, her hands clumsy with panic. She was still kneeling as she tried to fit the key into the lock. It was upside down. She tried it the other way, but it still wouldn't fit. The footsteps came closer and stopped on the other side of the door.

And the handle began to turn.

Farnham was back in the incident room before he could deal with an anxiety that had been growing on him since he had found the link between Mel Young and the gallery murders.

How had those photos got into Eliza's flat? Had Eliza gone to her friend's as she had planned? After a moment's hesitation – of course she'd gone to her friend's, what was he worrying about? – he rang the gallery. It would be typical if she'd decided to work late. He was reassured when he got the answering machine. He tried the number of her flat. The phone rang twenty times. Nothing. No reply. She must have left. He relaxed slightly, then he tried her mobile number – belt and braces. He wanted to be certain.

He got the message service. That was understandable – after the night she'd had, she'd probably switched her phone off and gone to bed. He left a message, asking her to contact him. There was nothing else he could do about it for now.

CHAPTER 18

Eliza scrambled back from the door, her hands reaching for something, anything, to defend herself. A vase, she gripped the neck, no, the table lamp, the vase dropping from her hand and smashing on the floor. She lifted the lamp, feeling its heavy base, its unwieldiness as she faced the door, backing away, the lamp held ready. The door was a glimmer in the faint light, reflections from the falling snow. She remembered the waiting silence in Maggie's flat, the darkness and the sound of the door latch in the night. Was that all she was going to see, a shape in the shadows, and then . . . ?

Everything seemed very sharp, very clear. She kept facing the door, but moved back carefully, checking the floor with her feet. To fall now could be fatal. She kept one hand gripping the lamp, but with the other, she felt along the surface of the table, books, papers, pushed aside and dropping to the floor.

The phone. She knocked the receiver off the rest and keyed the number in, 999, her fingers clumsy with urgency. How much more time did she have? She picked the receiver up and was speaking as she lifted it – 'Police! Quickly! The Second Site Gallery, the gallery by the canal he's here, he's here . . .' The phone was silent. She pressed the rest, and pressed it again and again.

The phone was dead. She thought she was going to be sick.

But the door stayed shut. She gripped the lamp again, and moved back, closer, quietly, listening. She could hear someone moving around. She could hear it through the wall now, in Cara's flat, muffled footsteps and a voice singing, absently, hummed snatches, occasional words, a strangely androgynous voice: *Girls and boys . . . Moon does shine as bright . . .* Silence. She pressed her ear against the wall. Singing again, to the same tune. *The grave's a fine and silent place, but none I think do there embrace . . .* a soft laugh.

Whatever it was, it was in Cara's flat. She could get out – straight through her door and out via the fire escape. The fire-escape door might make some noise as she opened it, but she would be well down the steps before anyone came after her. Straight out and run, straight to the nearest phone, the nearest person. Straight out and run.

She put the lamp down. Silent now. She mustn't be heard moving near the door. She reached out and gripped the handle. Turn it slowly, very slowly, very gently so the latch doesn't click. She had it turned to its full extent. Now, very gently, very slowly, pull the door open, make sure it doesn't creak or . . . The door wouldn't budge. It was shut tight. But it wasn't locked, she hadn't managed to lock it, she'd dropped the key on the floor in her panic and backed away from the door as it started to open. She tugged harder, then jerked the handle in case the door had stuck. But it wouldn't shift. It was locked.

Her key was on the floor where she'd dropped it. She picked it up and tried to fit it in the keyhole, but this time, though she'd got it right, this time, though the key should have slipped in, something was jamming it. There must be a key in the lock at the other side of the door. She was locked in. The lights were turned off, the electricity, the phone. She couldn't get out. She turned the locks in the security bolts. Now, no one could get in. Impasse.

She tried the phone again. No dial tone. Could she attract attention from the window? They were high up, double-glazed. What were the chances of someone being on the towpath, looking up, seeing her in the darkness and being aware of the meaning of her signals? Break the window, start shouting? How easy was it to break toughened glass?

The footsteps were moving again now. Someone was walking to the door of Cara's flat, walking into the corridor, walking towards her door. She closed her eyes, like a child pretending she wasn't there. *Don't attract attention!* The door was bolted. It couldn't be opened. The footsteps paused, then moved again, along the corridor towards the gallery, towards the stairs. She heard the footsteps fade away.

OK. She fitted her key into the lock again as far as it would go, and started jiggling it, trying to dislodge the key on the other side that was preventing her from unlocking the door. Just a gentle push to dislodge it and then work it free. It might be stuck, but if it wasn't . . . She could unlock the door and get out while the going was good. Patience. She had to be patient. The key shifted a bit. It was working! Now she needed to be careful. If it slipped, it might jam itself in the lock, leave her trapped. She jiggled the key gently again, feeling more movement. Better if it didn't fall out completely and clatter on to the floor.

She felt as though she had been kneeling there for hours, gently working at the lock, but it couldn't have been more than ten minutes. Her key was fitting into the lock now. It was going to be OK, she was going to be able to open the door. She pressed her ear against the wood. She could hear the sound of things being moved around downstairs. What was going on?

She turned the key slowly, silently. She felt the lock release. She turned the handle carefully and pulled on the door. Nothing. Of course, the bolts, she hadn't released the bolts. She opened the top one and was about to open the bottom one when she heard the sound of footsteps again, coming up the stairs, and then along the corridor. She froze, then she stood up, very quietly, and re-bolted the door. She pushed her key more firmly into the lock, to make sure it couldn't be dislodged, and sent up a silent prayer that the key on the other side hadn't fallen out.

She could hear whistling, low and meditative. She could hear footsteps again, moving towards the fire escape. *Please go! Please go!* And the cold wind began to blow under her door, like the cold currents in the canal, like the flow of cold that had woken her, twice now, as the night air was drawn in. The outside door was open.

Eliza released the breath she didn't realize she'd been holding. She was cold. She was frozen. She stepped lightly across the flat to the window. She wanted to watch the entrance to the stairway. The snow was still falling, the night seeming lighter in the white reflection. She pressed her face against the glass, waiting for a figure to emerge from the bottom of the steps.

The canal below her was in black shadow. A single lamp shone on the towpath, its light casting a faint gleam. A boat was drifting along the canal, barely moving. It bumped against the side, turned slightly, drifted imperceptibly, stopped. It looked low in the water. No one had come down the steps, but she could see someone on the towpath now, a shadow in the shadows that moved forward as the boat bumped against the bank, jumped aboard. The light caught the figure briefly, illuminating the neat head, reflecting from the glasses. Jonathan.

She watched, but her mind was detached from

what she was seeing. Because she was aware of something now, something that her subconscious had been aware of for a while, something that . . . Her heart lurched. The smell of burning. The stinging, chemical smell of industrial burning.

She ran to the door and undid the bolts, her hands shaking in panic. The smoke was curling under her door, thick and black, and the draught was like a chimney, pulling it into her flat and into her lungs. She pulled the door open, and a great cloud of black, greasy poison engulfed her. She staggered back into her flat as an impenetrable darkness enveloped her. She couldn't see, she couldn't breathe. She reached out, trying to get her bearings, and everywhere she moved she came up against blank walls. She couldn't get out. Her heart was racing and she needed air and there wasn't any. Her chest was on fire and there was a buzzing and a roaring in her head. She tried to draw in a breath and was retching and choking as the smoke froze her lungs. The air was gone.

The phone rang. Farnham picked it up, convinced it would be Eliza, but it was Tina Barraclough. The cabin cruiser, the *Mary May*, was missing from its mooring. The death boat – what had put that melodramatic phrase into his mind? – was out on the canal.

OK, it should be simple. They had her trapped between the canal basin and Tinsley locks. But searching the canal wasn't an easy task. First thing – get the helicopter up. The helicopter could search the length of the canal more quickly than anything, with its searchlight and its night-vision cameras. It could be in the air in ten minutes. And he needed to get people on to the towpath – there was access at various points all the way along. Fast movement along the towpath? Low-tech solution the best – bikes. A boat? The chances of the official patrol boat being on this stretch were remote. He needed to get a boat on that water. If the *Mary May* was on the canal, they would find it.

How long was it since the *Mary May* left her mooring? How much time did the killer need? He was making the calls as his mind worked, getting the team assembled, getting people out along the canal. Who was at risk? Who was the killer's next target?

Kerry. If he was right, and Stacy McDonald had died a victim of mistaken identity, then one attempt had already been made on Kerry's life. If the boat was abroad, then she was in danger, now. He needed to put her somewhere safe until this was over. What was holding them up at Meadowhall?

Was there anything else? Something was trying to get his attention, something he'd missed. He'd checked on Eliza earlier – she was away from the gallery and she wasn't on her own. She should be safe. After the other night, she wouldn't take any stupid risks. So why was he jumpy? Why wouldn't his mind let him drop it? He went over what he'd done. He'd phoned her at the gallery, which was shut. The answering machine had taken the call. He'd phoned her at the flat, and there had been no reply. Fair enough. Except . . .

A picture was forming in his mind. He could remember standing in the doorway to her flat, looking round, noting things almost subconsciously with the eyes of an investigating officer, eyes that knew the importance of small details. And he could see it clearly, the phone and the answering machine beside it, and he could remember the almost automatic way Eliza had checked it with her eyes as she went past, zero, no messages. She had an answering machine, she used it, it had been switched on.

But he'd let the phone ring over twenty times before he'd been satisfied there was no one there. The answering machine should have taken the call. Unless she'd decided to stay at the flat after all and had unplugged the phone so she wouldn't be disturbed. But why? She could just turn the ringer off and let the machine take all the calls. Unless . . . He phoned the operator and got the woman to check the line.

'I'm sorry, sir,' she came back with after a short, but infuriating delay. 'There's a fault on the line. I'll report it.'

Shit! It could mean something or nothing, but he needed to get there, to get someone there. He had no one else to send. The phone rang again. It was Dave West. 'We've found Kerry Fraser's friends, sir,' West said. 'But she isn't with them.

446

She got off the tram before Meadowhall, some-where around Don Valley Stadium, a good hour ago.'

Christ on a bike. The stadium was near the mooring where the *Mary May* had been. Kerry had been missing for over an hour. The helicopter was up by now. They'd have the boat located in minutes. Eliza? What could he do about Eliza? He remembered Barraclough, in her car, heading back towards the city centre. He phoned her as he was pulling on his jacket and running to the car. They had to be in time!

Tina was heading for the gallery. Farnham's message had been quick, curt. Get there, check that Eliza Eliot was gone. The gallery. Everything that had happened was associated with that place, with that exhibition. She was aware of Calloway following her as she ran to her car, but she didn't have time to worry about that. The traffic was moving, the roads were fairly clear, though the snow was still falling. She tested the grip. The roads seemed to have been gritted. She put her foot down, remembering the sudden light of excitement in Calloway's eyes.

Excitement? She could remember when it had felt like that, rather than the sick apprehension she was feeling now, the apprehension that came from knowing what she might find, where her mistakes might lead. She followed the road round, round past the old market, the hotels, past the old station and under the bridge that marked the end of the gentrification.

The roads were darker here, the old streetlights more vulnerable to vandalism, less quickly repaired. She slowed then speeded up past the brick walls of the old factories and warehouses until the gallery was in sight. The sky was suddenly lighter, as though the lights here were working better, casting an almost orange glow up towards the sky as the snow fell monotonously, heavily. Then she realized what she was seeing, and was on the radio as she came alongside the gallery.

It was ablaze. Smoke – thick, black smoke – was pouring out of the building, and she could see the red of flames deep through the smoke, the ground floor, the first floor, and the first tongues starting to flicker through the roof. The sky lit up and the air filled with the throbbing sound of a motor. The helicopter. It was hovering above the canal, the other side of the gallery, the searchlight illuminating the building, the car park, throwing the detail into relief, the falling snow, the smoke exuding through the windows and the walls and the doors and curling thickly into the air.

She looked up. The flats. The fire was already in the roof at the front. She listened for the sound of the fire engines, but there was nothing, only, over the sound of the fire, the helicopter, closer and closer, so loud that nothing else could be heard. Eliza. Farnham thought she might still be in there.

She was on her radio talking to control as she ran. There was no time to wait for the fire engines. If Eliza was in there, she had minutes, less than minutes. It was probably too late already. The door on to the stairway was locked, but it gave way to one good kick. The smoke wasn't too bad on the stairs – they were open to the air on the landings. She tied her scarf round her mouth as she ran.

The water seeped through Kerry's clothes, seeped around her, making the rug under her sodden, then a pool, and she rolled over, trying to get her knees under her, get her face clear. Cold was creeping through her, chilling her flesh, her bones. The tape round her body meant she couldn't use her hands to help her, and she fell forward again, her face under the surface of the water for a choking moment, her hand crushed. The boat had moved after he had gone, as if he had pushed it away from the side. She could feel it rocking slightly with the gushing of the water, and it would sink and it didn't matter that the canal wasn't deep, the water would fill the cabin and she'd choke and drown and rot. She tried to stand again, but the stabbing pain in her ribs made her curl up, tears filling her eyes, clogging her nose. *Help me!*

Then – it was very faint, a thump, a judder, and she was listening, still, intent. There was someone on the boat, someone walking around. Her heart raced. The boat was rocking slightly. She couldn't hear the engine. It was hardly moving at all, as though it had been pushed off and left to drift.

A circle of light dazzled her. She screwed up her eyes and turned her head away. 'Ellie . . .' a voice said. Then, 'Oh, Christ, oh Christ!' There was someone crouching over her. A flood of relief rushed through her as she realized it wasn't the person with the clown face, it was someone else, someone come to help her. But he'd called her Ellie. He sounded as though he was crying.

'The water . . .' His voice sounded odd, far off. Why wasn't he pulling her out? Why wasn't he helping her? He stood up, moved away and she felt the water swirl round her and splash over her face. *You'll choke and you'll . . .* Her face was under the water. She struggled against the tape that held her arms.

Then he was back, pulling her head up. 'I didn't mean to hurt you, Ellie. I truly didn't. I scared you. I'm sorry. I just wanted to explain. I wasn't going to hurt you.'

Kerry was still struggling. She could hear what he was saying, but it didn't make sense, and the water was rising now, faster, and she was going to drown, they were both going to drown and rot in the mud. 'Ellie!' There was panic in his voice and she felt his hands gripping her throat, tighter and tighter. She made herself lie still. She made herself lie very still, and his hands slowly relaxed.

Then she realized he was talking, he'd been

450

talking for a while. She kept very still, listening, the cold fingers were round her neck, the water rising inexorably around her. '. . . Why did you think I was going to hurt you? It was so lovely to see you when you came back to the boat. I'd been watching you.'

The last day. He was talking about the last day. He was talking about Ellie. And as the cold water rose up around her, Kerry suddenly realized what had happened. They thought the boat had gone away, but what if it hadn't? What if Ellie had gone back to the boat? She didn't like using the bushes. She was shy. But they'd seen the signs on the water-bus and Ellie had gone there, after everyone thought the water-bus had gone. It hadn't been her dad. It had never been her dad. They might listen now, but it was too late.

There was a moment of blackness, and then Eliza was on the floor, and she could breathe. Her mind was starting to work again. She must have fallen into the cleaner air beneath the smoke. She had to get out.

She was in the corridor. She crawled towards the door. The air above her was thick and toxic. *Keep down. Keep low.* But the smoke was everywhere. Her head swam as she tried to reach up to the handle, to push it down and release the lock.

Her arm was hurting. Something was burning her arm. She was in the corridor outside the flat and she had to get out, get down the steps. She had to reach the handle, had to pull it. She couldn't do it, her legs were water, her head was on fire, but just a short way away, just down the steps, the car, safety, people, Roy, Daniel . . . *Un cuadro interesante, no?* Daniel in the Prado, watching her, intense, smiling, smiling.

And the handle was down, but the door wouldn't open. She couldn't force it open. She pulled herself upright and pushed against the door. The fire roared behind her. Down, she had to get down. Down was easy, except when your legs gave way, except when your hands forgot to grip and the canal, no, the river, it was flowing fast so it had to be the river, was underneath and there was something in the water, something with tangled hair and empty eyes staring up and the sky where the ravens of the valley shall pluck them out, and she was by the canal and it vanished into the distance that way and this way and the lights of the bars and restaurants flashed blue and red and green in the night and she could go in and it would be *fun, fun, fun* only her legs weren't there any more and she was hot except she wasn't sure if she was hot or if she was cold and it was all going away like a rush she was rushing away on a boat to the river on the canal far away and she was falling, falling . . .

It was like climbing a tower block, a block of flats, the functionalism of the concrete, the grubbiness of the bricks, the cracked treads. And a face was looking down at her, white in the darkness. But this wasn't the tower block, no one was standing high above her, looking down, assessing the drop. Tina reached the first landing. A discarded mask lay on the ground, a clown face, grinning and weeping as she ran past up the second flight, up the third and she was at the next landing and the smoke was pouring out, but she could see now that the fire was at the front of the building rather than at the back. That was why no one had seen it. It meant she might be in time.

The door was shut. Someone had jammed a wooden bar across it. Anyone trying to open the door from the inside would fail. She put her shoulder against the bar and pushed, but it wouldn't budge. The smoke was making her cough and she tied the scarf tighter round her mouth. She could hear the sound of the fire engines in the distance. No time! She braced herself against the brick, and kicked the bar. Her head jarred back against the wall. God, she would end up punch-drunk. But the bar had shifted, slightly. Two more kicks, and it was loose. She worked it free. Now the door. It opened outwards. If it was locked, then it was up to the fire fighters to get through, but in that case, Eliza Eliot was dead.

The door opened, then caught on an obstruction. Smoke poured out, making her choke even through the scarf. She crouched down, pulled to free the door, feeling the obstruction move. The smoke was much less dense here, but she could feel the heat of the fire. The door was blocked by something jammed underneath it. The more she pulled, the tighter it became wedged. But she could see someone inside now, someone slumped on the floor. Tina pulled the door again and managed to grip one of the arms of the limp figure as she called again on the radio for help. The door was sticking, nothing was moving, the smoke was thick and impenetrable.

Then she heard the sound of feet on the steps behind her, and someone was kicking the door free as Tina struggled to pull the unconscious woman clear. Then there were more footsteps, and someone pulled her away, someone else was past her and she was being hurried down the steps, struggling to get back to Eliza, who she couldn't leave, not now, now that she had come so far.

The water was getting deeper. As it rose, he lifted her head more so that she could breathe. But they needed to get out, they needed to escape before the water came too high. She struggled, making muffled sounds, and his eyes focused on her again. They looked dull. 'You aren't Ellie,' he said. He gripped his arms round Kerry and tried to stand her up. Her legs wouldn't hold her, and they both fell. He tried again, but the weight of the water seemed to wash her over, her legs too numb to feel where her feet were, and the water was getting deeper and deeper.

It was lighter in the cabin. It must be getting to morning, but the light was all wrong, it was orange and it moved. He looked out of the window behind her, and made a strange sound. 'It's all finished,' he said. A loud roaring filled the air and the boat rocked. His hands seemed to drop away from her and she fell again, sliding helplessly under the water. Her eyes were open and she saw the cabin flooded with light, a brilliance that cut through the night, through the water that was swirling above her and through the blood that was trailing away in streamers, floating, curling around her.

The boat lurched again. It was going down, it was sinking, and she didn't want to die, not here, not in this water, not where he was. And there were people on the deck. She struggled, breathing half water, half air, and she was coughing and retching, but the cabin door was open and strong arms were pulling her up and out and then she was out of the cabin and the sky was orange flames and a hard stabbing light, and the *thump, thump, thump* was loud in the air where something black hovered, and she had died and gone to hell. *Kerry Fraser . . . love is as strong as death is.*

CHAPTER 19

Jonathan Massey had fought with the men trying to pull him out of the sinking cabin cruiser. He seemed, one of the team said to Farnham later, to want to go down with the boat. 'Not exactly the sinking of the *Titanic*,' the man said cheerfully. 'Swamped in a few feet of canal water.' Though it would have been deep enough to drown anyone trapped in the cabin. Water had been gushing into the boat from the open seacocks, which looked as though they had been sabotaged, but they'd managed to shut them off before the boat sank.

Massey had been caught with the missing Kerry Fraser; Kerry, trussed up with tape and helpless. No wonder he hadn't wanted to be taken. Now, Kerry Fraser was under sedation in hospital. Her sister, Mel Young, was with her. Her mother, Judith Martin had informed Farnham without expression, had 'self-sedated into oblivion' at home. And Eliza was in hospital being treated for the effects of smoke inhalation. He put that out of his mind. There was nothing he could do about that for the moment.

But Massey was Farnham's main target. The search of Massey's office at the gallery hadn't produced anything new, and the search of his home had been ambiguous. Farnham knew what he was looking for now. He was looking for evidence of a predatory paedophile.

He didn't find it, just hundreds of photographs. They were of children, girls, on the cusp of puberty, playing, laughing, riding bikes – everyday, outdoor pictures. And some portraits – private commissions, maybe – misty, soft focus: a girl cuddling a kitten, a girl holding a rose to her face. Photographs parents might cherish. And some pictures showing a darker side of childhood: monochrome, children on the streets, young prostitutes, a group huddled together in a drugged or drunken sprawl.

Evidence of obsession, Farnham thought, unhealthy obsession, but not the evidence he was looking for. Farnham looked at the man sitting opposite him in the interview room. Massey had recovered from his brief immersion. He was huddled into the white coverall as though he was cold. He'd lost his glasses in the struggle and his eyes looked naked. He kept touching his fingers to the bridge of his nose.

He still denied any involvement with Cara's death. 'She was a prostitute,' he said. His voice was bitter, incredulous. 'Anyone could have done it.' His hands moved nervously to touch his missing glasses.

His alibi for the night of Cara's death still held.

Patricia Carr was emphatic – Jonathan Massey had spent the night with her at her flat. 'Kerry's talked to us,' Farnham said. Massey tugged a cigarette out of the carton in front of him with shaking hands. Farnham offered him a light. In fact, Kerry hadn't said anything yet. She was behind an impenetrable shield of medics, but Massey needed a bit of encouragement.

He looked at Farnham now, his eyes bloodshot from the canal water. 'I thought it was . . . for a moment . . . it would all be OK,' he said.

'For the tape, Jonathan,' Farnham said. Though the other man was only a couple of years younger than him, Farnham had found that Massey responded well to a slightly fatherly tone, as though something in Farnham's role gave him an authority that Massey could relate to. 'Tell me exactly what you thought.'

'I thought she was Ellie,' Massey said. He touched the bridge of his nose with his fingers, wiped the back of his hand across his eyes. 'I thought Ellie had come back. I thought it was all a bad dream.'

There it was! Farnham kept his voice level, his expression neutral. 'Tell me about Ellie, Jonathan,' he said.

'I never meant to hurt her,' Massey said. The lament of child killers everywhere, Farnham thought, as he listened. Massey had been on the river that day with a friend of his. 'He was working on the river for a few weeks – running one of the boats between Sprotbrough and Conisbrough, taking people up the river. I joined him for the afternoon. The guy he was supposed to work with hadn't turned up. I stayed in the galley – I wasn't really supposed to be there.'

'Tell me what happened to Ellie,' Farnham said.

Massey's eyes were pleading. 'You've got to believe me!' he said. 'I didn't . . . I never meant . . . I was watching her. She was wearing a yellow jersey and little blue shorts. There were two of them. I could hear them running around and laughing. And then she was leaning over the side of the boat and trying to splash her hands in the water. I took some photographs. So beautiful.' He looked at Farnham, and there were tears in his eyes. 'Everyone got off the boat at Conisbrough. We were supposed to go back to Sprotbrough, take back the people who'd done the trip earlier – but there wasn't anyone. So we moored up a short way along the bank. It's beautiful there. The trees come right down to the river. I stayed on board.' He closed his eyes. 'It was like a dream. I looked up, and she was there. The sun was shining on her hair and she came jumping down the steps – they never walk anywhere, have you noticed, little girls? They skip and they . . .'

He looked at Farnham. His eyes pleaded for understanding. 'I only wanted to touch her,' he said. 'But she started screaming and I panicked. I tried to stop her. And then . . .'

'You killed her,' Farnham said.

'He helped me,' Massey whispered. 'After I'd done it. When he came back to the boat, I thought that was it, I thought . . . But he looked at her, and then he put his fingers on her neck, on her pulse, you know. He said he'd met her on the path and told her she could use the boat, told her where it was. And he knelt there for a bit. Then he said he'd help me. He said "You'd better leave it to me." And he made it all go away.'

'Who, Jonathan?' Farnham leant forward, close, confiding. *This is just between you and me.* 'Who took you on the boat? Who helped you?'

'Ivan,' Massey said. 'Ivan Bakst.'

Ivan Bakst. The artist whose name had been on the flier they'd found in Cara's flat. The man Eliza had seen with Massey in the gallery, the evening after Stacy's disappearance. *Shit!*

Massey picked nervously at his lips, at his fingernails, as he watched Farnham. 'I first met him when I was at art school,' he said. 'It was exciting, the art scene. There were ideas and people and we were all going places. And there was Ivan. He was an artist – he had these amazing ideas. When I graduated – I was hot in those days, I did my post-grad stuff at the Slade, and everyone thought I was going places – after that, Ivan took me on the canals with him. We went along the Grand Union Canal and then to the River Trent. We were in the veins of a corpse, he said.'

Farnham had had enough of this arty-farty

stuff from Eliza, but he nodded as though he understood.

'They were starting to renovate the canals. Ivan said – I've never forgotten this – he said it was like embalming a corpse, but it was all decaying anyway. "You can't stop it," he said. He said that the empty buildings, and the old machinery were the bones. "Just the bones left now," he said.' Suddenly Massey was lost in his story. 'I took photographs all the way. Did you see them? That summer, I really thought I was going to make it. That exhibition. It was the best stuff I'd ever done.'

Farnham needed to let Massey talk now. 'And then . . .' he prompted.

'Oh, I needed to work, you've got to live. But I kept in touch with Ivan. We'd come up as far as South Yorkshire, and he said he wanted to come back. He liked all the old industry, the way everything was falling apart. That's what he's into. When I got the place in Sheffield at the art school, he heard about it and he turned up one day, got his boat moored up near Rotherham. And he kept on coming back. Until that summer . . .'

Among the things found on the *Mary May*, apart from a stained plastic sheet neatly folded away in one of the storage units, and a tiny earring, its sparkle dulled, caught in a gap between the seats, were two cell phones. One was in the bag Kerry Fraser had been carrying. The other had been discarded on the deck. This phone was registered

461

to Mel Young. Farnham had looked at the exchange of messages stored on the SIM card when the information landed on his desk the following morning and despatched Tina to the hospital.

Tina remembered Mel from the gallery, a young woman who projected spiky, gum-chewing hostility. When she arrived at the hospital, Mel was sitting by her sister's bed. Kerry Fraser was sleeping. Mel's fingers were gently untangling the knots in the fair hair that spread across the pillow, matted and dirty. As Tina watched, she smoothed the hair away from Kerry's face. Then she looked up and saw Tina, and her expression changed. 'What?' she said. Her eyes narrowed. 'You leave Kizz alone.' Her voice was low but furious.

'It's OK, it's you I need to talk to.'

Mel Young looked at her, looked at Kerry, shrugged and came to the door. They sat on chairs outside the ward, Mel glancing through the doors as they talked.

Her eyes were more interested now as she looked at Tina in the bright light. 'I remember you. You got off with Daniel Flynn at the private view,' she said.

'I'd like you to have a look . . .'

'You should have seen her face! Eliza. She looked like . . .' Mel screwed her face into an expression of fastidious dismay. 'Cow,' she said.

Tina assumed that was aimed at the absent Eliza, rather than at her. 'This phone,' she said.

Mel glanced through the ward doors again. She saw Tina watching her and shrugged. 'She's such a div, Kizz,' she said. 'It's always me has to pick up the pieces.' She looked at the phone Tina was holding out and frowned. 'That's mine,' she said. She'd lent it to Cara, she told Tina, the night Cara died.

'You knew Cara, then?' Mel had claimed little knowledge of the dead woman outside of the gallery.

Mel's gaze drifted away. 'When I left home, I went to this hostel,' she said. 'It was OK. Cara was there, so I kind of got to know her. My family were in the news, on the TV, you know, all the Ellie Chapman stuff, all that stuff about *him*. She thought it was cool. We hung out a bit, you know, but she was a bit of a div. Don't get me wrong, she was OK, really. She got me the job at the gallery.' She was quiet for a moment. 'Anyway, she said she'd lost her phone so I lent her mine.'

She rolled her eyes when Tina asked her why she hadn't told the police. 'Like that was anything to do with it,' she said. 'I'm not stupid.' She'd seen what police involvement had done to her sister.

She and Kerry had kept in touch after Mel had left home. 'I thought your mother . . .' Tina searched for the words. She'd heard that Mel Young's mother had thrown her out.

Mel's face hardened. '*She* wanted me out. But I would have gone anyway.' She'd gone into a foster home briefly, then to the hostel where she had met Cara. Her mother wouldn't have her near the house, and didn't want her and Kerry meeting. 'I didn't want to get Kizz into bother, so I'd phone when *she* was out. And I'd meet Kizz in town, things like that. Or down the canal basin, when I got the job. Then *she* couldn't even pay the phone bill. She's a waste of space. They got cut off. So I got Kizz a phone, but I made her promise not to let *her* have it.'

She hadn't seen Kerry for over a week, she said. They'd met the Thursday before Maggie Chapman's funeral and they'd had a row. 'About her pervy dad,' Mel said. Then she'd lost her phone. 'So I didn't call. And it was all, you know, about Cara. I didn't want Kizz around that. I called her from the gallery,' she said. 'Yesterday. I left her a message telling her to call, but of course she didn't.' She looked at Tina. 'Have you got a kid sister?' she said.

'No.' Tina had brothers.

'You're lucky.' She looked through the list of messages they'd found on Kerry's phone: *c u @ caff usual time don't b l8*; *dont b a div kizz bunk off*; *c u fday same time caff*; *dont let the cow get u down*; *2sday 7 caff.*

'Yeah. We text each other. Eliza used to get a face on if I got calls at work. And Kizz gets into bother if her phone goes at school. And I wasn't going to let *her* find out Kizz'd got a phone. No way.'

She shook her head over the other messages: *its*

464

abut yor dad meet u at the cafy 7 dont b l8; RUOK?;
FDAY SAME PLACE 5.00.; OK. DONT B L8; WHO R U?;
WHR R U?; WHR R U?; MT U ON TOPATH RLY BR 7.30
RGNT DNT B L8.; WR R U? 'I didn't send those.'

'What about that one?' *its abut yor dad meet u at
the cafy 7 dont b l8* Tina could see the difference
in the other messages – whoever had sent most
of them didn't know how to make the phone use
lower case – but that one looked no different.

'Oh, please,' Mel said. 'I do know how to spell.'

That left Cara. 'Did Cara have the number of
Kerry's phone?'

Mel shook her head. 'Why'd she want to get in
touch with Kizz? No.'

So if Cara had wanted to get in touch with Kerry,
and didn't want Mel to know, then she could get
the number from Mel's phone. But why was Cara
arranging to meet Kerry? 'Did she know something about Mark Fraser? Cara?' But Mel looked
as baffled as Tina felt. 'You know that he probably
didn't kill Ellie, don't you?' Tina wasn't sure if she
should say that, but she wanted to find out what
exactly had been going on in the Fraser house
before Ellie's death. Fraser had never been
convicted of abuse, and if his appeal was successful,
he might be coming back to his daughter.

Mel looked at the floor. 'That's not my fault,'
she said. She looked at Tina. 'He's a pervert. He
was always touching. Always putting his arm
round me. Just because my dad forgot my birthday
or something, as if I cared. *Never mind, Mel, I'll*

465

be your dad. He was always going on about that. He is *so* not my dad. He's such a loser. And he came into the bathroom once when I was in there. *Lock the door, Mel.* As if he didn't know. And when Mum went out, you know what he did? I used to watch. He'd get dressed in her clothes. Her undies, even – *yuk!* – and her skirts and he'd put make-up on. And he'd walk round in front of the mirror. He was such a pervert. And Mum wanted to leave Kizz alone with him.'

After Ellie Chapman had gone missing, Maggie Chapman had defended Fraser against police suspicions. They were wasting valuable time, she'd proclaimed, looking at Mark, when someone had kidnapped her daughter who might still be alive somewhere. 'She *so* didn't get it,' Mel said. 'Letting that perv take those kids out. So I went and told her that he was a pervert, that I'd left home because of him.'

Tragedies arise from such mundane things. Mark Fraser had wanted too much from his step-daughter. He'd wanted to compensate for the break-up of her home, had wanted to be her father, but he hadn't been sensitive to the needs of an angry and resentful child. And he'd had a minor kink. A harmless one. But to Mel, for all her air of streetwise sophistication, cross-dressing and paedophilia were two sides of the same coin.

Mel looked through the ward door again. 'She's waking up,' she said, and was back at her sister's bedside before Tina could say anything. Tina stood there for a few minutes watching Mel sitting with her sister as she stirred on the pillow. Mel looked up and saw her watching, and rolled her eyes. Then she turned away so that Tina couldn't see her face.

They had got to Ivan Bakst's boat with a search warrant within an hour of Farnham's interview with Massey. The boat was moored above Rotherham. The other people using the mooring described Bakst as quiet and inconspicuous. They said he'd spent a lot of time on the boat, reading, carrying out routine maintenance. 'Because we live on the water,' one of them complained, 'doesn't mean we're criminals.' Farnham could sense the first signs of closing ranks.

In the compact, meticulous living quarters of the boat, they found carefully stored sets of photographs and some books. There was very little that was personal, no letters, no diaries, no address books. They also found a small supply of heroin, very pure.

The books were mostly art books. One was a copy of *The Artist's Handbook* by Cennino Cennini, which fell open at a page with a heavily underscored passage:

> *How to paint dead flesh.*
> *Do not apply any pink at all, because a dead person has no colour; . . . and mark out the outlines with dark sinoper and a little*

black . . . and manage the hair in the same way, but not so that it looks alive but dead . . . and so do every bone of a Christian, or of rational creatures' . . .

In the margin, someone had written *Crap!*

And the photographs seemed to support that succinct rejection of Cennini. Among the prints of derelict buildings, abandoned waterways, industrial concrete, were photographs of a child's body. The face was hidden, but it was the body of a young girl, pre-pubescent. The prints explored the processes of post-mortem change: the white and shadows of purple spreading over the flesh; the greenish luminosity; the creeping blackness; the blurring of the fine lines as the body distended, as the soft tissue liquefied. The sequence ended with bones, animal bones, showing the green of moss marring the fine whiteness.

Farnham remembered the flier they had found in Cara Hobson's flat:

Gonna roll the bones!

'Entropy' is an intriguing exhibition of film and computer images that is worth a visit. Ivan Bakst's time-lapse animation, and the reworkings of stills into abstract designs turns the process of death and decay into something that has a strange if macabre beauty . . .

The exhibition had been dated 1999. Had Bakst disguised what his photographs actually showed, presented them as abstracts, turned Ellie Chapman's body, in fact, into a work of art? Farnham had heard of artists working with shit, with piss, with dead animals – so why not the corpses of murdered children? It seemed about par for the course to him.

And *The Triumph of Death*? What was it that had brought Bakst back to South Yorkshire, back to the canals, back here to kill?

'He never left me alone,' Massey said, when Farnham resumed the interview. 'I went away after . . . but he stayed, for a bit. Then he went, and Ellie came back.' He picked nervously at his lips, at his fingernails, as he watched Farnham.

Farnham was making the connections now. 'Did you introduce him to Cara Hobson and Sheryl Hewitt?' he said.

'They met,' Massey said. 'I didn't . . . Cara didn't have much to do with him, but Sheryl was always around him. She's dead now,' he added.

Found dead of an overdose on the derelict boat where addicts used to meet. Farnham was thinking about the heroin found among Bakst's possessions. If he was in the habit of bringing heroin back into the country, he may have gone with Sheryl to make contact with other users, with other potential buyers. He would have seen the deserted place,

469

seen the dense undergrowth on the canal bank, seen its potential as a place of concealment. Bakst had left the country before Ellie's body had been found, left around the time that Mel Young had made her accusation against her stepfather and moved into the hostel where Cara was living. Cara had been impressed by the second-hand notoriety that the Ellie Chapman case gave. She would probably have mentioned to Bakst that her new friend, Lyn, was the stepdaughter of the accused man. Bakst would have wanted no contact with Mark Fraser's stepdaughter.

Massey was speaking again, the words tumbling out in a jerky torrent. 'And then Flynn wants to have his exhibition here, wants Eliza to put it together. She was a friend of Maggie Chapman. It was the nightmare starting all over again. I kept thinking Maggie would come to the gallery. I would have gone mad. I couldn't have coped with that.' His voice was shaking. He took a deep drag on his cigarette.

'Then – about a month ago, he came back. He said he was going to have an exhibition and I was going to help him. It was called *The Triumph of Death*. I didn't understand what he was talking about. That was Flynn's exhibition. He just laughed and said it was OK, the show was all in hand. I didn't need to do anything.' He wiped his face. His hand was trembling. 'He came back later. Eliza saw him. I was terrified he was going to say something, start her asking questions.'

He nodded. 'Go on,' he said to Massey. 'What happened to Cara?'

'When Eliza started doing a lot of evening work in the gallery, I began taking Cara to my flat.' He looked at Farnham. 'To pose,' he said. 'And she started looking at things – she was always into things. And there were some pictures, nothing bad, lovely pictures. They were of Ellie, on the boat. She found them. She must have realized what they were. And she took them. I don't know why.' His hand touched against the bridge of his nose, reaching for his missing glasses. 'I didn't know what to do. I told Ivan. He said he'd talk to her, sort it out. I gave him the gallery keys, the codes. He said he needed them.'

'And you didn't do anything, even when Cara turned up dead?'

Massey shook his head. 'I couldn't!' he said. 'You've got to understand that. I couldn't. But he said it was all right. He said he hadn't hurt her. He said he'd talked to her and she hadn't said anything. She was just puzzled. I wanted to believe him. I *did* believe him.'

Cara must have been on a cushy number with Massey. She had rent-free accommodation, regular money without having to do much for it. And she hadn't been particularly bright. When she found the photographs of Ellie in Jonathan's flat, she probably didn't realize their significance. It had worried her enough to want to ask questions, but not of Mel – bright, stroppy Mel who might cause trouble, disrupt the life that Cara had made for herself and her baby.

Who better to ask than Kerry? Kerry had been there. Kerry would be able to explain how Jonathan came to have photographs of that fatal day on the river. Cara's fingers had been twisted and broken. Her killer would know what she had done. He'd gone to her flat that night to retrieve the photos. And they weren't there. But he had what he assumed was Cara's phone, with the exchange of messages. It must have looked as though Cara had managed to fool him, that she had a far closer relationship with the girl than she had admitted to. Kerry knew too much.

How dangerous were the photographs to Bakst? If anyone had done what Farnham had done, and compared Jonathan's photographs with the ones Fraser took, then it would become clear at once that there was someone else on that boat with an interest in the children. So if the photos were missing, then the next step would be to destroy the other set to prevent that comparison being made. Eliza had mentioned the concerns of Maggie's landlord that someone was hanging around her flat – but of course the photos weren't there. Eliza had taken them. And then she took them back.

He looked at Massey. 'The day after Stacy McDonald was found . . .' Massey nodded, kept his gaze on the desk in front of him. 'Did Bakst know that Eliza had gone to Maggie Chapman's flat?'

He nodded. 'He phoned me after your lot had left the gallery. Said he needed to talk to me. He wanted to know if the coast was clear. I told him that Eliza was up at Maggie's but it wasn't safe for us to meet.'

So Bakst must have gone back to see if the photographs had been returned, and Eliza may have disturbed him as he searched. He would have had no time to sort out the photos he was looking for. So he'd burnt the lot. Farnham looked at Massey. 'Tell me about Stacy McDonald,' he said.

Massey covered his face with his hands. 'I knew then,' he said. He took a deep breath. 'I knew he'd killed Cara to keep her quiet. And somehow he knew she'd been in contact with . . . Mark Fraser's daughter. The second little girl. He asked me if Cara talked about her, if she'd ever been to the gallery. How would I know? Of course she hadn't. Why would she?

'I couldn't take it any more. That night, I was going to end it. I'd got the pills, and I'd got the vodka. I was going to do it at the gallery. Only, when I got there, Eliza was still around. And then I saw him. He was getting off this boat. I knew he was coming to the gallery – Eliza was there – I had to stop him seeing her. I managed to get her to go upstairs and I got out, before he came in. I didn't know what he was going to do, I swear.'

'Why did you get on the boat, Jonathan?' The one possibly mitigating factor. He could have run away, but he'd got on the boat and found Kerry, trussed up, injured and drowning.

'It was . . . he hadn't tied it up and there was something about the way it was lying in the water. There was something wrong. And in the Brueghel, in the background . . .' He caught Farnham's expression. 'I knew. I know that painting. I'm a trained artist for . . .' He stopped, then said, 'In the background, there are boats foundering in the water. Dead people, drowned people. There was someone on that boat – I knew. Someone else he'd killed. And it had to be that little girl, the second little girl, Ellie's friend. And it was my fault. I thought I could die too, with the pills and the vodka, die on the boat, like I deserved.'

He'd taken no action when he realized that Kerry Fraser's life was in danger, had run away and left Eliza alone with a killer.

But without him, Kerry Fraser would have died.

A week after the fire at the gallery, Tina Barraclough was surprised to see Daniel Flynn waiting in the car park, leaning against her car. He threw away his cigarette as she came over. 'Hello.' He looked unsure of his welcome.

'How did you know I was due to leave now?' she said.

'I asked. I wanted to talk to you.' She wasn't particularly pleased to see him, but she had no grudge against him. He'd done his best not to shop her to Farnham, and he'd kept his mouth shut about the drugs.

'OK,' she said. 'But I haven't got much time.' She was meeting Steven Calloway later. They were going drinking, and maybe clubbing after.

They went to a wine bar close by, which was quiet at this time in the evening. He bought a bottle of wine, and they sat in silence. She waited to see what he wanted. 'I'm sorry I had to tell your boss about that night,' he said. 'You didn't get into trouble, did you?'

'A bit,' she said. 'but it's sorted. It's OK.' Farnham had reprimanded her for keeping information back, and seemed to have dropped the matter. He didn't ask her again about the pills. Maybe he'd decided not to ask the question when the answer was going to be something he didn't want to hear.

'I thought I was going to get banged up for murder, otherwise . . .'

'I told you, it's OK. I should have told him myself.' There was an awkward silence.

'Ivan Bakst,' he said after a moment. 'I know him.' He ran his fingers through his hair. 'I can't believe he . . . Do you think he always . . . Did he do it?'

Bakst had been in custody since he'd been arrested on returning to his boat the morning after the fire. Tina shrugged. 'It'll be months before it comes to trial,' she said. 'He's been charged. It's up to the courts now.' And up to Farnham to put together a cast-iron case.

He poured himself another glass of wine. 'I can't believe it,' he said again. 'This place has never been any good for me.'

She remembered that he came from Sheffield. 'So why did you bring the exhibition here?' She had heard about Flynn's manipulations to get Eliza Eliot to put his exhibition together for him. She wanted to hear what he would say about it.

'It was . . .' He poured more wine into his glass and offered the bottle to Tina. She shook her head. She'd be drinking later. 'I had a sister,' he said.

He'd been thirteen when she was born. 'God knows who her father was,' he said. 'I don't think my mother ever knew.' The girl had died of a heroin overdose in 1998. The year Ellie Chapman died. 'There were a few people died of overdoses then,' he said.

Had Bakst brought that lethal supply of pure heroin? Had he been responsible for the recent deaths? That was something they would probably never know. Tina remembered the photograph in the exhibition. 'Are you saying that Sheryl Hewitt was your sister?'

'Sheryl Hewitt? Oh, you mean . . . No. I used her picture. I didn't have one of Julie. She'd been in care since she was thirteen.'

'How old was she when she died?'

'Seventeen. She'd been in trouble for years.'

Tina frowned. Flynn would have been twenty-six when his sister went into care. 'Why didn't you have her with you?' she said.

His eyes slid away. 'I couldn't,' he said. 'She didn't really know me.' He drank some more wine and refilled his glass.

'But later,' she said. 'When you had got to know her.'

'Look,' he said, 'I was in London. She was in Sheffield.'

She didn't react, waiting for him to go on with his story. 'I wanted there to be something,' he said after a pause. 'No one knew anything about Julie. She was just another dead addict. The Ellie Chapman killing. Nobody talked about the Julie Iqbal killing.'

'Iqbal?' Tina said.

'One of my mother's marriages. He wasn't Julie's father. He was OK, but he bailed out before she was born. I was in London when she died. I was the only person went to the crematorium.' He looked at her. 'I know I let her down,' he said. 'But there was something I could do for her. The *Triumph* could be her memorial.'

And about as much use as a three-pound note, Tina thought. It was easy to be sorry after the event, easy to make gestures, but it didn't mitigate the effects of what had gone before. Daniel Flynn hadn't made a memorial for his sister, he was trying to assuage his own guilt. He hadn't even gone public with Julie, hadn't even included her in the exhibition. He'd used a picture of one of the other victims instead. He wouldn't have come out of the story too well. Maybe he was hoping for some kind of sympathy from Tina, but if so, he'd come to the wrong person.

'What are you going to do now?' she said, deliberately changing the subject.

He looked at her, then shrugged. 'I'm taking the exhibition to New York in the autumn,' he said. 'And then there's a European tour in the offing.' His voice was cold.

'But it's gone.' *The Triumph of Death* had been destroyed in the fire.

'It was photo-montages, reproductions, things like that mostly. A bit of painting. I kept everything. I can recreate most of it – maybe even better this time.' He frowned. 'I've got the parts. I need to make it into a coherent whole.'

'Take Eliza Eliot with you,' Tina said. There was some malice behind that.

His face went carefully blank. 'Why Eliza?'

'Why not?' she said. She was pleased to have got under his skin. 'She'll be at a loose end now.' She finished her glass of wine. It was time she was off. She left Flynn sitting at his table in the wine bar, staring moodily at the wall in front of him.

She put him out of her mind. It promised to be a good evening, but she was feeling tired. Maybe she ought to look out some kind of artificial stimulus; nothing much, just a bit of something to carry her through.

Life was getting back to normal. Life was OK.

CHAPTER 20

The sky was heavy with storm clouds that turned the late afternoon into evening. Eliza parked her car outside the cemetery gates. She pulled her bag off the back seat, hesitated, then picked up her umbrella as well. She didn't want to be encumbered, but it was going to start raining soon. She had a long journey ahead, and she didn't want to get soaked at the start.

The colour of the grass was dulled by the grey light, and the flowers on the graves looked dead. The chapel of rest was closed and deserted. She walked along the path, towards the corner of the graveyard where Maggie and Ellie lay. She could see the green of the laurel gleaming in the half-light, the shadows that obscured the polished granite of Ellie's stone. *Roses are red...*

From this high point, she could see across the city, the houses running down into the valley and up the hills on the other side, the sky disappearing in banks of dark cloud. The first spatter of rain blew across her face. She stood for a few minutes looking at the graves. The mound that marked

Maggie's had sunk, though the earth was still bare. She read the epitaph on Ellie's stone, the fading gold lettering: *Ellie Chapman, 1989-1998. Love is as strong as death is.*

It was some weeks now since the fire at the gallery. She still saw the hanging figure above her in the darkness, still felt the choking smoke in the night, but the memories were gradually being blunted by time. And now she was leaving. Her job was gone, she had two-months' salary in her pocket, a ticket to Naples where she had the promise of work in a private gallery, and she had time. She had paintings to finish. She could have gone sooner, but there was one thing that had kept her lingering. Roy Farnham.

He had come to see her the morning after the fire, as she waited in the high ward of the hospital for the doctor to tell her she could leave. He pulled up a chair and sat down. 'You're lucky to be alive,' he said. Then he told her. Told her that the man who had been her employer and her mentor had killed Ellie those four years ago, spreading destruction through the lives of all the people the tragedy touched, Maggie, Mark Fraser, his family, now scattered and destroyed.

'Mark Fraser,' she said. 'Maggie hated him for all those years . . .' He was out of prison on bail, trying to reconstruct his shattered life. Stacy's family had lost their daughter, and Briony Rose . . . She could still remember Cara tucking the shawl around the baby as she put her in the

480

chair. Briony Rose would be adopted, but her mother was dead.

She knew that Bakst had been charged with the abduction of Kerry Fraser, and with the killings of Cara Hobson and Stacy McDonald. But it had been a month before Roy talked to her about it, a month in which Daniel had left, gone to recreate the now infamous *Triumph*, and to capitalize on the notoriety that the exhibition had acquired.

A few days before he left, Daniel had come to see Eliza at Laura's, where she was staying while she decided what she was going to do. After some hesitant talk about her welfare, her future, he said, 'I'm taking the *Triumph* to New York in the autumn.' He looked out of the window. 'You could come with me, if you wanted.'

'I've got other plans,' she said. Daniel Flynn was no part of her future. She still regretted the man she'd thought she had known, but that wasn't Daniel Flynn. That man didn't exist. There was nothing she wanted from the real Daniel.

'I'll miss you,' he said.

She laughed, and he looked hurt.

He'd left Sheffield not long after that visit. She thought about him a couple of days later. She was with Roy. They were grabbing a few hours from Roy's hectic schedule to spend some time together. 'Daniel knows how to ride high on other people's ideas,' she said, as she ran that last meeting through her mind.

'Mm.' He didn't really listen when she talked

481

about art. He was half asleep, lying back against the pillow. Music was playing, something jazzy that she didn't recognize, his choice.

'My ideas, Bakst's ideas.'

'Mm,' he said again. He was tired. He was working long hours, putting together the case against Ivan Bakst.

'He still won't talk to you?' she asked.

'Oh, he'll talk,' Roy said. His eyes were closed. 'He says it was a work of art. And that's all he'll tell me. His brief is already pressing for psychiatric reports, hospital . . . It might not come to court, if he can play the insanity card. But that doesn't explain Cara and Stacy.' He wanted to see the killings as utilitarian, he wanted to see Bakst as an evil man, not as a mad man. He wanted someone to blame and someone to punish. And those deaths had been utilitarian, it was true, but they had also been material that had come Bakst's way, material to be incorporated in his final piece. His triumph of death.

The madness of artists. She could understand. *The Triumph of Death* was never Daniel Flynn's. He came to Madrid with Bakst, but it was Bakst who'd come to see the Brueghel – I should have realized when I was talking to them. Bakst knew about it. Daniel didn't. Everything that Daniel did was based on ideas that Bakst had given him, and some that I'd contributed. He told me, Bakst, that we had a lot in common. I didn't realize what he meant.'

'Bakst did all this in revenge for Flynn stealing

his idea?' Roy was fully awake now, listening to her.

Eliza shook her head. 'No. But Bakst is obsessed with death. Everything of his I've seen is to do with death. I told you about those pots he made. And then . . .' But she didn't want to talk about Ellie. 'I don't know what his original idea was, but his *Triumph* would have been nothing like Daniel's. He'd never have put all those paintings and photographs together like that. Then when Daniel stole the idea, that must have given him the shape he wanted for his own version. Bakst's *Triumph* was the gallery. The fire – the derelict buildings, the canal, all those symbols of death lit up by the destruction of the gallery – fuelled by the kind of art he despised. A triumph.'

He was quiet after she'd finished speaking. 'So that's art,' he said after a while.

But she had seen his expression change as she spoke, as he realized that she understood Bakst's concepts, and she knew that she had stayed too long. It was time to go.

And now she had one last thing to attend to, here in this burial ground. The rain was getting heavier. She put her bag down beside her and got out the small shrub and the trowel she had bought. She didn't know anything about planting things. The man at the garden centre had said that the shrub, a forsythia, was hardy. When she'd first consulted him, he'd talked about soil preparation and planting mix and pruning and things that had been a foreign language to Eliza's ears. She'd explained what she wanted to do, and he'd looked embarrassed and suggested the forsythia. 'It'll flower every spring,' he said.

She was having trouble now co-ordinating the umbrella, the plant, the trowel and the bag. She put the umbrella down. She had to kneel on the wet ground to get enough leverage to dig into the hard soil of Ellie's grave.

She took the small package out of her bag, tissue paper, old, slightly discoloured. It contained the locks of hair and the infant tooth she had found at Maggie's – Maggie's last relics of her daughter. She left them wrapped in the paper and put them carefully in the ground. Then she tipped the plant out of its container, teasing the roots free as the man had advised her.

The rain was falling hard. She could feel tendrils of wet hair dripping down her neck. She put the plant firmly in the hole and pushed the soil in around it. The man had said something about watering, about wetting it thoroughly, but it looked as though nature was going to take care of that. She wished she had some religious belief so that she could say a prayer, something that would mark the moment, but she couldn't find any words.

Roses are red, violets are blue . . . love is as strong as death is.

And love leads to the grave.